THE ANNIVERSARY

THE
ANNIVERSARY

A NOVEL

STEPHANIE BISHOP

Black Cat
New York

First published in Great Britain in 2023 by Weidenfeld & Nicolson
an imprint of The Orion Publishing Group Ltd.

Published simultaneously in Canada
Printed in the United States of America

First Grove Atlantic paperback edition: July 2023

Library of Congress Cataloging-in-Publication data is available for this title.

ISBN 978-0-8021-6167-3
eISBN 978-0-8021-6168-0

Black Cat
an imprint of Grove Atlantic
154 West 14th Street
New York, NY 10011

Distributed by Publishers Group West

groveatlantic.com

23 24 25 26 27   10 9 8 7 6 5 4 3 2 1

'To be sure, the future of the woman I have been may turn me into someone other than myself.'

– Simone de Beauvoir, *All Said and Done*

Book One

I

We must have taken fifty photographs for that book jacket. At least fifty. Go on, my husband said, Do it for me? Say it?

I rolled my eyes, and then did as Patrick wished. Honey-honey-honey. I said. Money-money-money. He clicked away. It was a joke, and it was true what he said – repeating the phrase made me laugh. It got him what he wanted, a sly grin of sorts, if not exactly a smile, a reasonable photograph. I don't know why they need a photo anyway, I said, complaining while I took up a new pose. You know why, he told me. Because if we make you look beautiful people will buy the book. And if the reader can't put a face to a character, they can at least give them yours. I know, he said. But we have to do it. Now go on, say it for me again.

I was nervous. I hated photographs. And soon this one would be printed thousands of times over. Patrick didn't know this then, or not exactly. Three weeks earlier I had received a phone call from my publisher who told me, in a state of great but hushed excitement, that I had won a major prize for the book that the photograph was intended for.

No, Ada said. I'm not joking. This is not a joke. She had entered it as a manuscript, the release date was not supposed to be for another four months. I'd not long ago handed in the final proofs, back in July. But now they would go to press earlier. Bring everything forward, increase the print run. The news, she said, was under embargo, you cannot tell anyone, not even Patrick, she warned.

Not even him? I said. Why?

Because he is a total gossip, and because he loves you so much. I know things have been hard lately, but he really does, and because he couldn't help but go tell people, and if word gets out that you've leaked the news – well, I don't know. She was speaking quickly, but in a whisper. Her office was made of glass, and although it was thick safety glass, if she cried out with joy she would arouse people's interest and suspicion.

Are you sure? I asked. This was not something I was expecting. It was a different kind of book to those I'd written before – more personal and sprawling, and it had taken a ridiculously long time to write.

My hands were trembling. I could feel sweat collecting under my armpits, my shirt dampening. Are you sure you're right? I said again. I felt drunk, unsteady, a little sick.

Yes, she replied. I have the letter right here in front of me. The awards ceremony is in New York on December second. They say they'll send more details in a couple of days. She had been speaking in a breathless gush, and now said, Wait, someone's waving at me: there's a meeting. Oh my God, I forgot about the meeting! I have to go, I'm so sorry, I'll call you back.

4

I kept my word and didn't tell Patrick, not before the photograph and not after. But I did tell my sister, May. After all, it was a book in which she herself featured as a character, a fact she liked to boast about even before the thing went to print. But I knew she could keep a secret if I asked her to. And of course I told Valerie, my agent. Normally, Ada had explained, the awards ceremony was held in London. But that year, in an attempt to curry favour with the Americans, it would be in New York. This was to the chagrin of many committee members, but somehow the power of American opinion held sway. It was, without doubt, the biggest event in the international literary calendar. The whole thing seemed so extraordinary to me, so unexpected. I felt almost afraid of what was happening, superstitious even, maybe paranoid – to the degree that I couldn't bring myself to say the name of the award aloud or even in my own head, less I jinxed it. In conversation with Ada, and in my private thoughts, I called it just The Prize. It made taking the photograph seem so much worse.

Come on, Patrick said. Just one last picture for luck. Smile for me!

My publishing house had offered to pay for a professional photographer, but I could think of nothing I wanted less. If anyone asked me to put on a smile the left side of my mouth froze and the muscle beneath my right eye started to twitch. I tried it once for a previous book at Ada's request, when I was too naïve to know I could refuse, and spent three hours in a room chilled by air conditioning, repeating this phrase, Honey-honey-honey. Money-money-money. It keeps your lips open at the right aperture, the photographer said. If you don't want to actually smile, I mean. Because you want to appear inviting, he said. Like you're about to speak, a slightly open mouth is what we want. Like you're talking to the person who is looking at the photo, confiding. Open, but not overly friendly, like that, yes, perfect, if you could just hold that. Then we changed position and I repeated my mantra: honey-honey-honey, money-money-money, as the camera clicked away. Later we laughed about it, Patrick and I. But you never say that for me, he said. Won't you, please? Go on. Say it, just once? Please? And then he did a kind of rumba in the living room, Honey-honey-honey, he said. Money-money-money.

So it was an old favour I owed him, to say these words while he clicked away. Afterwards we looked through the photographs together. Whatever, I said. I hate them all. You choose, I told him in the end. I really don't want to know. And don't tell me – which one, I mean.

This was in early October, a month before we were due to depart on a cruise that I had booked for our wedding anniversary, and I had other things to see to: visas to organise and insurance forms to fill out – that photograph was just one more task to deal with. We were coming up to our fourteenth anniversary, although we'd been together in one way or another for a couple of years longer than this, and that year I had wanted us, just once, to have a proper celebration. The cruise was elaborate: eighteen days and starting from Alaska. We were to fly out from London then board the ship at the port of Homer before crossing the Bering Sea and travelling down the coast of Russia towards Hokkaido, in the north of Japan. From there we'd head south, ending up in Osaka, where we'd take the train to Kyoto. I had planned all this very carefully so that we would arrive in Japan in time for the last of autumn. We would celebrate in the gold and crimson forest and he would kiss me as red star-shaped leaves drifted down and landed in my hair. I only needed to tweak the itinerary a little to get a flight to New York, in time for the prize ceremony. I was going to surprise him with this.

It would have made more sense, I suppose, to start in Japan and sail to America. But that would have meant celebrating our anniversary at sea, which wasn't what I had in mind. Not for such a special one, fourteen being the year of ivory: patience and stability. A lucky year, some say, because the number is made up of two lots of seven. More to the point, I'd booked the cruise before the news of the prize came in. And although I had thought about trying to reorganise the trip, in the end I decided against this. The timing was tight but we could make it; we'd have two full days in Kyoto before I needed to be in New York.

We'd not done anything like this before, never been so extravagant. In fact, we'd hardly celebrated the date in any way. Each year, when our anniversary had come round we'd been too busy to do much more than have a meal out, maybe see a movie. Everything so casual. We talked about work. He was a film director with an honorary position at a prestigious university, and over time, as his films gained attention, pressures increased. Everyone wanted something more from him. Give something up, I'd said, over and over, let something go. He was exhausted.

And things hadn't been easy of late. Something needed to change. He would have been the first to admit that his schedule, at least initially, was a question of personal choice: doors were being opened, he had to step through them. If a script or a storyboard treatment was requested, he would deliver it. An occasional film became regular films, short films became feature-length films, each one accompanied by increasing publicity: interviews, panels, columns in the newspaper. It was, he explained without shame, just a case of capital. In those corridors one had to fight to make one's name ever bigger and louder, more widely known – laying claim to the territory, buying it up, seizing power when necessary. Our anniversary was at the end of November; it had been a beautiful autumn wedding, but at that later stage in our marriage it meant the date fell in the middle of the pre-Christmas rush to meet release dates set for the new year, and Patrick was always too frantic to go away. So we would just eat out, maybe have a couple of drinks, and he'd fall asleep on the couch watching television. But that year I insisted on something else.

When I suggested the cruise, he was close to being completely burnt out. He'd let his hair grow long. He didn't shower as often as he used to. He was important enough by then that these things didn't matter so much. Really? he said. You really want to do that? He was reluctant at first, claiming that a holiday was too much effort: to pack, to travel to the port and stand in queues, deal with strangers at mealtimes and at the pool. He wasn't up for this.

When we first met, he was one of the most beautiful

8

and elegantly dressed men I had known: crisp shirts and shiny Italian shoes. A leather jacket for the winter and the rain. Now, just the feeling of a shirt collar made his shoulders tense and caused a pain down the left side of his neck. The collar need not be tight, just the possibility of something constraining him in any way was too much to bear. He turned up to major meetings in a T-shirt, jeans and sneakers. We made light of this, citing for each other Virginia Woolf's diary entry where she pines for a pair of rubber-soled shoes so that she might go walking in comfort without her feet getting wet, and in this way we elevated my husband's sartorial standards, describing them as an act of artistic emulation. Really, it didn't matter that much to others, he could show up in whatever he wanted and still be admired, still taken seriously. Sometimes his T-shirt even had a hole in it. On his favourite black one the neck ribbing was coming unstitched. But between us we recognised the depth of his exhaustion. Let's take those rubber-soled shoes travelling, I teased, just as Woolf would have liked.

Although it wasn't only work. We had both been strained lately and things were bad with his son, Joshua, who was spending more and more time at our house. This too was taking its toll. At that point, we were living in a terrace next door to a vet. It was in a busy residential pocket of the city. Up the hill were rows of grand houses, owned by celebrities and bankers, all of whom possessed at least one very fine pure-bred dog. They were perfectly groomed, both the dogs and our neighbours, and perfectly trained: well mannered and chic. Down the hill the properties deteriorated, but the bookshops and cafés continued to proliferate, and everybody who visited these cafés also owned dogs, although these were mutts, as they say, rattier and less well behaved: bohemian dogs. So it was a crowded vet's practice.

In recent months Joshua had started to throw horrifying tantrums. He was seventeen at the time and a late bloomer. His tantrums were those of an enraged teenager: hostile, sensitive, at odds with the world in the worst way. He hated easily, trusted no one, blamed his father, You ruin everything! he screamed. Up until this point he had been placid – even-tempered and amenable. Always a gentle child. But lately that persona had fallen away and he had become someone I hardly recognised. The smallest thing could set him off – a meal he didn't like, the music his father played, a request to wear a jacket in the middle of winter – and he would start to yell. How much he hated us. How fucked up everything was, how everything was a fucking joke. It's all your fault, he said. Patrick's attempt to reason him down only made it worse until Joshua would just scream. These were not ordinary screams. They were not shouts of refusal or cries of protest. They were sustained, grating, high-pitched screams, animalistic yells that were uttered incessantly; louder and louder, almost without a breath between them. They were terrifying to hear, so full of adolescent pain, as if occurring in response to a repeatedly inflicted wound. At the commencement of these tantrums Patrick would speak calmly, asking Joshua to please quieten down, It's OK, he'd say. Tell me what the problem is and I can fix it. But the problem was not the meal, or the jumper, or the blunt pencil or whatever object Joshua had projected his misery on to, the problem was the existence of his misery, something he struggled to articulate and could only express by fixing it to an inanimate thing in the world. The more Patrick tried to appease him, the worse Joshua's tantrums became, until the volume and pitch of the screaming grew too much to bear, and Patrick would start to shout back. This only made it worse, the two of them eventually yelling insensibly at each other, beyond all control. Joshua did not respond to Patrick's fury by calming himself, allowing himself to be shouted into submission. And Patrick's rage only continued to escalate, until, in order to expel the demon, he'd leave the room and punch a door frame or kick the wide skirting boards, letting Joshua holler himself into exhaustion as if he were a small child.

The side effect of this was the issue of the dogs next door; the many dogs that were boarded at the vet's. In the opening bars of Joshua's tantrums the dogs paid him no attention: his voice expressed ordinary human rage. But as the tantrum progressed, increasing in volume and rising towards its sustained, sometimes unending crescendo, the dogs became distressed. They yelped and whined and howled. Between the noise of the animals and the noise of my husband and stepson, the situation was unbearable. I would sit at the kitchen table with my hands over my ears and cry.

It was in the summer when I came home late to one of the most extreme tantrums: I heard the shouting halfway up the street, the wind carrying their voices. This was only a couple of days after I'd handed in the final manuscript for the book, and I was feeling dazed and tired, absent-minded. When I got to the front door, I realised I had forgotten my phone and keys and that I must have left them at the house of the friend with whom I'd spent the afternoon. I knocked, but no one answered. I pressed the doorbell, but the battery was flat. I knocked again and again, louder. Still no reply. They were so consumed by their anger they couldn't hear me. It started to rain. I banged and banged on the door, but still nothing. Eventually I accepted defeat and crossed the road to the phone booth and called the landline. Patrick answered and then let me in. But still the arguing continued – between Joshua and Patrick and then between Patrick and me because I'd told Patrick he should calm down – until at last a neighbour, the old woman from the adjoining terrace, knocked at our door. While Patrick dealt with this, Joshua wailed for me, and I went to him. Look, he said, pointing to a red welt on his calf. Dad hit me with a rolled-up magazine, he cried. He whacked my bare legs.

Did you? I asked Patrick when he stepped back inside, stunned at the vision of this, at the possibility.

He looked at me, his gaze loose and dark with exhaustion. I really can't remember, he said.

Joshua went back to his mother's house then and it was some time after this, later that day or maybe the one following, when I said to Patrick, Look, you might not want a holiday, but I have to get away from all this. For my sake – can you agree for my sake? He rubbed at his forehead, and at the skin just above the bridge of his nose. Yes, he said. I can do that. In his perpetual exhaustion, Patrick had become averse to adventure. What I would have liked more than anything was for him to have said,

I'm so sorry for all this, for everything, I know this is not what you want. Let me take you away. Instead it fell to me to reply: Good then, I'll make the arrangements.

2

There is something unimaginable about setting sail, the vast ocean stretching out ahead. It can make you feel that your whole life still lies before you — the blue vista bewitches. Our ship was named *Adventure of the Seas*. We stood on deck in the sunshine sipping our drinks and thought of this: what the future might be like. He had his arm slung about my waist, his hand rested on my hip. I could feel the heat of this, his body close to me. These were our halcyon days when real life could not touch us, although I knew it would have to begin again soon; I had promised him that we would be back for Christmas. Despite their arguments, Joshua had asked if he could spend those few days with us, much to his mother's dismay. She makes too much of a fuss, he had said, with the meal and the presents, still insisting that they wore the stupid paper crowns that were always too big and slipped down to the bridge of his nose. He liked all this as a kid, but now it was just embarrassing. Patrick and I, on the other hand, went to no such efforts, preferring a walk in the park and a movie at home. I had always enjoyed these quiet days when we could be alone, but Patrick was flattered that

Joshua wanted to spend the time with us. He liked the idea that his son was coming home for Christmas; there was something filmic to it, archetypal, even though Joshua lived in the same neighbourhood and we really didn't do Christmas at all. But that was Joshua's point, the thing that pleased him, and Patrick wanted to make amends.

For now, though, the wide blue world was all ours. We sailed for days in the sun. How many exactly I'm not sure. One day slipped into the next and time lost its hold. Sometimes the ship stopped, but we didn't get off with the sightseers. Instead we lay about, drinking, reading, sleeping. We travelled through the Gulf of Alaska and across vast miles of ocean. For days there was nothing but dark water all around and after a while the very idea of firm ground seemed miraculous. We stared at the water and the sky for so long that the possibility of land started to feel like a mirage, a thing we would never reach.

Meanwhile, the weather was almost too good to be true. Strange, one crew member said as he bent over to refill my glass while I lay by the pool, Normally we travel through at least a bit of rain and swell. You and your husband are bringing us good luck, he said, smiling as he passed Patrick a martini from a silver tray. At that point we must have been sailing for two weeks or so and I was beginning to imagine what it would be like to arrive in Japan.

Patrick was lying in the sun, spinning those little paper parasols that come with the drinks. Pink and yellow. Blue and green. Round and round they went. Seagulls flew overhead. I was next to him, reading a book. You should put some sunglasses on, Patrick said, reaching over to trace a line along my collarbone. Hm? I replied, a little drunk and sleepy. Later, I followed him down to our cabin and we made love. The sex had always been good, but on that day it was something else altogether. The pleasure so intense I could hardly feel the edges of my body – all my limbs and the surface of my skin seemed to be tingling, almost dissolving. At one point the pleasure had been so great that I felt on the cusp of losing consciousness. Afterwards we lay listening to the bass of the music from a party that had started up above us. I rested my head on his shoulder and he held me close. Sweat beaded across his chest. Looking up, we saw a reflection of ourselves in miniature in the dome of the cabin ceiling light. Patrick ran his hand down my thigh.

He was older than me by a good twenty years. When we first got together I had just celebrated my twenty-fourth birthday. He was forty-five and a professor in film studies trying to make his big break into directing features. Back then I was his student, and he'd not long separated from his first wife. He'd left her, although I didn't know this at the time, when she was pregnant with Joshua. I met Patrick as he was trying to escape all this, having taken up a temporary post in Australia as a visiting scholar in the Department of Cinema Studies and Moving Image. I took his course in film history and theory, then another called Living Cinema. I always loved cinema. I loved the mystery of it and the ritual, the way it evoked for me all the most magical feelings. I enrolled in his courses because I wanted to understand that world, because I wanted to inhabit it, and because it seemed to me that my own thoughts so often took the form of film images: how did an idea become a picture? I wanted to know this. The cinematic image seemed the one image that could give me the world whole. A trembling, incandescent image that created a universe of feeling parallel to and sometimes stronger than my own. It was as if they were somehow prophetic, those images. As if the cinematic image could not only translate my own inner state but magnify and expand it, lift it right out of me and make it live.

I was among the quieter students, wearing my fringe long and tugging at the stray ends by my jawline. His verbosity made me nervous, the way he paced and pontificated to great effect, all the while coming across as friendly and eager to hear from us. There weren't many like him, lecturers who seemed to care about what you thought and said. I idolised him. We all did. Everyone was in love with him in one way or another. When he gave a lecture the theatre was always packed, and it was not uncommon to find students sitting on the stairs.

He never used notes when he gave those lectures, but talked fast and with a great deal of energy. Everything seemed to matter to him, everything was connected to something else. It was exhilarating to listen to this, to discover these connections. We all wanted to feel ourselves the subject of his attention, to bask in the glow. I didn't mind back then, the volume of his thoughts. We assumed that this was how we acquired knowledge, how we came upon it; by absorbing everything he told us. Besides, I myself didn't have much to say. Of course I'd seen his short films and read his essays, and when I did put up my hand to speak I sometimes referred to this. I knew I blushed every time I opened my mouth. I blushed at the very thought of opening my mouth. The blush broke out first on my chest and then spread up my neck in bright-red blotches until it reached my cheeks. I could blush just listening to him. And when I did start to say something, to respond to something he said, or to develop a point he might have raised in class, my thoughts came out in such a quiet voice. Sometimes he interpreted my slowly raised hand not as a raised hand, but as a hand going to my hair or shirt collar. He would ask this. Is that a raised hand, or are you just about to touch your hair? And I would be too embarrassed to say that yes it was a raised hand and so instead I would shake my head and drop my hand, blushing again. He encouraged informality and interjections. Speak up! he'd say. Interrupt! Tell me where I've got it wrong! But when I tried this, my voice was so soft that even when he was looking at me and could see my mouth moving it was as if he didn't really hear me; or he only tuned in to hear me after he had finished the long sentence he was in the midst of when I first started to speak. I didn't mind. None of us did. This was his prerogative, as a professor. He was American-born, but his parents were French. When he spoke, certain vowels retained their accent. French cinema, he told us, was in his blood. We all loved to listen to him talk. Later I would have a lot to say, too, and I would learn how to say it. But I didn't then: all I knew was that I wanted to be a writer, only I didn't yet have all the words and didn't know how to express the ones I did. At that time, it was all still in my head.

Things changed towards the end of the semester, when posters started to appear around campus advertising a public seminar that he was to give. Are you going? Who's *not* going? If you go, can you take notes? This was what everyone asked. What everyone said. You know, I heard a student say to him at the end of a class, you look a lot like Keanu Reaves? Yeah. You know the thing he does with his hands, in interviews? Like that interview when the person asked him what he thought happened to you in the afterlife? His hands are so beautiful, man. But you, you look a bit more like a Californian Keanu, a beach-bum kind of Keanu. People were signing up for the seminar just to say they were there.

On that day, the day of his talk, it was raining heavily. There was wind too, strong enough to turn umbrellas inside out. I arrived early despite this, running through the rain to get to the lecture theatre. Some people were already there, sitting in the front rows and chatting, laughing. There was cask wine and plastic cups. I found a seat up the back, unbuttoned my coat and hung it over my chair to dry, aware of the musty animal smell coming from the damp wool. Every sound echoed in that large space – every footstep, every cough. I took a pad of paper from my bag, and a book, and pretended to busy myself until the seminar commenced.

Looking back, I can't remember exactly what he said. He paced the small stage while uttering complex phrases that were full of words like dissemination, radicalise, inequality, matrix. His voice boomed low in his chest. I remember more the feeling of elevation, of enthrallment, of sensing a whole world of thought opening up in front of me, a parallel dimension that was not my future but which was infused with the same pull, the same anticipation of brilliance, glory, joy. Even if that's not true, even if that's not what happens to any of us in our real futures, this was what it felt like to listen to him speak, to follow that train of thought which seemed to reconfigure the order of the universe as I understood it then. Because there are points in one's life when revelations occur, when the force of revelation befalls one, and there isn't any other way of explaining the power of this event. I wanted to think like that. I wanted to know how one became able to think like that. I wanted to write poems and books and stories that would have inside them this force, this energy, this intensity, that would preserve this for me. I didn't take notes, but scribbled phrases. I could feel myself sweating. My hands were clammy. In front of me sat a tall, thin woman who did not move or fidget or adjust herself once for the whole hour. She kept her jacket on, perfectly tailored, and seemed to hardly breathe. One row down from me and to my left sat one of my lecturers from the previous year. He was a ruffled professor of nineteenth-century verse and perhaps not a film enthusiast, for he sat there picking what I think were pet hairs off the woolly jumper that he held in his lap. From a dog maybe, thin white stripes of hair diagonally placed – proximate in form to the scansion lines he spent his days scrutinising.

At the end of the talk there was a heavy round of applause, followed by questions. My heart beat hard in my chest, I felt breathless – how much I wanted to ask something. Only my thoughts didn't break down into a smooth question. There was too much I didn't understand. I wanted to show my eagerness, but not reveal my stupidity. I half lifted a shaking hand at one point, but then, instead of raising it above my head, brought it to my neck. At last I held up my hand properly, and he pointed at me and in a trembling voice I asked my question. He cupped his fingers to his ear to indicate that he couldn't quite hear me, and I repeated my question, louder this time, my face burning with shame. Patrick – or Professor Heller as I called him then – thanked me generously and answered at length, making a show of the question's brilliance, although I didn't know if this was genuine or whether it was just to make up for my obvious embarrassment. Then it was over. The theatre emptied. I stood up and pulled on my coat, avoiding eye contact with my poetry professor in the row below. Then I joined the queue heading out of the narrow door. It wasn't until I'd made it down the two flights of stairs and through the passageway and the foyer that I realised I'd left my umbrella behind. The rain could be heard pounding on the roof. I hurried back, but the umbrella was gone. Of course it was: a cheap black thing that looked like any other of the dozen or so umbrellas left on the ground or leaning against the wall once the plastic bucket intended for such objects was full. Many of the men, I noticed, had large, long-handled umbrellas – the size of golfing umbrellas, that meant they preserved a dry force field all about them of almost a metre and half in diameter. When these umbrellas were closed, the men walked with them as a dandy might have a good century before, flicking the umbrella out in front and letting the pointed tip tap the pavement, the smooth wooden handle, glossy from use, swinging easily in the loose cup of the hand. My umbrella was of the kind women carry: small, light, readily stowed in a handbag. The kind that even I, with my petite build, had to shrink in under, the canopy of such an umbrella being so limited. A polite umbrella that did not take up space and which always left the arms of my coat and the side of my handbag darkened by rain. I walked back down the stairs.

Outside, the crowd had cleared. All, that is, except for Patrick. I did not think of him then by that name, of course. But it feels strange, even inappropriate, almost a sexual masquerade to refer to him now as the Professor, or even Professor Heller, or Professor H, as some students liked to call him. He was standing there on the pavement watching the oncoming traffic, waiting, I guessed, for a ride. His rebel leather jacket was zipped up and he was holding above his head a giant, man-sized umbrella which bore the logo of the Hotel Intercontinental. The kind of umbrella, I later learnt, that a wealthy but impractical man, a well-heeled man who likes to think of himself as bucking the system, steals from a five-star hotel. He noticed me standing under the awning debating whether to run to the bus stop or wait for the rain to ease. Come under here! he called. It didn't occur to me that he could have walked towards me and led me out under the safety of his huge umbrella. So I ran. I dashed out from under the awning and across the pavement to where he stood. He held the umbrella aloft for the two of us. He thanked me again for my question and asked if I was going to the pub with the others. I made some excuse and garbled a long-winded compliment about his talk, his films, whatever.

You're not going? I asked. To the pub, I mean.

No, he said, I have a plane to catch, or not, if this weather doesn't improve.

He had ordered a taxi. As he spoke he stretched out his arm, flagging down the vehicle that was just arriving.

Hop in, he said. Let me drop you off somewhere. And instead of leaving the shelter of his umbrella and running for my bus, I slipped into the back seat beside him.

That day on the boat we lay together a little longer in our cabin, then he rolled away and got up to shower. Afterwards he pulled on his swimming trunks. I wanted him to stay with me, but he seemed suddenly irritable, fidgety. I just need to cool off, he said, get some air. Are you coming? he asked.

Maybe, I said. I'll follow soon. He took a bathrobe, pushed his feet into the complimentary slippers then headed for the top deck where there was the pool and the casino.

The sea was so still. Outside, I imagined the air to be soft and balmy. I thought I could stay on the ship forever, travel around and around the globe, become accustomed to no longer feeling the earth beneath my feet, and in this way turn leathery in the sun while feasting on pineapple and mango and melons. I did not follow Patrick immediately – I was sleepy from our exertions, and after showering I lay down to rest a while. I had a book and although I intended to read, I must have scarcely made it through a paragraph before I fell fast asleep. When I woke it was dark, and the ship was tilting this way and that. Our porthole was just above sea level, and as the ship heaved I saw first the sky, then just ocean – the porthole like a wounded eye that swings down over and over again into a basin of cloudy water. Then up again, to blink. Patrick wasn't there. I pulled on my clothes and went above deck in search of him.

We were sailing past the Kamchatka Peninsula and towards the Sea of Okhotsk. As I climbed the stairs, an announcement came through the speaker system. The crew asked that all passengers return to their cabins, as a storm was about to hit. There was no way to sail around it, the swell was already high and the water rough. But when I reached the lido deck there was still a cluster of people out by the pool and plenty by the bar inside, so I too ordered something, thinking why not, thinking it might at least dull the nerves, as I looked about for Patrick. Behind me a fat man was laughing loudly, smacking his thigh with his hand. Maybe it was just precautionary, the warning. A formality for insurance reasons, or something like that; once the risk was stated, the responsibility would be ours alone. Then I spotted Patrick near the roulette table – he was gesticulating, making a bet it seemed. When I reached him he put a finger to his lips, his eyes fixed on the wheel as the ball went round and round then settled. He whooped with glee and swiftly placed another bet, pulling a wad of cash from the pocket of his bathrobe to exchange for more chips. He was drunk, he must have been up there on his own for hours while I slept, his hair damp from swimming. His chest and face were sunburnt from the morning. He leant on me as he eyed the circling ball. And then he lost. He was insistent that they keep playing, that he place another bet although he had no money and no line of credit to hand, and so became aggressive: loud, wild, roughly spoken.

Then the storm hit. It was sudden and extreme. No one had predicted the size of the waves: ten metres, with winds up to eighty kilometres per hour. So they told me later. I had just picked up my drink when the furniture started sliding from one side of the room to the other, there was the sound of glass breaking, people screaming. Tables and potted plants crashed first into one wall, then the next. I held on to whatever I could: benches, a pillar in the centre of the room. Outside there was the flash of lightning. Then everything went very quiet, very still. I could hear a woman crying. I crawled towards Patrick, clinging to the broken furniture. People were starting to stand and brush themselves off. Patrick had been slammed back against the wall when the storm first struck and now, as I reached to help him, he pushed me away. He scrambled to his feet and started to head back to the bar. Then, all of a sudden, he collapsed into an armchair and closed his eyes. I had taken my anti-nausea pills but Patrick had not, and the storm, mixed with the alcohol, overwhelmed him; a moment later he pushed himself up to standing. I think I'm going to be sick, he said as he stumbled towards the deck, the ship still tilting this way and that. The door was unlocked, I saw him shove it open and step out into the darkness. What was he thinking? I watched him for a moment, wondering if I should go to help, knowing he'd prefer to throw up on his own because he never liked anyone around when he was sick or feeble. I'd hurt myself when the storm first struck and felt a little stunned. Then the ship listed again, more violently this time, and I heard Patrick calling to me. J.B., he called, as he liked to call me, using not my real name but my middle initials under which I published. J.B. Come out, J.B.! His voice cut through the noise of the storm, as it has always been able to cut through anything. The sound of glasses shattering. The sight of the looming dark waves outside and then water crashing down over the railings. I followed him.

As I reached the door I lost my balance, slipping on the wet floor. Outside, the night was cold and the ocean loud. I found him bent over, one hand clinging to the railings. I went towards him, but he brushed me away. Only once before had I seen him vomit from drunkenness. Generally, I discouraged him from drinking more than a glass or two. While it made others relaxed and convivial, after a few drinks he would get cranky. Or maybe tetchy is the word. Sometimes mad. And so I'd often quietly draw his glass towards me and, while he was talking, finish it myself.

The storm was getting worse. Patrick! I called. What are you doing? We've got to get you inside. I reached out to him, but he pushed my hand away. Some dark change had come over him, one I didn't understand. He lifted his face towards me then and said something he perhaps would not have said were he not so drunk. Something he must have been storing up. Something he must have been trying not to say. Something he must have thought of frequently, but at intervals. Something terrible that I would later try to forget.

You don't mean that, I said. You're drunk. You're really drunk. Then he yelled it again. I stepped back a little, scared and disbelieving. He moved suddenly then, as if to take hold of me – a tiger lashing its paw. The boat tilted. Patrick slipped and vomited once more then wiped his mouth with the sleeve of his bathrobe. We've got to get out of the storm, I yelled as I stumbled towards the door. But he moved fast and grabbed my wrist, his grip hard. What are you doing? I said. He spat at me then and I pulled myself free. I screamed at him through the wind and rain, but he wouldn't have heard me because just then came the crash of thunder. He took hold of me by the shoulders as a dark wave loomed up beside us, its white froth and marbling visible in the flash of lightning. The boat lifted and dropped, throwing us off balance. My gut lurched as though on the dip of a rollercoaster. He let go of me and I scrambled inside. Then the ship tilted and the heavy steel door slammed shut, separating us. Patrick! I shouted, as I struggled with the handle, but when I finally managed to push the door open he was nowhere to be seen. The waves looked like giant dark mountains, streaked with snow. Heaving, slamming against the ship. The lights on the balcony caught the sea spray and made a halo of it. The boat tilted again. I held on to the railings and dragged myself further along the balcony. But still there was no sight of him. I kept going, holding on and shouting his name, the railings slippery in the wet. It was soon after this that I heard the first call, Man Overboard, Portside.

In Shostakovich's cello sonata number one in E flat major there is a moment, perhaps a third of the way through the second movement, when the cellist must hit the strings with her bow. She hits rapidly, creating short, jarring sounds – part slap, part splintering of dense material. You cannot play this piece on a gut-stringed instrument but only on a metal-stringed one, lest the beating of the strings should cause them to snap – which sometimes happens anyway. It is a powerful part of the music, terrifying even – reminiscent of boots marching fast towards their target, of something being broken to pieces over and over again, attack, collapse, the failure of resistance, of terror coming back and back and back in the mind of the beholder, like a dream of falling when you fall and fall again and never hit the bottom. To make these sounds the cellist must unleash such force upon the instrument that she can appear at times to be almost whipping it, flaying a flagging beast. But in the process of this, the cellist's body appears to relinquish all effort, to give itself entirely to the bow, to collapse into the instrument, to collapse around it, on top of it, hanging her body upon it. She looks to be falling into the sound – the sound of terror and of the Russian winter and of the long, deep cold, the darkness, falling over and over again.

The call was repeated. Man Overboard, Portside, as one crew member after another yelled it out. I didn't know what it was at first. It didn't register. It certainly wasn't for me because I was there, squinting against the oncoming rain. A whistle sounded, followed by an alarm. Then an announcement came through the PA system. I was disoriented by the unsteadiness of the boat. As the storm eased, people came rushing to the railings. It didn't make sense then – it couldn't, for whom would this ever be real – that this call was related to Patrick, that he might be the one who fell. Then the ship cut its engines. I couldn't see him anywhere. I called out. I ran down the side of the ship, slipping, looking for him. I saw someone throw a white life float into the sea: the circle of it drifting down through the dark, spinning, getting smaller and smaller and smaller still until it was swallowed up by the water. Visible every now and then as a white speck in the waves. Women were crying. A searchlight swung back and forth. Further along the deck was a cluster of official-looking people, in the centre of which stood a man, pointing. Ah, I thought, there he is, and a cry escaped me. I ran up to him, pushed through the crowd. But I was wrong – Oh, I said. Oh. I thought you were— It was only then that I understood what had happened. Of course he was the one they were looking for, no one else had been out there. My husband, I cried out, I can't find my husband—

Twelve decks he fell. The CCTV wasn't monitored, nor was it connected to an alarm system. The footage was grainy: the white side of the ship, the grey sea. In this his body appears black, it looks like he's bouncing off the side of the boat, or trying to cling to it, like a cat leaping, tumbling. Later, on the television news, they made a spotlight around his body as it fell, a lighter, brighter circle that made his outline clear. They slowed the footage down, zoomed in. Repeated it from the beginning. It didn't show the top railing, the one he went over, just the side of the ship. Not the beginning or the end of the fall. Like in a dream.

Someone was holding me up. A crew member stepped closer to me, We are doing everything we can, they said. Action has been swift, immediate. Lightness in the legs, tingling, some swooning feeling that was not love. I don't remember collapsing. Here, a voice said, She's in shock, let's get her inside. A man gathered me up, one arm under my shoulders, the other beneath my knees. I could hear a woman calling, wailing. Come now, the man carrying me said. Let's lie her down.

We had drifted some way from the site of the accident. It took time to turn the ship around, and then move back so that we could weigh anchor closer to where it was hoped we might spot Patrick, waving, calling out, clinging to the tiny white life ring. There used to be an advertisement for these. For the life ring sweets that came wrapped in striped paper, orange and purple and green, and when you peeled back this coloured paper there was silver paper underneath, and when you peeled back the silver paper you found a neat roll of sweets, orange and purple and green. Life Savers, I think they were called. The advert would make my mouth water. I thought that the different colours signalled different flavours but then they all tasted the same, too sugary and slightly fizzy, and you had to be careful to unwrap them very slowly so that all the neatly aligned sweets, circles with the middles punched out, didn't fall from the packet to the ground. I remember watching the life ring grow smaller and smaller and smaller still, or maybe it faded in the dark, or perhaps it just disappeared in the white froth of the water. Everyone had rushed to the deck to help look into the sea. I was placed on a lounger, lying down, a soft blanket over my legs and chest. A woman in uniform tucked in a loose corner as she crouched beside me. I'm sorry, she said, but I have to ask you some questions.

I gave her all the information I could. How he called for me. How I followed him then came inside. The moment when the door slammed shut. Did he say anything to you? she asked. It was loud out there, I replied. He wasn't making sense.

She looked at me strangely, something flickered over

her neat features: her upturned nose, her almond-shaped eyes. But why did you leave him there?

I didn't, I said. I mean, I went out there because he called me and then I tried to get him to come inside, and after the door swung shut, he wasn't, he wasn't— I started to cry. She put her hand on my leg for comfort.

I'm sorry, she said. You don't have to talk about this now. Let's just get you settled. I'll take you to your cabin. Do you think you can walk?

I felt light-headed and was still visibly shaking, but the last thing I wanted was to remain there in a public place while everyone stared at me. I think I can, I said, yes.

In the cabin I was trembling too much to take off my sandals, and so the woman bent down to unfasten the buckles and helped me into the bed that now felt hard and uncomfortable – I couldn't fathom how I had thought it otherwise, how I had ever slept in it so easily, how Patrick and I had ever experienced such pleasure there.

I hoped then that I would drop down into a deep slumber: an unbearable weariness was moving through me, making my limbs feel so heavy, as if I had been drugged – a heaviness that came close to numbness. A terrible sinking feeling. But instead I lay wide awake, shivering although I was not cold, the sensation in my body approximating the kind of strange, unstoppable quivering that comes after anaesthetic has been administered through a spinal tap. My teeth chattering and my whole body trembling uncontrollably. I heard then the first of the helicopters as the search began in earnest. I lay facing the porthole. The sea was still rough, the sky dark, but every now and then I caught a glimpse of the spotlight as it scanned the waves. Do you have any questions? the woman in uniform had asked me. I shook my head. I did have a question, of course I did, but it was not one that I could bring myself to ask. How long, I wondered, how long could someone survive in that rough and freezing sea? How many hours or maybe minutes did we have? The helicopters continued on outside. Back and forth, round and round.

3

By morning the storm had passed and the sea was quiet. The air felt very cold, as if winter had come without warning. In daylight they thought they might have a better chance of finding him. I didn't know where we were exactly when he fell. Later I was told that we were in Russian waters and that they were Russian helicopters that continued to fly overhead. It was on the news now, someone told me. An image of the deck crowded with onlookers: holidaymakers with their birdwatching binoculars, deployed for a different purpose. Since the fall, the atmosphere on the boat had changed – this was no longer a party trip, hardly a vacation. The ship stayed put, small boats went out to expand the search. I remained in my cabin, except for a brief time early in the morning when I went to the top deck to look for myself. He didn't know, the captain told me, how such a thing was possible. The railings came up to the height of a man's ribcage. Everyone speculated: Maybe it was the freak giant wave; or else he could have been leaning over the railing, to vomit into the sea; unless, of course, he jumped. Rumours, all of them, but I considered every whispered possibility as a near-truth, a likelihood, the real story. If nothing showed up the ship would have to move on, but it would not follow its usual course. We would dock at Otaru in Japan and I would get off there. Then the ship would turn round, go home the way it came. In Otaru, the captain said to me that morning, there is some information the officials will need from you. About your husband's circumstances. Mainly for insurance, he said kindly. Nothing to be alarmed about. I wept continuously as he spoke; I was exhausted and confused – I did not understand what was supposed to happen next: to me, to the boat, to the other passengers who would soon head for home. I had not slept that night, nor did I sleep the following one when the ship started to move again towards port because nothing had been found. I'm afraid, the captain told me then, that the chances of him having survived now are almost zero. In that swell, in those temperatures. The language of the search changed accordingly: they were no longer looking for a man, for my husband, for Patrick, but for a body.

It took all night and the best part of a day to reach the port. By the time we arrived it was afternoon and very cold. I had packed my coat but didn't then have it with me and shivered in my flimsy jumper as I was escorted from the ship by a steward, his hand resting gently on my elbow and guiding me as if I were blind. I knew I needed to talk to Joshua. It was possible that he'd seen the news already. I was told that they had released Patrick's name. The steward took me to a taxi and gave a quick flurry of instructions to the driver. From there I was taken to a police station in Sapporo, where I was asked to make an official statement. I assumed others were being asked to do the same: the crew, the captain. The officer in charge was Japanese and spoke only halting English. Further questions, he said, would need to be asked. An interpreter had been sent for. Everyone was very gentle with me. My eyes stung from crying, the ground tilted with lack of sleep; I wanted only to keep vigil, to remain alert and watchful, on guard as they say, in case he reappeared, washed up and stumbling home. But how would he know where to find me? What if he didn't know where I was, where I had been taken? That I was already here? Which was not where we were supposed to end up. I was filled then with the heightened sense of life, of living, that accompanies certain states of deprivation. I have heard women who do not eat describe their hunger in these terms: as a brightening of the world, a sharpening of attention, a quickening of all feeling. The very air seemed thinner, lighter, pure in the nostrils like the chilled air of high mountains. The northern sky appeared brittle, made of fine blown glass.

I was on the edge of delirium, but not quite there. Enough, though, to feel sufficiently disinhibited when I was led to the interview room for questioning. My own biography was already part of the press coverage. I saw this just briefly, when something came through on my phone. The wife of the missing and the maybe dead. The newspapers reporting on the accident pulled the photograph from my publisher's website – the photo Patrick had taken. My image slightly blurred and too dark. 'It is like being like,' my students used to say, when they started a sentence. Not like being. Like something like. Meaning, the comparison was twice removed. The experience of being was only proximate, increasingly distant. Not the being of likeness, but the likeness of being. Or rather, the likeness of being like being. Which was how I felt then, bleary and slightly out of focus, as I took my place at the small wooden table in the centre of the room. I sat down, the investigating police officer stationed himself across from me and placed a tape recorder between us. Then the interpreter arrived. He bowed and introduced himself in a voice so soft and quiet it might have been a whisper, his glossy hair falling over his face. He pushed his fringe back as he too sat down next to me. The officer immediately said something to me in Japanese, watching me closely. A moment later the interpreter repeated his words: So, you say you were with your husband most of the afternoon, just before the accident. Can you tell us what you were doing, how he seemed to you?

My mouth was dry. I found it hard to speak. I turned to the interpreter. Can I please have something to drink? I asked. He nodded and stood up, making some gesture to the guard, who came over to us. They spoke quickly and the guard in turn opened the door and uttered some order to a woman in the next office. The three of us sat in silence while we waited. Soon the woman returned with the water, carrying the glass carefully with both hands. She placed it down in front of me, bowed slightly and backed away. I drank, then, lifting my forearm to my face, wiped my mouth with the sleeve of my jumper. The officer said something in his own language, and the interpreter relayed this: Please continue, he said. I nodded, looked around. The room where we sat was painted white, dark scuff marks on the walls where a table had scraped against it, or where a black-soled boot had kicked at the corners. Through the vents I could hear the wind picking up, the whining air.

We, I said, I mean I. I had wanted— The interpreter waited for me to finish my sentence. I felt sick. I leant over and placed my head in my hands, then, as the room began to spin, I leant down further to put my head between my knees. Take your time, the interpreter said. When you are ready.

There were things that I wanted to say. Things I knew I couldn't say but needed to tell someone. And then the things I knew I should say. What they wanted to hear. There is never only one version. Even in that room I could not know, exactly, how my words were being reconfigured as they passed from one language into another. I could not tell them that all too often I doubt my own version of events. There are things I did not wholly remember, but which I am sure did happen – there is an outline of them in my head, but the content is missing. There are things I am sure I once remembered differently to how I recall them now. And not only about my husband. Just tell us. If you can tell us. Take your time, the interpreter said again. My hands were shaking. Once, someone had asked me this question about my mother. Years ago, when I was a child. Just tell us, tell us what you remember. The last time, from the last time you saw her.

She too had vanished one cold, wet night, and in that small concrete room in the north of Japan the memory of this flashed up in the dark of my mind, overlapping with the more recent events. The captain's voice coming loud through the speakers of the boat, fading and growing close, fading and growing close as I ran along the deck looking down at the water, and my father, years before, calling out in the street below the hotel where we were staying as he too ran back and forth, asking people if they'd seen a woman in a coat and hat, but it was winter – everybody wore a coat and hat, or a *hoat and cat* as my father, in his distress, started saying: *A woman in a hoat and cat? Have you seen her?* But no one had seen anything, everyone had seen nothing.

I shook my head, reached up and pinched the bridge of my nose, near the inner corners of my eyes. Little colours sparked against my closed lids. The wind was blowing harder. I opened my eyes and could see, through the window, trees leaning. The threat of rain.

We drank on the bed, I said, champagne, still in our swimsuits. He'd already had a martini up on deck. I remember this moment, I told the interpreter, because it surprised me: how quickly he finished his first glass down in the cabin and poured us both another. As if he were feeling in himself already the desire to obliterate or be obliterated. While he sipped this he reached over and ran his finger around and then over my nipple, which was hardened from the chill of my damp costume. I lifted his hand away and put his index finger in my mouth. When we were children, I think I said, my father used to take us to the beach in the summertime. I was never a strong swimmer and disliked the waves, and so would explore the rock pools while my father and sister waded out into the ocean. I would search, in particular, for the anemones that clung to the edge of the rock pools. They were maroon, almost black, the colour disguising them against the rock. Sometimes they were closed up, like little humped growths. At other times their mouths stood open, their short velvety tentacles, a little like the edge of frayed cloth, waving in the gentle current. I would reach down and push my index finger inside the creature so as to feel it close its soft body around my fingertip, sucking a little, and as I pulled my finger away the tentacles, or whatever they are called, would cling on and try to retain me. Afterwards the anemone would revert to a small, silky growth, hard to the touch. I took one finger into my mouth, then the next. He shut his eyes and arched his neck in pleasure. Then he slipped the bikini top from my breasts, put his tongue to the dark circles of skin. I pulled his head in closer to my chest, then removed the bottom of my swimsuit and shuffled my legs open so that I could put his thigh between mine, pressing myself into him.

In that interview room the air was dry: a small vaporiser stood in the corner puffing a jet of white steam into the air. I swallowed, my mouth feeling clammy, and reached forwards to take another sip of water. The investigating officer coughed and looked away. There was a delay, only fractional, but a delay all the same, while the interpreter repeated my last phrases. It was not simultaneous translation, so there were breaks between my speech and his. In this brief hiatus of understanding I watched the investigator's face, who looked from the interpreter to me and back again. The investigator appeared puzzled, unsure: as if the words the interpreter was repeating could not really have come from my mouth. At one point he held up his hand, indicating that the interpreter pause a moment, and he asked a question in his native language. I knew it was a question because of the inflection, and assumed he was checking the accuracy of the interpreter's words. Continue then, he seemed to say, waving his hand as one might do when conducting a line of congested traffic. They were waiting for me to tell them what they needed to hear. An admission. Or a declaration. A point of fact. Go on, Patrick said. Or did he say, I can't hold on. Or was it, Come on, come here. Fuck, he might have said, cursing through gritted teeth, holding back.

I let him in an inch, then lifted off, then in a little more, then lifted off. I could feel myself opening. I waited for this. Then I let him in a little further still. And lifted off, very slowly. I could feel the deep centre of my body that he was heading towards. A dark, hidden core that otherwise went untouched; I craved the pressure of him there. I lifted off again, then lowered myself a little further. I can't remember where his hands were. Not on my hips, because, if there, he would want, by instinct, to push me gently down on to him, and I wouldn't have that.

I was so thirsty. I leant forwards again for the glass of water. I didn't know how much of this I was only thinking to myself, how much I was saying out loud. It seemed unreal that the accident had occurred only two nights before. That we were together like this only three days ago. My hands were shaking and I lifted the glass carefully to my mouth. But it didn't matter how much I drank, my mouth remained dry. So different from my mouth when Patrick kissed it. We kissed like teenagers. I kissed him like I was still in high school. Like I kissed on those long, hot summer afternoons when my boyfriend's parents were not yet home, and we would sit on the couch with the television on, or music playing. Sometimes we would eat something: a packet of crisps, or biscuits, and almost always I ended up sitting on his lap. He would have run his hands up and down my legs, admiring my smooth, freshly shaved skin, letting his fingers stray just under the hem of my skirt and then slinking back down to my ankle. I would have eventually chosen to act on this, and, while kissing, swung one leg over on to his lap and pulled myself in closer. The feeling of our physical proximity was overwhelming. Our lips swollen with kissing, our mouths full of saliva. I could smell his sweat. I could feel his lumped erection against my pubic bone, my cotton knickers sticking to my own wetness. He would run his hands over my top, then let his calloused fingers wander up my back, feeling for my bra strap. I let him do this, unhook it, so that I might feel the weight of my breasts being let free, then lifted so gently by his hands. I could hardly breathe. His own breath was rasping, shaking, a kind of guttural drag at the back of his throat. He would move my skirt away and push his fingers in beneath the elastic of my knickers at the edge of my inner thigh. Oh, he said, his fingers peeling back my layers of skin.

It soon became uncomfortable, though, the way my boyfriend's fingers were pushing about inside of me, without real direction, without knowledge. And with my underpants still on, the movement of his fingers was restricted. He caught my pubic hair by accident. The edge of his nail was suddenly sharp against my labia. As his own desire reached its peak, he had become careless. I pulled away, the discomfort suddenly extinguishing my desire. What? he said, breathless, What's wrong?

Nothing, I replied.

Did I do something?

No, I said.

I wasn't sure, and perhaps have never been sure, how to explain that it was less what he was doing and more a problem of what I needed him to do, what I wanted him to do, while feeling unable to utter instructions. My greatest desire was for him to simply intuit the routes to satiating me. Instead, I turned the situation back on myself: I just don't think I can do this yet, I said. It was easier to explain the sudden cessation as my own failing. A scenario that would then leave me in the role of having to calm him and reassure him of his prowess, and of my willingness to comply with his desire: soon, very soon, I'd tell him. I was still seated on his lap. But we're so close, he gasped, holding on to me. And no one will be home for hours. I thought you wanted this, he said. I do, I replied. Just not like this. I knew the lines by heart: it was what we girls, or young women, were all meant to say at one point or another, the polite refusal, the suggestion of a collective female fantasy that none of us properly understood. But it was, is, what we offer at one point or another in order to back out unscathed, in order to re-enter the domain of dialogue and barter. But instead of conceding, he said to me: You have to do something. It hurts.

What hurts?

It hurts, he said, when a guy gets this turned on and then can't do anything with it.

Oh, I replied.

It aches like crazy, he said. Please, he begged. If I can't go inside you, will you give me a handjob?

My husband and I, I said to the officer, had a conversation similar to this one early on in the cruise. Only it was me then who was aching, physically aching, as my boyfriend must have once ached, and I wanted Patrick to attend to this. We were in bed and his desire had suddenly flagged, as it had occasionally started to of late. This time I was the one asking. Please, I said. You can't just stop like that. I was angry when he refused to touch me any more, angry and offended, especially when he said to me, slightly surprised, that he didn't realise women could ache in that way, inside, and so in the cabin that afternoon, on the day of the accident, we—

The investigator nodded and got up out of his chair, I could see him blushing. He walked backwards and forwards behind his desk, then strolled towards me, his head down, demonstrating by way of this performance the act of deep thinking. He rubbed the stubble on his chin. Instead of pausing in front of my chair, he walked behind me. I uncrossed my legs. My stomach tilted: a rush of nausea. He stopped where he was. Against my neck I could feel the heat coming off his body, he was that close. Then he reached out and put his hand on my shoulder. I flinched.

He started to speak again and there was a slight pause while the interpreter translated this. I want to skip forwards a bit, he said. When you last saw your husband, where were you standing?

I beg your pardon?

Were you in front of him, behind, or to the side?

Where was I standing?

Yes, if you were standing. On the deck.

I was standing. I think I was in front of him. His back

to the railings. The investigator lifted his hand away and returned to his seat at the table.

Actually, no. I think I saw him from behind, I said.

My mind moved restlessly over this gap: the space between the moment he spat at me and when I tried to go inside. It was so dark. There was all that ceaseless tilting. I blanked out. Even now, the smooth progression of the scene pixelates in my mind, halts. As if my connection to this event were unstable, like that alert one sometimes sees on the screen when a loved one's face freezes and their words blur. In poetry there is a name for this kind of experience: the caesura. The point in a line of verse where there is a break in the continuity of the metrical structure. A momentary suspension, a banking up. This is not a syntactic pause, and not to be confused with an ordinary pause between phrases. Nor is it a rhetorical pause, although one will hear it in performance. It is a musical rupture. A moment of disassembling. In times past such prosodic junctures were assigned a gender: you could have a masculine or feminine caesura depending on where it appeared in the line, relative to the strength of the preceding syllable. Naturally, a feminine caesura came after a weak stress not counted in the metrical pattern.

There was a poster high up on the wall depicting snow-capped mountains and cherry blossoms. As I talked my vision drifted towards this. One of the top corners was peeling away from the wall. The investigating officer spoke again and the interpreter relayed the question while wiping his forehead with a very neatly folded handkerchief. You are, it says here, a British citizen?

Yes, I replied.

You do not look British.

The investigator put his tongue to the corner of his mouth. I saw there a tiny spot of dried toothpaste. He looked me up and down, wondering, I guessed, what kind of woman confessed in the way I just had, where such a woman came from. I recrossed my legs, looked at my hands – I was twisting my wedding band around and around my finger, an ongoing nervous tick.

Let's go back then, to your own account, in the cabin on the day of the accident. After this, he said, after this episode was over, what happened?

I don't know quite what I said then, but his own face was animated: much rising of his eyebrows, squinting in concentration, tightening and stretching of his lips. Was he mirroring my own expressions? Did I do all that with my face while I talked? It appeared almost farcical, this exaggerated display of attention, sympathy, shock. In the fleeting moments between the shifting of his features his face returned to neutral, and I noticed that although he must have been in his late forties, perhaps fifty, there was not one line or crease in his skin – as if he never moved his face at all, never frowned or expressed surprise, or grimaced as he did then, sitting across from me. And so it seemed that his expressions were carried out in mockery, an exaggerated performance of understanding – an attempt to disguise his own prudish view that we had been having too much sex, and that my own version of events was too emotional. Inside his own head he might have been stringing together a completely different story about the beautiful young wife of the rich white man who drowned. I started to cry, my words garbled.

The officer passed me a box of tissues. I thanked him with words he could not understand and blew my nose. I felt a headache coming on. The fluorescent strip lighting was flickering. I reached down into my bag and pulled out my sunglasses. I'm sorry, I said, and tried to indicate by way of gestures that my head was hurting. I could have said this, but for some reason didn't. Behind the dark lenses I closed my eyes. Heard the whir of the gas heater. The officer adjusting his weight in the squeaking chair.

Not long before we left for the cruise I had started suffering from the most terrible migraines. They began behind my left eye, deep in the socket, and slowly spread back through one half of my skull. Before this, when I heard people say that the pain they felt was blinding, I had thought the phrase to be merely a figure of speech. But once the migraines hit, I understood it to be a literal description of an experience: I couldn't open my eyes, I couldn't bear the light. The pain was a blade working its way through the fat and bone of my head. I breathed slowly, pressed my cool fingers to my temples.

After a little while someone said something to me. I thought they said this in English and that I had missed their meaning. The pain in my head was worsening. Then the phrase was repeated in what really was English and I understood. I think we are done here, the interpreter said. Someone will be in touch if we have any further questions. For now, he told me, you are free to go. The officer passed the interpreter a card and said something. Then the interpreter gave the card to me. It was for a local hotel. You will be comfortable here, he said.

Thank you, I replied, and bent down to gather up my things.

It was cold and blustery outside. I pushed my sunglasses back into my bag and took shelter under the awnings of the bus stop outside the police station. I held out my arm to flag down a taxi. Then I slipped into the back seat and passed the driver the card, pointing to the picture on the front. I pointed to my chest and then the picture again. Me, there, I said.

4

It was dark and raining when I arrived. The taxi pulled up on the corner and I stepped out into the drizzle. Up ahead I could see the flickering neon lights of the hotel sign: something something Garden Inn. If I wore my glasses the rain only made a mess of them and prevented me from reading any sign whatsoever. But without them I could only recognise very bright capital letters. I rubbed the lenses clear on the hem of my cardigan, then crossed the car park and pushed open the heavy glass door that led into the lobby.

It was the kind of hotel one expects to find in a B movie. Worn and grimy carpet, harsh lights, the smell of cigarettes. Too far from anywhere; the kind of place you come to when you have travelled as far as you can, when you have gone as far as the road will take you and your body has started to turn against itself, when even the landscape has shown you its back, even the weather. The kind of place you come to when you're half out of your mind with fatigue and disorientation, dizzy and thirsty and with the wrong loose change in your pocket, not enough for the stiff drink you really need, and although you have a credit card you can't remember your pin and you're too tired to sign your name in any reasonable fashion and when you try no one believes that it is really you, that you are who you say you are. They look at you with suspicion as if you might have travelled all this way in order to buy a single whisky on someone else's money, and the exhaustion you feel is only compounded by the fact that you've arrived in the dark so that you can only get your bearings by the dim street lights and the sign above the bar, the kind of place that leaves you feeling crazed by the endless logistics of travel, having long forgotten what mad impulse, what desire, what terrible set of events might have provoked such a journey in the first place. After all that, the traveller arrives at this hotel.

I pressed the bell at the reception desk and a woman came to take my details. Then she passed me a tarnished key attached to a plastic tag on which my room number was written, and I took the stairs to the fourth floor.

The room smelt of ancient tobacco and the kind of cheap air freshener used to mask the smell of shit. I dumped my bags by the door and gathered up the bottles from the minibar: the tiny gin, the vodka, the slightly larger bottle of red wine and then white, the champagne. In my handbag my phone pinged. Then again and again. I had already missed several messages from earlier in the day and now came a steady stream of calls from London that I wouldn't or couldn't answer. I put my phone on the counter near the kettle, and while I tossed back the drinks I watched it light up and vibrate over and over. It would be near midday in London. Word of the accident would be spreading through the industry. There were people,

I knew, who wanted to talk to me. Patrick's people: his manager, his editor, the production designer that he had been due to meet with by phone some hours ago – even on holidays work still followed him. Then there was Joshua, and his mother, Trudi. I couldn't think how to say the words that needed to be said. I knew I would delete the messages without listening to them, that I couldn't bear to hear their questions, to be the one who had to confirm the news. Part of me thought that maybe it wasn't true after all. Maybe they had the wrong person. Maybe he did make that phone meeting after all and just forgot to let me know where he was. He could be like that.

Outside, the rain had turned to sleet. The ceiling light was full of dead insects. The room was overheated. But still my hands were cold. I rubbed them together. I felt strangely hungry, almost hollow. On the sideboard there was the phone, a pen, hotel stationery. No room service menu. A map and a hotel plan which included a list of what one could find on each level. I stared at it, feeling vacant and curious. The question inside me: what would happen next? To me. To my life. I had asked, upon arrival, if there was anywhere I could walk to for some takeaway, anywhere I could buy Band-Aids, as the shoes I had bought for the cruise had given me a blister on my left heel. The woman to whom I directed these questions flapped her hands briefly in a display of mild alarm and hurried to get the attention of her superior, who was filling out paperwork behind a second counter. This larger, older woman came to my aid. I'm sorry, she had said, My colleague doesn't speak English. I'm afraid there's nowhere here. No shops in walking distance. A taxi could take you to the nearest town, but it would be a half-hour drive. There is food here, she pointed behind her, in the restaurant. Dinner. And breakfast is from six. It had been days since I'd last eaten properly but I couldn't bring myself to go down to that restaurant, to feel people staring.

Instead I ran a scalding bath and lay in this as long as I could, tallying up the time over and over again; the ship, the hours with the investigator, the taxi ride here. Three days, I said to myself again and again. Patrick had been missing three days. The knowledge kept coming back to me but it was so strange, so foreign, that it made a gap in time that I couldn't assimilate, was comprised of a series of hours that made no sense. When I at last stepped out of the bath I was overcome by a wave of such intense exhaustion that I slipped, still damp, into bed. The mattress was too hard, the pillow too soft, a feather pillow that rose up around my face as if to suffocate me.

Through the ceiling came the sounds of fellow travellers: footsteps, a toilet flushing. The reading light was angled in its fittings to shine directly in my eyes. I rolled on to my side, and from here saw a flyer I had not noticed before. It was made of hard, glossy cardboard and propped up by the bedside for better viewing. On this, in English, it read: Massage Service Dial 4702. Underneath were listed the prices, based on timing: 6,000 yen, 6,700 yen, 10,000 yen. Then, in smaller print a series of bullet points: *The staff will visit the guest room. Massage will be done from above the clothes. A young lady will not ask. I will not do any sexual services.* It seemed the wrong way round – surely the admonition needed to be reversed: you cannot ask the young lady. Or did it mean that one cannot expect the young lady to ask you what it is you wish for? What had he wanted me to do? In our cabin, on the ship, I stripped him of his trunks and went down on him, touching myself. Then, when he couldn't hold out, he lifted me up towards his face and we kissed, his fingers fluttering inside me, his mouth, just for a moment, hot and wet in my ear. The young lady becomes me: I was once the young lady. The syntax of the flyer worked this way, unravelled. I don't know, I told the investigator, I can't remember. As you wish. I think this was what I said, to Patrick – playing coy, playing a character. As you wish – after all, this was a phrase from one of his favourite movies and he always was a movie man.

I lay there then waiting giddily for something: I waited for him to clamber over the mountains, waited for him to come find me waiting. I felt crazed: exhausted, drunk, unreal. It is, an officer on deck had said at one point and unofficially, not entirely inconceivable that your husband has survived. The life ring was there. The water was calm by morning. We were not so far from fishing waters, where many small boats trawl the sea for their catch. I knew he was indulging me. That he was being the gallant figure peddling false hope. Countering the captain's warning. But nonetheless, I wanted to believe him and he knew I needed to believe in something, that I needed this for just a few days in order to keep moving, eating, breathing. I was thinking of this conversation when I saw, through the hotel window, the torchlight – low down near where the main road met empty fields. At first I assumed it to be a reflection in the glass – the bare light bulb above the minibar and the kettle. But then it moved closer, wobbling a little. The wind picked up and the torchlight disappeared for a moment before showing itself again, slightly higher up now, as if the person was climbing the hill towards the hotel. There were no other street lights nearby, no other house lights. There were the small, glittering lights of a town, miles away, but no traffic lights or cars. Then the light started to climb in earnest: a bright white circle in the dark. I closed my eyes, I waited for a knock at the door, for the torchbearer to arrive, for me to open the door and find him wet and bedraggled and desperate, but alive, Dear God, I would say, You are alive. I waited and waited but no knock came, and eventually I forced myself to get up and close the curtains. After this I must have fallen asleep, the deep, numbed sleep of the recently bereaved – the sleep that is both sorely needed and much resented, resisted all the while because, of course, you have to wake up from it, you know you will have to wake up from it.

Still, the night passed. I woke to the sound of the hotel phone ringing. Light seeped in at the edge of the heavy curtains. I reached across the bed and dragged the phone towards me. Yes? I said, sounding hoarse.

I'm sorry to disturb you, madam, came a voice. Male, unfamiliar, a thick accent. I tried to rouse myself from the fug of alcohol and reached over to feel for the switch on the stem of the lamp. There was none, and in the gloom I patted around for the wall panel where I thought the switch must be. Behind the nightstand, flush against the bedhead was a rectangle of light switches. I pressed one, but instead of it providing a soft glow the entire room flashed into fluorescent brightness; the four overhead lights, the bedside lamps, the entrance light near the door. I swore and pressed one button then another and another again, until the room fell back into darkness.

Madam? the man asked. Is everything all right?

What? Who's this? He gave a name but I didn't recognise it. There was a brief silence, then he continued. It was an officer from the police station where I'd been the day before. I pulled myself up to sitting, suddenly sober.

Yes? I said. How can I help you? I looked at the clock; it was later than I thought.

I need to tell you that they have found a body. Washed up further along the coast. North of here.

I reached towards the glass by the bedside, the water now full of stale bubbles as though it were effervescent. Sparkling, people often call this water, the little pockets of air catching the light, should you be sipping it in the sun, in the piazza.

We would like you to come see, he said, I mean, to identify.

To identify? To identify what? I asked. My mind moved slowly, I didn't want to understand what he was saying.

The body, he said. Your husband.

I misjudged the distance between my hand and the water and knocked the glass to the floor. Oh shit, I said, the water pooling down on the papers and books I had left there the night before. I pulled the sheet across and tried to mop the spill.

Pardon?

Nothing, oh shit. Nothing. Yes, yes of course. I felt nausea rising up inside me, sudden and intense. I'm sorry,

I said. Hang on. I dropped the receiver on to the mattress and ran for the bathroom, where I leant over the toilet bowl. Afterwards I flushed, rinsed my mouth, and returned to the phone. He was still there.

Although he continued to speak, I don't remember what he said. When he stopped talking there was a long pause. Madam? he asked. It is a long train journey, not unpleasant. There is snow, he said. You can see it. Through the forest you go. Someone will meet you. He gave me a number to call, should I need anything. Thank you, I said. Then I heard a click and the dial tone, indicating that the man on the other end of the line had placed the phone back on its cradle. I continued to hold the receiver to my cheek, feeling the cool, smooth disk of plastic marked with all those tiny black holes through which my voice travelled. There was the sound of a vehicle reversing far below, a high mechanical whistling that could have been a child's toy or some piece of faulty machinery or a bird, despite the absence of trees. A human voice far off. Tonal variations in the traffic. The thick, oily smell of meat cooking on a grill.

I took a taxi to the subway, bought a ticket north and hurried up the stairs to the platform. I wasn't hungry but knew I should prepare myself for the journey ahead. Further along, near the departures board, was a kiosk that sold bento boxes and snacks. Maybe that's all I need, I thought – a cream puff or a packet of sweets. It was busy, and travellers took their time selecting. Eel, tofu, omelette, salmon, squid. I knew I only had five minutes to spare and waited impatiently, shifting from one foot to the other. It was cold, and as I went to pull my scarf from my bag I accidently tugged out a packet of tissues which fell to the floor. Bending down to pick them up, I noticed the newsstand to my left. Japanese papers, some business periodicals and there, towards the bottom, right across from me, a British tabloid. I startled – on the front was a photograph of the ship, bright-yellow headlines running diagonally over the image: *Icon Patrick Heller Lost At Sea!* Suddenly I couldn't breathe. How was this possible? How was it real? For the news to be here, and like this. I choked for a minute on my own spit. I knew reporters had been covering the accident and attending in detail to the layout of the ship and its safety failures, I knew the story had been on the television and in the papers, but I didn't realise that the attention had already become so focused on Patrick, and that this had now gone mainstream and been picked up by the trashiest outlets. That the story was everywhere. It only happened four days ago. Only three nights. I hadn't even seen the body. Maybe it was conjecture, the bold type implying his death. Surely this was something I was still to discover, still to confirm. Maybe it wasn't Patrick after all, the person I was on my way to identify. My hand shook as I reached out to pick the tabloid off the stand. I felt light-headed, distant. As if at a remove. I could have been an actor in one of Patrick's films, hesitating, trying to find within herself the feeling she needed in order to carry on. He would have liked the colours – the acid-yellow of the headline against the concrete of the station platform, the sound of the train bells in the background, her ragged breathing. It wasn't journalism. I knew that. It was all talk, hearsay, even libel. The mention of Russian waters, the Japanese coast, the Norwegian ship – it was made out to sound like an international heist, the storm sensationalised, the accident described in tortuous detail supplemented by reports from the crew. Further down there was a longer section about Patrick's notoriety. I skimmed the rest of the page – certain words leapt out at me: shockwaves, reeling, disbelief. Of course I knew the rumours that followed Patrick, that clung to him. Over the years there had been so many. I tried not to pay attention to any of this, and especially not then, in fact for years I had made it my business to ignore these – it was the language that surrounded any famous man. The white noise of his public persona. But the gossip was exaggerated here, and my eye caught on the final paragraph: how he was survived by his young wife, his second wife. Or maybe it was worse than that, couched in bad grammar: survived by his ex-student, whom he had married. Now a writer of women's fiction. There were details regarding our years together and my childlessness. Then some final quote from a passenger: his wife seemed nice, she was pretty. I mean they seemed to bicker, at breakfast anyway.

Of course we did. Patrick wasn't a morning person. He preferred to be alone then, to work quietly while the caffeine made its way through his bloodstream. He could get very angry if he was disturbed and didn't like talking to anyone much before midday. This was a difficulty of the cruise I hadn't foreseen. Her eyes were like, really puffy, the passenger reported. She looked sick, I thought. But maybe that was afterwards, you know we had to change course to let her off? Some holiday, poor thing.

I put the tabloid back, my fingerprints greasing the

front page. I felt then too ill to eat. Not a cream puff, not sweets. The announcement for my train came through the station speakers and I excused myself to the others in line as I edged my way out of the kiosk, dragging my suitcase.

5

The train sped past grassy embankments and ploughed fields as it headed north into the forest, just as I had been told. It soon started to sleet. The further we travelled, the colder it became, until heavy snow weighed down the trees; it clumped on the foliage and lined the branches of the birches and conifers. It clung to the brown winter grasses that grew by the tracks. From every direction the white landscape glared at me.

I was not running late, but still worried that I would miss something, that there would be some inconvenience or delay. My watch was set five minutes fast. I have always set it so, out of an instinct to possess more time than I really have. The intention is to be early for everything, arriving in time to collect myself, as one says. Instead my earliness often leaves me pacing or fidgeting in a chair, or pretending to be interested in some notice pinned to the wall, trying to find something to do and not appear conspicuous or too eager. But, never having liked the condition of idleness, I only get myself more worked up than I might have if I just arrived when expected. For in the end I only ever need the extra time to calm myself; to urinate because I have made myself nervous by hurrying, or to find a glass of water because I have exerted myself by walking too quickly out of fear of being delayed. Both these things posing the risk of making me late for the appointment that I was, only moments before, too early for. I looked out of the window. Here and there fires smouldered in the fields of farms, the incineration of garbage, crop waste. I could hear ice spattering on the glass as we drove on. In my mind I kept seeing the tabloid photo of the cruise ship and that bright-yellow headline. It would only get worse, the coverage. There would only be more. At some point I would have to face the press. Have to say something. Account for myself, describe the ordeal all over again. Be in public what I had now become: his widow.

When I slipped into the back of that cab with him all those years ago, maybe I only wanted to want, but did not really know what it was, exactly, that I desired. Maybe I thought that, as a younger woman, wanting was what I should do. I craved the presence of some huge feeling in me, for this to mark my aliveness. Abstract appetite, the expectation of hunger, subsequent pain of deprivation. The experience of youth. We are prepared to expect all this in some form.

The rain was torrential. He paid the taxi driver in cash, then wedged open the car door enough to push his umbrella though the gap. I remember how he held his small suitcase in one hand while he ran round to my side and lifted the umbrella over both our heads as I stepped out. There were two keys to the entrance to that building in which Patrick then lived. One for a new deadlock, the other for the old flimsy lock that you had to jiggle before the key would turn. The foyer smelt of old damp shoes and bleach and on the far side of the room stood a line of silver mailboxes, built into the wall. Won't be a moment, he said, as he flicked through his bundle of keys. While I waited for him to check his mail I read the notices on the board provided for residents; on this was pinned a postcard from Holland, a reminder to lock the fire escape, a brochure for takeaway Indian and a flyer announcing a lost cat with a reward for its safe return. I heard the mailbox open and close. On the ground, near the door, were three dying pot plants: a spider plant, a rubber plant, a large monstera. All right, he said. Then he pressed the button for the elevator and we waited side by side listening for its slow, clanking approach. When it finally arrived there was a long pause before the doors slid apart. Inside stood an old lady with her bag of garbage, bringing it down to the bins. She blinked at us, then said, Patrick! beaming at him, her teeth very white and straight. He bent down to let her kiss him on each cheek.

Now, Mrs Treel, we can't have you lugging this, he said, pointing to the garbage. Let me help. He reached out and took the garbage bag while I held my finger to the button that kept the elevator door open. Just a second, he said to me, and ducked out of the front door through which we had just come. Oh isn't he a dear, the old lady said. And then, Are you his niece? You must come and say hello properly. I dropped my hand from the button and let her take the lift back up. A moment later Patrick was again at the front door, working his key into the lock. He was soaked. Come on, he said, putting his hand to my waist, so lightly that it could have been a stranger's hand accidently brushing against me, only it moved a little too slowly for that, his hand sort of tracing my waist as he pulled me towards him a little, showing me the way. Let's take the stairs.

His flat was very neat. There was a plastic container by the front door ready for his wet umbrella. Next to this hung a long shoehorn and a clothes brush. In the kitchen the counter was clear of appliances and clutter. There were no dishes draining on the sink rack. At the edge of the counter, near the refrigerator, was a blue glass bowl that held three freckled bananas. On the kitchen table a pile of papers neatly stacked. I opened the fridge, looking for a snack. There was butter, fish, Brussels sprouts, eggs, chocolate, some cans of beer. I took the beer and the chocolate. Want some? I said. I hadn't asked if I could take these things. I cracked open the tab on the can and while I drank wandered through the living area, running my fingertip along the edge of the bookshelves where all the titles were arranged in perfect alphabetical order. I pulled a couple out, flicked through them, pushed them back. There were tiny yellow Post-it notes placed carefully next to important paragraphs. He followed me. I stopped in the corner of the room by the large window, where there stood a houseplant whose foliage appeared diseased, covered in tiny brown spots. Some pale withered leaves lay on the ground where they had fallen. The soil was flaky and very dry. I circled back to the kitchen, looking for a glass. I opened the cupboard in which he kept his plates, then the one for his pantry items – rice, pasta, sugar – before I at last found the one stacked with cups and glasses. I took a tumbler and filled it with water from the tap. Then I returned to the living room and poured the water slowly on to the soil of the houseplant, letting a little sink in before pouring on some more and checking if any came out from the bottom of the pot, not wanting it to leak on to the carpet. My gesture of house-keeping charmed him. He came up behind me. Again ran his fingers along the edge of my waistband, through the thickness of my jumper. Then underneath the jumper. We finished the beer. Outside the rain continued. Later there were hailstones. His silver suitcase, small enough to pass as carry-on, remained unpacked in the corner of the bedroom.

I can see now that I shouldn't have stayed. But I did and it changed everything. What do you want? he asked me. I wanted. I want. The single verb that causes the present and the future to overlap. We drank vodka. I liked the way it made my body feel soft but kept my mind alert. You're so wet, he said, not because he was practising a line on me but because it was true. Unpicked unstitched unpacked unmet. My breasts were large and heavy, and when I lay on my back they fell to the side, like a woman in a painting by Lucian Freud. I rubbed his semen into my chest and we kissed. He had the body of an ageing rock star, the tall frame thickening across the waist and over the shoulder blades. It was not fat exactly, this gentle girth – it seemed almost muscular but not quite, as if his internal organs had themselves expanded with age and power. This girth looked like a kind of dense hide, or rind, a thickness that gave shape to an otherwise angular form and which I found appealing, almost moving, the way this both softened him a little and increased his stature. Previously the bodies of young men had often frightened me. They had hard hip bones and too much gristle. Their abdominal muscles, of which they could be so proud, made them appear reptilian to me. But Patrick was different.

In the morning he said, Don't leave. He said it as a gentle request at first, or so I thought of it, and then almost as a piece of advice, a warning. Don't leave, he said again. Today. It's probably not a good idea to leave the flat, he said. Sorry? I replied. I had a lecture at midday. It's complicated, he said. If someone saw you, I mean. Leaving. Or entering. Given how close we are to campus here. Maybe even close those blinds there if you're going to read at the desk. He was already dressed for work, damp hair at the nape of his neck, minty breath. He ran his fingers across my bare shoulders as he said this, so that I was more aware of the tingling of my skin than I was of this strange command. OK? I said, pulling away from him. His hand dropped to my waist and he tugged me back towards him. Please, he said.

At that age, at that time of my life, refusal involved a kind of strategising for which I lacked the language. I didn't understand how to negotiate my own disavowal – of food choices at a restaurant, of which movie to see, of which route to take through the city, of anything to do with sex – because I didn't know my own desire, I didn't know the limits and contours of my own wants, or the boundaries of my own comfort. Or how much another might press these. Because in its best sense refusal is relative, always secondary, always an after-effect of desire or predilection, or just a logical response to the insistence on self-preservation, to life and its livingness. But at that time I had no internalised repertoire of the preferences against which I could measure and assess his requests. Or if I did, I hadn't found a way of articulating them, of expressing them, of saying with my body or otherwise: This is how I feel. This is what I want. This is what I'm going to do.

Please, he said again.

I suppose I don't really need to go anywhere anyway, I replied. If you really think.

I do think, he said. He kissed me then, his soft lips opening on to mine, our mouths gently folding and un-folding around each other. After he'd gone I peeled an orange and ate it standing over the kitchen sink. Then I showered, made coffee, flipped through his vinyl collec-tion and CDs. The air in the apartment was stale. I could only sit and read for so long. I needed to take a walk but was afraid of his command. Afraid he knew something that he wasn't telling me. I didn't know then how to question his views, how to even consider the fact that he probably would have no idea if I left the flat or not, and that a walk outside would feature as nothing more than a white lie later in the evening. If I stayed that long.

But I courted his opinions. I admired and collected them as students sometimes will, passing off a professor's view as their own. There were plenty for me to choose from; he had strong opinions and knew what he liked. Because of this I could, in turn, play to these and please him. In all fairness, in those early days it pleased us to please each other. In that way we were not so different from any couple in love. Even his efforts to control me could be interpreted as a form of flattery. A service. Although I didn't think of it as control, not back then. It felt more like being guided, stewarded, directed. We were complicit in this: what was to his liking was generally to my liking too, at least I came to see it this way, and if not at the time, then after the fact. Once I had the dress on. Once I'd tasted the meal he'd ordered on my behalf. I was grateful for this – for the pleasure and the education.

So instead of going for a walk I pulled out the small exercise trampoline that I'd found behind the linen chest – a rebounder, I think they called them – pressed play on the stereo and turned up the volume. I must have been jogging on this for some time when I heard the knock at the door. I stopped jogging and turned the music down. The knock came again. I dared not open it. I stood very still, hardly breathing, wondering if whoever it was on the other side had a key. No one called out. I heard no voices. It was obvious that someone, meaning me, was in the apartment, obvious that I wasn't opening the door to whoever was on the other side. I waited. And then, eventually, after how much time I don't know, I heard footsteps moving along the corridor before descending the uncarpeted stairs.

He came home that night with a bunch of carnations. Besides a rose on Valentine's Day or a birthday bouquet, no man had ever bought me flowers. Not on a whim, not as a gesture of adoration at the end of a long day. I had always thought of carnations as supermarket flowers, cheap, skinny bunches wrapped in crackly plastic and padded out with what they call baby's breath, the carnations more stem than petal, not splendorous enough to cause a reaction either by perfume or design. The kind of flower that exists almost as a symbol, as an idea of flowers in general, as an unassuming blueprint for the more generous and dramatic bóuquet one might have chosen had one the money and the inclination to spend it; the closest a real flower could come to imitating a fake one. The kind of flowers one finds at hospital gift shops, the bucket of wrapped carnations positioned next to the helium-filled balloons, or outside service stations, the flowers wilted by sun and petrol fumes, and chosen, generally, for their value for money, being so long-lasting – stoic flowers that withstand dirty water, heat and cold. That was, of course, until he gave me these, the largest bunch of carnations I had seen, and arranged by the florist in such a way that they fanned out in unison, their blooms just opening and so densely gathered together as to appear lush and thick, so many that I could even detect their fragrance, the fresh, greeny scent of dewy grass and something sweeter. The pink petals flecked with white. From the Latin *carnalis*, he said. Meaning fleshly, or of flesh. Carnivorous, carrion, carnal and carnation. The original French word denoting pink, before the word pink came into existence. Charnel, he might have also said, or carnage. But in that first flush of love – there the image of blooming reappears – we were focused on other matters. I went back to my room in the shared house to get some clean clothes and returned to his flat. I never did ask him why he insisted I stay inside all day but was happy for me to walk home in the dark.

On campus we carried on as if we hardly knew each other: he went to his classes and meetings and whatever else, and I kept to my carrel in the library. Although it was hard to concentrate. I was tired from our nights together and distracted by the memories. Sensations I had never imagined. Feelings in the body that originated from invisible sources. How he touched me here or there, pressed here or there. Such pleasures are no small thing. When we had exhausted ourselves, we talked. And when we had done talking, we read, and when we had done reading alone, we read aloud to each other. I continued to attend his lectures and sat up at the back in the seminars that followed. I was as studious and diligent as ever, although it did seem that he called on me more often for answers, or asked me to elaborate on my answers, and when I did he offered me high praise of the kind that was rare and verbose and which was recognised by the other students, which drew attention, but maybe this was my own imagining, my own paranoia or fantasy. What was the difference? By then I couldn't tell. When our mid-term essays were handed back to us he paid tribute to mine in front of everyone, and in a dramatic gesture pretended to pass me a cluster of grapes and other tropical fruits with which, he said, I might decorate my hypothetical mantelpiece. I had no idea what he meant, and I assume no one else understood either. In his presence we believed in our collective ignorance and assumed his flouncy rhetoric to be making reference to some ancient text or another about which we had no knowledge. It never once occurred to us that it might be performance for its own sake, a joke, a display of wit that played out in its own echo chamber as we sat mute, in fear of revealing our stupidity.

I blushed horribly and mumbled some kind of thanks

as he put the essay on the desk and pushed it towards me. Then he returned to his position at the front of the classroom and, after shuffling some papers, announced that he would be away the following week as he had to go into hospital for unexpected surgery. It's nothing to worry about, he told us, clearing his throat and noting the alarm on our faces – for no lecturer ever spoke to a class so openly about their private life, their bodily life, in this way. Never admitted to bodily urgency or bodily needs. On campus, husbands did not mention their wives. Fathers did not speak of their children. He had not told me about this, the surgery. I had thought he might have. Although I couldn't yet lay claim to the right to know, and while I didn't question this withholding, some part of me felt the snare of this secrecy, the sting. We all wanted to know what was actually wrong, and of course he could not and would not tell us. I did try to delay it, he said, until term break, but they told me it had to happen immediately. I'm very sorry for the inconvenience. But class will go ahead, he continued, and Miss Blackwood here, he said – attempting to grant me mock authority – will be your tutor for that day. That's to say, I'm nominating Miss Blackwood to be your tutor, so you'll be in very safe hands for your discussion. I'd hate for you to miss anything, and it would be hard to make up the content for that week if we just skip it. I don't want anyone to be inconvenienced or disadvantaged when it comes to the final exam.

My mortification knew no bounds. I did not need to look up from my papers to know everyone was staring at me. Rage and embarrassment rose in me as solid nausea.

Anyway, he said, noting the time, the readings are listed in the course outline so please make sure that, as ever, you come prepared, and I will see you the week after. Then in his customary flourish he waved his hand as might a magician, or an actor playing a film version of his real self, and called out, Class dismissed!

I hurried away so as not to hear what the other students were saying, and so as not to be caught alone with him. I went back to my own room that night. But the following day he found me on campus and convinced me to return to his flat. To be honest, it didn't take much. Despite the feeling of being unworthy and ill-suited to the task that he had so publicly set me, I was also aware of how this had immediately changed the way the other students looked at me, the way they spoke to me, greeted me, the way they asked about my plans for the weekend. He didn't tell me then what he was going into hospital for. At the time I didn't know for a fact if he even went to hospital. He just packed his little suitcase, left me with a spare set of keys to his flat and disappeared for four days. I took the class, or rather, it might be more accurate to say that I turned up for the class only to find that most of my fellow students had decided this was one they could miss. All in all there were six out of fifteen, including myself. I timidly posed some questions about the readings. There was a lump in my throat and my voice came out in a whisper. I asked the same set of questions again. They all looked intently at their books, quite determined that under no circumstance would they meet my eye. A thick-set girl with mousy-coloured hair eventually spoke, and a boy whose name I didn't know replied to her. In this way a limping set of responses ensued with long pauses between each. It was too much for all of us. I didn't want the authority. They didn't know how to pretend that I had it. After forty minutes I said, Well, seeing as it's such a small class today maybe that's all there is to say. Again, no one responded. They didn't know whether they were supposed to utter a verbal agreement before I told them they could leave, or whether they were in fact always free to leave at any time – whether this gnomic phrase of mine meant that class was over, or whether it meant they ought to find something else to say, to make up for all those who were absent and to fill the time that was left. Someone flicked through the pages of their book, another swung on their chair. OK, I said. I think you can go now. And in a flurry of papers and bags they left the room as quickly as they could.

When he came back I looked, but never found the mark on his body that might indicate the surgery he had undergone. Keyhole maybe, or something in the mouth or throat. Even the eye. So many parts of the body, so many lines of secret physical history that I was not privy to. You don't want to know about that, he said when I asked. It's all fine now. And a few days after this he returned to work, with me officially and quite publicly elevated to the role of disciple.

The rumours soon started. We were seen together too often. He had lent me the keys to his office one day when he was at a conference and I had stopped there between classes. We had been up most of the night, as was our custom, and I was tired. You're not coming down with something, are you? he asked, very tenderly, that morning. You look a little pale. So instead of thinking to lock his office door behind me I took off my glasses, lay down on the carpet and fell asleep. It was very quiet in there. Just some bird calls from the tree outside the window, the sound of a football game on the field. The room smelt of pencil shavings and dust and paper. Sometime later there was a knock and the door opened. I stared up through bleary vision to see a woman standing over me. I scrabbled for my glasses, but by the time I had found them and put them on she had gone. Panic rose up in me. I stood quickly, feeling a little dizzy, shoved my things into my bag and hurried out of the building.

It was not long after this that I came to understand that his appointment at the university was nearing the end of its term. I had thought it might become permanent, he explained. I hadn't meant to not tell you. That had been the intimation, he said, the permanent bit. Originally, he told me, it was a year-long post as a visiting scholar. If there was the money, and general willingness, the suggestion had been that this would become something more further down the track. But realistically, he said, I don't know if that would have worked out anyway. He had a small child in London, a baby in fact. This too was news to me at the time. Then he said something I wasn't expecting. Come with me. Why don't you just come with me? he said. The academic year was nearing its end. I would graduate in a few months. There's no reason not to, he said. And it was true. There was nothing waiting for me where I was, and after our affair – as it came to be called – became public everyone hated me anyway. They hated me for different reasons – because they thought I'd used the relationship for my own advantage, or because I had kept it a secret, or because they didn't understand why of all people he chose me – whatever the reason, they hated me all the same. OK, I said. I will.

Even back then my desire to write and to become a writer was unwavering, a single and overriding ambition – something I wanted more than anything else. Writing was what made me feel most alive, and from the start Patrick admired this drive and encouraged it. He seemed, to me, to have all the knowledge that I wanted for myself, that I needed. He knew what books I should read and what places I should visit, the films I should watch. He prided himself on giving me experiences, he took pleasure in this. He wanted me to use these, incorporate them, become someone because of him. He never thought that he himself might be one of those experiences about which I would one day write, long after he had changed the course of my life.

So I followed him to London. First impressions: damp air, excessive greenery, thin brown houses crowded together, spotted dogs, and golden foxy dogs and fat limping dogs on leather leashes. The lumpy grey sky and the rain then the not rain then the rain again, then the soon-to-be rain but not quite, the any-minute-now rain. The sight of the gutters and the flat, soggy leaves on the footpath, especially the ivy growing over the walls, the variegated kind where the green appears to have been loosely painted on to the creamy surface of the leaf, and that also happened to be heart-shaped – all this had the effect of stilling some cog that whirred away deep inside me, catching on a memory but not igniting a memory as such, not hauling it out but touching it, making some passing contact. I felt at home there, like I had come back to something.

I started to see Patrick in a new light. I loved him already, but I came to love him more. He appeared increasingly gentle, open, inviting. There was no one there who knew our history or who could criticise us for our choices, who could accuse him of wrongdoing or inappropriateness. It was a whole new start, and once we were living together he let me in on everything, shared his life so completely as to make it not his but ours. The timetable of his day, the people he needed to meet with, the books he ordered: it was all plain for me to see. He noted his appointments on the kitchen calendar. He took his calls on speakerphone, so I often overheard everything. If I was writing I would sometimes put in earplugs: his laugh was loud and gener-ous. Full-bellied. Later we'd recount our days, breaking it all down. He had a small pocket diary that he carried to work, and sometimes, while he was cooking or if his hands were otherwise full, he'd ask me to make a note in this: an appointment he mustn't forget or someone he needed to call in the morning. There was nothing I couldn't see, nothing he needed to keep from me. Even the surgery he'd had and about which he'd been so secretive was later explained: a laparoscopic procedure to repair a hernia. He felt embarrassed, he told me – after all, he was ageing and I was not. Or at least not then, anyway.

When I look back, I see this as the beginning of one of the richest periods of my life; a phase in which my life seemed at last my own; my own to have, to live, to feel. My body felt continually light and open. My mind clear. Every sensation, every impression lodged itself, sank in and opened out – as a feeling in the heart, as a thought, as a rush of energy. At the time Patrick had a permanent post in the Film Studies Department at UCL which kept him very busy, and he'd leave for work early while I took my time readying myself for the day. Each morning I would shower in very hot water followed by cold, and make a pot of strong black coffee. I would cook two pieces of toast and eat them with a thick layer of salted butter, then take the coffee to the desk by the window. I had the upstairs front room of that flat as my study. Patrick had bought me a green velvet sofa, and we moved the desk so that it looked out over the street and the rows of damp plane trees. On either wall were bookshelves. A worn Persian rug was spread on the floor. I never sat down straight away but stood by the edge of the window drinking that first cup and watching the fat ginger cat that lived across the street, where it spent its days sitting on the lid of a metal garbage bin. I had tried to befriend it when I first arrived, calling to it and rubbing my fingers together. It had jumped down and taken a few careful steps towards me, but a shiver ran up my spine as the cat's gaze met my own, and instead of rolling over or pushing itself up against my legs it let out a long hiss. I noticed then how matted its hair was, how wild its eyes – pale green, as if they had once been very deep and bright in colour and had now been strangely bleached. I backed away and instead watched it from the window as it hissed, each morning, at one passer-by after another. A school bus stopped a few houses away from the cat, and it was heartening somehow to watch the children arrive and get on the bus just before I sat down to write – to see their eagerness and think of lives beginning as much as days, the smell of lead pencils newly sharpened and of old bananas left in lunchboxes, bread crusts and clean fresh paper and the sound of chalk making letters on the board. This is nostalgia but I am entitled to it, as we all are once something is long gone. I knew it was not shared by these children, this feeling, some of whom clung to the legs of their mothers during those first weeks of term and did not want to get on the bus, for mostly they were very young, maybe five or seven years of age and they always came with their parents, some of whom gathered together to chat while others stood alone, beside their child. When it was raining, which was often, the children came in brightly coloured coats. One of them had a clear-blue plastic poncho and I could see how pleased she was with it. It must have been new, the way she flapped at it, making it puff up and down as it caught the rain like some strange jellyfish. She kept checking the other children, not really talking to them because she was preoccupied by her poncho but wanting to make sure they had seen it and admired her. My favourite child, however, was a small blond boy who was too young to take the bus and possibly not at school yet. He came holding his mother's hand as she accompanied two older children to the bus stop. They were also very blond, one a head taller than the other, and I assumed they were all three of them siblings, given the neat descending heights and the straw-coloured hair.

I noticed the boy straight away – it was impossible not to – because he never stopped jumping. The family would appear on the corner of the opposite side of the road, the side on which our house stood, and cross the road all holding hands together. All the while the boy would leap or try to skip or jump or hop, or sort of jump-jog next to his mother, who kept a tight hold of his hand, sometimes his arm when he wouldn't hold her hand, his blond hair flapping all about. Sometimes she would carry him, holding him close. I would watch this child a while, until the coffee had brought on a rush of words in my head, then I'd sit down to write.

Patrick was so encouraging at first. So excited about whatever I was working on, so happily surprised by the outcome, as if he were the lucky man who got to see what was inside of me, things he had never thought possible, new things he hadn't seen before that no one else knew. In the evenings he would read my drafts in his armchair, smoking, the cloud of tobacco drifting upwards and turning the white lampshade a dingy yellow. Sometimes, if he was especially tired, he would sit in the armchair smoking with his eyes closed and I would read my pages aloud to him.

While he listened, he tugged at his collar to loosen it. This was before he stopped wearing button-down shirts altogether. Before he threw away all his ties. Before he started to feel his body chaffing, failing, aching with fatigue, heavy. The crick in the left side of his neck, the twinge in his right knee. He got my pity. I brought him heat packs and ice, tending to the pains of age that I could only yet imagine.

I sometimes wrote about things we'd done together or seen, describing events that were like those in our own life but not quite. One day I might have read him a story that began with a scene like the one I came to find myself in: in that foreign train travelling through the snow, the promise of a journey. He'd have liked that, I thought, as we at last slowed and pulled into the station. I felt dazed and tired, and not exactly sure where I was. I'd lost track of the hours. A light ringing of bells came through the speaker system, followed by an announcement from the guard. He spoke first in Japanese, then in English: Please make sure your children step off the train in safe. Please make sure the elderly also step off in safe. We offer you nice day.

What did I love back then, in those early days with Patrick? I loved his hands, his long, elegant fingers, the way they held the cigarette. I loved the scent of his jacket, how it smelt of tobacco and sweat and whatever leather smells like once it has grown soft and old. Sometimes I could smell other things on him also: women's perfume, exhaust fumes, aftershave. The smell of the city. Of being pressed up close against grime and strangers. I loved this too. I loved his accent, audible only on certain words, caught in certain inflections. I loved the way he blew into his hands on a cold morning to warm them, how he leant back in his chair after a good meal, how he tore apart a piece of bread as if it were the first and only piece of bread he would ever eat. As I read aloud he used to mutter sounds of approval. In those days he was the most attentive listener, nodding at the passages he found especially moving or powerful, furrowing his brow a little in concentration so as to hear my words more clearly. What more, I thought, could a writer want?

Just imagine, Patrick had said, what you could become. What we could become together.

Of course I married him.

6

In all our years together I had imagined many things, but never this – stepping off that train into a blizzard without him. The fourth day, I said to myself, counting time as a child might keep a tally of the days leading up to their birthday, or Christmas, only my counting worked in reverse: the days since, the days gone, the days that make up whatever life is, afterwards. Although the name of the day itself eluded me. Monday? Thursday? I had no idea, although I knew what I had to do, what I had come there for, and felt instantly sick at the thought of this.

The station was surrounded by a ring of black mountains, high and ragged and capped in snow. The train line cut through the flat basin between these and disappeared. To the west was a cluster of buildings: three car rental companies, a car wash service and a small hotel. There was no green anywhere in sight – everything black, white, grey and muddy-brown along the edges; the roads and paths. Although the place must have had some loveliness to it in the summer; the island was commonly known as the land of milk and flowers. Cheese and tulips, ice cream and lavender.

I made my way to the information desk in the station foyer where, I'd been told, I could organise a rental car. There was a queue and I waited in line. I heard the south-bound train pull in, heralded by a cheerful flourish of music – the promise of which is that you will have a good and happy journey, a peaceful journey, a journey full of fun and adventure and that this is what we wish for you, what we all wish for you all the time, forever and ever and ever. Around me, the foyer was already decorated in preparation for Christmas; a large plastic Christmas tree stood in the corner, replete with shiny blue baubles the size of tennis balls, while carols played through the station speakers. The foyer reeked of disinfectant and tobacco; just behind me was the designated smoking room, its door propped open. Once, a long time ago, I too had been a smoker and in that moment – impatient to get going, nervous about the car rental and the directions – the old urge rose up in me and I turned to look. It was a small, dark, glass-fronted room, brightened only by the blue and yellow glow emitted by the drink-vending machine. There was a handrail running along the walls on which three men leant, each stationed in separate corners. They watched me watching them while they smoked slumped in their spots – one arm in the pocket or crossed over the torso, the cigarette pinched between finger and thumb. The tune of 'Hark the Herald Angels' floated out around me as I stood in line shifting my weight from one foot to the other, irritated by the delay.

At last my turn came. I collected the key and signed a form. Then I picked up the hire car, and with the map gripped in my right hand drove slowly through the icy streets to the morgue.

Inside there was a reception desk with no one behind it, and to the left of this a long corridor. I pressed the small silver bell on the desk and a woman in uniform came out from behind a wall of filing cabinets.

Can help you, miss? she asked in faltering English.

I nodded and stepped forwards, clutching my handbag to my stomach and limping a little because I had hurried from the car park and slipped on the ice. The woman and I exchanged words that neither of us properly understood.

She looked down at the papers in front of her. There was a yellow Post-it note stuck on the top left corner of the uppermost sheet. She peeled this off, looking at me, then back at the Post-it note and then at me again. She spoke gently and I nodded, agreeing to whatever kindness she seemed to be offering but which I did not fully understand. Then I was escorted to a small waiting room and ushered inside. The door closed behind me. The walls were painted lime-green. The air smelt of fried fish. I picked at my nails, watched the small blue flame flicker in the gas heater. There came a knock at the door. Without thinking I replied, Yes, come in. It was the same woman. This time she was holding something in her hands. I stayed sitting on the bench. She bowed her head in greeting and held her hands out to me. For you, she said. In your condition. I startled at this. What did she know about my story? What about my condition? She passed me a bowl of warm rice with butter, and a ripe persimmon. I could tell, she said, by your colour. It's true I was very hungry, having not eaten properly in how many days – some salted peanuts on the ship. The complimentary hotel cookies. Then she backed out of the room, bowing again. I ate, suddenly ravenous, then placed the bowl on the bench beside me. In the distance I could hear someone whistling. The whistling moved closer, grew louder and then a man called my name.

He stood at the entrance to the room, and when I did not immediately step forwards he called my name again and gestured for me to follow him. I greeted him in Japanese and he mistook this for fluency, talking quickly and without making eye contact as he opened the door to a stairwell and indicated for me to go ahead. I explained that I did not understand him. I tried to do this first in his language, and afterwards in my own. There was no interpreter in sight, no other English speaker. At the bottom of the stairs was another corridor and we followed this, first right, then left, until we came to a metal door. He said something I didn't understand and made a series of gestures: hands in a fist, the fist on the palm, some kind of cutting action against the body. All the language I had was about desire, about want – the language of the tourist, what Patrick and I had prepared ourselves for. *Sumimasen kore kudasai?* Can I have this, please? Can I have that over there, please? I would like to eat, I would like to drink. *Tame mass, Nomi mass. Chotto ii desu ka?*

I knew no words for repulsion, for dislike, for ignorance, I never learnt how to refuse something. It never occurred to me that I would need this. No, I wanted to say. I am not ready, I do not want to look, I do not know if I can do this, I know I do not want this. I cannot do this on my own. Could I phrase it in this way: I want *not* this? I stepped into the cold room and the man checked his clipboard. A younger man in scrubs came forwards. He bowed to me and greeted me in English with an air of apology. Then he said to me, Madam. Your husband this way.

Both men walked ahead and I followed. Together they talked, pointing and checking the clipboard. The first man, who did not speak English, turned back to me briefly then said something to his colleague. The second man laughed. One made a gesture of springs coming from the head and I would have thought this to be referring to my wild curls, an oddity in that country, if I had not known it was also a sign for stupid. I felt myself blush. The other man said something more quietly and then the two lifted their chins a little as if to compose themselves and picked up speed. In the background, music could be heard: 'Morning Has Broken', dubbed in Japanese. The English-speaking man turned to me and said, Just down here, madam.

Patrick's body, the officer told me on the phone, had been carried by the current from the Kamchatka Peninsula down to the northern tip of Hokkaido and was spotted by a fishing vessel in the area. The authorities had been alerted and now I stood over the bag in which his body lay, ready. One of the men unzipped this halfway, from the feet up. Then the zip caught. I closed my eyes, my head slightly bowed. I didn't direct my attention in any conscious fashion; I just saw what was before me. I did not see anything else. I could not bring myself to. I could not look, as they say. I just saw something. In the background the music had changed: a pan-piped version of 'Greensleeves'. I asked if they could please turn the music off. One of the men grunted, but I was wrong to take this as assent. The other replied that this was where they worked, and they liked to work to this music, it helped them concentrate. I didn't argue. They unzipped the bag a little further. I steadied my attention. I saw a patch of his chest, curls of dark hair. A pimply rash across the surface of the skin. By this marking alone I knew.

Yes, I said to the two men. This is him. For months before our trip this rash had been the bane of his days. It sounds petty, but it was true. The rash drove him mad. It itched and burnt both day and night. The doctor said it wasn't eczema, but what it was he didn't know. An allergic reaction to an insect bite perhaps, a food intolerance. But antihistamines had no effect, nor did eliminating lactose or wheat. Patrick scratched until he bled, and then had to tape pads of gauze over the worst sections to protect the skin. This, however, did not ease the irritation and maybe only made it worse, because of the way the skin sweated under the gauze, and then because when he removed this he had to rip away some of the chest hairs too. The rash started to spread from his chest and appear on his back as well, in places that were hard to reach, and so he'd rub himself against the corner of a wall or beg me to scratch the point between his shoulder blades. At last he went to a dermatologist, who looked him up and down very slowly, then said to him, Don't wear black. What? Patrick replied, You think this is some kind of cosmic joke? Too much accumulated negative energy? The dermatologist glanced at his papers, then continued, If you wear light colours, white, cream, yellow, it will go away very quickly, he said. Patrick snorted. You've got to be fucking kidding me.

It's the toxicity of the dyes, the dermatologist continued. Dark navy and black clothes leak toxic dye on to the skin and are more heavily dyed, obviously, than white clothes. I'm afraid, he said, pausing to check the information in front of him, Professor – Professor Heller, I'm afraid that it's not candida or any food allergy. It's just chemicals that should never be in contact with the skin. But they're cheap and fashionable and we generally have no idea how anything is made or what constitutes it. But I assure you, if you wear only white clothes, and soft cottons especially, the rash will disappear in a matter of days.

Of course Patrick would not do this. Even I had rarely seen him, at least not for many years, in anything other than his black or navy T-shirt and black jacket, maybe a shirt for days when he had a really important meeting, but even this was generally of a dark hue, or else he wore a dark T-shirt underneath a paler shirt. He couldn't turn up to work in soft white garb. People would think he'd lost his mind. This was what I joked, anyway, because there were people who wanted to claim this, who'd take the smallest suggestion of infirmity or immorality to bring him down, and if not totally then at least a peg or two. He was one of those kinds of men by then. A cult figure. I would be a laughing stock, he told the dermatologist.

Take some time off, I suggested, and wear the white clothes at home. And then what? he said. The doctor had told him that his system had developed a cumulative intolerance for the dyes, and that any contact would trigger this reaction from here on. The discomfort was unbearable. I don't know, then, I replied, feeling a little weary. You could wear the white clothes under the dark ones, so that no one actually sees them.

He thought this a good compromise, but by the time we left for our holiday the rash had still not abated. So when my gaze fell on this section of his chest I recognised him immediately. I told them so, the men standing behind me. Yes, I said again. This is my husband. There was still a small hairless patch where he'd last torn the gauze off, the patch pink from sunburn. But you have only looked at one little part of his torso, one of them replied. I know, I said, just from that. To an uninformed eye it appeared as if he had been trying to tear his own heart out, or as if someone else had: the deep scratches over the left-hand side of the chest, near the nipple.

We need you to look at the face.

I don't want to look at the face.

I'm afraid you must.

I heard the zip unfasten further up, towards the top of the bag. Please, madam, when you are ready.

7

I didn't take the train back to Sapporo that night as planned. Instead, the woman who had brought the persimmon booked a room for me at a nearby ryokan. You can walk, she said. It is very close. Leave the car in car park here. Someone will collect, she told me, as she drew me a map. The fresh air would do good, she said, pointing to the paper and where I needed to go. There were three entrances off route 479, she explained, but only one took you to the ryokan proper. The first led to a hill that was so steep no car could easily make it and was only traversed by foot. The other was a false entrance – while it appeared on the map as the most obvious route, in reality it was blocked by a gate that could only be opened with a key from the municipality. The third appeared on the map to be a forest path; it was marked as yellow rather than blue, and anyone who did not know the area well or who did not frequent the cemetery through which the path led would not consider the possibility that this was the best and most direct route. This one you take, she said.

I left the car where she told me and followed the path. In my handbag my phone rang again. I still hadn't returned any of the calls from the day before. As I feared, that tabloid article was just the beginning and now everyone wanted to talk to me, not just Patrick's team. Journalists, friends, associates. But it was impossible to think of talking to anyone. How could I say out loud all the things that needed to be said, and then to think of repeating these words to so many different people? Around me crows fed at the graves where mourners had placed offerings of sweet rice cakes and salted meats, disregarding the sign that instructed visitors to take care when leaving food, lest it be poisonous to beasts and creatures. This was the direct English translation, as I was later told: beasts and creatures, not animals and insects, or birds and bees. I climbed the hill towards the guest house, pausing halfway to catch my breath. While I rested an old man overtook me, walking with the aid of a cane. At the top of the rise stood a shrine, and in front of the building was a large, gnarled maple, tied with rope and strung with paper prayer flags. I watched the old man lean his hands and face against the tree and whisper his devotions into its bark. I envied him, imagining the sense of divine order that he carried around inside him, unpunctured. The scent of incense wafted towards me.

At the ryokan, I removed my shoes and stepped through the doorway into the hall. An old woman came out from a back room carrying a pile of threadbare white towels. We greeted one another; the woman at the morgue had phoned ahead and so my arrival was expected. I was shown the way upstairs and given a key to a small beige-coloured bedroom that had a large window looking out on to the mountains in the distance. There was a kettle in an alcove by the bathroom sink and next to this a hotplate with a saucepan, should I want to heat up food of my own. She did this for Westerners, the woman told me, who always like to eat packet soup at midnight.

I hadn't said why I had come to that northern town, and she didn't ask. But she saw something in my face then that made her own soften as a mother's might when looking upon a child's suffering. She passed the towels to me and, bowing her head a little said, Here, you need tea and a hot bath. Then rest. I will go now. Later I will bring you food.

I did as she said, filling the kettle and putting the water on to boil. I felt weak with exhaustion. All distinctions between wakefulness and sleep had been eroded: I was a misplaced creature in the daylight, a nocturnal animal wrongly passing through hour after hour in which the world seemed too bright, too strange. I was, again, queasy with fatigue, disorientated by my new location. I could be anywhere, I felt I was nowhere. How many rooms had I slept in since we departed for the cruise? It had been three weeks since I'd lain in my own bed and now I was somewhere so unfamiliar that I did not know where to buy milk and food, how the garbage was collected, what plants were in season, how to turn the heater on, whether I could drink unboiled water from the tap, how to get a subway ticket, if there was a subway. How to get home. I heard a knock at the door. When I opened it the old woman was again standing there, this time holding out a shiny pink paper bag with ribbons for handles like the kind in which one might place a birthday gift. Potatoes for you, she said. From the garden. In case you get hungry in the night and have no soup. We eat many potatoes here. I thanked her, then she bowed and turned away. The bag was heavy, full, as she said, of unwashed potatoes that smelt of damp earth. Behind me the kettle clicked off. I rested the party bag by the hotplate and pinched out some green tea from an open packet left in the small cupboard under the sink. I dropped this into the bottom of a large earthenware mug and filled it with water.

In my handbag my phone rang again. It rang and rang; whoever it was wouldn't take no for an answer, they knew I was there. All day it had been the same number, no caller ID. At last I reached past the papers and the scrunched-up tissues and the tangle of headphone wires and pulled out the phone.

It was Max, Patrick's manager. I had his mobile saved in my contacts, but he was calling from home.

I don't know, I said, when he at last coughed out his question about the funeral. The very word made me feel ill, as if a strange pressure were closing in around my head and chest. I really haven't thought that far. I mean, I can't—

Because it would be good to have it nearby, and soon, he said. I mean if you're not up to this, I can . . . I know he wasn't born here, but there's just so many people. And this was his home. If you let me know what his family, I mean what you decide, then I can get started. It's just that, things are heating up here, the news of it is everywhere. I'm really sorry to have to ask this but it would be great if you could say something, do a brief interview perhaps, put your voice to the story. I know how hard this must be. And yes, we need to decide about the funeral.

We. I. Me.

God, Max, I said. I really can't talk about this now. I've just come from— I can't think . . . The line's bad and—

Outside, in the streets below, I could hear sirens. One after another and another. Max started talking again. I walked over to the window. In the distance I could see a mass of grey swelling and moving towards me. I didn't know if it was rain or smoke and watched, transfixed, as the haze engulfed the village below, and then the trees on the hillside, and eventually the ryokan. The room that was, only moments before, lit by pale sun now grew suddenly cold. I took an old cashmere jumper from my suitcase and put Max on speaker while I tugged it down over my face. As I did so I caught the residue of Patrick's cologne. Last signs. Last traces. The horror of human ephemera. Listen, he said. I was talking with Carla and she thought we could maybe fit—

Carla?

The second assistant. The new girl. Woman, I mean.

Oh, right, of course.

She thought we could book the—

What he was saying made no sense to me. I was finding it hard to follow. All the names and the numbers. The mention of caterers, venues. Something about the possible order of service. Heavy rain started to fall. Somewhere below, the landline was ringing. Then I heard the old woman clambering up the stairs, calling my name.

Look, I said to Max. I'm sorry, I've got to go, there's someone— and before he could answer I hung up.

Miss Blackwood, the old woman called again. A telephone, she said, from international. My stomach tightened. I left my mobile on the windowsill and followed her back down to the small table by the entrance where the phone sat. I held the receiver to my ear for a moment before speaking. On the other end of the line there was static which sounded, at first, like distant frogs or crickets. Through this someone was breathing, a stiff inhalation followed by a sigh. A person waiting. Hello? I said.

Oh my God, she said. It's you. Oh my God, I'm so sorry. It was Ada, my publisher. I just heard yesterday, she said. I don't know why I only just heard, and it's been a total nightmare trying to find you. No one seems to know anything. There's no record of anything. I've been trying to call. I phoned, like, every hotel on the island asking for you. I even called your sister, she said. I thought she might have known how to get hold of you, but it was even hard to get in touch with her. It sounds like she's been unwell? I'm not sure of the details, but she really wants to talk to you. And your mobile, what's happened to that?

Of course it was Ada who tracked me down. We'd worked together for nearly a decade and over that time she had become one of my closest friends.

I'm so sorry, I said. There had been so many calls. At some point I couldn't look any more, couldn't answer and must have forgotten—

Listen, I'm flying out now to come get you.

You don't need to do that, I said.

Rubbish. I do. I'm coming to get you whether you want me to or not.

I'm sorry, I said. I'm so sorry. I mean I don't want to be—

Don't be stupid, she replied. What the fuck, I mean

98

what the fuck happened?

I started to cry then and through my tears blub-
bered something about how, yes, please come, actually
please do, about how I hadn't even thought of how to
get home, that I was so exhausted. But what I couldn't
say because I didn't understand it yet was that over the
course of the last several days I had become irremediably
alone, permanently alone, alone in the deepest and
strangest parts of myself. Just as Patrick was – alone when
he fell, alone when he drowned, alone when he passed
over into the afterlife or alone when he did not, and in
my aloneness I could keep the idea of him company,
keep faith with his final state. On the table where the
phone sat someone had placed a small vase of flowers.
I picked the petals off a daisy. Loves me, loves me not.
Loves me.

Wait there, Ada said. Just wait there and don't do anything and don't go anywhere and I'll be with you soon.
We can talk about all this then. I've spoken with Valerie,
she's going to call. There's other things too, that we need
to— Hang on, wait a second. A car horn could be heard
in the background. Sorry, she said. That's my lift. I'll be
there tomorrow.

It was mid-morning when Ada arrived. Oh darling, she
said, over and over again, hugging me tight. Oh darling,
I'm so sorry. Now you just sit down here and let me look
after you. She fussed around with the little saucepan,
finding food somewhere from downstairs, pulling other
supplies from her handbag. She cooked me rice and eggs,
and while I ate she ran me a bath. Oh shit, I called out

to her, suddenly remembering. What about the prize? I hadn't thought about this at all since the accident.

Just forget about it, Ada called back. You don't need to think about that. That's the last thing you need to think about.

But what will happen?

I'll talk to them, she said, stepping out of the bathroom.

It was going to be a surprise, I said. For Patrick, I mean. I hadn't told him. Even the shortlist wasn't announced until after the accident.

Oh honey, said Ada, and she reached out and put her hand on mine. We stayed that way for a minute while I let this sink in. Then I finished the last of my coffee and Ada went to turn off the bath water.

I want to do it, I said when she came back. I want to go.

You don't have to, you know, she said. It's only been a matter of days, hardly a week. Valerie's worried about you too. We both thought that maybe we should just do this one quietly, step back a little.

No, I said. It's better for me if I just push through. You know that. And I don't want to drop the ball now. I want to go big with this. I want to put everything behind it. Can we do that? It's what Patrick would have wanted too.

I knew what I was in for: the prize and the publicity that would follow – interviews and panels and all the rest.

Can you go ahead and organise the events? I asked. Whatever they are. Really – I need to. Please.

Hang on, said Ada, let me think. It's what, just gone ten here and we're thirteen hours ahead of New York. If we leave like, now, and get a flight today we'll fly in on the afternoon of the awards ceremony. We might just make it. She looked at me and squeezed my hand. Are you sure? Are you really sure?

I nodded. Absolutely.

It's too early over there to call Valerie now, she said. It would be what, two in the morning or something. I'll text her from the airport, or on the plane. OK. You go have a bath and let me make some calls.

While I lay soaking in the hot water I heard her re-packing my bags, doing up the zip and re-clicking the florescent safety straps that wrapped around my suitcase. When I got out she passed me a pill and a glass of water. Valium, she said. Take it. You can do this, she told me. I know you can. You're so brave. And you've worked so hard. To be honest, I don't know anyone who has worked as hard as you. Everything is set. You just need to get yourself dressed. And when it's all done, we'll get you home. I swallowed the pill and dried myself, pulling on a pair of jeans and a shirt that belonged to Patrick. I knotted the long tails at my waist and left the collar open. Then I sat by the window in my dark glasses and stared at the sun while I waited for the drug to take effect, for the chemical tang to sprout in my mouth, the sharp, slightly acrid taste spreading across my tongue. I felt my muscles begin to slacken, and slowly all nearby sounds – bird calls, human voices, cars passing on the road below – drifted into the background until they smoothed out and became continuous. Ada leant over me and lifted my sunglasses away: Are you ready?

She held my hand during take-off. I had the window seat and as we rose up, higher and higher, I peered down at the forest, at the island, at the sea. Far below the shape of the land revealed itself: oval, rising up to a range of green mountains in the middle. But what stunned me was the way the island faded into the sea at its edges – the water transparent in the shallows, then turquoise, shifting to dark blue where the ocean deepened. From my vantage point, the portion of land that was above water appeared tiny, its existence so fragile – how close the sea was, how far it spread, how easily it would re-consume dry ground. A sense of vertigo overwhelmed me, a feeling that had nothing to do with being in the air and looking down, but which was caused by the sudden comprehension of this tenuousness, the sense that liveable earth was just an afterthought, sheer chance – the island balanced so precariously in the great mass of that cold and ever-moving water.

We took a budget flight because it was all that was available at such short notice. It didn't land at JFK but at some smaller airport upstate. While we were waiting for our luggage Ada's phone pinged. That woman is amazing, she said, looking down and scrolling. The message was from Valerie. She'd booked our hotel and organised a driver. He should be waiting, she wrote, just outside the baggage collection. Sure enough there he was – I could see him past the barrier holding up a placard with my name on it. We followed him out and he swung our heavy bags into the boot while we slipped into the back seat. I fastened my seat belt and closed my eyes while Ada made small talk so that I didn't need to, then she unwound the window a little so I could smell the grass and the farmlands. You just rest there, she said. I turned to stare out of the window.

I dozed and woke, and after we had been travelling for some time a series of signs appeared at the side of the road advertising a kiosk half a mile ahead. Ada asked the driver if we could pull in here and stop for a break.

The cab dropped us off at the front then went to park, the dust billowing behind it. A cool breeze blew. The place looked as if it hadn't been touched since the 1950s, the building having been made of old weatherboard and corrugated iron. Hanging along the guttering was a long strip of bunting fashioned from small triangles of decorated vinyl or plastic, as if some bored housewife had cut up all her outdoor tablecloths and then gone on to make milkshakes. The bunting flickered in the wind, the sound of rain, the sound of applause, and we stepped under this and through the fly-screen door.

Ada ordered a coffee. I ordered a strawberry milkshake. I hadn't had such a thing since I was a child, but the milkshakes, I could see, came in those large metal cups with striped paper straws – red and white, pink and blue. Patsy Cline was playing on the radio. We sat at the counter, a high bar with tall stools. Once perched there my feet didn't reach the ground and I rested them, like bird claws on a branch, on the narrow metal railing that ran between the legs of the stool. I was going to send Joshua a message while we waited for our drinks, but as soon as I turned my phone on it started pinging with missed calls and new messages and I got distracted.

God, Ada said, you're a wanted woman. She watched as I deleted most of these and only skimmed some. Everyone sent their condolences; each message was prefaced with shock and sorrow. But there was also work that couldn't and wouldn't wait. The last few months had been frantic for Patrick as he raced towards the deadline for a new film. Before we left, he'd signed over the final tasks to his editor, who now wanted to talk to me. Scenes needed to be reshot, and because we'd developed the early drafts together the script supervisor wanted my opinion on the suggested changes. Worse still, the film's financiers were getting cold feet in the wake of the accident. And reporters kept on texting and leaving messages. These were not anonymous journalists calling me, but people with whom I'd had contact before and who therefore had my number; journalists who must have interviewed me at one time or another, whom I had spoken to over the phone. But now the less I said the more they hounded me. It was this that I really couldn't stand.

Our drinks came. I sipped at my milkshake and kicked lightly at the metal wall behind the bar. Ada reached over and stroked my hand very gently. Years before, at a party, she'd flipped my hand over and read my palm: a long and happy life, full of glory. She tipped back the dregs of her coffee; I'm just going to freshen up, she said. And then, as an afterthought, watching me diligently work my way through the giant milkshake, said: Don't go making yourself sick there.

When she came out of the bathroom we nodded to each other: yes, we were ready to go. The bell above the door tinkled as we left. Ada waved at the cab, which soon reversed, and we repositioned ourselves in the back seat. You should get some more shut-eye, she said. Shut-eye. A phrase I hadn't heard in how long? My father's second wife used to say this, my Joany. But something about the way

Ada said it, the concern in her voice, made tears spring to my eyes. I brushed these away. I knew I had to keep it together. We had a tight schedule – the driver would drop us at the hotel and I would have maybe half an hour to get myself ready for the evening and hop back into another cab. We turned on to a long, empty freeway and Ada asked the driver if he could speed up a bit, explaining that we were pressed for time and actually, she realised now, we probably shouldn't have stopped just then. I was shaking a little – I thought perhaps it was the drugs, one Valium before take-off, another once we were on the plane and a third halfway through the flight. They're a pretty weak prescription, Ada had said, as I washed down that last pill with a cup of Shiraz. My throat felt tight. Saliva sprang up at the back of my mouth. Then it hit me. Oh God, I said. Oh God. Oh God. Stop the car – I said, leaning forwards, I think I'm going to be sick. Ada reached across and patted the driver on the shoulder, Pull over! Pull over! she cried. But he'd heard, all cab drivers must be highly attuned to those words. He skidded on the gravel at the roadside and I stumbled out into the dust. I was close to throwing up but not quite there, and in my dazed state I wondered about looking for a spot to vomit when really it didn't matter where I vomited so long as it was not in the car, or on my person, or anyone else's person. But, like an animal looking for a safe place to give birth or a quiet place to die, I moved this way and that, searching for something to lean against while my body spasmed. I stopped at a tree, crouched down with my hand against its trunk and spewed up a long stream of bright-pink milk. I was dimly conscious of Ada behind me, rubbing my shoulder, holding my hair back. There, there, she said. There, there, as a mother might. And when it was all over she passed me a tissue from her purse. You know, she said, laughing a little, as I sat down and leant my head back against the tree, You're elegant even when you're being violently sick. I flapped her comment away and closed my eyes. I'm so sorry, I said. I'm so, so sorry. You don't need to do this. I'm sorry you had to see that. I started to cry.

Now, she said. You know what? I'm just going to phone and tell them you can't make it tonight. I'll tell Valerie too. This is too much. Just too much. No one should have to do what you're being asked to do, to live through what you have to live through – what you are living through, I mean, right now. This is ridiculous. This is so fucking crazy. The whole thing is totally fucking nuts. I'm so sorry, she said. She squatted in front of me and passed me another tissue. I blew my nose, the last small bits of vomit honking out. I tossed this tissue into the grass. No, I said. It's OK. I want to do it. I have to. Besides, what am I going to do otherwise? I mean, really? Really, what will I do? What am I going to do? What do I do? And then I sobbed, wailed even, in the dirt at the side of the road. Ada pulled me close, rocking me until at last I caught my breath enough to stand and brush the dust from my clothes and get slowly back in the cab. The rest of the journey was a blur: the trees, the farmlands, the river when we glimpsed it.

In the city, roadworks had made a mess of things. The traffic was bad. It would be tight now, I knew that. We shouldn't have stopped. If I hadn't got sick. After all this, if

I didn't make it in time. While we drove, Ada checked her phone compulsively. Her screen went to sleep after about thirty seconds of inactivity, and whenever it went black she pressed the button to light it up and see the time again.

Shit, she said. If it comes to it, we could get changed in the loos at the prize ceremony. I mean I hope it doesn't, but this isn't looking good.

The car idled, not moving. All around us vehicles sounded their horns. The street we needed to turn down so as to be dropped outside the hotel was closed. I'm sorry, the driver said, waving his arm at the barricades, the roads are blocked off to eastbound traffic, I'm sorry. I can't take you there.

What? said Ada. What do you mean?

I mean no go. I mean, the road is closed. Look, he said, drawing a map in the air in front of him, I can go this way then that way then this way then that, and then I can get you a little bit closer.

How long will that take?

Maybe twenty minutes, half an hour. Depends.

And how far away are we now, if we just walk?

Hm, maybe ten minutes, fifteen?

OK, just drop us here.

Here?

Yes, just here's fine.

Here then, he said.

I stepped out into gritty white sunlight. As I did so a small man in a fedora gave a deep bow and said, Welcome to New York! The cab waited, idling, to check we crossed the road safely and walked in the right direction. My unsteadiness was that obvious. At first there seemed to be only noise: engines, horns, music thumping from dark cars. A flock of grey pigeons flew upwards and spread out beneath the sound of an onrushing siren. Men stood under shop alcoves sucking at their cigars, eyes squinting closed. On the sidewalks bags of garbage were piled as high as my waist and the fuggy air through which I walked smelt of bile and decay. I could see darker patches of ground where sprays of vomit had dried up or been hosed away. A truck reversed. A police siren started up. At my feet a beggar woman shaking a plastic cup of coins. The cup made a high, light noise, like tiny bells, as if there might only be ten of those small copper-coloured one-cent pieces. I had no change. I felt a little faint. I thought maybe we had taken a wrong turn after all, or that the cab driver had been mistaken and we had walked in the opposite direction to the one we should have gone in. We thought we should be there by now but couldn't see the hotel sign anywhere. I walked on through clouds of cigar smoke and across dark streaks of dog piss, my suitcase banging against my leg because one of the wheels had broken.

Book Two

8

OK, Ada said at last. This is us. A concierge opened a very clean glass door fitted with a brass handle and I stepped inside. The sounds of the city fell away. We checked in then took the elevator to our floor. In my room I unlocked my suitcase and lifted out the dress I had packed to wear. It was a little black dress – the kind that can be crushed into the corner of a bag, left there for weeks, and when it's at last pulled out there's not a single crease. The fabric was glossy and heavy – draping in just the right way, skimming the curves of the body. Pockets. No zip. Machine-washable. I showered, brushed my teeth and tugged the dress on over my head. I took one last look in the mirror and suddenly worried that I'd have been better off wearing something with long sleeves. But there was nothing to be done about it then. I slipped my plastic room card into my pocket and hurried to meet Ada in the foyer.

As I stepped out of the elevator my phone pinged. It was Valerie texting to say she was caught in traffic and might be late. Then Ada was at my side, steering me towards the door and passing me a piece of paper. Here, she said, I've written you a speech. I thought it might make things easier. It's just simple, she told me. I held onto this until we arrived at the awards reception, where I glanced at the note.

It was written in black ballpoint on the pink-tinged hotel stationery. Ada had lovely handwriting: a touch of the copperplate that she must have been raised on as a child and which had since deformed into an elegant bohemian scrawl. The sentence structure was not mine, the clauses too short. But it was efficient, brief, it would not make me cry, I would not ramble, I would not repeat myself or forget what I was supposed to say or why I was there, and so it did what I couldn't have done myself at that time. Thank you, I said, refolding the paper and slipping it into my pocket.

Now you stay right there, she said. I'm just going to find us a drink.

I hovered, feeling nervous. The winner hadn't yet been announced, which only encouraged speculation, and while I waited for Ada, a writer whom I recognised but didn't know very well came up to me. She looked much older than her author photo, and despite the loss of youth I had heard through the grapevine that she was a favourite among the punters, touted as a sure winner. She had large dark eyes that glossed with tears as she reached out and touched her warm hand to my arm. I'm so very sorry, she said. I heard just yesterday. I thought she meant the prize at first, then realised of course it couldn't be this and that she was referring instead to Patrick.

I was taken aback. I suppose I should have expected it, the sympathy. The accident was common knowledge now. Yet for some reason I thought I'd be immune from it here – an arena I had sought to make my own, one not beholden or attached to the details of my life with Patrick. I didn't think I'd see you, she continued. I mean, I don't know how you're even standing up. If I were you, I'd just want— at that moment Ada returned, smiling, and I gratefully took the drink she offered.

No, I said. I mean, thank you, yes. The writer looked at me gently, as if I were a pitiable child, and I found myself suddenly blinking back tears. Ada noted my discomfort and stepped in. Sorry, she said, there's someone we need to meet, and I let myself be led away. As we headed towards a darker, more private corner of the room I turned round and saw the same writer waving to another shortlistee somewhere behind me. I heard her calling out, Congratulations! Oh my *God*, you *so* deserve this!, something she had entirely forgotten to say to me.

There was a chair in the corner and Ada sat me down in it. I swallowed my drink quickly. We were near the speakers, and the music was too loud. She leant close and said into my ear: When they call your name and say the title of your book, you will need to stand, walk up to the lectern on the stage and read from that piece of paper I just gave you. She was talking very slowly. Saying her words very loud and clear. I watched her bright-red lips move in and out of shapes: rounder, less round, closed, open. Her lipstick made her teeth appear slightly yellow. Now, she said, we should fill up that glass again and toast you properly. I know you don't feel it, but this is huge and you're amazing.

A bell chimed then, and the MC asked us to please take

our seats. Just before we did, Ada said, Wait a second, there's just something I should add to that piece of paper. I passed it to her. She rustled about in her handbag for something, made a note, then gave the speech back to me and I once more shoved it into my pocket. The formalities began. Waiters roamed the room. Every time my glass appeared a little less than full, some beautiful young man leant over my shoulder and topped me up. Eventually Ada put her hand over my glass – She's fine thanks, she said to the waiter. I sipped my water. I'd already drunk too much. Above me, bright and coloured spotlights moved over the ceiling. It felt vaguely like a scene from an Italian nightclub, remembered from my youth. With Patrick. The speeches went on, I heard them as a kind of hum in the background, my mind loose and tidal as it swung from one sound to another, jolted every now and again by sudden applause.

Soon, Ada said, nudging me, Are you OK? I nodded and took a deep breath as I tried to gather my thoughts, be ready.

I well knew that all literature has a form to which it adheres. A map of sorts that indicates how movement will occur and therefore how time might be experienced, how in it we might live. Sometimes our allegiance to form might, simultaneously, be a dismissal of it, a refusal. In this case form is the parent that the child rebels against, but still needs in order to live; what the child will come back to when they feel they are really losing control, when every limit has been exceeded.

If all literature adheres to a form – even the form of contesting form – so does life. I, of all people, well knew this. We are always on the cusp of its reinvention, or so it feels. We are always in the grip of its repetition, or so it feels. Each of us on that shortlist had lived out our books in one way or another, had sought to align our chosen forms with the content of our lives, or vice versa: the exchange is ever present and only differs by degree. My preference has always been the omnivorous beast that is the literary novel: where you can have something of this, a bit of that, a pinch of whatever is over there. I liked it because it is the form most approximate to the unruliness of living, and the book for which I had won the prize was a book of this kind – one that had been touted as a novel for our times, a book *about now*, about this moment *we are now living in*, about the present, the *times we are going through now and so much more*. Well, Ada had said, nowness is a kind of thing. There is no real market for the literary novel anyway, they told me when I signed the contract. But still, they worked at it – the campaign was clever, soothing the literati who wouldn't risk being seen with a novel of feminine bearing while catering to those always eager to keep abreast of the bestseller list and the recommended holiday reads. Like some kind of subliminal programming, the publicity material used the word *now* at every opportunity. *Now* it was a way of turning something that was essentially unfashionable, unnecessary, unfamiliar and undesired into its opposite: *now* something of the absolute moment – unrepeatable and therefore urgent, essential, cutting-edge and completely necessary if one were to have any chance of successfully navigating *this moment*, such a bewildering moment, one never lived before; a moment we might learn to live with and through only by reading this book, *now.* The logic of this was a mix, it seemed, of self-help meets Hegelian snobbery meets fashionista. Whatever, I said to the team when they were putting the publicity together and working out the mock-up for the cover. Just no half-faced swooning woman, the image so often selected in preference to the aerial shot of the building in which she lives; the God's eye view that the female novelist is commonly denied. Just no embossed gold, I said. Please. And no high-res popping white font.

In the end I got both these things, the gold and the white, but offset, Ada reassured me, by an endorsement from some megastar emblazoned on the front. This happened to be the white bit. The books by the shortlisted authors were displayed on stage. They were right: you could see the high-res font from where I sat, it appeared luminous without making any sense: without my glasses on I couldn't actually read it, but I didn't need to – I well knew what it said. Because the idea is that women should write about women without sentimentality, that the feeling body should be anatomised with a cool eye, a rational eye, a detached eye, the eye that is thought to belong to the male, historically speaking. And if there is anything in a woman's work that can suggest an alliance with this view she is celebrated for, to quote the cover of my own book, 'a bracing lack of sentimentality', a sign that she has emerged at last as the victor of her own feelings, having vested herself of them, mastered them, separate from them now and watchful of how they operate in others. It is the ultimate corseting of the female novelist; if she is to be taken seriously there are so many ways in which she should not speak, so many things about which she cannot write. So many directions in which she cannot look. Not the house, that goes without saying. And not to the past – a prohibition that is plainly selective: what is derided as nostalgia in the work of a woman is celebrated as a talent for counterfactual thinking and lauded as a rare feel for the historical moment when it comes to the work of her male peers. I suppose that in my books I could have tried irony or satire: that was a way of performing an emotion without having to inhabit it, a way of giving readers just a taste of the feeling while keeping its real power at bay. Or I could have moved towards non-fiction. But I wanted more than this: I craved the intimacy, dissolution and transferral of self that occurred through deep contact with the most powerful works of art. I wanted to be swayed and changed, and I wanted my books to do this too. This last one more than any that had come before.

I thought of what one of my old teachers, Mrs Harley, used to rail against, the quote on the front of a paperback she once lent me. It was a book she loved and a quote she despised: 'The most perfect English prose any woman has written' – this quote being offered, quite naturally, by a man.

The quote on my book was slightly longer, a few extra words for context on either side, but the *bracing* and the *lack of* was the important bit. The bit the publishing house wanted. Once again, the woman's victory is marked by a definition in the negative, by the idea of an absence. It is unflinching, unsentimental, uncompromising, rather than being labelled for what it is: tough, hard-headed, gritty, piercing, robust, muscular, searing, bold, etc. I could go on. All those positives that are given to the men.

We, on the other hand, are defined once more against the expectations of our sex, the assumed lack.

I suppose this approach offered something of a catch-all for a book that was hard to classify even within my own oeuvre. For while there were historical sections in this latest novel, and many sections of straight realism generous in nature and feeling (these, I discovered, were the parts that seemed go down well in any public readings), the bulk of the book occurred in the near-present and attended to contemporary events in a way that none of my previous novels had done. Because of this the judges, in their citation, couldn't help but commend it for its importance, without being able to say what, exactly, was pressing or necessary or relevant in any of the words I had written. I hated the cultural valorisation of issues so much – not on principle, there were many things I believed in quite passionately, but because so often it was a hollow valorisation, one that required no artistry and which saw books and paintings and whatever else lauded for the ability to make certain noises, to sing the right words however out of tune – that I had sought to write a book without issues and now, somehow, this was what people loved. Only they didn't phrase it like this exactly, and maybe it was the case that I had only fooled them and even they could not see this: the work was so utterly contemporary, so shaped by its own time, that they assumed there must be issues in it, even if they couldn't say exactly what they were. As a result, the novel had been deemed complex and multilayered. Ada took my hand and leant over to me. Remember to breathe, she said.

9

Music started up, heralding the announcement of the prize. Around us lights shifted from purple through to green and then yellow, flashing and circling on the ceiling. As I tipped back the last of my wine I watched the lights spin. Valerie slipped into the empty chair beside me and took my hand in hers. *Now,* said Ada, squeezing my upper arm, they're going to call your name any moment now. And sure enough, the man announcing the prize looked down at a piece of paper identical to the one in my pocket. Pale pink, palm sized, the same hotel stationery. He read it slowly, as if he was not quite sure of its meaning, or perhaps the script was illegible, or maybe, I thought, there had been a mistake. Then he cleared his throat.

And I'm pleased to announce that the winner of this year's prize is . . .

He paused here a moment. I was sure he would say someone else's name. In fact I hoped, prayed that he would. I didn't think I could stand up and walk to the stage. I didn't think my legs would hold me. I surely couldn't take from my pocket the piece of paper, unfold it with my sweating, trembling hands and read. The microphone was set too high for me, at the level of this tall man's mouth. Who would adjust it? Other people had given long, profound speeches and if I said what was on the piece of paper I would sound miserly, short, ungrateful, out of date. The MC had very white hands, they looked luminous, almost fluorescent under the spinning lights. He opened them out to the audience. Then he said my name: J.B. Blackwood.

A cry went up. The room was cheering. Ada helped pull back my chair. I stood at her behest and took a few steps. The heels of my shoes sank into the carpet. The music was too loud. The lights were bright and flashing. Flashing then spinning. Spinning then flashing. I couldn't see a path through the chairs although there must have been one, crumbed, littered with a trail of bread and spilt wine and dropped napkins and handbags shoved against chair legs. I took a few steps, smiling. Everyone was turning towards me. My eyes watered, people's faces swooned in my vision. I balanced myself by holding on to the chair backs as I went. The lights flashed again, flashing then spinning. Spinning then flashing.

I don't remember taking the stairs to the stage. I was just suddenly there, behind the lectern, and the spotlight shone into my eyes. I looked out into the audience for the sight of familiar faces, but the stage lights prevented this: all the people were small lumps of black in the middle distance. My heart beat so hard I thought I might pass out.

I knew all too well that I was seen as the dark horse of the shortlist. It wasn't that I was not known, but that in this particular arena I was thought unlikely to succeed. Maybe I was thought to have enough readers already. Maybe I had published too many books for my age. Maybe they were the wrong kinds of books, all along. And while I had been very successful, my success had not come without criticism from certain corners. Up until that point, I had been known as an author of taut and compelling novels that indulged the anti-hero. Slim books that tended to hone in on moments of disaster or transformation in an individual's life. But just as they were praised for their acuity, my books were sometimes criticised for being, what some called, forbidding. They were the kind of books that made the reader feel a little uneasy when they weren't expecting it – books that contained or provoked too much feeling, and often feeling of the wrong kind: exposure, violence, guilt or tremendous love that shifted into something dark and murderous. They were, in essence, too pointed in attitude and too confronting – abrasive, some critic once wrote. Difficult, said another, referring not to the words themselves but to the sentiments evoked.

But however my work had been described, my fans well outnumbered my critics. My publisher played to this, they knew my readers had an endless appetite for protagonists that were obsessive and rich. In the end, though, the words used to describe my writing were eventually the same ones used to describe me, and so despite increasing success – sales, adaptations and all the rest – I somehow found myself drifting away from the particular kind of critical acclaim that relies on gusts of easy reading buoyed by good cheer.

I knew all this. As did the audience sitting at my feet that night. And I knew I had won despite this. I could feel everyone waiting on me, the heat of their attention.

I took a deep breath, lifted my hands to the microphone and tried to angle it down towards my mouth. I pushed it too close then and my breathing, amplified, crackled through the room. The piece of paper Ada had handed me was still crushed in my pocket. I rubbed at the paper as one might a tissue. My hands were sweaty and I could feel them turning the paper damp and soft. I took it out then and, standing at the transparent lectern, smoothed the paper as best I could. I wasn't quite sure what I was seeing: a sheet of yellow foolscap with the address of a hotel, and what looked like a shopping list: milk, tomatoes, cat food. I didn't think the handwriting was mine, although I couldn't be wholly sure. I knew I didn't own a cat, that I didn't like tomatoes because they gave me a rash on the edge of my lips. I looked up and stared into the lights. Ada must have passed me back the wrong piece of paper in the dark. I was trembling. In the lead-up to the ceremony I had asked whether or not there would be a lectern because, I explained, it helped me to decide what to wear, and it was good to know whether or not I had anything to hide behind. And although they told me that, yes, there would be a lectern, no one thought to add that it would be made of clear plastic, and therefore rid itself of the function I expected it to serve, which was to shield me, to give me something that I felt I could at least partially cower behind. Instead, it existed merely as a tall transparent shelf on which I could rest my crumpled piece of paper and, if careful, I could balance my hands just behind this on the narrow ledge so that their shaking might be slightly less visible. Next to the lectern, on an ordinary wooden stand, someone had placed a glass and a jug of water. A young woman stepped up and filled the glass for me. I took a sip, swallowed carefully so as not to drip the water or cough, and put the glass back down on its cardboard coaster. The room fell silent. I looked at the words printed on the paper; some of them were blurry from being caught in the lines of a hard fold, some had small tears through them. I had no idea what to say.

I knew, though, that whatever I said up there on the stage, there could be no middle ground. Too much feeling and I'd be criticised for being soppy and over-emotional. Too little and I'd be, as I sometimes was, accused of a clinical attitude and described as cold. How I longed to be treated as Patrick was, to be granted without question that kind of artistic authority that let him say and do as he pleased and be applauded for it. I had mimicked his persona, to a degree, in the hope I would be treated the same way. For both of us, this inflated and armoured presentation was a cover – a way of existing as an artist in the public arena, establishing a stance or attitude that set the tone for any further critical debate. At home we could be different creatures, a couple who liked to watch baking competitions on television if only to see grown men cry over split batters and soggy bottoms. But in the literary world, well.

I smiled at the audience, then glanced down at the piece of paper. My book had been placed on the stand beside me, next to the water jug, and its bright lettering glittered under the lights. It still seemed strange to me, that I had written this – an expansive and digressive fiction more personal than anything I'd done before. A book I was compelled to write, so compelled in fact that there were times when I felt a little afraid of what I was doing. In the writing, whole scenes would come to me at once, as they had never done before, and I would have to rush to get them on paper. Or I would be going about my business, only to be floored by a sudden memory that surged up so vivid and intense it could hardly be distinguished from real life, and I had no choice but to transcribe this, knowing, as I wrote it down, exactly where it needed to go in the novel. And not only was the material on which I was drawing strange in its vividness, but the sentences that communicated these scenes were made of a different substance entirely. Even I did not know how to properly describe them.

Up to that point my sentences had been tightly focused and well aimed; they satisfied the need of an impatient reader. I had deliberately nurtured a certain androgyny in my writing, eager to uphold the idea of a universal and sexless sentence. Now, though, I see the ruse of this, that the unisex sentence is just the male sentence assuming its universality. For these new sentences – the sentences in that prize-winning book – were languorous, multi-jointed, threaded through with double and triple thoughts. I felt the thick ribbing of their musculature, the weave of tendon and tissue, I felt the strength of this pulsating, tugging, lifting and bending however it needed to make the leap, accommodate the consciousness of the subject. They felt, finally, to be my very own sentences, uninherited and wholly inhabited at last. Everything living seemed to speak to me and through me when I wrote in this way. It was as if this was the book I was always meant to write. The book I lived to write, the book I was born for. I'm not exaggerating when I say that it changed me in the writing of it and made me at last into the woman writer that, for one wrong reason or another, I had long thought I ought not to be.

I cleared my throat. I could feel everyone waiting for me to speak. I knew I had paused too long. I knew that what was written on the piece of paper Ada had passed me was all wrong, that it was not the paper she had meant to give me and that she must be wondering why I was stalling. I pushed my hands back into my pockets and there I felt another piece of paper; this was the dress I had worn on the ship, the last night we went up for dinner. Patrick had gone to fetch our drinks and was delayed by a conversation at the bar. While I waited, I took my notebook and pen from my handbag and started to write a draft of the speech, but because I was not happy with the result I tore the paper from the notebook and, having no bin in which to throw it, shoved it into my pocket as Patrick returned, jovial, with our negronis. It was this piece of paper which, standing at the lectern, I now pulled out of my pocket. Dazzled by the lights and knowing a speech was required, I started to read.

They were not complicated, the words. The sentences were neither long nor polished. There was very little punctuation other than full stops at regular intervals and the occasional comma. Although I had marked, with an asterisk, a section where I could pause and used this then to take another sip of water, before looking out into the audience and remembering to thank everyone who needed to be thanked, using the stock phrases that you hear at the Oscars about the risk of having overlooked someone important and the hypothetical apologies if that did happen to be the case. I had forgotten exactly what I had written that night on the ship, forgotten what was coming. Forgotten that I'd mentioned Patrick in his living state, that I had, in one long and indulgent sentence, thanked him for always being by my side, for always being my biggest champion, my first reader, for being there with me tonight. I thanked him for showing me how to see things through to their end. I thanked him for all his love and care. I had already stumbled into this sentence before I understood what I was saying, and by then, halfway through, it was too late. I couldn't unthank him. I couldn't acknowledge to the room that he was not there, no longer alive, not anywhere. Instead I had to just finish it, I had to plough my way through. Pretend the accident hadn't happened: this one now, and the one on the ship. It would be far worse if I stopped where I was and explained my error. I knew I couldn't do that, that if I did I would break down and need to leave the stage. To pause there and begin again would mean acknowledging his death and my widowhood – things that I knew everyone was thinking about anyway, but to survive that moment I needed to make-believe, at least temporarily, that these things hadn't really occurred, or that they were irrelevant in my own moment of glory – that my grief didn't exist then up on that stage, that it wasn't my own, that it didn't become me and was something I could learn to do without. And so I continued to work my way through that long and gracious sentence that dripped with thanks, even though I knew it risked making me look deranged, out of my mind, in the grossest state of denial.

When at last that part was over, I took a deep breath and started to wrap up. Around me a new hush had fallen. In those final, closing remarks I said nothing about theft or corruption, I made no political point, I did not signal my virtue through the support of good causes. I completely failed to advocate. In short, my words bore no resemblance to the speech I thought I might one day give, that I had so often, in moments of rage or splendour, imagined myself giving – the grown-up equivalent perhaps of the teenage girl's daydream in which she sees herself spotlit on the dance floor, the crowd clearing a space for her, her white dress glowing fluorescent under the neon lights, her hair flapping around her body as she performs gasp-inducing moves. After all, it would be only a slight exaggeration to say I had been listed for prizes more times than I could easily remember, without ever winning. Some of the rumours among the literati suggested that this was due to my marriage: I could not win a prize without this bond being cited as cause for my own rising prestige – that I, in short, had married into direct privilege, into another man's money, money that had bought me my time to write, that paid for it in the early days, and it would look bad and rouse suspicions if I were to ever be the recipient of the prize and given money which others thought I did not need – charity and merit blurring in the minds of the panel.

Patrick was, after all, my own origin story. Or one of them. It was under his tutelage, before we were a public item, that I researched my final academic project on contemporary noir romance and alongside this wrote, without Patrick's knowledge, a novella that extended the thesis in dramatic form. I bought into the genre, quite literally, too young to query this, too impressionable, too beholden to my future husband's praise. It had been some time before this that I'd confessed my desire to write, and he'd encouraged me.

For a while I kept that novel a secret, wanting some things just for myself and thinking, for a long time anyway, that it wouldn't be the kind of story Patrick was interested in. Then I showed him part of it one day, on a whim or out of frustration because there was a passage that wasn't working – not smooth enough somehow. I didn't expect him to read the whole work, just the section I had circled. Can I keep this for the night? he asked, as I was stepping out of the shower at his place, about to get dressed and take the bus home.

OK, I said, but just that bit. I only need help with that section.

Sure, he said.

He called me early the next morning to ask if I'd let him turn the novella into a short film. Do you know how good this is? he said. It has all the right qualities, he told me. It might even get picked up for the festival circuit. Of course I said yes. And then yes and yes again to all number of things I might have refused. The film became a small sensation. We were in London by then and popped champagne in his office when the first reviews came in. Something changed in that strange, buzzing atmosphere of my sudden success. I say 'my', but it was only this in private. It was not in the interests of publicity, they told me, to broadcast the fact that the film was based on my thesis, or to widely publicise that the writer was me. They would instead, for obvious reasons, draw attention to the stars of the film, the beautiful men and women, and to Patrick as the director. They had to change the end to give it more finality and make it a little less morose, more of a sting in the tail kind of thing they told me, but otherwise they reserved the good bones: the storyline, the features of the main character, the clever plot twists.

His movie, people came to call it in the press, and in those many corridors through which he walked. On that day when, in celebration, we got drunk in his small, very un-soundproofed office, I gave him a blow job while he relaxed in his wingback chair. Towers of books were placed around my feet. I shuffled sideways a little, to get a better angle, and knocked a pile over. Afterwards I sat in that same chair and he took a photo of me. I look a little flushed, rather pleased with myself, a flash of wickedness in my slightly raised eyebrow, my tilted head. My lips look glossy, almost doll-like, and this became the photo that was used on the dust jacket of my first book, a slim volume published by a tiny independent press. Not the novella, which as a text never saw the light of day, but the one after that. Anyone who knew my husband in his capacity at that university could recognise the scene of the photograph, the scene of the crime: the bookshelves in the background, the filing cabinet, my slight frame too small in the man-sized chair. It had never occurred to me not to use this photograph; my publisher was only thinking of how I looked, the image they wanted to present. I didn't know any better and no one thought to suggest that my alliance with Patrick would pit people against me, form quick and powerful enemies: the rogue scholars who would sit on the funding boards or chair the prize panels, the women who were outraged by what they considered to be Patrick's moral laxness and who made the assumption that I was wilfully benefitting from this liaison. After a certain number of years spent passing through one prize list and another, I came to expect to be overlooked in a certain kind of way.

None of this was written on that damp and crumpled piece of paper that I was reading from. And in reality I well knew, and had always known, that this was not a story I could ever tell. At that moment, standing under the lights in front of the crowd, trembling behind my transparent lectern, part of me wanted to say, Here, keep the prize. I needed it years ago, but not now, because my life now is another story, one I do not know, one I have not imagined, one I could not have foreseen, one I cannot write, and cannot tell you about, because I am in a place I cannot speak from, because the struggle is too great, because it is all that I can see, all that I can feel and I have no idea, any more, how I am supposed to hide this, what I am supposed to be for you. I had mustered such will. I had had to find within myself such endless reserves of strength, casting the bucket down over and over as one might into a deep well so often low in water, the cavity dug into the side of a rocky hill in an arid landscape where there was rarely rain, but still I went to it, thirsty, determined, finding at long last what I needed in order to finally write the book that brought me to that moment in my life, standing behind that lectern, accepting the prize. I lifted my chin a little and steadied my gaze. I felt the audience staring back at me, stilled, stunned even. And I understood that in this moment of greatest triumph I was again – and perhaps always would be – overshadowed by Patrick, maybe now more than ever. Even in death he had the power to eclipse my own achievements. For as I looked out over that room of people, I knew that they were only partly thinking of the book I had written and of my achievements as a writer. Worse yet, perhaps they were no longer thinking of me as a writer at all. I realised then that in the wake of the accident I had become his widow, above and beyond anything else.

I lifted my glass, toasted the crowd and drank. Someone turned up the music.

IO

I woke the next morning in my hotel room, the alarm ringing. Daylight sheared the edge of the curtains. Had someone carried me here? I wasn't sure. I couldn't remember. My muscles felt so heavy. I rolled over – dim memory of the things said the night before – and pulled the crisp white sheets up to my chin. The pillowcase was cool and smooth. But maybe I didn't say them. Maybe those words were only thoughts. Through the fug of sleep I was aware that I was still in my party clothes: dress, stockings. I pressed the snooze button. My head hurt, the bones around my temples ached in a strange way. I remembered the lights shining in my eyes. I felt incredibly thirsty, my tongue rough and thick. I needed water. There was a glass there, on the nightstand, half full. I remembered drinking the other half hours ago, just before someone switched off the light, after the pill got stuck in my throat, its bitterness rising up. I had swallowed it down hard and then a woman's hand – Ada's I assumed – put the glass back on its coaster, under the lamp. The alarm went off again. Through the crack in the curtains the day looked too bright. I felt the headache start to spread into the back of my skull. I was so tired. So very tired. I couldn't think. The alarm went off again. And once more still. I moved slowly to the bathroom and peed. Then I lay down again. I reached for the water beside my bed; a piece of paper was tucked under the glass. I pulled it out: Call me when you're up. Love A xx.

Ada was booked into the adjoining room. If I'd had the energy I could have just banged on the wall as Proust did when he needed the attentions of his grandmother. But I'd slept so long that by now she'd be out on business. Images from the previous night came back to me with a sickening turn of my stomach – that woman touching my arm, her look of pity – and I thought of the reading I had promised to do that lunchtime. And then what? I had hardly considered this. Hardly had the chance. I didn't want to think about it. I pushed off the covers, ran the shower until the hot water steamed up the glass then scrubbed my body under the scalding jet. My untouched body. My untouchable body, rendered so by grief and cataclysm. My single, widowed body. I turned up the heat as far as I could handle it: burning, dizzying. Then I wrapped myself in the hotel robe, opened the heavy curtains and phoned for room service.

Valerie arrived just as I was finishing my coffee, breezing into the room with a paper bag of pastries. She was tall and always wore some extravagant architectural coat over a sack-like silk thing that on her looked incredibly elegant.

Oh goodness, she said to me, slipping off her coat and hanging it over the back of a chair.

I just can't believe all this – how are you feeling? Did

you get some sleep? Last night was pretty rough on you.
I'm really so sorry, she said. You know you don't have to
do all this, if you want to just call it quits you can. I can
easily rearrange things. Or just do the bookshop reading
today and maybe leave it at that. You should consider it,
she said as she brought the pastries to the small table by
the window and sat down.

I understood what she was saying. I realised that the
awards speech had been a disaster. But I had already told
Ada I wanted to go ahead, and I still did. No, I said. Not
after all this time. All the work that has gone into getting
me this far.

She knew what I meant: after all, she'd been there for
most it, we had come this far together. Valerie and I had
met years ago, at a writers' festival when I was still what
they call up-and-coming and Valerie was just starting out.
At that point I was represented by someone else, but was
less than happy with this arrangement. Valerie and I were
brought together by chance in the green room, when
there was some mix-up over the schedule. Our names
had somehow been swapped so that I was accidently listed
on her panel, and she on mine. But it was one of those
fortuitous mistakes – because after meeting her I never
looked back. Neither of us did.

Look, if I could make it through last night, I said, I can
make it through the rest. I know I can push through, I
told her. I want to, I need to.

You've seen your schedule though, yes?

I nodded. I can do it, I told her. Besides, it's better
this way. She tilted her head a little, as if she herself was
undecided.

Well, either way, she said, you need to eat. Valerie tore one end off a croissant and popped this neatly into her mouth, somehow avoiding crumbs sticking to her fingers or her fuchsia-pink lipstick. Still, she wiped her hands neatly on a paper napkin. She was impeccable and economical in all her habits, restrained, one might say in everything other than her glamorous clothes. She nibbled at the other end of the croissant in the same way. I'd never seen her finish an entire meal.

Listen, she said, I spoke with your sister. Ada gave me her number. We're trying to work something out. Some support. It's all going to hit you hard pretty soon, she told me, getting up to fill the kettle. You really have got such a full calendar up ahead. Even if we carry on, as you want to, it would be good to have some further wriggle room and I've negotiated something of a grace period – a week or so before the schedule really kicks in – but you know, to say there's a lot of interest would be an understatement. And not just in the prize, I'm afraid.

The press had been hounding James, my publicist, along with Valerie and Ada, asking to speak to me. All three answered in the same way – saying that I was not available for comment at the moment, equivalent to saying that the lady of the house was not at home, indisposed. Perhaps they used that word. It was the kind of thing that James might say. Still, the calls kept coming. You'll have to say something sooner or later, Valerie said. If you talk to them, they'll pretend they're calling about the prize but then you know, don't you, that they'll dig for something on the accident. For your own good you should issue a statement, a press release, at least get them off your back.

I didn't know what to say. I didn't want to say anything. What did anyone put in such a statement? I worried that whatever I said would sound false or be misconstrued. I knew how easy it was to use a quote for purposes other than that for which it was intended. The seemingly harmless appearance of ellipses that omit crucial words. You need to just get it over with, Valerie said. I'm happy to draft something.

For a long time I had thought of Valerie as my guardian angel. She had an uncanny knack of pulling the strings behind the scenes, of knowing whom to talk to and when. And of knowing, as she did now, when I should withhold comment and when I should speak. She took a pack of Beroccas from her handbag and dropped an orange lozenge in my glass of water. Here, drink this, she said.

After the reading today – are you totally sure you can manage that? – after the reading we can pack your bags and get you ready. Your sister really wants to talk to you. I think she's going to try calling tonight. I've got a meeting before the reading but I'll be there. Oh, and there's a last phone hook-up with that journalist from the *New Yorker*, for the profile. It shouldn't take long, she said there were just a couple of final things she had to check with you. But after the interview and then the reading we'll get you ready. We've organised your flight. I wish I could take you myself, only there's business here I need to see to. I'll be back in London in a week.

Ready for what? Travel to where? I asked, confused.

Home, she replied. You need to go home. An image flashed through my mind, as if we were still children, my sister and I, looking for home together, wondering what this was, where we should find it: babes in the wood.

Oh, I said, glancing out of the window, the sky striped with white cloud. I was holding a copy of my novel; I knew I still had to choose a section to read for the bookshop event.

Anyway, Valerie said, checking her phone, We'd better hustle. The phone interview is in a few minutes actually. So you just finish that pastry there and I'll get you some more water and maybe some camomile, what do you think? Then I'll message to let her know you're ready.

I pulled the chair up closer to the window and cleared my throat. You'll be brilliant, she told me. Because you always are. And remember, don't answer any question that you're not comfortable with.

Very soon the phone rang. I let it ring three times and then I picked it up. A man from reception spoke: I have an incoming call for you, madam. Just a moment, please. There was some static and a radio station started to play, indicating that I was now on hold. Then a woman began to speak. Yes, I replied. This is me. Valerie hovered by the door. She gave me a thumbs-up sign to check that all was in order, and when I nodded in return she let herself quietly out of the room.

The journalist, whom I could name but won't – the piece is still out there for anyone to see, but not me, I don't want to ever cast eyes on it again – offered her congratulations. She sounded warm, and genuine in her enthusiasm – after all, she knew me well by then. Our conversations had started some months before when she'd

contacted Valerie to ask about doing a profile. It seemed
perfect timing, with the book coming out, and this was
before we knew about the prize. I met her first for coffee,
and suggested a café near my house. I said I wanted just
to meet initially to see if we connected. It was late spring.
We sat outside. I was nervous; she was younger than me,
and remarkably self-assured. I knew from experience that
she would write to please her peers, or whoever it was she
admired most in the world of journalism. I was wary of
this, of her. Still, she knew my work well, and her initial
questions were smart and interesting. She hadn't been told
to cover me, either – she'd asked to do it herself. So I
agreed. After that coffee we met several times. She was
American, but living in London. We had lunch at some
old-fashioned Italian restaurant, drinks at a bar. There
was a quietness to her that gave her a sense of composure.
She had a calm, open face.

Sometimes I think she roped me in from the start.
Knew what would compel me to open up, without me
even realising it was happening. I should have been more
alert to this. I usually was. But during that last conversation in the hotel room my guard was down, or else I
couldn't keep it up for as long I was normally able. We
began in the usual friendly way, but then the conversation
took a turn I wasn't expecting.

I just want to get inside your head on this one, she told
me. To really get a sense of your process. I know we've
talked about this before but there were just a few things
that we didn't quite get round to last time we spoke and
that I wanted to take a little further. In one of our earlier
conversations you mentioned you mother's disappearance.

I know that this same kind of dramatic event has often featured in your novels, changed the life of your heroines. We haven't talked for a few weeks – since before the, well, the terrible recent events, and I wanted to ask, it must feel strange, she said, now, to be suddenly living—

I was taken aback by the brazenness of this and cut her off. No. I said. It doesn't. It's not. I could see where she was heading and I didn't want to go there. Didn't want my story to be the answer to her question, and so better if she never got to ask it. She was right, none of this – what was happening to me now – was entirely unfamiliar. But I wouldn't talk about Patrick. Not then. Not to her. I knew, though, that my abruptness made me sound callous and unfeeling and that I needed to correct this, so as to avoid it being emphasised in the piece.

Yet it is true, I said, making a concession, backing up. For a while, I told her, my mother's disappearance was everywhere. It was on the radio, in the newspapers – it was awful. Not something you forget, or ever outlive. Especially as a child.

Of course, she said.

I reached for the tea Valerie had left me and scalded my tongue. The journalist seized on this momentary pause and spoke quickly, making clear her own knowledge, her own expertise – a woman who had done her research and who would not be shrugged off or redirected. I was stunned. She knew things about my past and about the book and to this day I still don't know how. Details about my life with Patrick. Things about my real mother. Information she must have been collecting, storing up, waiting to use and now ambushed me with, wielding her knowledge as if in an effort to force my hand. But why? There were certain phrases I remember her using: hungry ghosts, behind the scenes, private demons. I don't know how she'd found these things out. Whom she'd spoken to, what had changed. After months of long, rambling conversations she was suddenly simplifying everything I had written by making it sound confessional, as if this had always been her plan: matching the dots between my life and my fiction, summing it all up. I was so surprised that I had no sound response, not then, not in my current state, and so I blindly stumbled on. Of all the words in my head at that time, I wasn't sure how much I said out loud.

But you're right, I think I replied – I suppose there is always an overlap. I could well remember posters featuring a picture of my mother's face glued on telegraph poles, and the news bulletin that my father would tune into on the little brown wireless. The static, the broken aerial. I may or may not have described these things over the phone. Perhaps it made no difference; that journalist knew my work, she would have encountered these details at one point or another. But the case was closed, I reminded her. Still, I'd be lying if I pretended that versions of that period hadn't been developed in one book or another. I knew that I had adapted true details in fictional scenes. It was a way of dealing with the fact that certain episodes continued to appear in my mind long after they were over in real life. The case was closed, not because we knew what happened but because an answer couldn't be found. I tried to live with this. I don't think I said that to the journalist. But I was exhausted, grieving, hungover. I can't be sure: what I said out loud to her, what I just thought to myself. No one ever came forth with any information, no traces were discovered. Either my mother couldn't be found or didn't want to be. We didn't know whether or not she was alive. It's better to think of her as dead, our father once said, when he wanted us all to move on, to put things behind us, as he liked to say. He could live like this: deliberately forgetful and selective. But what person can pretend the death of a parent, when even a real death is something whose existence is called into radical question, perpetually doubted, a fact that one seeks to reject or refute or disbelieve at every turn, despite evidence. An impossibility. I glanced out of the window; a vapour trail crossed the blue sky. As children we couldn't do it, couldn't imagine it. So I learnt to live with not knowing, to live with a lack of resolution that could sometimes be reconfigured as hope: she might be dead, or she might turn up on our doorstep at any moment. I learnt to live inside a profound uncertainty, I think I might have said, understanding my own past through this heightened state: was she alive or not alive? In existence or not in existence? This is not so very far from the question of was she real or not real?

I was holding the phone so tightly that the fingers of my right hand were feeling tingly, slightly numb. A fire engine with its siren on went past in the street below. Ms Blackwood? The journalist said. Are you still there?

Pardon? Yes. Yes I'm still here.

She asked something else, and from a new angle, her question made of double and then triple links. I suddenly felt so tired and struggled to keep up with what she was saying, felt myself slipping into the need to pretend coherence. I would not let her think I couldn't follow what she was asking, that I didn't understand, that I was scattered and vague. All of these things, I knew, could come back on the page. And so I talked. I talked to show her that I was still capable. That I could respond to her complex question with an equally complex answer that she herself might struggle to keep hold of.

Yes, I said to her, although as a child I wasn't sure what I was aggrieving with. Sorry— What did I just say? I mean agreeing with. In terms of what my father asked of us, that is. I cleared my throat and started again. You know I have often thought, I told her, that my becoming a writer was a side effect of an essentially fictional habit of mind designed to manage this uncertainty around my mother's disappearance and preserve her. I spent a great deal of time as a child, and then as a young woman, expanding on hypotheticals (what if I hadn't, what if she had, what would it be like were we to, maybe she's, I could). In this way I learnt to cultivate and sustain a certain psychic energy that was concerned with the conjectural and the putative and discharge this to a point – energy that I associate, now, with the kind needed to make fiction. A form of negative culpability, perhaps. I mean capability. As a child I drew on this energy to keep the idea of my mother alive, to maintain an intensity to her image, her moving image – sharpening the recall of small words and ways of speaking, her ways of moving, the details of her face. I could give her reality by making her seem alive. Or: I could make her seem alive by giving her this quality of appearing real. In essence, she became the first character in my head.

The journalist murmured something on the other end of the line. But I didn't quite catch what she said. Her voice was soft when she needed it to be and she had a tendency to lean forwards a little, making me feel that she was really listening. I imagined her doing that then, even though we weren't in the same room. Due to various interruptions the whole interview process had taken much longer than I thought it would, but I was also flattered by how much time the journalist was prepared to invest. She worked hard to gain my trust, something that I now know I should never have given. But I had always felt bad, almost grubby, when I resisted any reporter's questions, as if I ought to be grateful that someone was asking. It was my own unwillingness that made me uncomfortable, I had often reasoned, not their prying. Which, in this particular case, was always done very gently. That *New Yorker* journalist, whose name I will not speak, had a habit of nodding slowly, even if I wasn't saying anything. It was like body-language code for *OK, this is good, I am with you here, we are good with this together.* She would just keep doing this as she sipped her drink and into this silence I would start to talk, because I felt a little nervous and I thought I could talk myself to a better place, to a more comfortable state, and because she kept nodding, encouraging me and agreeing at the same time, as if she was already in agreement with whatever it was I was about to say but hadn't yet, and because she seemed pleased by my words, which was the kind of flattery I was a sucker for. Afterwards I always worried about what I'd told her. I could never quite remember, the lunches or drinks always went on for longer than I anticipated.

There's one question, she said on the phone that day, that I haven't yet asked about this particular book, this story, although I know we've covered it for much of your other work. I guess it's a simple question really, but essential.

★

For all my writing life interviewers have wanted to know why I keep returning to the same themes, why in so many of my books someone suffers a terrible injustice – abandonment or ruination – and perhaps even experiences what one calls a breakdown, although the reasons for this differ. Some readers and critics disagree that the things I have described constitute a breakdown. Some say that whatever these people do, and how they behave towards others, is a natural and even expected response to the things that have, in turn, happened to them. A reasonable reaction even, given the circumstances. Others prefer to accuse these figures of neglect and see them punished, even if only through the hatred of the reader, made manifest in the public declaration that they despise the character I have created and that they rue his or her fictional existence. Several times such people have turned up at readings just to tell me this. They have sat through a whole hour of me talking and then waited in line for another half-hour just to stand before me and tell me how much they hate the person I have invented. While they say this, they clutch the book that I have written close to their heart, refusing to hand it over. No, they tell me, I don't want you to sign it.

I'm sorry about that, I say. I mean, that you don't like the character.

But perhaps I shouldn't apologise. For in the end there are those who are compelled to cast judgement, and others who are prone to abstain.

I have no idea how I answered the journalist's question that day. I knew I talked too much and too fast. True to form, I tried to talk myself out of the question I was trying not to answer. I didn't decide, I tried to explain – I hunted it, or discovered it. Or maybe it discovered me. My voice cracked and I fell silent. Oh, she said. I'm sorry, I didn't mean to upset you. You don't have to—

No, no, I said, taking a breath. I'm fine. I'll be fine. Valerie had left a plastic bottle of water on the table. I went to open it but the lid was stuck. I wedged the phone receiver between my chin and shoulder and tried with both hands. I felt so dehydrated from the night before. The lid shifted, the plastic serrated tab peeling away. I drank. She must have heard me gulping.

I was known to have once hurried out of an interview before it was over. I remember how I made some excuse, left the café, crossed the road to the car park where there were public toilets and shut myself in the far cubicle. I leant against the door, closed my eyes and tried to breathe deeply. I remember walls painted a lurid yellow, the colour of bile. Parts of this – the story of my abscondment – appeared in the final article. And subsequently – as damage control, and to offset a tendency of mine to over-talk, lose the thread and then descend into quivering nervousness – Valerie had come up with a series of elaborate justifications in an effort to protect me, and, like a politician, took to giving me a series of sound bites that I used as needed. I memorised these for one book after another. The novel was *magnifying an experience one-thousandfold* until it became fiction, or else we said that it was only *drawing on real experience*, or that it *explored the limits of memory* – thereby proving that there was a tipping point at which the work became unreal, not true, false. Although the more elaborate this secondary publicity spiel became, the more I started to wonder whether I had only repeatedly disguised the truth – as I understood it, as I believed it – because I am a woman, or whether it was because I was afraid, as artists often are, that if I understood too well the creative source of my work, if I became too conscious of it, it would dry up and vanish. Or maybe I went along with all this because within these competing versions – the books themselves, then the publicity material in the background, and the afterlife of all this – I started to lose sight of the real thing I had been trying to speak of, losing sight of it to such an extent that I couldn't speak of it if I tried. Or – and this was the version I started to err towards, to rely on, to fear above everything – maybe it was because there was something that I needed to lie about after all. But I only started to think about this after the accident happened.

I know your husband only died, what, is it eight days ago? the journalist said. I'm so sorry. I can't imagine—

I let my gaze drift out of the window, while in my head, as if to calm myself, I played and replayed the car stunt scene in Truffaut's *Day for Night*. I played and replayed the playing and replaying of this scene, as it happens in that film. At what point do you know that something terrible will occur? A death is imminent, only whose we don't know. It is distant from us. In the film that the film is about, *Meet Pamela*, Pamela herself will be killed in a car accident, although we never see this happen It doesn't matter. Instead we see a stuntman drive the car, dressed up as Pamela. He jumps out at the last minute, the car spins off the cliff and falls down the rocky slope to land in the water. They get it right in one take. We watch the character of Ferrand edit this, running the scene forwards and backwards and forwards again at speed. The car moves in reverse, disappearing behind the blind corner, then shooting out again. The stuntman jumps. The car flies off the cliff. Then they reverse this, so that the car floats upwards out of the water, then they drop it down again, crashing. They play the scene over and over, looking for the sequence of moments that will make Pamela's death appear genuine, convincing, an accident after all and not a carefully orchestrated scene. Only this doesn't satisfy us, because we know it is not real. Because we know it is a set-up. Yet still, the expectation of a tragedy has been established, we have been prepared for this and so we wait, despite not knowing what it is.

No, I replied. You probably can't. But that's why you're on the phone now, asking me about these things. Asking me why I imagine, how I imagine. I heard her shuffling papers, possibly scanning her notes while she considered which question to ask next, or whether there was anything she'd forgotten. I was feeling agitated. It was taking longer than I thought it should. I still had to get dressed for the bookshop event, decide what section I would read and remember to mark it up so as not to look a fool flipping through my own book in search of something I had lost. But I knew I couldn't risk hurrying her.

II

By the time the I finally got off the phone I was running almost half an hour late for the reading. I jumped into a cab and Valerie met me at the other end. In the bookshop they had cleared a large space and set out rows of chairs, all of which were full. Someone passed me a glass of wine as Valerie ushered me through the crowd and led me to a makeshift stage. My hands were clammy. I brushed down the front of my dress and took my seat. Beside me was a small table on which rested a glass tumbler, half full of water. I put the wine down next to this and tucked my hair back behind my ears as the facilitator came up to me. But instead of reaching out to shake my hand, as I expected him to, he touched me lightly on my shoulder and leant down close to my face.

I can't tell you how sorry I am, he said softly. Are you sure you're OK to do this? I had already talked too much to the journalist on the phone and knew if I tried to say anything else at that moment I would cry, so instead waved my hands in front of me as if it all meant nothing and reached for the glass of water. I looked out over the audience. I felt everyone's eyes on me, watching in anticipation, wondering if I would hold it together. My heart was beating too fast and hard. It occurred to me then that maybe everyone thought the prize had been given to me out of pity – the widow writer, whose pain turns out to only add to her glamour. What if that was true? But it couldn't be, I reminded myself, because I had been told of the prize before we even stepped on to the ship, weeks and weeks before the accident. I took another sip of water. The glass smelt slightly eggy. On its edge I could see fingerprints and the lingering stain of another woman's lipstick against the rim. I flicked though my novel. The pages I planned to read from were marked with yellow Post-it notes; I had chosen them in haste, in the cab in fact, as I rushed from the interview to the bookshop. Now I worried I'd picked the wrong sections. The facilitator adjusted my microphone. How much time do I have to read? I asked. I thought it was twenty minutes.

Yes, that would be perfect, he replied.

I nodded. He tapped the microphone and the crowd fell silent. Then he gave a few words of introduction, followed by applause. I smiled at the audience. Thanks everyone, I said. It's lovely to be here. I know we're running a bit late so without further ado I'll just begin at the beginning, or not exactly at the beginning but quite near it. I won't explain anything, though, I don't want to, um, plot-spoil for anyone who hasn't read it yet. Then I cleared my throat and opened the book.

I started with a passage about the day my mother disappeared, and that terrible morning when the policemen trawled through the shallows. The river had been drained and in their blue plastic gloves the men carefully removed certain items from the mud and sealed these in transparent bags. A shoe, I was told. A pair of reading glasses. A belt from a coat. Other bulkier objects appeared as sludge-covered lumps lodged in the riverbed: numerous Victorian safes all busted open, broken bicycles, sheets of corrugated iron, school chairs. The smell was terrible – the stink of green weed exposed and rotting in the air and the shallow pools of black water with their blooms of algae. Dead grey trees raised their branches from the silt. I had leant out of the hotel's open window and called for her. My mother. But my voice was small and high in the gale, the wind rising. It must have been sometime around then, I think, that they cut my fingernails – before or after – cutting them so short that they clipped the soft pad of pink, untouched skin where the underside of the nail meets the fingertip. Someone held my hand, and their grip tightened when I flinched. They did this because I had scratched at my face until I drew blood. Then they let me go. All done now, they said, and I ran to the window and I opened it and I called out into the wind. Someone reached down and carried me away. Afterwards they put my hands in soft woollen mittens and gave me a cup of warm milk that had a medicinal tang to it, To help you sleep now, they said, and then Look at the cup! What's Peter up to now? Naughty Peter – the cup decorated with a faded painting of Peter Rabbit in his blue coat eating carrots stolen from Mr McGregor's garden. Naughty Peter, they said again. Peter with his buttons missing. The cup had a handle on either side so that a very small or fraught child might grip it easily. I did not recognise the cup, it was not mine, but it must have been washed frequently and very thoroughly, a favourite cup scrubbed with a scourer until the picture of Peter started to pale and disappear. By the time they put it in my hands just his tall ears and blue coat were visible against the white background.

I then explained that only later did I realise that it was my father who slipped those mittens on and passed me the warm milk, laced with brandy and honey. Then he pulled the curtains closed, making the room dark. She'll be back, he'd said. Just you wait and see. My voice cracked as I read this section. I felt oddly nervous. It was harder than I thought to revisit this material, to describe it out loud. My hands started to shake. The feeling of being stared at was somehow alarming, even though I knew it shouldn't be. To deal with this I decided to just talk to the room directly, befriend my audience, so to speak. At least try this. I closed the book for a moment, leaving my finger in place to mark the page.

You know I should probably tell you, I said, just to offset the inevitable question at the end and to give some context to the nature of this novel, that Henry, the father in this book, is a man who is very much like my own father, and only in some ways not. The odd thing is that my father actually had a different name, and I could have given this name to the character, only in a weird kind of way I came to spend so much time with this fictional version of my father that I found myself referring to the real man by the name I had given to this avatar, Henry. Funny, I said, as if to myself, because it was strange. Although other characters, I continued, people rather, have kept their own names – I have let them keep these, I said, laughing a little. And no, I didn't ask their permission.

Anyway. This is just a bunch of things I figured I might tell you because it tends to be something I get asked about. Of course, I'm happy to speak more to this later, I said, remembering, with a withering kind of horror, that interview only an hour or so ago, and those other questions I tried so hard not to answer.

I opened the novel again; it was my reading copy, dog-eared and stained. I turned the page. In the end I decided not to refer to the scene where our mother said she had left something in the car, a present for us each – a scene I had revisited in a number of books, albeit in different ways. In this book, the scene came not long before that girl clung to the frame of the open window and called out, before she was drugged to sleep. I'll be back in a moment, my mother had said, *in a jiffy*. I promise, she told me, winking. And then she slipped out of the door and never returned.

I didn't refer to this in the reading because I didn't want to give too much away. It would risk spoiling something were I to detail that scene and go on to explain how my sister and I then waited and waited, eager to discover what the presents would be. *She promised*, I wailed. She promised! This word, how it exists as a golden charm for a child, a word that marks an almost magical bond, unbreakable and glowing with power until it is sullied. Every child remembers that sinking of the heart, that sudden knowledge of adult life as a chain of deceits: you said you would, you promised I could, you told me when. I turned the page and took a deep breath.

Before the accident on the cruise ship, Ada had suggested that for the upcoming bookshop events I read the section where the girl and her sister find themselves in the midst of the investigation. Ada liked that bit – she thought it was a good hook, that it drew people in. But I knew that in my current state I couldn't humanly do this, not now. I couldn't even look at the section where the police arrived at the hotel where the girls and Henry were staying. It was during breakfast hours, and all the guests sitting down to their buffet of eggs and sausages turned to stare. I knew this section by heart. I could almost have recited it without glancing at the page, and the more I tried not to think of it the more my mind turned to it. They had wanted, that morning, to search our room for any signs our mother may have left, and my sister and I were sent off to wait while they did this. I remember a lady officer sat May and me down in a set of club chairs in the foyer and a waiter brought us each a hot chocolate, which I didn't touch, instead letting the milk fat form a yellowish skin over the surface while the drink turned cold. They questioned our father for a long time. I could see him, over in the far corner of the room, his head in his hands. Hotel patrons stopped to stare or came over to say how sorry they were. Older women who wore too much perfume on the inside of their wrists left the residue of this on our bodies, wherever they happened to touch us: stroking our hair or putting a hand to our shoulder. It was not a comfort, all this concern, but a terrible and sudden invasion. Even as a child I understood the immediate loss of our private life. As if a kind of puncturing had occurred and all the breathable air had suddenly been let out.

I was only five, maybe six, and I struggled to follow the officer's questions. Or was I younger than this? Eventually they just repeated the same thing: 'Just tell us, tell us what you remember. The last time, from the last time you saw her.' But I didn't say enough, and then I said too much, and then what I said at first didn't match the thing I said after that, and when they asked me again – a different officer this time, a man – and again still, for what felt like the hundredth time, the man's voice changed. He sounded cross and I didn't know what I'd done wrong and was afraid that maybe I'd done the same wrong thing that they thought my mother had done, whatever that was, or that my father had done, and suddenly I couldn't talk any more because the words wouldn't come out because I was breathing too fast and crying too much and because I couldn't swallow the spit down and so I started to cough and gulp and eventually a woman came up and put her hands on my shoulders and said to the officer, That's enough now, don't you think? Outside, police vehicles had lined up along the kerb, and sections behind the hotel – near the river – were being roped off. Through the front windows of the foyer I could see cars slowing down to look. Our club chairs were quite close to the window; they were the chairs guests liked to sit in of an evening and watch the bustle of the street. But that morning it only made me feel exposed. I heard a tapping on the window and lifted my head to look. A sudden flash then, as a reporter took a photo – the one that appeared in the papers the next day, the two girls sitting in the oversized chairs, alone now without their mother. Nothing would ever go back to the way it was before.

I didn't discuss any of this, though, and instead cut ahead to explain that we stayed at the Royal three more days, in the hope that our mother might return to us. My father begged the police to expand the search. He always had the capacity to hold a good poker face, but in those early days this started to show its cracks – his eyes narrowed in an effort not to weep in front of us, he forgot to shave, and the cuffs of his shirt were marked with stains. After this we became itinerant while, for a time, our father tried to search for her on his own, moving from place to place until he too gave up and found somewhere that seemed right for just the three of us – that small cottage in Oxfordshire.

I stopped where I was and reached forwards for the glass of water. The room was overheated. I had planned to keep on and read ahead to the end of the chapter. But I felt myself flagging for some reason – it all suddenly felt flat, the writing duller than I remembered, not the right section for a reading after all.

Valerie was to my left, at the side of the room. She always made sure I could get a good view of her at these things so that she could signal to me if needs be. She had one signal for 'time's almost up', another for 'keep going'. The keep going signal was a slow nod or tip of the head and could be used for a variety of purposes. I was, then, expecting her to give me this if only to offer some encouragement. I needed it. But Valerie made no such gesture. Nor did she hold up her hand to let me know that time was running short. Instead she gave a tight smile and glanced down at her phone. I wasn't sure how to interpret this, so I continued, cutting to the section where I relayed my sister's conflicting version of events. She had told me that on that final day, after our mother went out to the car to fetch the gifts, she came back. I couldn't remember this, my sister said, because I had already fallen asleep. Apparently our mother sat at my sister's bedside and stroked her hair. But then our father came into the room. Our parents argued in fierce whispers, and our mother left again for good.

My sister said that our father made her go, that he pulled her purse from her hands and rifled through it before throwing it at the door. She did have gifts, after all: some sweets in a small jar that she placed on the bedside table before she left. After she had gone, our father went into the bathroom and sobbed while May, seeing the jar, took it and opened it and stuffed her mouth with sweets. Most of these were striped white and pink or white and blue and without a wrapper, but there was one, she said, that was a kind she hadn't seen before and perhaps ended up in the jar by accident. It was larger than the others and wrapped in a twist of waxed paper: she opened it and popped it in her mouth. A soft caramel. When she woke up, the jar in which the sweets were held was gone from the bedside table, but in her hand she still clutched the square of waxed paper.

I didn't know whether or not to believe her. Then look, she said in our bedroom in Oxfordshire, when our father was at work, pulling a fragile square of white paper from her dress pocket. Smell it. The paper was creased from many folds, and darker in those creases where the wax had collected. The paper was as soft as tissue from being excessively handled. I turned my head away. Go on! she said, Smell it! She reached out and put the paper to my nose. You have to breathe in, she said. We all know, even if we do not think about it, that we take a breath because we feel, just before it, the pressure of suffocation – there is the instinct to live on, and on and on. And so I couldn't help but smell it, the rich odour of burnt sugar ingrained in the paper, preserved by the wax. How do I know you didn't get it from somewhere else? I said.

There was no way of knowing if May was telling the truth. That wrapper was shown to me as evidence and I wanted to believe her, to believe that we were worth coming back for. Or that May was at least. She was the one my mother spoke to. It was her side of the bed on which my mother sat that night. Because why would she want to sit with me, wake me, run her cool palm over my forehead, pushing back my hair to feed me sweets? After all, I had been the one to ruin things.

I took a sip of water and cleared my throat. Time, I read. Time, in anyone's mind, can be both stretched and compressed. Looking back, scenes slip in and out of place, rearranging themselves. Call this a tendency, a reflex, an instinct, maybe a weakness – a human fallibility, one that in a child is often grossly exaggerated. Our very earliest sense of our own humanness – our sense of self – comes from the stories we hear and the stories we tell, it emerges through our ability to absorb and then deploy the tropes of fiction. I suppose I was practising this when I ran the story of our abandonment through my child's mind, playing it over and over again. In this way I sought to rectify my mistakes, the things I had said and done in fits of wild rage. I always believed that I made her go. That it was my fault that she left us. That I was too much. That I behaved too badly.

I could feel something caught in my eye: a speck of

dust, some city grit. I removed my glasses for a moment to rub at it. It wasn't an exaggeration to say that my child-hood tantrums had long been part of family lore – my refusing to sleep, or eat, or screaming myself sick. A child of uncommon outbursts, until there is a last straw. My long hair, with the plait matted at the back. The after-noon sun coming bright through the bedroom window as I kicked and wailed, pulling away from my mother and dodging the brush until she took the small sewing scissors and hacked my plait off.

It was because of me, I always thought, that she disap-peared. What did she say once? *You will be the end of me,* and for a long time I thought that I was, or had been. In one form or another, this was what I continued to believe. I could never shake the sense of my inadequacy; that I was in the wrong and therefore not loveable enough, or not loveable enough and therefore wrong. As a child this belief in my own insufficiency was a source of shame, and in turn that shame gave way to a feeling of culpability: it was my fault that I was this way, and not another. She vanished because of me.

I never said any of this to May. But my badness was something I could never forget, never forgive myself for. I suppose I hid this over and over again in the various characters of my books.

I blinked a bit. The grit had gone. I replaced my glasses and read out a passage about Joany – the nanny who even-tually came to help after our mother left. She was a large, cushiony woman with such enormous breasts that the buttons of her shirt strained against the flesh inside, giving me a peek of a white undergarment. I mention this as her

chief identifier because it was the thing I often took most
pleasure in: the comfort of being squeezed against her, of
climbing on to her lap and sinking into the warmth of her
body, completely enveloped. There was a soft line of black
down above her upper lip, and her skin was so translucent
I could see a network of thin blue veins on her face and
neck. I would put my small fingers to her top lip, to the
white skin, and let them tingle against the velvety hairs of
her moustache.

Meet Mrs Charleston, my father had said on the day she
arrived. And we squeaked something in reply. But to us
she simply became Joan, or Joany, or our Joany. It wasn't
long before our father married her.

After relaying some of this, I flicked ahead a few
chapters. I'm just moving along now, I explained, to the
last section that I'd like to read tonight. It's quite short.
I won't explain anything. Unless I say . . . but no. That
would probably give too much away. Anyway, here it is.

I read for a little longer, then closed the book. There
was a moment of silence, as I knew there would be. Readers wanted to know about the sisters and what happened
to them, but they were less prepared for the section about
the disaster that derailed their adult lives and to which
I had just referred. I didn't give much away, just gave a
taste, and the silence around me was one of surprise and
hopeful expectancy: would I read on, tell them more,
was I really going to leave them hanging like this? The
sentences in that part of the book were long, full of com-
mas and conjunctions – they were hard to read aloud, and
although I'd practised this, even then in the bookstore
I found myself running out of breath. I had to speed up

to reach the end of the section, I couldn't pause in the middle of the action, the pace was paramount. But this made it sound as though I myself were anxious, overly invested in the story I had written, and had to break off so suddenly because I couldn't go on, when it was really just the syntax that made me speed up. Of course, if they had read the blurb they would have known something of the terrible event at the heart of the book that I had stopped just short of. They would have bought the book or opened it because the mentioning of the event sparked curiosity; only the book never read quite like the blurb, the two didn't fully coincide. This was in keeping with how many of my books had been pitched or blurbed – emphasising the car crash, real or metaphysical, or the fire or the shooting. One of the sisters in this particular novel had made a horrible mistake. And while the questions asked at book clubs emphasised causation and motive, the beginning of a moral inquisition – why did she do it? – I was always more interested in the aftermath. I knew the audience would come away and forget the details of what I'd just read, but they'd retain certain impressions, certain images that would float up, dreamlike, at some other point long after I had vanished from their lives: a woman running through the airport in blue trousers, or a man slamming his fist into a wall. They might remember these moments and forget the connection between them, forget which one came first.

It only took a moment, though, for the audience to recompose themselves and then everyone applauded. I reached over and took another sip of water. Not because I was thirsty, but just to wet my mouth. I put my other glasses on – one pair for reading, another for looking about – and saw the clock on the wall. I'm sorry, I said quietly, to the man who had who introduced the event. I think I read too much. No, he said, blushing. Not at all, you were great.

There's only time for three questions, he said to the audience, so make them good.

12

The following morning I took a flight home. In a story, I had explained to my audience that previous day during question time, the feeling of not knowing what happens next is often a thing of pleasure – the cornerstone of our delight. If it is well executed, this not knowing doesn't feel like a plateau, nor a hiatus – it does not feel like an absence of life, but is experienced as a moment of elevation, of suspended animation, a feeling enabled by the certainty that something else will happen, by a belief that significant events are yet to unfold because the conditions for this have been set up earlier on. At some point such unfolding of event, the action of a life, becomes inevitable: a forceful living-out of energies earlier established. The feeling of not knowing is, at the same time, a desire to know, a belief that this desire will be fulfilled, that it has to be fulfilled and that a greater part of life is yet to occur, still to be realised.

But the same feeling of not-knowing, as it happens in one's real life, is rarely so pleasurable; the belief in continuity rarely so assured, so manifest. I knew it was time to go back. I did not know what happened next. It seemed impossible for something else to ever happen, for things to go on happening. And so I could only do as a traveller does. Take a bus or a taxi. Get the next flight out. Focus on logistics. Fasten my seat belt. Avert my gaze from the safety demonstration. Make my way through dark space. Float, zoom, hover – the idea of escape.

I had a window seat, and as the plane gained altitude I looked down to the sparkling city below. Slight queasiness, tilting of my stomach, steeling myself to look. They use the acronym MOB – man overboard – even if the person who has fallen is a woman. The officer who questioned me in that small concrete room in Japan was balding, and so had shaved the whole of his head, which was covered then in a fine stubble. I remember looking, very closely, at the pattern of freckles on his skull. According to the literature, the officer told me, vertigo is simply a way of disguising a real desire to jump.

In the summer, my husband and I used to go swimming in the river. At the beginning of the season the water was always very cold – so cold that the pain of it could be felt deep in the muscles. I knew this, and in knowing it chose not to draw the agony out by entering the water slowly but would wade in up to my knees and then, very suddenly, without hesitating, dive in, going right under and opening my eyes a moment in the murky depths before shooting up to the surface. When I broke out into the air I would scream – a scream of cold and relief and delight because I had done it and now could either swim on or retreat, no matter, for the victory was mine. But Patrick's nature was otherwise. He would strip off, then stand a while looking at the surface of the water before stepping in just to his ankles. He gasped at the temperature; really, it was too cold to swim. But I had done it, and he would too. So he went in a little deeper, up to his knees. He stood this way for some minutes more, debating whether to go further. He does, did. Up to his hips. He always started to gasp at this point, the numbness reaching his thigh muscles, climbing up from the soles of his feet which he really couldn't feel any more, or perhaps just a little – the silty riverbed, some small stones. I swam on, back and forth, my body hurting from the cold, my breath fast and shallow. I watched him going in, inch by inch. As he did so he let out a guttural, very constrained yell that sounded full of effort – as though he would like to scream but was fighting this, holding it in, trying not to abandon himself to the cold. It was the same sound he would make when trying not to orgasm, either for my sake, because he was waiting for me, or because the pleasure was so great he wanted to yell out, only his son was sleeping in the next room and he was mindful of this, leaving us to have sex which, while pleasing, did not end with total abandon, with forgetfulness. The cold took all thoughts from my head, but I was aware of this sound and its familiarity – how proximate physical expressions of pleasure and pain can be. I wanted him to not make this sound, just to throw himself into the water and swim with me, but still he went in slowly, stepping forwards bit by bit so that the water crept up his groin, then his abdomen, little by little. He said he was acclimatising himself to the water, and I replied that this wasn't possible because it was so cold, he had to just do it, and besides, I would be getting out soon. Hurry up, so we can swim together, I said. He splashed the water on his arms, still groaning and occasionally panting. And then he ducked under, holding his nose, and when he surfaced – exploding up through the river as if he had pushed himself off the sandy floor – his eyes and mouth were wide open, but not a sound was coming from him. It was, I realised, the exact look his face sometimes had at the moment when he could no longer hold back after all, he couldn't wait, it had to be now, he couldn't help it and would come anyway, silently, inside himself, looking shocked that this thing was actually happening to him. The sound escaping like a long wheeze through the constriction of his throat, mouth, jaw. I am the river, I thought. The river is me. And then, of course, there was the sea.

The plane reached a level altitude. The seat-belt light switched off. I started to feel intensely sick – the knowledge of my reality slowly sinking in, the fact of my going back, alone. I pressed the button on my armrest that summoned a flight attendant and asked for a red wine. Maybe I just needed to relax. She brought me a small bottle and a plastic cup. I ate the last of the potato crisps given to us earlier and poured the wine. Maybe I would have another after this, I thought, and fall asleep. Movie credits were running on the screen in front of me. I drank the wine while I looked out of the window: clouds, sometimes a glimpse of water. The wine made me drowsy but did not lessen the nausea, and all of a sudden I realised that I was actually going to vomit. I could not get up out of my seat in time and make my way down the aisle to the toilets, and so pulled the paper airsickness bag from my seat pocket and threw up into it. The flight attendant returned. The two passengers to my right were relocated to other seats, and when I had finished retching I wiped my mouth with a paper napkin, dropped this into the bag and folded the top closed. The attendant took the bag from me, holding it away from her body, and after a sip of water I reclined my chair and fell at last into a deep sleep.

Hours later, I wobbled through the arrival gate, bought a packet of aspirin then stepped outside to join the taxi queue. A woman in an orange safety vest directed me to the appropriate bay and soon enough a maxi taxi pulled up. It was too big for me, but I hopped in anyway, hauling my suitcase into the cabin space.

Must be glad to get home, the driver said, flicking his indicator after I gave him the address. No one coming to meet you? he said, smiling in the mirror. What you need is a big bunch of flowers. Some of those helium balloons. Every woman likes a welcome party, I know my wife does.

I nodded politely and blinked back the sting of tears. A welcome party, he said again, as he shifted lanes, someone can give me one of those any time, after a long day at the wheel. Imagine that.

I tried. It was hard to look out of the window, to see the roads which Patrick and I had travelled down together and that were now mine to travel alone. I had only come here, to this city, to this country, because of him. He was the one who had made it my home. I only stayed because he was here. I gave the driver a tight smile and pushed my sunglasses on, fiddling with my phone.

There were several missed calls that had come through during the flight. And now, as I checked them, my phone rang again. It was Patrick's agent, Robert, who wanted to know on behalf of Max what we were doing about the funeral. I can't imagine what this is like for you, he said, we really do just want to help. Time's running short, he reminded me, and I made a mental tally: the accident had happened only, what, nine days ago? How could time run short? How could there be not enough time when it felt to me like all I had now was endless reams of hours without him? Outside it started to rain. A light pattering. Are you there? Robert asked. I cleared my throat. He would have to put a press release together, he said, if I didn't want to say anything. I understand, he told me. But he would need to send out invites soon. There was also an obituary he wanted me to check, or Max did, and Robert was now passing the message on. And when you've got time, he told me, Max wants to talk to you about a possible special screening – over the holiday period, he was thinking – a proper send-off. The rain grew heavy, and the windscreen wipers whipped back and forth. No matter what Robert said I couldn't do it, couldn't talk about those things. Couldn't say yes.

While he was talking another call beeped in the background. I'm really sorry, I said, desperate to end the conversation. I'm afraid I've got to take this one, let me ring you back. I hung up quickly, but instead of answering the next call I pressed the phone to silent, letting it vibrate in my lap. Eventually the cab driver glanced in the rear-view mirror, Don't mind me, he said, I hear all sorts here. Everything comes out in the wash in the end, he said, smiling. And so I answered: it was Patrick's cousin, Nick, the one living in upstate New York.

God, he said. It's just unbelievable, totally unbelievable. I've been trying to track down your number for days.

I had answered on speakerphone and quickly changed this. Patrick? he said, as if he were talking to him, as if Patrick were there in the cab. Patrick was, like, immortal, he said. I mean, obviously not, but I just can't believe it. I murmured my condolences; somehow I had become the one who answered the phone not to immediate sympathy but to expressions of disbelief, I was the one who had to be a stable and calming presence, the voice of truth, the living confirmation, and never more so than with the calls that had started to come in from his family. He wasn't close to any of them. If anything, he'd moved away to get some distance, his mother doting and nosy. The driver took a left and then a right. We weren't far away now. I said this to Nick, Sorry, I told him, I've just got to— I'm in a taxi and—

Look, I said. I'll let you know about the funeral. I'll ring. Then I ended the call and pushed the phone into the back pocket of my jeans.

Here's fine, I said, as the taxi neared our house. The driver pulled in at the corner and I passed him my credit card. While I waited for the receipt, I noticed the pot plants on the upper balcony in need of watering, junk mail sticking out from the letterbox. Signs of life. From the outside it all looked the same, but as soon as I opened the door I sensed the difference: the smell of air freshener, cleaning product. I dumped my bags near the shoe rack – my suitcase, my handbag, the tote I'd been lugging around. Ordinarily our house had a slightly dry, yeasty smell – a mix of dampness, dust, the softening apples in

169

the fruit bowl. But the bags and coats were hung neatly on their hooks in the entrance, the mail stacked in an ordered pile on the sideboard. There was the lingering sense of a visitor having been in the house, a well-intentioned help-er. I went to the bathroom; the sink had been scrubbed down, the soap scum removed from the glass door of the shower, fresh towels had been hung on the rack – two of them. I felt a little dizzy. I sat down on the closed lid of the toilet seat, tried to focus on my breathing, rubbed at my face as one does when waking from a strange dream, and as you see people do in the movies, as if this contact had the power to reaffirm one's living presence in the room. Then I noticed the hinge on the window – an old window made of frosted glass, two panes that swung outwards into the side garden, so that from the bath one could look out over a wild tangle of buddleia. The win-dow hinge had been broken, as if by some kind of wedge, a chisel, and then carefully put back together, the side of the window leaning into the frame but not properly attached. I panicked then; I shut the bathroom door and locked it and pressed my ear to the wood, afraid that someone was in the house with me, that they hadn't heard my return, or perhaps they had and were then waiting for me to wander through, unthinking, oblivious.

Unless he had somehow survived, come ashore, found his way home, or been brought home, disoriented, and dropped off here, and without a key, with no luggage, found a way to break into the house. And now where was he? Resting, perhaps, on the sofa by the long window. At his desk, making notes. Both possibilities filled me with terror. I listened carefully, but all I could hear was the mag-

nified sound of my own breathing, my heartbeat. I waited
a while; perhaps we were testing each other's patience,
like children, each waiting for the other to come out of,
or find, the secret hiding place, and like the children who
are unable to bear the possibility of discovery, we might
eventually be compelled to declare our presence. There is
always one player who gives up the quest, and someone
else who gives into a certain impulse ahead of the others:
I'm here! I'm *here*! But this would not be me, it would not
be me, it would not be me, I said to myself as I slumped
down on to the tiles.

How long did I stay there? I grew cold, and hungry.
In all the time that I sat there I didn't hear a thing, other
than a bird scratching in the gutter, traffic. Voices in the
street. I pulled myself to standing; my lower legs and feet
had grown numb and as the blood returned, the feeling of
pins and needles overwhelmed those body parts. I shook
my legs a little, shifted from side to side. In the hallway
the phone rang. I stood silent, waiting to hear if anyone
picked up. Intruder, visitor, husband. Eventually the answering machine clicked on and I could hear, very faintly,
a woman's voice. I opened the door and let myself out of
the bathroom just as the call ended.

All around me the house was not just quiet, but still.
This felt so different to how it was before. Even when he
was at home, working or reading, I could sense the fizz
of Patrick's consciousness. The energy of it. I never liked
to disturb him; the very labour of his thinking could give
the air a certain density, a certain charge. A preciousness.
Now all that was gone, and I felt the strange slackness of
the atmosphere. The total emptiness. The fridge hummed.

The sound of the clock ticking on the wall seemed louder than I remembered. Now I wanted more than anything for him to step out of his study, for him to stand in the doorway and say, Oh, you're home. I didn't hear you. And I'd go towards him as he put his arms out, letting me lean in against his wide, tall frame, my cheek pressed to the soft fabric of his T-shirt, a spattering of dandruff over his shoulders, and he might lift his hand to my head and gently stroke my hair before leaning down to kiss me. Are you hungry? he would say. It was impossible to think of his consciousness as having just disappeared, evaporated. Please, I wanted to call out, as if I were still that child caught in the game of hide and seek, Give me a clue! Just a clue! Then a murmur or a whistle might come from behind a drawn curtain, leading me to his hiding place.

I was aware then of my breathing, how it had become very shallow, and that I was feeling a little faint as a result of this. I knew I had to look. I knew I had to check the bedroom, I knew I had to at least eradicate for myself the possibility that there was still someone lurking in the house, or that it was him, that I had to look upon the place where we had, for so long, lain together, my husband and I.

Normally we left the internal doors of the house open: bathroom, study, bedroom. As there were no children or pets, there was nothing we were trying to keep out of any one room or another. And so it took me by surprise to find the bedroom door closed. I tiptoed up to it – perhaps, I thought, whoever had so thoroughly cleaned the house was now sleeping off their work, having a quick lie-down before gathering up their things and letting themselves out. It was a heavy old door that got stuck along the side near the frame – the door swelling in the damp weather so that after turning the handle one had to shove one's shoulder against the wood until it gave way and swung free into the room. Although part of me knew what to expect – that in keeping with the rest of the house the bedroom would also have been methodically cleaned – I was not prepared for the effect of this. The sheets and duvet cover had been changed, our clothes that had lain in a crumpled heap on the floor had been washed, ironed and hung up in the closet, the piles of books on the bedside tables had been stacked neatly, the ones on the floor re-shelved. Our shoes were lined up in a row under our shirts and the mirror had been polished. The air smelt strangely of vanilla. I startled then at the sound of a chair pushing back against wooden floorboards and spun round – only to realise that it was just the neighbours, their movements audible through the upstairs common wall.

Still, there, above the shelves on the far side of the room as if watching me, was the face of Patrick staring out from my favourite photograph – of him as a young man in a student play. The picture often tipped sideways a little because the wire at the back of the frame was loose but now, I saw, it was lined up straight. He didn't want that photo, he'd found it one day when he was sorting old papers and had tossed it in the bin. I fished it out and kept it for myself, as an image of him before I knew him. As a way of imagining myself into his history. Because of course I didn't know him then. I might not even have been born when the photograph was taken. I don't know what character he was cast as, but in the photograph he is staring intensely into the middle distance, not talking but holding a finger to his lips. It is unclear whether this gesture is meant to silence someone else on the stage, or whether the finger is lifted in accusation. Something was about to happen, was happening all around him, and I would never know what that was. I never asked. Or maybe I did, and he himself couldn't remember. His face was pale, his jaw very clearly defined, his eyebrows heavy in an expression of serious intent. I imagined that at his waist hung a sword in its hilt, that his other hand rested on the handle of this, waiting for the moment to act, dive forwards, spear the opponent, the traitor, the spy who was going about his evil business on the other side of the stage. His white collar was starched and buttoned, while behind him and to the sides the scene was dark, empty, more blue than black and not uniform but rough and grainy, patchy in parts. I loved that photograph. He must have been the same age in that as I was when he first met me. A young man on the cusp of great things. I was what came later. Fate or the mistiming of it.

A wholly new and unexpected pang of grief moved through me, as if it were coming up from within the earth itself, through the soles of my feet, up through my legs and gut and heart and face, each body part that it touched rendered weak by the force of it. I fell forwards on to the bed and sobbed into the clean pillowcase – denied even the last vestige of his body, the smell of his hair on the cotton. I recognised that the gesture was well in-tended – that the house had been cleaned in my absence precisely to spare me the pain of having to re-encounter the signs of his living presence, to relieve me of having to tidy up after him, one last time. But how I craved this – all the souvenirs of his days, the things that would make up a story of their own, a catalogue of essential details by which to decipher the last actions he took before leaving the house for the final time. What book was on the top of his bedside pile? What page was he up to? What shirt had he worn before showering, what shoes? I needed to touch these things, internalise them; make up a story of what his day was like, the normal day he had, just before we departed, before everything changed. Now I had been denied the chance of greeting the phantom of his body – he had been eradicated from my life in more ways than I could bear.

I crawled under the bedcovers, fully clothed, even my shoes still on, and wept. I felt hollowed out by my longing, eviscerated. I wanted just to reach out and touch Patrick's hand, warm, lined, larger than my own, to listen to his gentle snoring in the early hours, to stroke the nape of his neck, that little soft pocket at the base of the skull. There was the terrible burning feeling that I had not made the most of him, of us together, that I hadn't remembered often enough to say how much I loved him.

Patrick had looked so tired when he headed off to work the day before we were due to leave for the cruise. He shrugged his leather jacket on to his shoulders very slowly as though the jacket were weighted, then neatened the pages of the script he was revising by tapping them on the table, squaring the edges. He slipped these carefully into his bag. There were some last-minute changes to be discussed, then a guest talk that evening which he shouldn't have to give, he complained.

But he was at his best that day, that's what people said later. What I heard. It was the jacket, he was always at his best in that jacket. He only needed to don his black leather to signal the impending performance. Everyone loved him for it, the monologue they knew was coming. He'd take a long inhalation, pace a little, let his breath out and then begin. Occasionally, when more official business was to hand, he would swap the leather jacket for a black blazer. What was not to love? He was the kind of man who, after a day's work, could come up with a string of possible jokes in answer to the caption competition on the back page of the *New Yorker*. And in the evening, after a drink, he was the man who could write the winning caption, five times over. I learnt this after that taxi ride in the rain. The picture was of a gingerbread man in a hospital bed, or was it the one with the pig at the complaints desk? Whatever it was, he made me laugh like nothing else, and this silly playfulness that he encouraged became part of the sex, or led into it, especially in those early days when my own self-consciousness was intense and when he wouldn't turn off the light, despite my asking. But this mucking about brought my guard down. He gave the impression of taking nothing seriously and of taking everything seriously, both at the same time. Or, to put that differently, he understood frivolity and anything on the frivolous spectrum to be significant, meaningful, worthy of consideration. This undiscriminating field of his attention was disorientating at first. Are you for real? I asked when he bought me a fancy-dress costume that took the form of a chicken suit and told me to put it on because we were going out to dinner. Jokes, for him, could be very serious business. At the same time serious business was often taken as a joke. It was hard to tell where I myself sat in relation to these two possibilities – it was hard to tell when he was joking, and when he was applying his critical faculties to the existence of a joke. When I didn't get it, when I trusted him blindly and put the chicken suit on instead of bantering back, I became the joke. But his giggling when this happened was so contagious, so intense, that I only caught the laughing fit, until we were both laughing so much we completely forgot what caused the hilarity in the first place.

At some point I must have fallen asleep because when I woke it was almost dark. For a moment I was disoriented, I couldn't remember exactly where I was, nor did I understand the new state of my life: there were just fragments, broken sections that didn't match up. Bits of memory. Then in a rush it all came back to me, the recalibration washing through like acid: I was alone. I was now his widow. I was no longer his wife. And I knew I could only be this way, existing as his relict if he was truly and properly gone. I had had a husband. I had been a wife. I never much liked the past tense, I always preferred the uncertainty and the immediacy of the present, the way it could make the banal accrue importance only because one had no idea where it would lead, but that tense was no longer my own, no longer fitting. I sat up and brushed myself off as if I had been lying on sand, or damp grass. Through the window I could see a soft evening mist had formed, shrouding the trees. There was the wisteria vine, winding its way over the fence and up the side of the house, and the orange flame of the persimmon tree clinging to the last of its brilliant foliage.

My phone was still in my back pocket and now it rang again. I pulled it out and knew this time it was Max. He started talking before I could get a word in. Listen, he said, I gather Robert spoke to you earlier. I'm sorry to call again but we really need to sort this out. Whatever we do next the green light has got to come from you. I've drafted a guest list for the funeral, and we need to think about the best location for the wake.

The wake? I said, uncomprehending, the idea impossible, unreal. He asked me something else then, about the remains. Of Patrick, he meant.

I'm not sure, I said. I signed so many forms, in Japan, after the body was found, after Patrick was— Valerie might know, I said. I mean, I assume the body has been cremated now. That was what he wanted, I said. But I couldn't believe that I didn't know.

I thought back; I was sure I'd signed something for that. I had asked about it – the cost and the logistics, the timing. I felt a little nauseous as I gazed out of the window, watching a cat creep along the top of the fence, towards the persimmon tree. A flicker of small birds.

Hello? Max said. Are you still there?

Yes, I said, wearily. Yes, I'm still here.

Well, he went on, Do you think you could just give me a bit of a heads-up now as to which direction you think we might go in?

Which direction?

I couldn't tolerate any more publicity, the thought of being surrounded by all those people, being watched, being filmed or televised or photographed in my grief, having my clothes commented on, my state of glamour or disrepair, my new circumstances, whatever they were. Other people's endless prying, their desire to own the story of Patrick and parade their small part in it. No. No, it couldn't happen like this. I wouldn't let it. I wanted to keep him just for myself. I had to.

In the end I said this. Look, I told Max. I don't think I can do it. I really can't. I think, actually, that I don't want a funeral. I'll leave it to you to organise the celebration of his work, but the funeral, no. I might just do a very small and private thing, and maybe later in the winter. Then I ended the call.

I stood a moment, a little dizzy, before making my way through the house, steadying myself against the wall. Some deep part of me knew I needed to keep on the move, that I couldn't stay here, in that house we shared, in that bed. And his ashes? I worried for a moment that there was something I had overlooked. But no, there couldn't be. Valerie was assiduous on every front. I seem to remember listing her as my alternative contact on one of those forms. It made sense, she had taken to overseeing all sorts of details about my life. I drank some water and listened to the messages on the answering machine.

They played in order, with the most recent message first. It was May. My God, she said. Where are you? I've been trying to get hold of you for days. If you're back at that house now, listening to this, I can only think that you probably really need to be somewhere else, anywhere in fact but there. I'm so sorry. I just can't believe it. Come and stay with us for a while, why don't you, get away. Call me? Or not. I'll call you. Or just turn up. Whatever. Anything you want, I mean. I'll try again later.

There was a pause, signalling the end of the message. This was followed by an automated voice giving the time of the next call, then a woman started speaking. Her voice sounded familiar, but it took me a moment to place: Trudi, Patrick's first wife and mother to Joshua. She offered effuse condolences, followed by an explanation. I wanted to help in some way, she said, and I didn't want to send flowers – besides I wasn't sure when you were returning, and thought it would be worse to come back to a dead bouquet on the doorstep. I remember how hard it was, after he left me, to keep stumbling upon his things in the house, how, each time this happened, I felt as though I reprocessed the whole story of our marriage and its failure and I couldn't stand this. Eventually I took all the things of his that had been left behind and I burnt them in the backyard. It was, really, a wonderful liberation, there is something very powerful—then the message cut out. She had run out of time, but must've phoned again to complete her monologue, because after the pause indicating the end of the message an automated voice gave the time of the next call and Trudi's voice continued: There is something very powerful, she said, in watching objects be destroyed by fire. I only wished I had done it sooner, rather than enduring the pain of accidently encountering his things over and over again. I didn't want you to have the same kind of experience, and so I organised for my cleaner to come and tidy the place up before your return. A total gem, that lady. Joshua couldn't find his key, and so we broke in through the bathroom window. I think the hinge may need a new screw, but otherwise it all looked OK. Although we left, obviously, by the front door, once the cleaner had arrived. I hope this has made the return easier for you. It would be good if you could talk to Joshua about what happened – at some point anyway, when you're ready. He has lots of questions. Anyway, I hope you're settling back in now. Everyone is thinking of you.

The whole time I listened to this, I stood scratching at my neck, at my throat, a nervous scratch. A clawing sort of scratch. Then, once she had finished speaking, I picked up the machine and hurled it against the wall. The damage inflicted set off the message signal inside it and the thing lay there on the floorboards beeping and beeping. Like a heart monitor, I thought. I kicked it a few times and the beeping stopped. Then I grabbed some extra belongings, shoved them in my suitcase which still stood where I had left it near the shoe rack, pulled the front door shut behind me and walked to the main street where I held out my hand to wave down a taxi. Then I phoned Valerie. I told her what I'd said to Max, and that I needed to go away now, to rest and just get as far from all of this as I could.

Of course you do, she said. Absolutely. It's all over now, you know. It really is. Take whatever time you need. And if anything does arise, I'll sort it out.

They say that after sudden bereavement one ought not to make any major decisions, nor should one be left alone.

This was what my sister had reminded me of in her message. Just call me, she had said. Whatever time it is. Just call me. Or just show up.

Book Three

13

Twenty-four hours later I arrived in Sydney. The sky was luminous, the sun unbearably bright. I took a taxi to May's house. Adam, her husband, met me at the door. This way, he said, apologising that May wasn't there to greet me. She's sleeping, he explained. The room he showed me to was upstairs and at the end of the hallway, behind the second bathroom.

It was the spare room, furnished with a single bed pushed up under the window and a tall bookshelf along the far wall, stuffed with paperbacks. There was a chest of drawers and a clothes rack, a vase of flowers – wild, spraying stems – beside the bed. The girls picked those for you, he said. I touched the white heads of yarrow. They are lovely, thank you. He had carried my suitcase for me, and now put this down near the bookshelf. Right, then, he said. I'll let you settle in. The girls are outside. May will be awake soon. She just needed to lie down a minute before making dinner. Anyway, he said, give us a shout if you need anything. I'll just be downstairs.

I rubbed my hands together – partly a nervous gesture, partly the chill of the room, the window missing the afternoon sun. Thanks, I said. I think I'm fine for the moment. Cool, he replied, and ducked a little as he left the room – a gesture that at first I took for a kind of misplaced chivalry, an abbreviated bow, then recognised it for what it was: the habitual dropping of the head to pass safely under the low door frame. The practical habits of the tall man mistaken for gallantry.

I closed the door quietly behind him and turned on my phone. A text message from Valerie pinged through: she'd told my publishing team in Australia that I would be arriving soon, just in case I needed anything. I typed back a quick reply, thanking her. I saw then, from my email, that she'd sent a longer message a few hours after this one, and one more after that, but these were slow to download. I tapped and tapped, waiting for the words to appear. The first one opened. The team in Australia has gone ahead and organised events, see attached. Sorry, she wrote. Didn't know about this. Am awaiting details. The next message failed to download. I tried opening it again and again; the subject line marked the message as urgent. Then my phone rang. It was Valerie, what was she doing calling at this time? I said this, It must be late there.

I just got your text, she replied, and thought it would be better to call and explain. I don't know what they were thinking, I really don't, but your publicist there has gone and confirmed a live interview on *The Morning Show*.

What?

I know, I know. If I haven't got my time zones completely muddled, it's actually booked for tomorrow morning, your time.

Fuck, I said. Valerie went on to clarify. Apparently, the

Australian team had overseen everything, but without once consulting her. She was furious.

You're under too much pressure, she said. I could see it at the reading in New York. You weren't yourself then. They don't understand this. They just think, Great, superstar. I mean, really? Now that you're there I suspect they want to reclaim you as their own.

Outside my window a lawnmower started up. I heard currawongs in the trees.

God, Valerie said, and of all things why did they book *The Morning Show*? Apparently it's too late to pull out now and it's all beyond my control, but they could have run it by me. I mean you'd think—

I knew I had to go through with it. OK, I said. It's OK. But can you make it understood that they're not to ask questions about Patrick? The interview must be about the book only. Seriously. I can't keep going over that night again and again. I just can't. Not any more, and not on television. We both knew that even before the accident it was rare for me to be asked about my work exclusively, the questions always shifting towards my marriage as the primary context for anything I wrote.

Of course, Valerie said. But really, I think this is just too much. I'm worried about you.

I know I shouldn't have read that last section at the bookshop the other night.

Look, she replied, it's all done now. Don't think about it. But I'm going to cancel the rest of your UK events, especially the ones booked for the new year, and maybe the ones leading up to Easter. The schedule was endless, we both knew that.

Sure, I said, as summer air gusted into the room, the scent of wisteria and jasmine. I agreed that maybe that was for the best, perhaps I might even stay a while. If I didn't have to go back. If there wasn't anything to return to. The sound of the breeze in the trees outside. All the sunshine. It had been so long since I'd last been here, properly, on my own. Patrick never liked to linger and hated the long-haul flight.

Yasmin, your Australian publicist, will be in touch asap, Valerie said. And I have a horrible feeling that they want to do some bookshop visits or something, after the interview. I'm really sorry, this is all out of my hands now. You must be exhausted.

It's fine, I said. I'm sure it will be fine.

Call me when it's done? she asked.

Of course.

Then I slipped the phone back into my purse, swept my hand over the bedcover – seersucker, lemony cotton – and lay down. I heard Adam moving around in the living room. There were small cobwebs in the corners of the ceiling near the open window. Through this came the smell of fresh-mown grass and the peppery crush of leaves on the breeze, rain, perhaps, in the distance.

Then I heard my sister's voice – deep, commanding, perfectly enunciated. Rupert! Rupert! she called. She was talking to the dog. Without even seeing her, if one only heard her from afar, one would assume my sister to be of regal bearing: tall, upright, chin lifted a little, high cheekbones perhaps, a good jaw. She had a deep, almost velvety voice, but one which seemed to emit at the same time a light melodic tone, harmonic almost. It was a voice that carried forth into the wilds without effort, one that easily summoned animals – dogs, children, men. A voice in which authority, and subsequent obedience, was implicit.

Sit! I heard her say. And she needed only say it once for the dog – a fine Dalmatian – to obey. I myself could never be a dog person for the very opposite reason: I did not like raising my voice or trying to exert authority, I had no desire to command a living creature, or to have to discipline and punish when my power or my voice failed me. My attempts to make an animal cower had never worked; the dog, any dog, sees through me – hears through me, rather. But in my sister's voice one could not pick a note of self-doubt; it did not waver, it did not drop in tone or force, it did not question itself, she never mumbled or let her sentences fade away. This seemed extraordinary to me, I who was by default what one might call a cat person, and for the very opposite reason: because one need only speak quietly to cats, one need play no part in commanding them, one lived with them as an exercise in mutual independence, mutual silence, with conversation limited to occasional murmurs and questions. I could smell onions frying, and then came the clatter of plates. My sister's voice calling again, this time to a child.

I lifted my suitcase on to the bed and unlocked it with a tiny silver key of the kind I used, as a teenager, to unlock my diary. I hardly ever wrote anything in that diary; I had very little experience to report, but I liked the idea of secrecy, of privacy. Back then it was not the experience that mattered, but the act of confiding. Now there was so much to tell, and nowhere to put it. Nowhere that I felt I could put it, no one to tell. My sister had cleaned out the top drawers of the dresser. It was of heavy oak and the drawers were stiff, making a rough squeaking sound when I pulled them open. They were lined with pale-blue paper like the kind we once used for letters that were to be posted overseas – extra-thin and very light paper that would lessen the cost of postage. I took my clothes out, refolded each item and placed them on this blue sheet. I heard footsteps on the stairs, then a knock at my door.

Come in, I called. It was Lexi, May's eldest. She was tall now, and lanky. An eleven-year-old going on fourteen. A spray of tiny pimples across her forehead.

Hi, she said. Mum said to ask you if you'd like a cup of tea?

Yes, thank you, that would be lovely, I replied. I'll be there in just a minute.

Lexi smiled quickly, a child who was not sure how to exit a room, not sure how to greet me, whether or not she should loiter and be nosy and watch what I was doing or be extra polite. Then she turned and ran back towards the kitchen. I heard her yelling out: She said yes!

I brushed my hair and changed my shirt. Then I too went downstairs.

Through the general din – children, the television voices, the jazz playing on the radio – May didn't hear me come in. Her back was turned to me, hunched over at the bench chopping herbs. The girls were arguing during an ad break, Lexi hit Jess with a cushion, setting off a high-pitched wail the exact timbre of an alarm which caused my sister to spin suddenly to face them, knife in hand, and then she saw me. The knife was a mere prop in that circumstance, but it had the effect of immediately silencing her children. When she noticed me, her face opened out in a grin. Putting the knife down, she stepped forwards, arms open.

Oh Lucie, she said, pulling me in close. We melted into each other, the shape of her body familiar against my own. Her hair felt soft and springy as it brushed my cheek. I breathed in the scent of her: soap and coffee. But it was the sound of my own name that undid the knot inside me: My Lucie, she said again, this time holding me at arm's length to better see my face. In hearing this all the years collapsed; the vast network of complex geography that had long separated us not only vanished but seemed never to have existed, as if no parting had ever occurred, no private singular histories ever accumulated, no adulthood ever properly acquired. It must have been, what, five years or so since I last saw her.

She seemed to have hardly changed, and at the same time changed in inexplicable ways, as if she had grown into her face somehow, the face our father had so adored. For him, May was the more beautiful: What lovely eyes your sister has, he would often remark. Her appeal was all the more apparent when set against my tomboy ways. Even as a child I hated dresses and made a mess of myself and always wanted my hair short. She pulled me in close once more and for a moment, feeling her body against mine, it was as if we were again those children, sharing a bedroom in that Oxfordshire cottage and whispering to each other in the dark. The sound of Dylan Thomas's *Under Milk Wood* coming faintly through the adjoining wall where our father slept, our voices and those of the poem weaving in and out of each other. Our father liked to fall asleep to this, drifting off before the record had finished its first side, so that if I snuck into his room late at night, because I needed to ask for more water or because I had to go to the toilet, I would hear the shuck, shuck, shuck of the dust-covered needle coasting over the ridges of the album, the sound magnified by the speaker. At first, before I understood what this was, I thought it to be the troubled sound of a stranger's phlegmy breathing, hiding in wait behind the door, and was too frightened to step into the room when I needed to, meaning that I returned to my bed and wet myself there rather than risk asking my father to take me to the bathroom. After being wrongly scolded, I explained what happened, and thereafter understood and came to love the sound of the record having run out of voices, the passage of the night marked instead not by the whispering of Welsh ghosts but by the needle's inevitable gathering of dust. Shuck, shuck, shuck. May was always such a sound sleeper, I doubt she ever heard this, and in the mornings I would sneak into my father's room and lift the arm of the record player very carefully off the moving album while my father and Joan were still snoring. Then I would pick the bits of dust from the tiny dark point that resembled the stinger on a bee – the proboscis, my father reminded me – the sound of my picking fingertips making a loud crackle through the speakers, causing him to wake.

May stroked my hair back from my face and looked at me quizzically. Every woman who does not have a sister wants one. Every sisterless woman imagines a kinship that fate has denied her. Once, when we were younger, I thought I would never marry but live as a spinster, that we might both live as spinsters together, upstairs and downstairs in a cottage surrounded by flowers and woodland. In that one moment when she said my name and held me close, I was again that child, that girl on the cusp of the rest of her life, a person to whom adulthood had not yet and might never come.

I'm so sorry, Lucie, she said again.

I took a sharp breath in. It was so strange to hear myself referred to by this name – hardly anyone called me that any more. I published under my middle initials, J.B. – short for Joy-Beth – and this had come to be what many people knew me by. Patrick sometimes took advantage of my middle name and shortened it further, turning it into a joke, a game: I was his joy ride, or he might ask me to ride him, or he might ride with joy, or ride Joy with joy. Hell yeah, he'd say, adding his own name, slightly adapted, to the mix. He was after all a boy who'd grown up by the racecourse, in a wealthy town in upstate New York known for its equestrian spirit. In that house by the racetrack, he told me, his mother used a dishwashing liquid called Joy. It was a yellow liquid in a clear plastic bottle that she kept on the window ledge by the kitchen sink. Non-Ultra Joy, Patrick said, to be precise. The 'non-ultra' printed in smaller blue letters beneath the brand name. I, of course, by comparison, was his joyful maximus. Ultra-ultra joy. And now what? I was myself again, here, for May.

She was thinner than when I had seen her before, although I stopped myself from commenting on this lest it be taken as criticism. I remembered then Ada mentioning that May had been unwell, but I'd heard nothing from

May herself. The skin beneath her eyes was puffy, her face looked drawn, fixed now in an expression of worry despite the smiling welcome. I did not ask then; it wasn't the time, the children were close by, and on the stove a sauce was thickening. She stirred this, then scraped the herbs into a small bowl.

Can I do anything? I asked. No, no, she said. But you could open a bottle. You choose – the rack is down there, she said, pointing to the banister past the piano, under the stairs.

They had moved since I last saw her, and I now recognised the scale of their luck: the real-estate man in the right place at the right time. Adam was local to the city, a child of a wealthy immigrant family, and knew the rising worth and benefits of the various neighbourhoods. The house was vast, larger than it seemed from its modest street frontage: a tall but narrow entrance replete with a glossy clipped box hedge and glass panelled front door. The rack was not a rack so much as a cellar, a deep alcove built into the wall under the basement stairs, where a cloakroom might once have been. The bottles were carefully arranged by type and year, the real heirlooms tucked away down the bottom, the dark glass a little dusty. It was cool there and quiet. I ran my fingers across the labels, looking for a picture I liked. It smelt good, the cellar – of old rock and damp, like the dim, unused regions beneath a house or at the back of a garage, the smell of earth, rain, oil. My sister and I were used to talking on the telephone, long rambling conversations across continents. It was strange to find myself now in the presence of her physical body, in the presence of her house and its accoutrements: children, food, wine. I didn't know, all of a sudden, how I could explain my life to her. What the disintegration of this would look like, here. I leant my face against the cool of the plastered wall and closed my eyes. The muffled sounds of the television came through the floor.

When we were children, Joan had plied us with food to put us at ease. She was not a cook of refined meals, but she liked her food to be plentiful and filling: roast potatoes, bacon and eggs, steak and kidney pies. Good old English stodge, my father would say, very fondly. Without ever asking us directly about our mother, she inquired as to our favourite meals, and I often found her leafing through the old cookbooks, the most used ones – the pages yellowed and dog-eared and dotted with the oily stains from batter or gravy, picking out recipes she thought we might like. I loved to watch her cook, and sometimes she'd let me sit up on the bench and observe her as she measured and stirred. But most of the time I preferred to sit on the floor, where I played with the cats who had come looking for morsels of food: the bits of cheese or fatty meat that Joan would sometimes give them while she went about preparing dinner. On the floor like that, I noticed her feet – how she always wore court shoes, or some slightly heeled equivalent, sometimes dark brown with laces. Her legs were thick, and the tops of her feet swelled up over the edges of the shoes, so that it looked like her feet were filled with air. I wanted to touch them, but dared not. Above me, Joan wobbled a little as she whisked the eggs.

I heard May calling from the landing. Lucie? Lucie are you OK down there? The dog, following up its mistress's question, trotted down the stairs to investigate, and when it found me nosed at my groin. Yes, I called back, just coming. I quickly chose a Merlot and a Cab Sav, unsure which would go better with the meal, and carried these back up the stairs. In my absence May had laid the table and set out the salad, along with a basket of bread. I watched her a moment, stirring butter through a bowl of green beans. Then I opened the Merlot and went to pour myself a glass. As I did so my sister whispered some-thing in my ear, before pulling away as Adam stepped inside. He said what returning men say: Smells good. May retreated to the kitchen bench. I watched him come up behind her and take hold of her waist, tugging her in towards him. He was gentle, but still she flinched. He seemed not to notice, or to ignore this – interpreting it as a self-preserving move on her part, ducking her head a little to avoid the heavy metal rim of the extraction fan where it jutted out over the stove.

When my sister first met him, she thought he was an Evangelical. She was working out at the gym, running on the treadmill. Beside her were the stationary bikes, and a man riding hell-for-leather, as she told me. He had headphones on, and she thought he was singing quietly to himself, in a kind of panted whisper. But as he continued with his routine, the whispering became more forceful. He was speaking quickly, and louder, as if giving com-mands. She made out the words: Stand up! Up! Come on up, people! She thought he was possibly crazy, and that his ferocious exercise was part of some delusionary phase. She watched him out of the corner of her eye, concerned. His gaze was intent, focused on the wall in front of him as though he could see something there. She slowed the treadmill to a walking pace and thought perhaps she should move; he was tall, well built, clearly very strong, and she didn't like the idea of being too close to a raving man of that size. Although he soon calmed down, the cycling became less frenetic, and he leant back on his seat to take a sip of water. But the return to some state of possession was sudden – a new song, perhaps, triggering the rise in energy. She listened more closely to his whispered mutterings, intrigued by the fact that he was either oblivious of this behaviour, or didn't see it as at all out of keeping with normal gym etiquette. Up! Up! he said, Everybody stand! He cycled very hard, and it was then that she heard him say, Jesus, Jesus. At that point she thought perhaps he was not crazy in the conventional sense, but very devout, and his utterances were intended as a form or worship, a self-induced state of exaltation, exercise as a means to possession. It was only later that she realised he was one of the gym class instructors, and that what she had overheard was him practising a new routine – when people should stand up on their bike pedals, when they should sit and race. This was before he changed direction and moved into real estate. He found the ridiculousness of her initial misunderstanding somehow attractive. She joined his classes.

Here, she said, unhooking herself from his arms and gesturing to the large cast-iron pot, hot from the oven, take this to the table.

Lucie, he said, come have a seat. I thanked him and took my place. The girls were fighting over who sat on which chair, despite the chairs being identical. Adam merely raised his voice enough to say, Hey! and they hushed down, squirming a little as children do when, in the midst of a party game, the music stops and they must settle wherever they happen to be, lest they find themselves excluded from playing.

May came, carrying the platter of green beans, and we all flapped our napkins out over our laps. Well, she said, grinning, Here we all are. So lovely to see you at last, she said, reaching out and taking hold of my hand. I smiled back and thanked her. Especially, I said, after everything that— But she quickly brushed this comment away, sweeping her hand through the air close to her face, as one might shoo a fly. It's nothing, she said. Please eat. It wasn't clear whether she meant that her hospitality was nothing, as in not an effort of any kind, or that her own illness was not of significance, or that nothing had happened to me either, to either of us in fact, that it was better to act this way, to say nothing. These were things, her gesture indicated, that one does not discuss at the dinner table. In front of the children. In this way May's own silence could be readily justified and reframed as a way of caring for others, a form of consideration.

Because this was what she had whispered to me while I was opening the wine before the meal – Just so you know, I had a hysterectomy, she told me. A few weeks ago. That's all. Best not to talk about it around Lexi though, she said. There were some complications and I had an infection but I'm fine now, just tired, she told me, her voice still hushed. But it really bothered Lex.

They had learnt of Lexi's sensitivity only after May first came home from the hospital. Explaining to the children what kind of surgery had taken place, Lexi leant suddenly against the shelf near which she was standing and said, Can you stop talking about that, please? I feel really strange. They looked at her and said, What kind of strange? But before she could answer she fell down in a faint. She came to fairly quickly, her gaze swimming around the room, her voice small. What happened? she asked. She had a headache. Lexi said that the mention of the surgery, and especially the word *womb*, had made her feel dizzy, then a little sick, and that was all she could remember.

I reached over for the water jug and poured too quickly. Chunks of ice splashed into my glass. Between my life and May's I could only think of all the things I wasn't meant to say. I was, in a sense, in a state of quarantine, my inner life fenced off by the collective onslaught of pleasantries in which I was complicit (*how is London, what year are you in at school, when did you move here*). I knew this to be a way of coating my own damage, of sealing it and preventing it from leaking out and infecting the people I was living among. They were afraid of my experience, I realised, and so dared not ask. Adam turned to take the other bottle from the sideboard, the Cab Sav this time. It had been, I calculated, nearly two weeks since the night Patrick died. Although this was an unreliable tally: I'd lost hours flying from London to Australia, gained some heading from Japan to New York, then there had been the flight in between, from New York to London. If I travelled in a certain direction for long enough it seemed possible to erase that terrible night entirely – such was my magical thinking at the time. And if May didn't ask about the accident, if she never spoke of it, perhaps that was because it hadn't happened at all.

I looked over at my sister. She perched on the edge of her chair and sat very upright, her spine straight in the fashion of an obedient schoolgirl. She always had been rewarded for her good behaviour – a child that wanted to please people. I was more tempestuous, and when we were young she had often witnessed the arguments that erupted between me and our father. May made herself different by being the good child. She made herself stand out in that odd way that brings praise when young, and invisibility when older. She didn't scream or make demands or speak out of turn. I had often thought what an effort that must take, but now I understood that this was easier for her – she didn't want to be unsettled. Maybe she never had those greater and disruptive feelings. Or if she did, they were feelings she must have pretended not to know, refused to tell me about. Held off for as long as she could. Of course we wouldn't talk about Patrick. Not now, maybe not ever. Just as we never spoke about our mother. Sometimes I used to try, when we were young and sharing a bedroom. I'd whisper to her after the lamp had been switched off, but she never replied. I knew she was still awake, I could tell from her breathing. I wanted to hear the story, the one she once told about our mother's return that night. She first told me this when I'd been ill. I'd had a bad fever, so bad in fact that our father said I'd been delirious, and it was while I was recuperating that May told me the story about our mother and the sweets. But you must never tell Father, she said, because he didn't know that she knew, and neither of us wanted to make him angry. After all, for a long time he was all we had. Later, I wrote about the scene that May had described, although May never commented on this. I'm not sure she ever read one of my novels cover to cover. Although she was happy to talk about them in generalities. In all truth, she once told me, the proximity between our own lives and certain episodes in my fiction unnerved her. I didn't exactly intend this; sometimes, when I write, I feel not so unlike that fevered child, the scenes that emerge coming hot from the mind – a strange fusion of wish-fulfilment and prediction, sometimes hallucinatory in their power. None of this was to May's taste; she preferred not to dredge things up, but to leave them unspoken. The child and now the woman still upholding her code of silence – keeper of the peace.

Adam pushed back from the table and, without saying anything, went to the fridge and stood a moment staring into its bright interior. May glanced at him, said nothing and dropped her head down a little towards her food, so as to look at the meat she was cutting. To the fridge, her husband said, Do we have any mayonnaise? May replied, as if to the dead chicken on her plate, I don't know, did you buy any? She carved at her meal as if it were made of some dense and resistant substance, requiring her full attention and preventing her from going to Adam's aid. Eventually, however, he found what he was looking for and returned to the table, sitting down heavily in his seat and letting out a sigh that could have been a sigh of effort or relief, it was hard to tell, and perhaps not an involuntary sigh at all but a sign or signal that belonged to the language of their marriage. My sister appeared to understand this sound because it elicited no response in her, no query, no concern; it was a familiar piece of marital code it required no interpretation on her part. Instead, she pushed some greens on to the end of her fork, so that they overlapped with a piece of roast potato, and lifted it towards her lips, asking me, How is the book going, and the prize thingy, sorry, I should have remembered – the name of it, I mean. It was a big deal, right?

She sawed at the meat on her plate. Then her knife slipped and a piece of roast chicken fell to the floor. Rupert! May called, without glancing up. The dog came padding in. My sister put one hand beneath the table and clicked. She did not even need to make eye contact with the dog for him to understand the message: food in waiting. It was a tiny piece, but still you could hear him slobbering all over the tiles, and then sniffing around at everyone's feet in case he'd missed something.

I pushed my food around, the nausea rising. Are you not hungry? May asked.

I think it's the jet lag, I replied, my body clock all mixed up. Sorry.

Lexi leant over and started to pick out bits of tomato from the salad, putting one piece after another on her plate. May reached across the table and smacked her hand away.

Hey! Lexi yelled. What was that for?

Use the salad servers, May replied.

They're too big for my hands.

Well you can't just eat the tomatoes. What about everyone else, what about Lucie? What if Lucie wants some tomatoes?

I don't actually— I started to say, but Lexi interjected.

There's still lots there, she said.

That's not the point, replied May.

You just said it was the point.

You know what I mean, can't you just have some manners?

What, like, for once?

I didn't say that.

But you were about to, right? That's what you say, *just for once in your life*, Lexi said, putting on a whining imitation of her mother's voice.

Lexi, please. I just mean—

I know what you mean, Lexi spat. For God's sake, they're just tomatoes. *Tom-at-oes*, she said, sounding the word out slowly and phonetically as if her mother were an idiot. Lexi shoved her chair back then she stomped off to her room and just before she slammed her door she shouted out, Why didn't you just stay in hospital? Everything was fine then.

We all fell into silence, chewing very carefully. May's face was flushed. Jess poked at the food on her plate while she kicked idly at the leg of the dining table. I'm tired, Mummy, she said. I'm not hungry any more.

I know, honey, May replied. Just eat this bit here, she said, pushing a small pile of potatoes to one corner of the plate.

I'm sorry, I said at last, excusing myself as a headache started to throb behind my eyes. The jet lag is really getting to me. I think I might have to lie down for a moment.

Do you want some more water? May asked me. Or a hot drink? She went to get up. No, no, I said. I'm fine. I'll be fine. I just need to lie down.

But you're not though. What about a hot-water bottle? Or just some paracetamol. Camomile tea? It was the language one uses when tending to a child. What does the child want? The child that exists in an endless state of wanting, then needing, then wanting again. Wanting so badly they feel it as a need, the ache of the body. It was the habit of maternal language. Not the language of the host. A host would say, Can I offer you a glass of water? Can I get you a cup of tea? They would never assume wants. Like a person who deals with financial matters but never utters the word money. Instead, they use words like lucrative, substantial, insufficient – descriptors of proportion or gain – or they might say something like 'the number is around two hundred'. One could entertain preferences, but not announce desires. There could be only approximations. The language of the host would work hard to efface their own labour, their own appetites, disguising any hint of the inconvenience that might be caused by fetching that water or that tea. Not so the language of the child or their weary parent.

Sure, I said. Actually, some more water would be great, thanks. The jug on the table was empty. I didn't say, in the returning voice of the house guest, Please don't trouble yourself, or, if more familiar with the environment, Don't you get up, I can do it. I drank the water in one go while May stood beside me, watching. I'm sorry, I said again. But I really think I have to lie down. Besides, I should get early night – I've got a TV interview in the morning.

Gosh, she said, you should have told us! Are you going to be okay to do that?

I'll be fine, I replied. It's not a long slot.

It must be good for sales though.

I shrugged and pushed my chair back from the table. Hopefully it'll be over before I know it, I said.

From my bed I could hear the muted sounds of the kitchen: chairs scraping on the floorboards, cutlery on plates. The jet lag made the ground beneath me feel unstable, whether I was standing on solid earth or lying down. Now, as I stretched out between the sheets, I had the sensation of sinking and turning. If I closed my eyes the darkness seemed to swell and shift. I drifted in and out of semi-sleep but couldn't settle. The plunging feeling of the jet lag was too much like the feeling of the ship tilting and dipping on the high seas. Somewhere in the room a fly was dying. It made a high-pitched buzzing, striking a note of frenzy. It buzzed and buzzed, unceasing. Eventually I reached over and turned on the light, then got up to look for it, hoping to set it free from whatever web it was caught in, but I couldn't see it anywhere. I lay back down. Its frantic noise sounded like a kind of plea. Why would the spider not come and kill the fly? I closed my eyes.

The air was hot and damp, too hot to sleep. Above me the ceiling fan turned slowly, pushing warm air from one part of the room to another, a sticky breeze moving gently over my bare shoulders, my face. Dull memory of his hands touching me there. The stroke of his fingers. During that first taxi ride, when Patrick didn't go to the airport, when he reached across to brush my hair behind my ear. He had confessed then that he was secretly writing a script which, he told me, was basically a love story.

I'd complimented him on the seminar, and he'd waved this away explaining that he wasn't all that into those ideas any more, that he was mainly working on this other thing. The love thing. Not a story exactly, more of an exploration. It's not going so well though, he said. I think I can pull the production funds together, but that means nothing if the script is crap. He sighed heavily. The windows were fogging up. Until that all gets going, what, I keep turning up to talk about this academic bullshit. Sorry, he said, I probably shouldn't say that. I mean, you're studying this stuff.

He rubbed a hand across his stubbled jaw. I dismissed his concern. Some of it is boring, I said.

They'll hate it, you know. My film. Everyone here, I mean. He worried that it would be deemed too emotional. Really? I said, when he confided this. But isn't that the point? And I mean, who cares?

Ah, he said. Now this is what I like about you.

Human beings are never so very different from the art they make, and he himself had a powerful effect – electrifying. If he worried that others might doubt him, even then I had every faith. What was there not to believe in? With his salt-and-pepper hair and expressive frown lines etched into his forehead like a grid. The ancient leather jacket that he wore then over a striped jumper. The jacket, I noticed, smelt strongly of tobacco.

He moved closer. The traffic was slow. The driver turned on the radio. As he lifted his arm to stretch it out over the back of my seat, I saw that the lining of the jacket was a little torn along the side seam. Somehow this made him all the more loveable. Like any great man, or any man who once did something great, he was vintage material of increasing worth. Or should that be value? He was the one who could always explain to me the difference between these things.

The nausea returned. It was more intense if I lay on my right side, slightly better if I lay on my left. The heat didn't help. On my back the dizziness was too much to bear. The sound of the trapped fly continued, but more intermittently now. I got up and tiptoed to the bathroom to refill my water glass. Back in my room I turned the ceiling fan on at high speed and lay down beneath its whirr. My body ached with an animal loneliness, a deep longing for his weight and girth. I heard his voice, as clear as if he were in the room with me, and my own voice replying.

You have nothing to worry about, I'd said to him in the back of that taxi while I let him touch my hair, still damp from the rain. If the film is successful, you'll be celebrated for having reached a mainstream audience at long last, for having captured *the spirit of the people.* We both giggled. But we knew that I was only partly joking. So many of us want the thing we pretend to hate. His fear was that the film would render him a laughing stock.

No, I said. Besides, he was an important figure. Or he was to me, even then. One day, he would be more than that, and to more people – I was sure of it, I said. But you know the only person, I reminded him, who gets to preserve their cult status is the one who dies before their time.

He snorted at this and glanced out of the window, through the rain. Then he reached over and tucked a stray piece of my hair behind my ear, slipping his hand along the back of my neck. Well, he said. We'll just have to see about that.

14

A car arrived early the next morning to take me to the television studio. Yasmin, my Australian publicist, was already in the back seat and she pushed the door open for me. Hi! she said, as I slipped in beside her. Oh god, I'm so glad to finally meet you! she cried, flicking her silky hair behind her shoulders. She was young and bubbly and had just joined the company after an internship. She couldn't believe her luck, she said, to think that she was the one who got to spend the day with me. So just shout out, she said, as she tapped away at her phone, if there's anything at all you need. I nodded, as I buckled my seat belt and let out a long, shaky sigh. Ok, all set? she asked, and we reversed down May's drive.

The car smelt of menthol and aftershave. Soft classical music. The driver told me I was welcome to take the bottled water nestled in my door compartment. My hands were trembling too much to unscrew the lid.

Here, Yasmin said, taking the bottle. Let me, and she twisted it open.

Thanks, I replied, popping a beta blocker from its blister pack and gulping half the water in one go.

Don't worry, she said. You'll be great. You must have done this kind of thing, like, a million times before.

Sort of, but that's not to say it's fun. I get very nervous, I said, waving the box of pills before I slipped them back into my bag. For live recordings only, I told her. My cardinal rule.

Don't worry, she said again. It really will be only about the book. They love it, we all do.

By the time I was in the make-up chair the beta blocker had started to do its work. The jeans and shirt I'd turned up in proved unsuitable and so they dressed me in a hot-pink suit which, they said, made for a striking image of feminine power. I protested, saying it really wasn't my colour, but by then we were running out of time for a wardrobe change. I came on set after a song break: some new pop star belting out her chart topper. The studio lights were violet and sparkly, the hosts – a man and a woman, *The Morning Show* marriage format – swayed to the beat. Then they took their positions on the sofa and I walked in. The camera didn't show my entrance, nor my face as the female host introduced me. One of the most celebrated writers, she said, known for her bracing take on modern life . . . her new book . . . alarmingly candid . . . please welcome . . .

I refolded my hands in my lap. Neatly, no white knuckles. The hint of a smile. I could feel the corners of my mouth spasming a little. I tried to look natural; honey-honey-honey, I thought to myself. Money-money-money. The first questions were routine, and I let myself slip into the zone: the automatic answers, easy and predictable. My motivation to write the book, the creative process, a brief debate over the poor life decisions made by some of my characters, and so on. I don't think either of the hosts had actually read the book. I assume they'd been filled in on the key plot points. It was possible they asked every author the same things – I didn't really know, I never watched morning television. Then something unexpected: It's been some years now since you've been home, hasn't it? What's it like, being back? I understand you just arrived yesterday. This question posed by the woman, with a little too much feeling. Something too earnest and searching in her voice. I garbled some reply: a busy schedule, commitments in the UK. And it's such a treat to have you here, she said, because it wasn't planned, this trip, was it? A surprise author tour!

Yes, I replied, I suppose you could call it that.

Well, we're the lucky ones. But I imagine, she said, lowering her voice, that you yourself don't feel that way right now.

Sorry?

Well, you've been through a lot in the last week or so, she said. I mean the prize is huge, just extraordinary. And that itself, it's a lot to take on board, to process. But even before the prize, I mean. In fact, many of our viewers who've been following the events are, as we speak, sending in messages of condolence.

The male host, I've forgotten his name, leant forwards a little, as if in confidence. Katie and John, or was it Sam and Kylie? Their names twinned, indistinguishable. If that had happened to me, he said, I'd want to come home too. Not the prize, I mean, but your terrible tragedy. His make-up had been applied very thickly, which gave his skin a rubbery appearance. He had the suntanned hue of a Ken doll, against which his white teeth seemed to glow. It must weigh on you, he said, the accident. I mean, I imagine it's something that plays and replays in your head. Even while you're doing your job, talking to us here.

I felt my eyes sting, my throat tightening against the tears. What's that like for you? As a writer, I mean.

What's that like? No one had asked me this so directly. No one had asked me anything much about how I was feeling. Everyone had been too shocked by the event and then too afraid or too worried about me. This was the first time anyone had put this question to me and expected a reply. How was I? How did I feel? It was almost a relief to be spoken to so frankly. For someone to want to know, to not hesitate to ask. To assume I felt something. But I couldn't answer this. I don't know if I even knew the answer then. If I could even come close to unravelling the mess of my feelings.

I mean, I began, then stopped mid-sentence. I felt suddenly very cold and dizzy. There was no way through this question. No way round it. He wasn't really asking how I was, what I was feeling. The strange sensation then, of someone digging about beneath my skin, prying. May said that when Lexi was pulled from her during the C-section she could feel the surgeon's hands through the anaesthetic, the dull pressure of them both on and inside her body, pushing and tugging, manoeuvring the child, a feeling she'd never forget. I was sitting too close to the man, I could see the make-up caking in the fine lines at the edge of his eyes. They had promised. I had asked

Valerie to make them promise. I mean, I said. What I'm trying to say is that—

There were meant to be limits around what questions were asked. Book stuff only. I paused, looking to Yasmin for a sign. I didn't know what to say. I wanted someone to end this. And to do it now.

It must have been terrifying, the storm, he continued. He paused. Did you actually see him go over?

I swallowed hard, a dry lump in my throat. No, I mean yes, I mean he was there and then— it all happened so fast. My heart flipped quickly, like I was running hard up a hill. An irregular thump in my chest, then my neck.

It did, he said. It did indeed. And we can get a glimpse of that now, he said, his tone changing as he swivelled back to centre and eyed the camera, addressing all those viewers at home. Let's take a look at some exclusive footage captured by a fellow traveller. Yasmin was close to the cameraman on my left, gesticulating, telling him, I assumed, to put a stop to this. Now.

Then the waves appeared on screen. Giant black mountains massing and rolling, the hand-held camera shaking. Sea spray. The call of voices. Glass breaking in the background. My breath lurched as my chest closed in, tighter and tighter. I couldn't breathe. I didn't know where to look. I thought I might pass out. The make-up artist stepped towards me. Close your eyes now, she said, as she dabbed at my cheeks, fixing the smudges where I'd wiped away tears. And just keep them closed a bit longer. A brushing of something else, a touch-up of the hair. A tissue to press against my lips. OK, she said. And five, four, three, two, one. Camera rolling. The presenters turned to me, smiling, with more questions.

Fuck, I said, as I ripped the mike off from behind my ear. I felt humiliated, exposed. I mean what the fucking fuck, I said to Yasmin once the slot was over and the show carried on with its next segment. Why the fuck I didn't just get up and leave the set when I could? Why did I stay on after that storm footage? There were meant to be rules, limits, I said. You knew this, they knew this. Yasmin was beside me, taking me by the arm and leading me away, Don't you worry about it, she said, We'll get on to this. Let's just get you out of here now, come on, the car's waiting. We're just going to drive for a while, OK, and let you chill out. I'm so sorry. God I'm so sorry.

The studio was on the edge of the city, near the old railway warehouses and the grain mill. We drove back the long way. I closed my eyes a while, then opened them to glimpse the city skyline and closed them again. We stopped for coffee. A café with tables on the sidewalk, in the sun. I wasn't hungry but Yasmin ordered food anyway. Are you going to be all right with the rest of today? she asked. I nodded. There was no real alternative. OK then, she said, pulling out a schedule from her bag. Normally we'd just do these mass signings in the warehouse, but the stores have put huge orders in, so most of the stock is on the shop floor. And everyone's really keen to see you, they're thrilled to have you visit. It's hard to get authors like you to drop by in person. We'll make the stops brief, I promise. And just say if at any time this feels too much.

I nodded, stirring more sugar into my coffee. I'll be fine, I said.

In reality I felt far from this. I was still shaking and had sweated right through my shirt. My mouth remained dry no matter how much water I drank. We got back in the car and drove to the first bookshop. The piles were ready for me on the counter and on the floor. Yasmin whipped a pen from her bag. I scrawled at speed, making small talk with the owner while I tried to concentrate on signing my own name. Most of the booksellers didn't know whether to say congratulations or I'm so sorry. At that first bookstore the man said both. At the second the woman said neither, explaining that she wasn't the owner but that she could show us to the piles that had been put out for signing. I'll leave you to it, she said. Just give a shout when you're done. I realised then that my experience was too much for her; my presence had this new effect – I frightened people. At the third, a kind woman sat me down at a small table at the back and brought me tea. She was older and had a soft, cushiony face. When she put the tea down beside me, she touched her hand to my hair. I could tell, just from the gesture, that she too had known great suffering and understood the impossibility of translating this into the practical language of ordinary life. You just go slowly there, she said. And if there's anything else I can get you, just ask. I'm right here, she told me, pointing to a set of shelves that she had been restocking when we arrived. Right here. I had to bite my tongue then to stop myself bursting into tears. My palms were sweating so much that I could hardly keep hold of the pen. By the fourth store I was getting muddled, writing down the first part of something I was saying to the shop manager rather than writing my surname, then getting the J. mixed up with the B. My hand cramped. My face hurt from forcing a smile. Yasmin spotted this and stepped up, moving me to a stool at the back of the next shop while she made conversation, then hurrying me out of there as soon as the books were done.

The jet lag hit hard by early afternoon – an overwhelming exhaustion, that feeling of the floor tilting, the desire to just lie down wherever I was and sleep. Is everything OK?' Yasmin asked. Just two more stores, she said kindly, then we'll head back to the office to freshen up.

Freshen up?

For the party.

There's a party?

Oh, did you not know? I thought Valerie had mentioned this. There's, like, our end-of-year do this evening. It's early, starts at half five and won't go for long – nibbles, speeches, a bit of mingling. The venue is only booked until nine. Although I think the plan is that some of us will migrate to the pub afterwards. Everyone's super-excited that you'll be there – our guest of honour!

Something in me started to crack, I wasn't up for all this. I couldn't remember then what exactly I had agreed to. Maybe I had said yes to this, when it was described to me in general terms, maybe I'd zoned out in the car on the way to the TV interview. Valerie would have checked with me about it if she'd known. For whatever reason the line of communication between the UK and the Australian team had broken down and I no longer had the energy to stand my ground.

Just then Yasmin's phone pinged. She swiped at the screen. Nice hands, manicured nails.

Oh, she said, look. The *New Yorker* profile has just gone up online.

I'd forgotten all about this, that last awful interview in the hotel room. I watched her face while she read, tight with concentration, then a slight downward turn of the mouth. Did she sigh? Was that it? A tense, almost wheezing release of breath. She scrolled quickly, skimming. Gosh, she said. It's long, as if this were reason not to read it properly.

Don't tell me, I said, turning to look out of the window, not even wanting to see her staring at her phone. I don't want to know.

Really?

Really, nothing. Not even the good bits.

But what about— she hesitated while she scrolled. You should probably hear this bit where it—

Nope, I said.

OKaaay, she replied, drawing the word out, while her fingernail continued to make a tapping sound on the screen. I mean, there might be things here you don't agree with, things, I don't know—

Like what?

You should probably just read it. Later I mean. Not now. It's really long.

Like what things? I asked again.

Hm? she said, still tapping and scrolling. Well, there's quite a bit about the, the um, your family and stuff. And then your books. Ergh, she said to the device in her hand. Go away! These ads are so annoying. She fell silent for a moment. Well, they do talk about the accident. But you know, it's hard for me to tell, I mean you'd know what they were when you read them.

Know what what were?

Well, whether it's true or not. The details. She sounded strange. Sorry, she said. I really shouldn't read in the car, I get motion sick.

At the office she showed me to the staff bathroom, where there was a shower, a hairdryer, a cabinet of toiletries.

My desk is round the corner to the left, she said. I'm just going to sort out a few things while you get ready.

I had no way of making myself more ready than I was. I was still dressed in the awful pink suit from the morning and my television make-up was still thick on my face. I scrubbed this off with paper towels and hot water. What had she meant – whether it was true or not? I prided myself on not reading these things. I told others that I paid no attention to reviews and the like, that I preferred not to know. But now I worried. Now I wanted to know. I couldn't really remember what I'd said to the journalist in all those meetings for the profile, in all the months of correspondence, the emails and phone calls, or what exactly I'd said in the hotel, perched on the edge of the bed, next to the vase of flowers, just after the accident. Particularly towards the end of the interview, when I was trying to wrap things up and make it to the reading on time. It seemed years ago, that hotel room. Some details came to mind, but maybe they were things I said that morning, after they'd shown the footage of the storm. The timing of events felt confusing. I remembered being quite short in that last conversation, in the hotel, and the journalist's questions feeling nosy in a way that seemed different from usual. Like she was hunting for something, not curious but eager. I couldn't help but think about it, about the things I didn't know, hadn't read.

I sat down on the closed lid of the toilet and punched in the code to my phone. I would just skim it. Glance over it. Check it for the worst. As if this would arm me somehow. But there was no signal. The bathroom was some mobile-data black spot. I stood on the closed lid of the toilet, lifted my arm above my head. Maybe I just needed to get higher. Up on tiptoe. Still nothing. I sat back down. I thought I could smell gas. As if there were a leak somewhere, a burner on without a flame. There was a knock at the door.

J.B.? It was Yasmin. We should get going in a minute. Can I get you anything?

All good. Sorry. I'm just coming.

I slipped the phone back into my pocket. I washed my hands out of habit. I tucked a few wisps of hair behind my ears. Then I unlocked the door and stepped out. Yasmin was waiting at the end of the corridor. Great, she said. Let's go?

The party was on the harbour, the restaurant's deck opening out high over the briny water. Yasmin hooked her arm through mine and led me through the crowd, stopping to take two glasses from a tray. She took me out on to the deck. I felt my stomach lurch. I tried to turn away from the sight of the sea but she was introducing me, or introducing others to me, drawing me into a small circle of women who were each holding a glass and laughing. All that bright lipstick and the small beads of sweat, on the forehead, above the top lip. The laughter stopped, they greeted me. I felt a tension in the air. Soon after, others saw me too, or noticed me, or I was led up to them in order to say hello.

The lower level of the restaurant was part of the old wharf and with the rising tide I could feel the boards shifting under my feet, the sound of the water lapping. I didn't want to be there, I wasn't up for it. Other people's eyes started to feel hot on my neck. I was aware of everyone glancing at me in the same way, nervous, a little wary, a look of concern. Yasmin continued to expertly move me around the restaurant, and as she did so it became clear that each time we arrived at a new group, the conversation fell silent. Lovely to meet you, one or another would say, a limp, sweaty palm offered in greeting. But their eyes said otherwise. Narrow, watery. As if they wanted to apologise for something. Glances over the shoulder. Muted voices. Or so I thought. It all felt to be happening at some remove. I felt unreachable. Sealed off. I knew then, as I made my way through the crowd, that everyone was thinking of what I had lost, what I must have suffered, how I must be suffering still; that same close and unbearable feeling of being scrutinised that I remembered from the night of the prize ceremony. It created a kind of awe – the sublime terror of someone else's pain. No one wanted to step any closer to the precipice that I represented. I felt them watching in case I stumbled or collapsed. And then I realised. It wasn't just that. Everyone had seen *The Morning Show*, of course they had. Everyone had read the *New Yorker* profile. These things spread quickly. I alone was on the outside, frozen in the headlights.

Something had happened. I didn't know exactly what it was, but could tell that I wasn't just being looked at now as Patrick's widow. With the television interview and the appearance of the article something had changed. I realised that I was being looked at with concern. Not admiration, but anxiety. As a woman on the cusp of breakdown, disintegration, adrift in hopeless sorrow. It was not sheepishness or pity that I saw in their faces, but doubt, fear – I was a walking tragedy they were afraid to touch. I had rarely been to a party like this without Patrick. Without his body to lean against, without his warm hand to pull me away or lead me to a corner so that we could kiss. Without him there to make apologies, so that we could sneak away early. I suddenly needed to get out of there. I said this to Yasmin, I'm sorry, it's been such a long day. I really think I need to head back now.

Oh, for sure! I'm so sorry, I should have thought. She was oblivious to my suffering or else embarrassed by it. Perhaps she thought it polite to pretend it didn't exist or maybe she just didn't know where to begin, what to say. I of all people knew how hard it was to find the words that could fit such an experience. But let me just introduce you to— She passed me another drink from a tray as she led me towards the railing, near the water. How many glasses had there been so far? Too many, I thought. I saw the sea loom up, the curve of ocean in the distance. I finished the drink and took another. I felt a little unsteady on my feet. Who was the man I was talking to? Yasmin was there, making small talk, joining the dots. I held on to the railing for balance. And just one more person who's been dying to meet you, I promise this is the last one,

Yasmin told me. Or maybe the second last. I handed my champagne flute to a passing waiter. I was wobbling a little by then. Yasmin took my arm just as I caught the toe of my shoe on something and stumbled. There was a smudge of lipstick on her front teeth. The sea slapping at the pylons beneath our feet, the smell of brine and rot, the call of night birds. Bats swooped out of the giant fig trees. It must have been later than I realised. City lights in the distance. The ferry boats in the harbour started to glow, rows of bright-yellow windows floating over the black water. It was hot. So hot. Sweat trickled down my back. I wished I hadn't come. What was I thinking? Just of escape. Being anywhere else. The gross regret turned in the pit of my stomach.

At last Yasmin put me in a taxi and handed me a cab-charge card for the other end. By the time I arrived back at May's house everyone was asleep – all the lights off except for the one in the kitchen. I was walking unsteadily towards this, along the path and past the swimming pool, when I heard Adam call out. I turned slowly in the direction of his voice. I had drunk far more than I meant to. Looks like a wild night? he said. I gave a kind of nod-shrug in reply. I needed to lie down. You must be hot in that, he said, referring to my suit. Come for a swim.

I looked up to the house.

The girls are in bed he said, meaning both his children and his wife. Early night. He was right, I was hot. I thought at first it was this that was making me dizzy. I could smell the sweat coming from my shirt, damp under the arms and across the back where it had stuck to the seat of the taxi. The water looked so inviting. Yeah, maybe, I said. I couldn't be bothered going inside. Getting changed. Coming back out again. I sat down on the edge of the pool, rolled my trousers up and dipped my feet in. The water felt amazing – the relief of it. I hitched up my trousers a little further, felt the water on my calves. Come on, he said. It'll clear your head. I told him the truth – that I couldn't be bothered getting changed.

Just come in in what you're wearing.

This? I said, pointing to my clothes.

No, the stuff underneath. Of everyone in my circle at that moment, he was possibly the only one who hadn't seen or heard of the television interview, the magazine profile. A person who didn't and wouldn't care. The water rippled. Sure, I said. Unbuttoning my shirt and standing to tug off my trousers. I could feel him watching me. I was too drunk to swim. I knew that. The dim, faraway knowledge that seems to belong to someone else. My toes were numb from the alcohol. I didn't feel sick, but I was dizzy. It would be fine, he was sober. The cold water would help. I jumped in. He turned the pool lights off so we could see the stars. Or this was what he said, anyway. I heard a splash and felt something slip past my body, eel-like, the current it made as it moved against me. As a child I could make myself panic by just imagining a shark in the water. Hyperventilate almost. The gulping of air, the sudden frenzy of kicking to get myself to the shallow end of the pool. Now the same feeling, the dark shape of his body coasting underwater, brushing past me, just touching, skimming. Watery contact of limbs, maybe accidental. He came up for air, plunged down again. The game children play, of diving between the other person's

legs and scooping back up. Adolescent pleasure of brushing against the wet skin, the surprise feeling. Where are
you? Where will they touch me, will they touch me, what
if? The moving shadow in the water. And then that
strange, sudden panic that I remembered from childhood.
I lifted my legs off the ground, pushed away, swam a quick
lap. Then I stopped, leaning on the edge of the pool, out
of breath and nauseous. Adam came up beside me.

You OK? he said, placing a hand on my neck. The
weight of his hand was enough to turn my face towards his.
He leant in to kiss me. I was drunk, slow, and so watched
this from a slight remove. The face coming closer, the
water lapping at my back. The bats. The dream from the
night before, of a mouse the cat had caught and left, Look
what the cat has dragged in, mauled and maybe dead the
mouse was, or maybe not, it was hard to tell. The delay
then of one second, two, enough to seem willing, partially so, not totally opposed, his tongue seeking something
out, curious. Then I realised what was happening, what I
didn't want, and I pulled away, stricken, clambering out
of the pool, forgetting to take my clothes with me as I
hurried through the dark and back to the house.

15

That night I didn't sleep. I knew what Adam had done, how it had happened and that I hadn't refused quickly enough. I knew how easily my slow reaction would be taken as a woman's ambivalence, and not seen as the paralysis of shock, drunkenness, dull surprise, the setting-in of disgust. And now I'd have to continue to face him and pretend for May's sake, carry on as if nothing had happened. Just the thought of it sickened me, the memory of how he leered, and the fact of May's unquestioning devotion. I tried to push the image of him away but it kept returning, and at last, after lying for hours in the dark, I picked up my phone for the distraction and eventually found myself clicking on the link to the profile. It loaded slowly. And then there I was, the long article accompanied by a cartoon portrait. The piece followed the usual format: recent acclaim, news of the prize, contemporary context, and then the slow trek back through my history. It was a format designed to tell the story of how the artist won, why she deserved to be celebrated, how she had been transformed. But not this time. Not in the way you'd expect. It gave the life summary: of my immigrant parents, my father who was a child of Partition, the early abandonment by my mother, the legacy of these traumas reconfigured in my books. Then the knife: the child's determination, the hot-headed teenager, the younger woman in love with her professor, following him to London as if she were a stalker and never looking back. The ruthless artist who doesn't ever see her father again, who refuses to come home even when he's dying. My monstrous ambition, the lack of children, the single-minded pursuit of my art – not talent, just grit and strategy. The woman who would not be where she was now had she not married as she did. I broke out in a cold sweat. How could she say these things? After appearing so friendly, calm, even generous. After all those conversations, all the emails, the months of going back and forth, my perpetual willingness to disclose, all those questions that she asked, sometimes the same one over and over again. The long lunches that we had in the beginning and my readiness to give extensive written replies. As well as the lunches and drinks, I had invited her over for dinner. Patrick had cooked for her, wooed her even. To think she hid her real feelings all that time, if these were real feelings. Unless I did something to change how she felt? Or was this who I am, who I was then? I felt strange. I should have put the phone down, turned it off. But I didn't. Instead I read on.

She described me as willowy. She debated the colour of my eyes, and whether or not I looked my age. She said that during our in-person meetings I twitched with nervous energy – a fidgety woman who somehow wrote tens of books but couldn't sit still for a coffee. A woman who chewed her nails. Who peeled a stray fruit sticker off the table, then stuck it back on and peeled it off again. A woman who sent her meal back because the meat was overdone. Someone who fussed. Who was not afraid to give orders, make demands. There was a quote from a previous colleague, unidentified: 'She is,' they said, 'a person with an instinct for her own survival.' In another context such a comment might be taken as a compliment, but it appeared here as a questioning of character. Inevitably she talked about Patrick. The journalist referred to something I had said in an old interview: 'He reads everything. I can't imagine how I would ever write a novel without him. His ideas have always been critical to the development of my work.' This was true, for years we had worked closely together and often collaborated. I'd helped him with his scripts just as much as he'd advised me on questions of editing. He had always been my first and best reader, but the article exaggerated this and made it sound as though he was the true conduit for my own work, its only reliable source.

And then it told the story of the accident. It told this in such a way as to make it sound like a section from a novel, 'exactly the kind that Blackwood might write', the article said, 'a scene she would plan meticulously before sitting down to execute it on the page'. Then it mused on the cost of this loss for whatever I might do next. Patrick as my single confidant, my ally, my better half, as I myself had once described him. It ruminated on the books I would not be able to write without him, my downward trajectory, the consequences of this loss. At the time of going to print, the article said, the accident remains under investigation.

My heart jumped in my chest. How did I not know this? I didn't know this, did I? He was dead – for me that was the end of everything. They had found him and he was dead. I thought that once I'd seen the body, once I'd answered all those questions and been told I could leave, everything was over. This was what I had assumed. All of a sudden I was finding it very hard to breathe.

When I went downstairs the next morning the house was quiet. The dishwasher hummed and there was a light turbulence to the air – the kind felt after a bustling and rapid departure. The smell of burnt toast. The girls' school bags gone from the hooks by the door. Adam's car not in the driveway. I stepped outside into the garden, and walked further to where the back of the property met the bush. The air was hot. I could feel the sting of the sun on my skin. I closed my eyes; some childhood recollection, of eucalyptus, heat. Around me the shrill call of the cicadas, rising then falling still. As if there were a disturbance that caught them unawares, made them watchful, suddenly silent. As if I were that thing, moving deeper and deeper now into the scrub; acacia, honeysuckle, bottlebrush, long feathery grasses against my legs. A circle of quiet opened around me. Then a sudden chill along my arms – the sound of voices, murmuring. From which direction? They seemed to be moving up from the trees, through them. Low voices shifting left then right as they found the path, or were they coming from behind? There she is. Or so I thought, so I thought I heard. Imagined, maybe. I spun to look. Nothing. Yet still the sound, the murmuration here, then there. As if something was about to appear, on the cusp of it. Then the dull realisation: blowflies buzzing, shooting left then right, then left again, their low and broken hum matching the tenor of a distant male voice, one then another. I shivered. The feeling, despite the naïve error, that people were talking. If Adam had said something. Or because of the things in that profile, what was written there about the case being under investigation. The neon glow of the woman's teeth, smiling at me while she asked me those questions on *The Morning Show*, Kate and John, or was it Sam and Kylie? Whatever they were called, the sweat beading on the investigator's bald head, in another country, another era almost, what felt like years ago then. Is now. How hard was it, that journalist asked, to become an artist in your own right? With being married to— Your own mother struggled in— that buzz again. Dry mouth. Whatever I had written in that book, whatever the book was, it had been overlaid now by the events of my life. It was treated as something like evidence – read backwards, against the grain. I had asked if I could publish the book anonymously, because there was so much of my own life in it, more than with anything else I'd written. This was before I'd even finished it. Ada and Valerie both thought I was joking. No, I said. I'm totally serious! Valerie looked at me; she understood.

But really, I said. Why not?

People would work it out, she said. All that would happen is that you'd be grilled about why you wanted to publish anonymously in the first place, which would be far worse. In the long run, anyway. Trust me.

Something stung my ankle and I took a step back, tripping on a fallen branch, catching myself on a sapling, then I heard May's voice calling. I had gone further into the bush than I realised. I've made coffee! she called. It was too late by then. Whatever I might have done, wherever I might have gone, the night before, in the dark. She called again. And once more. The tone rising. Where are you? For a moment, voices collapsed in on one another: her voice so like that of our own mother, all those years ago. Tones overlapping in my mind. I can remember that sound, feel it in my body. Even now. We must have been playing by the river. Or digging in the backyard. Somehow out of sight. She'd call: Lucie! May! And after she left, I kept hearing this, her voice. Then I'd look up and find it to be another woman calling to another child, down in the park, at the water's edge, the inflection identical. Women say all children sound the same when they call for their mother. When they cry. The reverse is equally true. In an instant I was ready to run to this voice, to see our mother walking towards us against the wind, her dress blowing back against her thighs. The blue dress with the white flecks, or spots or maybe flowers on it. Only to see someone else standing on the grass, or on the footpath, or in the sand, their body dense and solid – the sight of which made me feel all the more keenly our own mother's vanishing, as if she'd stepped off the edge of a flat world. No message, no traces, no signs. Did she or did she not make it? Did she get what she wanted in the end? In that article, the journalist asked this same question about me. I felt something then: small dark ants crawling up my leg. I reached down to smack them off. There you are— She called from high up, on the balcony. May's voice again.

I've been calling and calling, she said. Didn't you hear me? Yes, no. I wasn't sure. My white shirt visible through the scrub. I looked up at her, she was smaller from this distance. Coming! I called back, as I bent down to rub a red welt forming on my ankle.

Hello stranger, she said when I stepped inside. I tried to wake you earlier, but you were out cold. I drank the coffee she passed me.

What day is it? I asked. In the background the dishwasher beeped out the end of its cycle. May tapped a cigarette from its packet. You serious, she said? She went out on to the balcony. I followed.

I didn't think you—

Desperate times, desperate— she began, breaking off to inhale. You know, she said, waving her lighter in the air while she held the smoke in her lungs, feeling its slight burn.

Measures, I finished for her.

She nodded as she let the smoke out. You've slept it off, the flight?

I think so, I said as I reached over and took the cigarette from her fingers.

God, she said. I feel a wreck. I'm sorry, you know, for all that on your first night, Lexi and stuff. Hardly a welcome. I mean, it would have been nice if we could have behaved ourselves, for you at least.

I laughed a little, breathing out the smoke. I felt queasy.

How was the party? I've hardly seen you. I mean, all that promotion stuff was yesterday, right? Was it fun? And *The Morning Show*? I missed it with the school run.

The air around us was warm and close, sticky. A small

breeze came up from the land below and cooled our faces.
I felt it first stirring at my arm, then my cheek. The breeze
subsided. I shrugged, sucking on the cigarette. How's
Lex? I asked.

Ergh, she groaned. It feels never-ending. You know, I
only have ask her to do something, like pick her top up
of the floor, say, or take her wet towel to the bathroom
and she gives me this scowl, like she thinks I am an idiot
and why on earth should she do what I ask of her, because
I've become, in her eyes, a new irrelevance. It's like she's
striving to make me irrelevant, because the alternative is
unbearable – like the process of self-definition happens
through the negative, by erasing me, working herself out
against me. Without this, what? To acknowledge me, *and*
to become herself – these two things are incompatible,
mutually exclusive. She hisses at me sometimes, you
know. She does it when she pushes past me, rather than
just doing the thing I've asked her to do. The whole faint-
ing thing – it's the thought of the inside of my body that
repulses her.

Somewhere nearby a small wind chime was disturbed
by the breeze, two bells lightly striking against metal. She
stubbed out her cigarette, swilled her coffee. I don't know.
Perhaps it's just the weather.

And it was true, everywhere was so hot; it was too hot
outside, too hot inside. The humidity made everyone feel
cramped and irritated – thick, damp air stuck to the skin,
and seemed to resist all human movement. Trapped you
inside it. On the horizon, mountainous grey clouds were
building. Maybe a summer storm, May said, later today.

I had come unprepared for daily life lived under this

kind of heat, bringing with me little more than I had on
the ship: some jeans, a bikini, a sarong, a dress for those
cruise dinners and the prize ceremony in New York. I
noted this to my sister, as we stepped out into the yard
with our cups, a layer of sweat like an oily coating, a kind
of film, springing up over the whole surface of my body.
It was almost eleven. Adam had left for work at first light,
he'd be back after dinner. We had the rest of the day to
ourselves, she said, as if our keeping company were somehow illicit.

I'm desperate to get out, she said. I really haven't been
out since the surgery. I asked her whether it wasn't still
too soon, but she said no. We should go shopping, she
said. Besides, you need things. Let me just have another
coffee.

OK, I said then, sure.

We parked in the underground car park and took the
lift to the department store, stepping out into a haze of
perfume and bright lights. I followed May, pleased for
the distraction of the outing, as she turned left then right,
taking the route as it appeared before her, the shiny white
path weaving through the merchandise. Black-suited
women hovered at the edge of this, watching for our approach and smiling their bright smiles. They encouraged
us with small rectangular flags of cardboard on which
they had sprayed their scent. Ladies? each one said to us,
holding out her card, Good morning, ladies, Welcome,
ladies, Can I interest you, ladies? I held my breath a little
and pursed my lips, offering a curt smile as we passed
through. I felt dazed by the lights and the mirrors and the

glow of the white marble floor. May walked ahead, sure of her way through the labyrinth of merchandise. Around us every brand of perfume – and behind this, deeper into the building, the skincare and make-up – had its own self-contained set of shelves positioned in formation within ornate carousels, each with its own inner chamber into which a woman could be invited. The marble path wound its way through these, leading this way and that, confusing me.

Over here! May called. I spotted her far off, near the hats, but wasn't sure which path would take me there most directly. I needed to find the womenswear section – I'd been living out of a suitcase for weeks, with my party dress crushed against a pair of sneakers and a plastic bag full of dirty underwear and socks. I looked around. There was surely an order to the layout of sections here, a path leading out, but when this was overlaid with vertical and oblique mirrors, some at shoulder height, some higher up, combined with the echo of piano music – all this made me disoriented. The sales assistants, they must stand in wait for this, they must come to know the appearance of sudden helplessness, of exhaustion, a moment marked simply by the woman, me, stopping, looking around, looking around again, and sighing deeply. She puts her hand to a tube of face cream or mascara while she wonders what to do next, where she was supposed to go, how she got here, what she came for in the first place. She touches it, the small tube in front of her. She is mildly curious, mildly alarmed – albeit in a distracted way – at the variations of the one product: mascara for curly lashes, for false-lash effect, in colours from black through to electric blue. I was just putting this back into its plastic hole in the display unit when a white-coated woman appeared out of nowhere and, waving her arm between my body and the row of eye products, asked if I needed any help. I must have appeared startled, for she smiled very gently, then held out an oval-shaped mirror so that my own fatigued appearance was made plainly visible to me. With her free hand she touched a palette of eye shadows. These colours would look stunning on you, she said.

I'm OK, I replied, snapping out of something. I just got distracted. I'm actually looking for someone. I turned round, peeked above the rows of shelves – my sister was nowhere in sight.

It's complimentary, the saleswoman said, noting my paralysis. The makeover. And if you buy one of the products you get another at a discount. If you buy three items, though, you get a fourth free. Here, she said, gently touching the sleeve of my shirt. Why not take a break? she asked.

I am tired, I thought to myself, I am tired after all, telling myself this as a form of justification as I sat down on the stool and arranged my bag on my lap. I could wait here, like this, I thought, and my sister will come back and find me. But if you see her, I said, she's wearing a pale-yellow dress.

The saleswoman seemed not to hear me. Now, she said, I'm just going to match the colours first. If you could close your eyes? I did as I was told. I felt the warmth of her face leaning close to mine, then the cool tip of a brush as it worked a creamy ointment into the crevices of my eyelid, then into the dip between the corner of the eye and the bridge of the nose, then across the deeper curve where the eyeball sinks back into the skull. I'm just getting rid of all those shadows, she said. The brush continued to move in tiny feathery motions over my skin. You want to get right in there, she said, and get rid of those darker bits. As if a face should be flat, without curvatures. Non-dimensional. With her free hand she placed her fingers against my temple, preventing my head from swaying away from the brush. Her fingertips were very cool, her touch very light. It was an easy touch to want more of. If you could open your eyes and look up? And close again? Beautiful, she said. Every time I opened my eyes she was there in front me, very close, I could see the fine, pale hair across her cheek, the freckles on the bridge of her nose. In that moment I was a child once more, standing still with my eyes closed while someone wiped my face with a warm flannel, gently brushed my hair, and helped me push my arms through the sleeves of my sweater – in that moment I was that very same person being so gently prepared for the world, made ready, loved. For how long had she been gone, that child? I wondered where my sister had got to, and if she was looking for me, but I couldn't open my eyes because the sales assistant was holding my chin with her free hand while she used a new brush, a slightly spongy brush, to work something into my lash line. When I was a child and couldn't sleep, Joan would sometimes sit at my bedside and stroke me in not so dissimilar a fashion, running her fingertips very lightly over the translucent skin of my eyelids. On those wakeful evenings I couldn't keep my eyes closed – I couldn't sleep, I said, because my eyes wouldn't stay shut, each time I tried to close them they would just spring open again although there was nothing in particular I wanted to look at, nor was I really even seeing anything when my eyes were open. The closing of the eyes and the keeping them closed was a basic law of sleep that as a child I easily forgot, and so Joan would come and gently remind me of this. She would pull the covers up to my chin and perch on the corner of the mattress, the springs creaking as her weight sank into the bed. The mattress would tilt a little, and I would roll towards her, my knees resting against her fat hip. Now, she'd say, close your eyes, as her fingertips glided down over my eyelids, as far as my cheekbones, where they would lift off and start back again above my brows. My sister would be sound asleep by then, giving out little snorts and snores, completely oblivious to my struggle. And Joan would say, as I turned my head towards my sister's bed, Now never you mind about her, it's you I'm interested in, and her fingers would glide down again over my eyes, and again, and again. At that time of the evening her hands smelt faintly of the washing-up liquid that she had squirted into the sink and of the rubber gloves that she wore to withstand the heat of the water. Over the top of this floated the sweeter scent of the cream she massaged into her hands once the kitchen had been put in order, and the slightly sour tang of the Vaseline jelly that she applied into her cuticles where they were often cracked and torn from the cold. Sometimes, during the day she would chew on the little tags of white skin that came loose from the edge of her nails, and when she had at last shorn them off there would be small red dots, like little pinpricks. Again and again and again her fingers stroked my face, just as a river might carve its way into the earth through centuries of rain, and beneath her fingertips I could feel my eyes slowly losing their hardness, I could feel my eye sockets loosening their hold, and I would fall asleep then under the spell of Joan's hands, under the fat padded fingers, a little greasy from the creams, sometimes puckered and creased on the tips if the washing-up gloves turned out to have a hole in them.

There, came the saleswoman's voice. She lifted the brush away from my eyes. I could feel the heat from her body close to mine, the intensity of her presence as she scrutinised her handiwork, my skin. You can open your eyes now, she said. Everything was blurry. A large silvery disk wobbled in front of my face: the woman, holding out a mirror. I blinked. She held the mirror closer, then flipped it over to reveal another mirror of greater magnification. Before I could get up she started on her monologue, explaining the prices and discounts and potential improvements to skin tone and other lasting effects of the product. I averted my gaze, stood to go. That's lovely, I said. Thank you. But I really have to find someone now. Where was she?

I could smell the make-up on my face. My eyelashes felt heavy with the triple coat of mascara. I couldn't see May anywhere. I reached for my phone then realised it was back at the house, turned off in the drawer.

Then suddenly she was there beside me. Found you! she said. She had got what she wanted. I'm so sorry, she told me, but we really have to go. Did you pick up the things you came for?

I had forgotten what I needed. Anyway, she said, if not, we can always come back tomorrow – it's just that Lexi has swim squad this afternoon. Normally it's on Thursday morning, but because of various Christmas events and school carnivals, they've moved this week to the afternoon. I'm really sorry, it totally slipped my mind, but I have to swing by the school and pick her up, I'm afraid we don't have time to stop off at the house. Do you mind?

No, I said, of course not.

Jess is going to a friend's place, Adam will pick her up on his way home. It's just Lexi. It should only be an hour or so, max.

As we drove up out of the underground car park I was dazed by the light. The fluorescent glare of the mall was one thing, the Antipodean glow quite another: luminous, almost other-worldy, the kind of light that penetrates every atom of the body, every cell, as if the body might be broken down by it. Thinned out. Disintegrated. I rifled through my handbag to find my sunglasses. Then I lifted them to the light, checking the state of the lenses, the smear marks. My shirt cuffs fell back from my wrists. The bruising was still there, fading, soon to be gone. How hard he'd gripped my wrists. Don't, don't do this. One of us had said that. Please. May watched the traffic, waiting for a gap that would let her turn out on to the street. A wide yellow circle on each inner wrist, a few small dark capillaries showing inside these, like something under a microscope. I pressed my thumb to the most colourful bruise, testing its tenderness. At the time of questioning no one had thought to ask me about this, there was no need to examine me – it was not, after all, the state of my body that was under investigation.

I wiped at the lenses and pushed the glasses on to my face.

16

We collected Lexi from outside the school gates and drove
to the indoor pool, dropping her at the entrance before
May found a parking spot under the shade of a tree. The
air conditioning in the car was cold, and stepping out into
the blazing sun made me dizzy. I felt a little sick again;
maybe it was the weather after all and not the jet lag. On
the road, patches of tarmac were melting in the heat. At
the entrance to the sports complex the automatic doors
slid open – a burst of humid, chlorinated air ringing with
the yells of children. We stepped inside and the doors slid
shut behind us. There was the smell of ice cream and chips
and instant coffee. May showed her entry ticket and we
walked through, finding a place on the damp metal bench.
Around us the air was thick and warm, tangy with chlorine. Lexi stood hunched over near the blocks, her arms
folded across her abdomen as the coach issued instructions
for the first laps. Her swimming cap was in place, her
purple goggles pulled down over her eyes and pressed to
her sockets. We could see her nodding, then pinching her
nose and blowing to clear her ears. Her legs were long and
thin with knobbly knees, and she pushed them together,

bending them a little in a posture that suggested coldness but could not possibly mean coldness given the soupy air of the building. She was making herself smaller, making herself ready, her muscles preparing themselves for the dive and the sprint to come, for the willowy slip through water in which her prepubescent body would be made almost invisible, just as she wanted it to be, a slick of blue lycra under ripples. Back and forth, back and forth she went. At the end of each lap she somersaulted underwater, flipping her body to face the other direction, and as she pushed off from the wall a silvery stream of bubbles floated out behind her.

In the wake of the prize I had been offered a generous contract for the next book and had signed under Ada's enthusiasm, feeling slightly delirious and not thinking about the fact that I had no real idea what I would write. But you're brilliant! Ada cried, and we love you and I know you'll do something amazing. I'd agreed to this without really considering the deadline and the reality of it was now starting to sink in. I thought of all the scenes I'd cut from the previous novel and wondered if I could use them in the service of a new work. They were sections that I'd cut at Ada's urging, and the book had gone on to succeed in just the way she hoped it would, but I still thought fondly of those scenes – so many of them loosely autobiographical. Orphaned scenes, one might call them, from a provincial life. Scenes that May had also wanted me to withhold when I told her about them.

She didn't like to think about these things. She certainly didn't want to read my version of them. Whereas I preferred to leave no stone unturned. Please don't, she said. Or maybe she said, I don't know how you do it. I thought about those deleted sections while watching Lexi coast back and forth, back and forth, soothed by the ease of her movements, the grace of them. It was hypnotising. I felt that heavy lull beginning in my head – the opposite of a migraine, the start of any work of art. A sense of being dazed, slow, too open, distracted by all things, porous. The mind a fat, heavy bee, its thoughts bumping slowly up and up and up against the glass. Although sometimes my migraines precipitated this feeling, exaggerated it, made me more attentive: how thin and white the light could be, the smell of the air, the strange new bitterness of certain foods that had tasted quite ordinary the day before. Cheese. Peanuts. Brown bread. Everything then seems easy to imagine, hard to realise. How suddenly the world can be made strange.

Whatever I wrote – however I had described it in one of those many scenes that were cut – it's true that Joan died suddenly one winter's night. It was an aneurysm, they said. She passed without a sound, and our father woke to find her this way in the morning. I'd expanded on this at one point, giving it extra colour in an earlier draft. But it didn't need it – the event itself was plain and terrible. There was nothing else to say other than that it happened. At least that was what we were told as children, and there was never anything that made me doubt the truth of this. It was a death too sudden for my father to make sense of, and he reached the end of his line. There are only so many losses one can bear, only so much that one can accommodate, internalise, carry. He had never intended to stay in England, and once Joan died there was no reason to. He booked us flights to Sydney, took a long-term lease on a tiny second-hand bookshop on the main street of what looked like a rural ghost town, and bought a corner of land that a farmer was selling off.

I'll never forget that first journey, no matter how many times I delete it from one book or another. To get to our new house we took that long road west for hours. At first there were various roadside stops; a fruit stall, a diner, public toilets in a park, but after that any building looked to be abandoned – its paint flaking off, rusted cars and machinery in the front yards, overgrown grass. Here and there poplars grew along the edge of the road, some tall and well established while others stood in small thickets, having sprung up wild. It was coming into autumn and the leaves on the trees were a deep gold, like the kind of leaves one reads about in fairy tales. After a time, the trees gave way to grass, miles and miles of dry grass, stretching out into the far distance. At certain points the road ran parallel to the train tracks and in these parts there grew tall, feathery grasses with white plumes, and smaller clumps of grass with purple seed heads. When the road did not run beside the train tracks it continued on by pasture and farmland, vast stretches of dry country fenced off with barbed wire. Here and there the barbs were snagged with clumps of sheep wool, or remnants of plastic bags flapping in the wind, as weathered prayer flags might in some other faraway place. At the side of the road, along the verge, the dirt was pale. Further on it gave way to grey, lichen-covered stones, and soon after that banks of red soil. Clouds cast wide, lumbering shadows. We drove for hours. We drove with the windows down, and hot, dry air filled the car. Dust rose up behind us. In that part of the country there had been no rain for months. What would normally be green pastures, full of clover and sorghum, was then barren, the ground hard and pale. You could kick it with the heel of a boot and not break through the surface.

Our new house was called Hilltops. It stood high up on a rise in a parched paddock, with a flank of forest running behind it. Once inhabited by a farm worker, the patch of land was now no longer fit for grazing, bare and eroded, and every time the wind blew, clouds of grit were carried in its wake. Behind the house was a large metal water tank, out front an abandoned vegetable garden. Bushfires burnt further north, with thick funnels of grey and orange smoke visible in the distance. Downhill there was a shimmer of water where the dam for the neighbouring sheep had shrunk to a small blister. Large, dead gums stood on either side, trees that would have once provided ample shade. White animals gathered in the mud to drink.

Patrick had read this early scene, one that was still in place right up to the fourth or fifth draft of that last book, and thought I should keep it all. What do you mean, he said, when I told him I was cutting out much of that childhood history. Not least the part where I had said to our father on the first long drive to the farm, Maybe Mummy will be waiting for us. Maybe she'll surprise us again.

Pardon? my father had said.

Like she did that time in the hotel, I replied. May told me.

I remember how my father gave a soft grunt: disbelief,

surprise, maybe the slight choke of shock. He tightened his grip on the steering wheel. You always did have an overactive imagination, he said, keeping his eyes on the road. Sweetheart, you haven't seen your mother since, what, since you were a tiny child. I'm surprised you even remember her.

But you can't do that, Patrick told me. You can't cut that whole scene, the drive and everything. I love that bit. I just shook my head, I found it hard to even think of that scene, to remember it. I couldn't have it in a book. I'd tried before and every time deleted it at the last minute, filling the gap with a bridging passage. Besides, Patrick continued, why is everything so ahistorical now? As if we're all made of fucking plastic, smooth and cool to the touch – which, you know, we kind of are, or will be, all those microparticles and whatever. Why not let her crap on? It's your life. Or hers, I mean.

OK, I said. OK. But Ada will hate it.

From the very beginning the collaboration between Patrick and me felt inevitable. The pleasure we took in reading each other's work, and in literally finishing each other's sentences – on paper and aloud – was profound. Our collaboration was, I thought at times, even better than the sex. The feeling of our minds being conjoined, thinking with each other, in sync. The transformation that I felt in the midst of this. The best sex, in fact, was when we talked, every now and then, over the top of our pleasure about some image or phrase, or asked the other a question which they had to answer, or were compelled to answer, while being touched in such a way that made it incredibly difficult to speak coherently. The contrast seemed to heighten everything, intensify every sensation: I'm sorry, he'd say. I didn't quite catch that. Could you just repeat that answer for me?

If full sentences were a requisite in that scenario, when we worked we often spoke only in fragments; he would raise a thought and leave it unfinished, distracted by something, and I would pick up the tail end of it and carry this along. I wrote the words, and he often filtered the larger ideas and the logic, while the mental pictures, the intertwining of visual features – this was the thing we did together. It was hard to imagine what any of my books would look like if it hadn't been for his editorial suggestions, such as I called them. His thoughts on my work had always been generous and lengthy; when reading drafts of my fiction, he would often stop to comment on sections that could possibly be expanded. Or he'd invent plot developments for the parts where I'd got stuck. He was especially good at that, imagining dramatic complications. I think there's room to add something more about the moment where, he'd start to say, and I'd put my hand up to stop him. Hang on, I'd reply while I picked up my pen and notebook. OK, I said, fire away, and he'd continue.

You know the moment when they arrive at the hotel and the porter, what if it went . . . Patrick could deliver in perfect syntactical form whole paragraphs, paragraphs that I noted down, sometimes pausing to pick up in speech where he left off. But then what if, I'd say, what if she didn't phrase it exactly like that but turned back a moment, went inside to get something and then . . .

He was nodding furiously. Yes, yes, he said, and that would mean the timing might—

I would then revise these new sections before adding them to the draft. There were so many of these collaborative moments in every book – not only paragraphs but long and complex sentences, striking phrases and larger sections, sometimes up to a page or two – that I have now lost count and would struggle to identify them. But they are there, like a weft thread running through the fabric of my work. He was my first reader and perhaps the only one that mattered. I hadn't expected to feel like this – I realised then that I hadn't really thought about how impossible it might be to try to write a book without him. Although it wasn't just the books that we had laboured on together. There were also the screenplays, guest talks, the occasional public lecture that one or the other of us had been invited to give. Working together like this was the closest I have ever come to feeling wholly and entirely understood. I had wanted to protect this feeling, this bond. I wanted nothing to disrupt it – not family, not weekend hobbies and least of all children. Joshua was already taxing in this way, taking up many of our weekends and evenings. I loved him to the extent that any woman can love a child that is not her own. But I would never pretend that I could mimic real maternal affection for him; I was an ally, sometimes a friend. He was always a little wary of me, sensing, as any child does, that I resented having to share Patrick, resented the time lost.

By the poolside, nausea was rising up in me again. It should have gone by now if it was, after all, due to the jet lag. I thought maybe it was the warm chemical air with its smell of chlorine, or the noise. I was often sensitive to these things. Speakers were positioned in the corners of the ceiling and an announcement bounced through, calling a number plate. Christmas carols started up over by the therapy pool, where an aqua aerobics class was about to begin. Children screamed. Somewhere else a radio was playing. One sound cut across the other.

May was talking but I struggled to keep up with what she was saying. Something about Adam, Lexi. My attention was dissipating. In the lead-up to the publication of the book I'd been finding it hard to concentrate, and now it was worse. My mind wouldn't settle. It was difficult to focus. If I was reading, the words seemed distant, muted. I was unable to sit still, to make myself comfortable. If I was listening to something or someone, I often vagued out. My thoughts felt disconnected. Even my handwriting showed this change: my words looked scrawled and flattened, as if there were letters missing, when previously my handwriting had been neat and orderly.

It's only natural, Patrick had said as the book started to take its final shape and the publicity geared up, to feel anxious about this one. But that was not it, I didn't think. Or not the whole of it. Although it might have been easier to put my state down to these more ordinary pressures, something that would pass in due course.

There's a lot riding on it, he said.

What do you mean?

Well, you've been working on it for a long time.

I work on everything for a long time.

Not exactly, he said. This one's different. I mean— his voice trailed off as he tapped at the computer keyboard, blue light reflecting off his glasses.

What? What do you mean?

He stopped what he was doing and looked up at me. I don't know, I guess I mean, I mean you've given things up for this one. He took his glasses off, rubbed at his eyes. Or however you want to say it. We both have.

I knew what he was referring to and I didn't want to talk about it, I didn't think it was possible that we could still talk about it. That there was anything else to say. It was late winter then and I was tired. The months of cold, wet weather made me feel low. He knew how much my work mattered to me, and I was tired of having to justify this, to explain again and again my reasons, to keep talking about the child I would not have.

But I thought, he kept saying, that you'd written that all out, got over it now. The old fear of repeating my mother's mistakes. We've been through this, he said, pages and pages and pages of it. Isn't it time to move on? We could still have this, together.

In the end my own mother had chosen against me. Or so I understood, so I had been told. Us, rather – May and me. I thought about this often, sometimes compulsively; I knew that my need to write was stronger than any other urge. I couldn't risk it, I had explained to Patrick, the repetition of that collateral damage that May and I had felt as small girls, the harm that came about as a side effect of our mother's departure. But Patrick was impulsive and didn't think about repercussions, or else he'd felt himself immune to these for so long that he no longer cared. Yet in my mind there was no question: my artistic ambition was paramount. It always had been. It still was, is. He knew this. I had thought that was what he loved. But how much ambition can a woman lay claim to before she is ruined by it? Unsexed, seen as living in error. Before it is challenged and held against her. Patrick, telling me how much we had both sacrificed. It was a question of valour, of giving up differently; one form of renunciation being more acceptable than the other.

He sighed, and went back to whatever he was working on. I had started the book when I was the same age my mother was when she left us – my sister and me. It seemed fitting somehow, this closing-up of numbers. To start where she finished – the same number marking both end and beginning. I wanted to give shape to the events so as not to repeat them, to tell what I knew of her story, or my version of it. It was a way of making her own life more distinct from mine, and of honouring it – because I couldn't shake the feeling that her unfinished story had been buried inside me and was waiting to live itself out – the child a vector for the woman. As I was growing up, my father often commented on how alike we were, mother and daughter. The spitting image, he'd say sometimes under his breath. His gaze a little dreamy. I felt frightened by this somehow, not proud.

Our father said that she left because she couldn't stand it any longer. But what she couldn't stand he was never clear about. Once he said it was the heat. Or the country itself, the one he had brought her to. Another time, when we were throwing some tantrum, he said, in a fury, No wonder she left! For many years her dresses stayed hanging in the wardrobe. She took her hairbrush but left her jewellery. Our father was a proud man, not one to admit to his own feelings. He was never going to say that she left because of him, or that it was his fault that she ran away – as he once described it, as though she herself were a small child. She made her choice, he said, and we're the ones that had to live with it.

But if I had started the book then, when I was in my early thirties, I stopped it soon after. It felt too difficult, too much. Too consuming. I couldn't live with this and so put it away, saved to some archive folder. Although in the end the story forced itself upon me – I tried diverting my attention by working on another project, and yet found this same old material pushing its way through, insisting. And so I gave into it. I did what I had to do.

May stood up. Sorry, she said, I just have to go to the bathroom. She was, she told me, still bleeding a little. The discharge on the sanitary pads reminded her of the watery pink fluid that you find on the synthetic rectangles lining the plastic supermarket packets of precut meat. The meat is very dead, very edible, she said, rifling through her bag to check for a new pad, and you don't think about this until you lift it away and realise it is still leaking.

In front of us a group of large women in bobbled bathing caps stepped carefully into the water. Their stomachs were round and their legs thin. The instructor stood on the edge of the pool and showed them the moves: a light jog to the beat of 'Jingle Bells'. Squats to the tempo of 'Dashing Through the Snow'. The women were singing along. The instructor wore a pointed red hat with a tinsel pompom on the top, and a T-shirt that read 'Santa's Little Helper'. I watched Lexi continue to move smoothly through the water, and a little while later, once May had returned and Lexi had done her laps, May hopped down to the pool edge and held open the worn beach towel. She wrapped this round her daughter's back before Lexi stepped away and pulled off her goggles and cap, her blond hair a bright, wiry mess.

On the way out I bought her an ice cream from the snack bar – The aunt's privilege, I said to May when she looked at me with disapproval. Then we piled into the hot car and turned for home, only to find the freeway clogged with traffic due to an accident. The sun started to sink down behind the ridge while we sat idling in the gridlock. I leant back, let my gaze drift to the side mirror. From where I sat I could see Lexi in the back seat, her eyes glazed over, sleepy. The side of her head rested against the seat belt. A horn behind us. A sign flashing on the roadside instructed all vehicles to merge into one lane. I need to pee, I said. How long do you think?

God knows.

The car idled. The lights changed to green but still we didn't move. They turned red again. Then green. The traffic was so heavy I could only just see the front vehicles, the ones nearest the lights edging their way slowly forwards. In the back seat Lexi had fallen asleep, her mouth slightly open and her cheek still leaning against the grey seat-belt strap. The driver ahead of us braked suddenly. May pressed on her horn. Hey, fucker! she yelled. Sorry, she said then, turning to Lexi before realising that she hadn't heard her swearing. What does she call me now? she said, squinting against the sun, which was coming in at an angle through the windscreen. Hypocrite, she says to me. *Don't be such a hypocrite. You swear,* May said, imitating her daughter. She sighed heavily.

It was different when she was very young, she said, when she was a newborn. All she did was sleep. We were in sync then, in our mutual exhaustion. People say that as a joke, don't they, 'to sleep like a baby'. But she looked so old and wrinkly and tired from the journey of just making it into the world. Now it's as if we are in sync again: exhausting each other by turns. May glanced in the rear-view mirror. She's out cold now. She even twitches when she dreams. Her and the dog both.

The traffic had stalled completely. May leant forwards on to the steering wheel. On her right hand, I noticed, she wore Joan's emerald ring, the one that had been a gift from our father and which she used to remove every evening and place in a glass on the windowsill while she did the washing-up. How had May got the ring? I was about to say something when she continued her line of thought: You know it's like some strange regression, she said, some inversion. If I drive, she sleeps. If I ask her to go to bed, she screams at me. I don't want her to hate me, I don't even want to consider the *possibility* that she might hate me, but sometimes I think she does, you know, and when she does I think that she doesn't really want to feel that way either, and then is so enraged and confused by her own reaction to me – the reaction that she had because of me – that in a weird, complicated kind of way she hates me more for making her feel these things in the first place and is almost horrified or surprised or somehow repelled maybe by her own reaction, and doesn't know what to do with the first feeling of dislike or the secondary one of repulsion so just throws them all at me. Like, what the hell. I don't know, she said, I mean I didn't think any of this was supposed to happen until she was older. She's only eleven, not even officially a teenager yet. I thought I had years before it all fell apart.

The traffic moved forwards, she accelerated too fast and braked hard. I watched her ringed finger glide over the steering wheel. The car behind honked. My window was spattered with white flecks of dried milk from where Jess had squeezed a drink carton and the milk had sprayed out. I reached up, picked at the flecks with the edge of my fingernail.

The highway, or the section of it that we were stuck in, was lined by palms, their wide fronds circling gently in the breeze. In the distance I could see as far as the blue ridge of mountains and imagined, behind this, the wide, vast country that we once used to travel through on the journey home from school, that dried-up corner of farmland still out there, somewhere. The flowers baked dead in the heat, broken down to dust and husk. No signs.

I never had been back there, to the farm. Not as an adult. I could still remember it, though, as clear as anything, how the eye stretched out across the paddocks to the far ridge in the distance. The ground of the farm was so hard and rocky, grazed for so long by so many head of cattle, that we were lucky if the perennial grasses came up green in the springtime. The earth there was tinged with red, and the bleached grass pale yellow, closer to white. I remember this, watching it, how it was smoothed in one direction by the wind. The grass short enough not to ripple exactly, but to be tussled a little so that you could see the gloss and shade of it – from far away it looked thick and dense, like the pile on a piece of velvet. Further out, behind the line of our property, white specks dotted the empty ground: the dry, parched bones of animals. In winter the house there was the coldest place I had ever known; the floor covered in brown linoleum and the windows fashioned from old, thin glass. In the kitchen the cabinets and benches were of lime-green Formica, and mice would take shelter in the corners of these, eating holes in the end of the bread, chewing through the cereal box.

It was true, in part, what that *New Yorker* reporter said. I hadn't gone back there even when my father was dying. We had fallen out badly many years before and both of us were too proud and too offended to make amends. Of course it wouldn't be me to whom he gave Joan's ring. He never met Patrick and didn't like what I told him, going so far as to blame Patrick for the books I wrote, the books that made me so successful and which my father despised. He thought I was exposing myself, cheapening my experience by writing about it so candidly, if not in the books then in the interviews that followed. During one of our last long-distance phone calls I tried to explain that it was fiction, or at least that any truth was conveyed with the aid of fictional tropes. It was designed to make the reader feel that it was all real – a lie told well should sound true. He particularly disliked what he perceived to be their confessional mode, despite me trying to explain that his very perception of this was a sign of their success. The achievement of believability. But I was his child, and he couldn't see the artfulness of this, couldn't see past the occasional facts that he alone could recognise. More to the point, perhaps, as an immigrant child he had so effectively mimicked the British character that the notion of decency and the overriding faith in the saving power of a stiff upper lip left him unable to tolerate my own more liberal choices. Maybe his incomprehension was something my mother had suffered from too. He never did understand why I took up with Patrick, why on earth I chose this.

Which terminal? the taxi driver had asked. Two, please, Patrick replied. But halfway there, with his hand on my thigh, he changed his mind. I'm sorry, he said, leaning forwards to talk to the driver. There's been a mistake. Would you mind turning round and dropping us off at a different address? I knew he was much older than me, but at the same time he seemed somehow ageless, as all new gods appear in the eyes of those who worship them. Of course there had been others before him, other boys mainly, boys who performed the act quickly with their sports socks still on. Sometimes their trousers scrunched up around their ankles. You know what you'll have to lose, one of them must have said to me – the first one, the boy I dated during the summer in that last year of high school. Or was it: Are you ready to lose it? Or even, You know what this means, right? We would have been in the cafeteria, eating hot chips with chicken salt and gravy. Afterwards I felt sick. He was annoyed that I didn't bleed, suspecting someone else had got there first. No, I said, but he didn't believe me. The water, as the car moved through a deep puddle, sprayed up against my window. A change of plan, Patrick might have said to the driver, not a mistake.

17

I thought it might have been May's driving that was making me feel worse. The way she accelerated with the small gaps in the traffic then braked hard, jolting us along. Or maybe it was the smell of the car: she had one of those air-freshener decorations hanging from the rear-view mirror. Either way, I really needed to stop to go to the toilet and get some water from somewhere. My mouth was sticky and dry. My throat tight. I'd long finished the bottle I had in my bag, the water lukewarm and tasting of plastic, and now felt woozy. May accelerated again and once more dropped her foot hard on the brake. I was close to throwing up.

It took nearly an hour to inch our way towards the intersection, the lights green then red then green again. There were blue patrol lights further along, marking the scene of the accident. In the back seat Lexi had woken up and was tapping on the window, keeping beat to whatever song played in her head. After the intersection it looked like the traffic eased at least a little; before the lights there was a merge, beyond this there was an exit. Where the accident had been cleared away, a cop was packing up the bright-orange witches' hats and waving people on. A line of indicators were flashing as cars veered right, away from the inside lane. May was drumming her fingers on the steering wheel.

She reached across to the glovebox. Sorry, she said. Could you pop that open? There should be a packet of candy. Since the surgery, she told me, she'd often felt a little unsteady. Blood sugar levels, they say. Squashed next to the car manual and a packet of tissues was a bag of boiled sweets. If you could just pass me one, she said. The bag was open and the smell was sickeningly sweet: mint and raspberry. The heat had caused them to melt and stick together. Don't worry, she said, a clump is fine, better maybe. I passed one to her.

God, I said, smelling my fingers and wiping them on my jeans. I don't know how you can eat those. Don't they just remind you?

What do you mean?

Of that night, I said. I glanced out of the window. When our mother came back with the sweets, at the hotel. You told me about it.

May frowned and checked the rear-view mirror before merging.

I mean, I know the scene from your novel, she said. I read that bit. But I took it as fiction. She opened her mouth as if about to say something more when the car next to us on the inside lane sounded its horn. Look! Lexi yelled, suddenly alert. Her palm pressing against the window. There's McDonald's. Right there, look! Can we go? Can we, Mum? I'm starving. I'm really, *really* starving. Please? Just this once? Please. This traffic is going to go on

forever anyhow. *Please*, Mum – I'm so hungry I'm about
to pass out.

I wanted to ask May about what she'd just said, but the
space for that question quickly closed up.

No way, May replied. You're not eating that crap. Besides, you just had an ice cream.

That was ages ago. And it's not crap.

There's plenty of food at home. We'll be there soon.

But Dad does!

What do you mean Dad does?

He eats it.

Well he shouldn't either, and anyway, he's not you.
Look, the traffic is clearing.

So? Even if it does it'll still be hours until dinner and I
really have to eat now. Didn't you see how fast I swam?

May glanced up in the rear-view mirror and caught
Lexi's eye.

In the end she complied, or capitulated – take your
pick. OK, fine, she sighed, raising her eyebrows. Just this
once. I felt a wave of relief; maybe some cold lemonade
would help the nausea. Maybe I just needed to get out of
the car. May flicked the indicator on. But never again,
you hear me? Then the bright neon sign overhead. The
arrows pointing us to the speaker where we would place
our order, then move forwards to the collection point.

But I don't want drive-through, Lexi replied, indig-
nant. I didn't say I wanted drive-through.

It's quicker this way, and you can listen to music while
you eat.

But I want to sit down.

Are you serious? May said. You are sitting down.

I want to sit at a table because the sauce always leaks and besides, I need to go to the toilet. I do, she said, I really do!

May grimaced a little then did a U-turn, so as to drive around the front to the parking bays. She reverse-parked and ended up at a bad angle, across the lines. Lexi and I got out while she straightened up the car. While I stood there, balanced on the edge of the concrete guttering, I had a strange sense of déjà vu, something to do with the mangy box hedging around the parking area, how the hedging plants were stumpy and not bushy at all, each an isolated and ailing plant that held inside it some glossier version of itself. The ground around each plant was pale grey in colour, not brown as one might expect of soil, and had the appearance of dirty sand. Cigarette butts were visible here and there, as were plastic and metal bottle tops. There was a garbage bin nearby, the lid covered in bird droppings. Already I couldn't think of what had happened that day, couldn't remember it clearly. There had been the bright lights of the shopping centre, neon on white, and the smell of chlorine. The impressions were intense but their timing obscure. Everything felt to have happened on top of itself, layered, when in truth I knew that the events had been spread out.

Lucie, Lexi called. Lucie! Are you coming? I had been dragging the toe of my shoe through the dirt, over and over, engraving a line. The others were ready. The car lock beeped and clicked, or maybe it clicked and beeped. Another car emitted the same sound, only in reverse, as its passengers made their approach after having eaten and were now ready to make their way home.

I went to the toilets then met the others at the counter, where May was placing the order. Lexi stood next to her, eager to make sure she got it right. But then, at the last minute, after May had ordered my lemonade and her coffee, Lexi decided that actually she wanted something else – not the regular meal pack, but the jumbo one, the one with the triple-layer cheeseburger and the extra-large thick shake. It was a special; the laminated ad was propped up against the cash register. May refused, brushing her away and placing the order as planned, but Lexi exclaimed that No, that wasn't right, that she hadn't seen the ad when they decided, when they stood back and read the board together, and that they needed to change the order, saying this directly to the cashier. My Mum's got it wrong, she told her.

Stop it, Lexi, May hissed. I've already ordered, she said, and Lexi elbowed her sharply in the ribs, a reflex action almost, as they were standing very close to one another. I'm sorry, the cashier said, Which size did you want? They both spoke in unison: Regular, Jumbo, and the cashier gave an embarrassed giggle as she looked down. Please, Mum. Please, Lexi said, her voice rising, drawing attention.

Go. And. Sit. Down. May replied, saying this loudly enough that others in the line could hear. Lexi flushed with rage. From where I hovered at the side, near the stack of brown plastic trays, I could see that she was itching to hit her mother and in the end expelled a small slug of fury by looking down and lightly, but quite fiercely, kicking May's ankle. I saw May steel herself in order to pretend, in public at least, that this hadn't happened. That she hadn't felt a thing. That it hadn't hurt. She didn't bend down to touch her ankle, didn't rub it, although from where I stood I could see the red mark. Then Lexi retreated. She found a table in the corner, took the seat by the wall and sulked. A few minutes later May came carrying a tray with the smaller-sized meal, not the jumbo, along with the chips and coffee. Lexi pushed the tray away. I'm not hungry any more, she said.

Oh really, May replied. Well, you can take this back and ask for a refund. You can explain. Lexi huffed and whispered something under her breath.

What was that? What did you say?

Nothing.

Tell me what you said.

I said nothing. Nothing. I didn't say *the word nothing*, I just said nothing. I sighed, she said. Is that OK? Am I allowed to sigh? Am I allowed to breathe in your company? Or maybe not, maybe I'm not even allowed to do that.

I saw tears well up in May's eyes. We came here because of you, she said, we came here because you asked us to. Look, she said, I hate McDonald's. The coffee is foul, the place smells, the lights are too bright. Lucie – just look at Lucie, the lights here make her look green. And you just kicked me. In public. And everything they cook here tastes of fucking gherkin, sweaty, slimy fucking gherkin.

She pushed her chair back. I've had enough. I really have. Lucie and I are going home now, she said, without looking at me. You can sit here and finish the meal you asked for, and after that you can catch the bus. Then she slung her handbag over her shoulder and made for the door. I looked at Lexi and said, I'm not interfering here, you better work this out fast. And Lexi replied, She's bluff-ing. She always bluffs. I raised my eyebrows at her, partly horrified by her stubbornness, partly full of admiration, partly afraid, and followed May out. She unlocked the car and we got in. She pulled the seat belt across her body and slipped the key into the ignition. The engine turned over and she put the car into reverse. Behind us, in the restaurant, I imagined Lexi sitting, still sulking, hunched over in the orange plastic chairs, her elbows on the beige plastic table – like something out of a Hopper painting.

You're not really, are you? I said. But May only reached forwards and switched the dial for the radio, swivelling it until she reached the classical station. Even though we'd hardly been inside the restaurant for more than fifteen minutes, the car was stifling hot. I felt faint. May turned on the air conditioner just as I unwound my window. Maybe I should stay? I said. But she only checked her mir-ror before reversing out of the parking spot. The fumes from the exhaust blew back into the car. She paused a moment, then started to move off towards the exit.

Really, I said. I could take the bus with her. Does she even know where we are here? Does the bus even stop nearby? It's just the highway. The radio station was break-ing up with static. She adjusted the dial and sat back. At the corner of the restaurant building, before the exit, was a zebra crossing. May drove slowly and stopped there for a family with three small children, the mother in the middle pushing the pram, and two children either side. Halfway across, one of the children dropped a toy – some small cloth bunny – only it wasn't until they had almost reached the pavement that they realised this, and had to walk back into the middle of the road, all three of them, to fetch it, and then once again make their way to the other side. The exit was visible ahead of us, the traffic looked to be clearing. May turned the air conditioning on to high and I felt goosebumps rise on my forearms. The car ahead of us moved out on to the highway. We were next. My sister flicked the indicator, released her foot from the brake. But at the very last moment, just before she turned on to the road, Lexi appeared, banging at the window. She was out of breath from sprinting and her face wet with tears. May stopped suddenly, and without saying anything Lexi opened the door and climbed into the back seat. I reached behind and patted her leg but she pulled away, curling herself up against the car door and the window, where she sobbed quietly. As we drove I tried to keep my eyes on the road, focusing straight ahead in the hope that the nausea was just motion sickness. But of course it wasn't. I passed Lexi a box of tissues. I knew now where it came from, I remembered what it was – how I'd felt it before.

18

I hardly knew about it, that first time, before I started to cramp and bleed it out. It had been an accidental pregnancy a few years earlier when I was just beginning work on the book, and I thought my ill feelings were simply due to my anxiety about the project. But the reality took me completely by surprise – it was something I had never planned, never wanted. I wasn't pregnant for long, though, eight weeks perhaps at most. I don't know why I didn't join the next dots faster: I'd been vomiting even before I arrived at May's house, the queasiness worst in the mornings. That first time, in the days immediately after the miscarriage, Patrick nursed me with great care, bringing me hot-water bottles, tea, painkillers for the cramps. Yet even then, seeing me like that, he wouldn't take it seriously when I said that this was never going to happen again. What do you mean? he asked. I thought this was—

No.

But what if we—

I said no.

I knew I couldn't live as May had chosen to, by making her own motherhood the central act of her life. We had both tried to exorcise this part of our history in our own way, May by living through maternal experience differently, living it out, and me by choosing against this. Each attempting to outwit and overpower that common past. I never could remember the name of the woman my mother left us with when she fled. Jan? Carol? I was crying. She picked me up and carried me to the kitchen. She had fat upper arms, and where I clung on I could feel the roughness of her skin where it was covered with tiny raised spots, some kind of dry rash.

You can't stonewall me on this, Patrick said.

I'm not stonewalling you. I'm just saying no. It would disrupt everything. Maybe it was meant to be this way. Maybe it was my body doing me a favour. Besides everything else, I couldn't tolerate the unpredictability that a child would bring to our lives.

But I want children, Patrick said. I want them more than anything in my life.

You already have a child, I replied.

That's different.

Why?

Because Trudi and I had started to hate each other even before Joshua was born. She never let me get close to him. Not really. Besides, he said. I want children that are ours. Yours. Mine.

You don't know what you're asking of me, I told him. I can't, I'm sorry, but I just can't. What about us, what we have together, and besides, how would I write?

How would you write? he said. Are you serious? If the situation were reversed, he replied. If you were the one who wanted this, I would do it for you. How can you say this, after everything that I've given you?

After everything he'd given *me*? I suppose he was referring to the house in which we lived, to the money and to the time this money had afforded me, the clothes it had once bought – before I made money of my own. In his eyes I was one of his investments and he now felt bitter at my failure to offer a good return, the return he was expecting. And what about everything I've given you? I scoffed, looking away. Some bachelors employ not just cleaners but women who go by the title of housekeeper. I cooked him meals every night, I stocked the pantry, I tended to his son, I opened the mail and paid the bills, I updated his insurance and submitted his tax returns. For a long time our marriage facilitated my ambitions and Patrick encouraged them, but I realised then that something had changed, or was changing; my success was an irritant, a source of resentment even.

I was fragile after that, after the miscarriage and the drawn-out nature of our argument, and for a while Patrick kept his distance. If I felt expectant it was really with the life of the new book, this last one, the prize-winner, the one that seemed to take everything that I had, like a small living secret growing inside me. I think he always assumed that he would persuade me in the end, that if he gave me some space I might change my mind and a child would one day be born. Because who was I to refuse him his desires?

On that first night, the taxi sped through the rain. The windows lit by droplets of water and the blur of city lights: neon shop signs, traffic warnings, street lamps. We turned out on to the highway, picking up speed, the scenes through the window moving faster now: five, ten, fifteen frames per second, depending on how you measured them. A wet palm tree, a row of terraces with chimney pots, a pedestrian crossing, the dark mass of a shrubby park. The images flashing past. The experience made continuous because it occurred at speed; his voice, the wet, black city, the windscreen wipers snapping back and forth. The white and orange street lights sliding over the side of his face. It's not far now, he said, reaching over to touch my hair. Just round this corner. He leant over and stroked my cheek and I felt some hard, compressed substance long buried in the core of me slowly start to dissolve. It was a very gentle touch, the light brushing of the back of his fingers over my skin. The touch one offers to a fragile and cherished creature: a child with a fever, a sleeping cat. A touch of comfort and curiosity. Of wonderment. Still, I flinched. Sorry, he said. I didn't mean to hurt you. You didn't, I replied. You didn't at all. The driver turned up the radio.

19

If the fabric of May's household was already fragile, the scene in the car park seemed to rupture it entirely. We'd hardly pulled into the drive when Lexi opened the car door and jumped out. She ran round to the back of the house and went inside through the laundry. Then she disappeared into her room. Later, when she came out, she argued with May about the air conditioning. It's too cold in here, she said, it feels like the middle of fucking winter.

Don't use that language.

You did, just back there, at McDonald's.

Adam heard this from his seat at the computer. McDonald's? he said, who went to McDonald's? And then Lexi let loose, telling him, in dramatic fashion, of her mother's attempt to abandon her in the parking lot.

It wasn't the parking lot, May replied.

So it's true, then? he asked.

No, it's not true, and the argument actually took place in the restaurant.

Then Lexi asked me to vouch for her. Tell him, Lucie – she might have even said Aunt Lucie at this point – *tell him what she did.*

We picked her up at the exit, I replied.

You picked me up! I was banging on the window!

Is this for real? he asked.

May turned away. She did bang on the window, she said. But the door wasn't locked.

The car was moving! Lexi replied.

We had actually just stopped, May said. I had pulled the handbrake on.

She's lying! yelled Lexi. She's always lying! All three of them then descended into a fight for the truest version of the event, a fight for ownership, for supremacy. There was Lexi's violence to be debated – how she kicked her mother (I didn't kick you, I *tapped* you). There was May's irresponsibility. There was the father's convenient absence – innocent by default because nothing could be proved otherwise. I retreated to the kitchen to wash lettuce for the salad, in case we did, after all, end up eating dinner together. A point of barter, and maybe kindness: Can you please pass me the salad, the salt, the bread. There was soil clogged in the crisp white base of the leaves. I tilted them to loosen the grit. It would be good at least to have food ready – for when people wanted it. Behind me I heard hurried footsteps, then the door to May's bedroom slam shut. This was followed by Lexi's heavy stomping, and the slamming of her bedroom door too. I attended to my task with great diligence; with head down I double- and triple-rinsed the last of the dirt away, feeling, at my back, the brittleness of the air. Adam resumed his activity at the computer, tapping away hard at the keys. A few moments later he pushed back his chair, its feet scraping at the floor. I'll go see what I can do, he said, sighing.

Soon afterwards I heard him shouting at Lexi, then another door slamming. It must have been at least an hour before he reappeared, only to say that May wasn't feeling well, and if I was hungry I should just go ahead and eat. Then he too disappeared. I tiptoed up the corridor and stood outside Lexi's bedroom, listening for sounds of life. I could hear her music playing very quietly, and every now and then the sound of a hiccuping sob. I went back to the kitchen, piled a plate with food – salad, and meat and bread with butter – then knocked on her door. Go away! she yelled.

It's only me, I told her. I brought you some food.

I'm not hungry.

You should eat something.

I'm NOT HUNGRY.

OK, well, I'll just leave it here, on the ground, and you can get it when you like.

I won't eat it.

That's fine. I'll come back later and take the plate.

Then I found the dog and led him outside by the collar. I shut the front door and poured myself a large glass of wine. I took the salad bowl and a fork and sat down on the couch. When I had finished that glass of wine I brought the bottle over, and when I had drunk enough to no longer notice the rage humming in the air, nor the dog howling at the door, nor the loud thumping of Lexi's music, nor May's weeping, nor the neighbour's car alarm, I rinsed my glass and retreated to my bedroom.

Later that night the house phone rang. I was still awake, and heard Adam answer it. Then his footsteps on the stairs and a knock at my door. Lucie? He said. It's for you.

London, I think. He says he's phoning about Patrick. About the accident. That there's something he needs to ask you.

Downstairs the house was dark except for the glow of the lamp on the side table near the phone. I picked up the receiver. Hello? I said. A formal, slightly throaty voice answered. Ms Blackwood?

He gave his name and his position, but spoke quickly and I missed it. Inspector someone, or did he say investigator?

Ms Blackwood, he said again.

Yes? This is me, I replied.

We've been trying to get hold of you for some time now. I'm afraid I have some news. The results of the autopsy are in. There was a delay on some test results, and then what with the business of locating you . . . I'm just contacting you to let you know that the coroner has called for an inquest following the findings.

My knees felt loose, weak. The autopsy? I said. I thought that had all been, I mean what findings did they—?

Yes, the man said.

There was a delay on the line so that what he heard lagged behind what I said, and then it sounded as though were both speaking at the same time.

You may be called for further questioning, he told me.

Can you tell me what—

Questioning, he said again, thinking I had misheard this, that I was asking him to repeat himself. I'm afraid I can't say anything more at this point, the man said. I just need to inform you. He went on to mention other formalities, emphasising due process, the precautionary measures, the suspicion of foul play. Explaining to me very slowly, very carefully, that the task of the coroner was not to accuse anyone, if this was indeed what we were looking at, but to establish the chain of causation so that the events leading to my husband's death could be placed in the right and proper order. The cruise line company had been amenable, he said. Given clearance on— but I missed the end of the sentence. All possibilities, he told me. If there was someone else out there with him. Although it's not personally for me to say, he stressed. Anyway, he said. I'll be in touch. Apologies for the timing, he said, meaning that it must be late there, where I was. The call ended.

I held the receiver away from me, then put it to my face. The earpiece that had been pressed against my skin was warm and smelt a little of wax. The dial tone continued. Beep beep beep. I listened for a while. One beep sounding longer and louder than the next, the two playing off each other in slight variation. I stood there waiting for a voice to come through the dial tone. To correct what I had just heard, to erase it.

Book Four

20

After I have written a book, once it is finished, I forget what's in it. I find myself daydreaming about it, or can only think of what I have written in a vague sort of way. The memory of the book and the memories of my life slide across one another. I can no longer tell if what I am recalling is a memory or a scene from the book, or if the scene from the book is a memory. Or if the memory has been adapted into a scene for the book, a fragment that has evolved into a story. The origins of what I see in my mind become impossible to trace. If there are repetitions across my books, it is due to my own forgetfulness. If I recall facts in error, it is never intentional. Over time, all borders break down or are breached; the artist wills this.

For years I read almost everything Patrick ever wrote: essays, introductions, early scripts, interview copy. I read and corrected and made suggestions – or additions, shall we say – on every draft before it went to print. He was busy, and at first I did this just to help him out and because I was interested – I wanted to see the work he was doing. I wanted to talk about it. Over time we grew used to this pattern, up to the point where he wouldn't sign off on anything unless it had gone through me first. Just work your magic, he would say, passing me a sheaf of papers.

This collaboration had started in our early days together, and only intensified when with his first feature film – three years after we moved to London – he found himself rocketed into the limelight. He left his teaching post at the university then, although he kept an honorary professorship, and his days became less structured than they were when we first met. Things came up. Invitations were received. He worked long hours, and obsessively. For some years he continued to keep a pocket diary, simply out of habit, but as his days became more hectic appointments were scribbled in, crossed out, overwritten. I couldn't always decipher the entries and I knew that, out of sheer busyness, he didn't list all his engagements and often rolled with things as they arose. Max kept tabs, tried to steer the ship, but Patrick was a free agent. His days became less and less predictable as his fame increased. No one could hold him to anything while at the same time a great array of tasks could appear, and whims could be passed off as leads. I made sure to keep abreast of things – of appointments and projects, timelines and due dates – to know his movements and plans. He used to come home alight with ideas, half-thought-out scripts, images that he would describe to me as if they were dreams. Sometimes I myself would then dream of the things he had told me of: a pale-blue corridor, a black door, a child hiding underneath a tangle of jasmine vine. Or I would draft a scene of my own in which I found myself replicating an image he had described to me, one he was putting together in real life for an upcoming shoot. There was often too much going on for him to keep it in his head and he would unburden it all on me.

During those years in which his fame appeared to know no limits, every college student wrote about his films, they were on every syllabus for cinema studies. I knew that he was heading in this direction when we met and over the course of our marriage his reputation only grew – the aura that accompanied his acclaim deepening over time until it developed a rich and manly glow.

It's fair to say that the term 'director' didn't do his work justice. In recent years people had started to refer to him as that other thing, an auteur. In the time it had taken me to stop and start and finally finish that prize-winning book he had become known as one of the most innovative film-makers of his time, devoted to the medium of cinema. He liked visually complex compositions, glamorous long shots, evocative landscapes. He couldn't stand fast trash. The question critics liked to ask was whether he was participant or impersonator. Was he living inside his stories, or did he tell them? It then fell to us to debate who, within the context of our marriage, could lay most claim to the rights of authorship. Whose form would best fit the subject, who had first say over how to use the things that happened to us, the life we shared? Because each of us lived for the sake of representation – as if living backwards, in the hope that real life might be perpetually reduced, flattened, rephrased and repeated, on page and on the screen.

Maybe, in my commitment to our partnership and my belief in our common vision, I overextended myself. Overstepped the mark. I wanted to do this, that much was true. For so many years I shadowed him; working hard to be both sounding board and repository for any ideas he might want to talk out or keep in mind. Eventually I convinced him to replace his pocket diary with an online calendar that I could access. I kept his notebooks sorted in chronological order because as a project developed he often found himself needing to refer back to earlier ideas, to the first manifestation. I filed his drafts. I even went so far as to read his funding pitches, checking his budget before he submitted it to whatever institution he was applying to. My maths was terrible, but what he wanted was my eye. I knew how much he was asking to spend on per diems and what hotel he was planning on booking into. I knew the airline that was flying him to this shoot or that one. I knew everything. Total knowledge. This was the thing he once wanted for himself, and yet in the end it was what he gave to me, or what I acquired. At least this was what I thought, until things changed.

In the year or so before the cruise, life between us began to feel strained and we had started to drift apart. I knew we needed to get away, to be alone together without the pressures of our day-to-day lives. I wanted to take him away from the gaze of others. More than anything, I wanted to find again what we once had: that heady combination of ease and desire. To have something of a new beginning. And so, as our anniversary approached, I insisted. Can you do this for my sake, I asked? For us? He was reluctant at first, but eventually agreed. I went ahead and organised the details, not knowing what lay ahead.

★

Countless other falls were captured on film before his. King Kong's fall from the Empire State Building in 1933 – the ape bouncing and tumbling off the tiers of the skyscraper, the body seen complete and from a distance. Although the proportions were not wholly convincing, nor the speed.

Or take *The Squaw Man*, from 1931. The man slips, clinging to a white rope, the cliff on his right. The rope is fraying and it soon snaps, the man plummets, and in the next shot he is tumbling head first, but the cliff suddenly appears on his left now, the camera angle having illogically switched sides as the man's body rolls into the dry tussock grass, the continuity of action broken by the angle change, as if we've missed something.

Then there are other scenes, without error, scenes of men falling, caught on film. *La Roue*, directed by Abel Gance in 1923: Elie holds fast to a tree root at the top of a cliff, his body small and black against the white background of an ice-covered mountain. Images flash rapidly though his inner eye just before he falls to his death, while the woman he loves runs to save him, but is too late, his body tumbling dark against the snow.

Or *The Matrix*, 1999.

Or *Lethal Weapon*, 1987 – Fuck you! I'm jumping!

Do you really wanna jump, you really wanna? Well then that's fine with me.

Come on then, let's do it, asshole, let's do it.

I wanna do it, I wanna do it – the men leaping out into the daylight, the camera angle first from beneath so that we see the soles of Riggs's shoes, leather soles, maybe white cowboy boots even, slightly pointed, then the camera angle from above, watching the first stages of the plummet.

Then there is *The Fugitive*, 1993, when Dr Richard Kimble, played by Harrison Ford, looks down into the frothing water far below and jumps the gun, plunging into the Cheoah Dam. His body falls fast, we see it from above as he tips over, going head first, and again the soles of his shoes – what is it with all the shoes? – visible for a second, white sneakers this time, before the angle changes and we see him side-on and from a distance, dark and tiny as he falls against the background of the white rushing water.

But perhaps my favourite scene is in *The Game*, 1997. Once more there is the shot of the shoes, heavier shoes this time, with good grip. Again we see the flash of a sturdy sole as the character of Nicholas steps up on to the roof ledge, then the shout which is like a gunshot, fast and loud. Christine calls out to him but it's too late, he has stepped off, away from her. He too falls head first; one hand reaches out, white and creaturely.

Women also fall, but not so often, and generally speaking a man is either trying to save her or push her off. She is helpless. She is not falling of her own free will. She does not jump. She does not take the leap. She is not asked to screw her courage to the sticking place. She is often part of those mass anonymous falls. Think of *Titanic*, 1997 – all the bodies that make only a small white splash, a little froth seen from afar, one after another and another. They are like little blips of light as they fall, these people, shooting stars against the night sky, bright against the black hull and the even blacker water. But what strikes me now is how every fall in cinema happens as if in a silent film: just the choreographed moment and the soundtrack. The fall itself a repeating trope.

The ship's CCTV recording was more limited than what we see in the cinema. It didn't show us what was happening at the same time as Patrick's accident; things occurring simultaneously but in different locations – the parallel edit. In literature we signal this by saying 'meanwhile'. Meanwhile, they asked me. Where were you meanwhile?

In the violence of that storm, chairs and tables had slid across the room and broken. Giant potted palms were rolling on their sides. The grand piano was fastened to the floor and so stayed where it was. I too had been slammed against the wall as the ship tilted. My head hurt. It hurt for days afterwards, accompanied by nausea and giddiness – a little like the build-up to a migraine, when my mind does strange things. During this phase, before the true pain sets in, random images flash across the screen of my closed lids. They are bright fragments, unconnected, and they move very fast, as if someone has accelerated the speed x5: a girl's feet in roller skates yellow flowers a woman with goggles a ferris wheel a racing horse in motion a painting of an iris in a gilt frame shoes splashing in a puddle of water cube of ice bicycle tyre lawnmower clearing a swatch of grass green tennis ball in a basket case of wine blossom tree. If I open my eyes the train of images stop. If I close them, the images start up again, increasing in speed until they almost blur. The migraine pain, when it comes, is just light – inhumanly bright light. There was the sound of glass shattering. Patrick had his back to me. I could see the waves looming, heaving. In Japan I had given the investigator one image then the next, just as he had asked. But accounts can change. Scenes can be revisited. There are precedents for this. Like in *Life of an American Fireman*, when the action is seen first from outside the burning house, with the firemen hosing down the building. Then one of the men appears at the window holding the woman in white over his shoulder; she has been rescued. Then we see the same time frame, the same actions, but viewed from inside the house, as the fireman again rescues the woman in white. We go back to the same event, to revisit it from a different perspective. Time repeats, replay after replay. Later, Edwin Porter edits this differently: we see outside the house, then inside the house – the woman suffocating is being rescued – then we see outside the house as the woman is carried down the ladder, and then inside again as the fireman returns to save the small child. Spaces replace each other, fracturing, spliced, intercut. Two or more actions in one scene. Events unfold as they happen, time is continuous, and to show this the cinematic space must break up. Then this, then that, then the other thing. One moment of life chasing the next, bumping up against it, the collision of instants.

I had tried to explain this at various points, as a way of justifying my account. Reaffirming it.

I needed to get to safety. He wouldn't follow.

I said maybe one or both these things. The motive for my action might differ but the result is the same. He was out, in the storm, while I got stuck inside trying to open the heavy door. Any appraisal of that which is occurring simultaneously is necessarily contextualised by the thing which came before. This is how it comes to matter, to be a moment, later on, of great or greater significance. But I have already said all this, here and elsewhere – Patrick and I both knew the theory well, knew the examples that went with it. What started the fire? That is the question. But if Porter had told us this, the film would be less about the American fireman and more about the woman and child.

21

Outside now, the season is starting to turn, heading into autumn. The leaves fall quickly. Come winter you can see further through the bare trees. At that time of year, when I go out walking along the marked tracks, I can see past the chain-link fence with its barbs and into the country beyond. There is not much there. A narrow, winding road. Fields. More woodland in certain directions. From the eastern corner of the boundary I can see through the trees to a neighbouring house, a fair way away but visible. Because this wasn't always the place it is now. There would have been neighbours, country folk, landed gentry. Although this house, the one I can see in the winter, might not have belonged to the latter. It is in need of repair. The front garden is wild with overgrown grass and cluttered with odd junk. One side of the house is clad in rusting corrugated iron in the manner of a barn. We are a long way from any town, and so whoever lives there occasionally puts out by the roadside the objects they no longer need and leaves a large sign on them saying FREE. Sometimes drivers pull over to look at these things and put one or two items in their boot. At other times the discarded objects sit there for weeks. Then they disappear, back into the house I suspect. I have never seen who does this, the person who carries the objects to the side of the road and then takes them back in again.

But I am interested in these goings-on, the discarded objects – among which I have seen an exercise bicycle, a TV cabinet and a rolled-up piece of carpet – because so many other signs of life have ceased. Stalled. Run aground. I can only watch these things happening on the screen from afar: the stock markets' plummet, the helicopters, the summer wildfires. The things outside. Here, on the inside, time is counted in an empty way, without event. During the day, when I turn up for meals and answer to the roll call and complete my duties, I do everything on repeat. The days are long and unvarying, by and large, unless I try hard to look at the small things: the changes in the garden, the sprouting of new leaves on the seedlings, the infestations of pests that I am charged to deal with: red spider mites, aphids, flea beetles. These are things of mild concern, relatively speaking. Although I have found that you can teach yourself to become interested in all manner of things, when you must. Otherwise I live, as I have always done, to write. To write and revise and then write again. I used to do this for Patrick too – I read everything of his, even the things he wished me not to see. He in turn left his mark on all my work. I let him have what we might call the power of attorney over my writing, almost up to the very end. But now I am free to say what I like.

There were questions, of course, that I didn't answer in that last book, nor in the one before. Threads that were left unresolved, whole periods skipped over in brief. In interviews I've often been asked about this. It always surprises me that readers think of my characters as real people and want to see their lives resolved. And then I think, why not? Real people, experienced in our head, and real people whom we've lost, eventually start to feel like characters. The dividing line has never been especially clear for me. Or rather, I've never been overly concerned with policing it. Patrick admired my fictional version of both Henry and May. Henry, he thought, was particularly lifelike, and maybe this was why he remained a character that people continued to ask me about. Even at that reading in New York, people wanted to know what happened to him, as though he were a friend they had lost track of. I told them what I knew, which was what I had made up, but also what I had come to believe, as if I had discovered and not invented it. This is what I think happened, I tell them. This was how Henry appeared in the second-last draft. This was my last sighting of him. He's still there, ghosting the pages in a file somewhere. Most of the time this seems to satisfy them. I used my father's letters as a springboard, and after he died I burnt these in the fireplace in the living room where Patrick and I often spent our evenings. A room that has featured heavily in all my books. A room I have described over and over again, with minor variations. People were always surprised when they saw it in real life. In that room Patrick and I often sat on the sofa together, which was positioned in front of the television. We liked to watch movies that way, curled up. On the sofa we took the same sides as we did in bed, him on the right, me on the left. Sometimes, after the movie we were watching had ended, we would sit for a while in front of the blank screen. Faint light came from the kitchen and this made our reflection visible against the dark glass. Two blackened figures, side by side. We would half stare for a while at this image, half seeing ourselves, half seeing through these reflections, able to look both at them and past them, noting the dusty and fingerprinted screen, part of our minds still dwelling on whatever it was we had just been watching. We stared at ourselves with some detachment, because each reflected figure lacked a face. The television was placed at chest height, so that when we sat on the sofa the images in the dark glass were of two headless people. It was a portrait. A portrait of us, the portrait of a marriage. Poets are discussed in reference to phases of style: the early, middle and late periods. A marriage, in the development of its language, might be classified in the same way. One becomes less aggrandising, less persuaded by a youthful tendency to swoon, the less bearable impulses are gradually internalised and weighted down. But we caught a flash of them then, in that portrait. The decapitated couple. The potential for violence and all the violent feelings, given back to us in that dark image. Just for a moment anyway, before one of us reached over and switched on the light.

Months before I even booked the cruise, I had asked him over and over again if he could please check my manuscript. For years he was eager to read everything I wrote, and I didn't understand this sudden reluctance. Things had been difficult all through the spring while I worked away to meet the July deadline. The novel had taken so much longer than I thought it should, and I just wanted it done. I also knew that I'd made many additions in a state of fatigued distraction, and because of this I needed Patrick's eye more than usual. He'd read an earlier draft, but I was unaccustomed to signing off on anything without his reassurance.

I only want you to look quickly at a few sections, to double-check some changes, I had said. But he was always caught up with other things.

I'm sure it's all fine, he replied. You're always brilliant, he said, sounding blasé, without being convincing. Just remind me tomorrow, he would say. Or, Remember to remind me. And I'd reply, I am reminding you. I reminded you yesterday too.

Just remind me again, he said. But day after day, reminder after reminder, he claimed never to have the time, or never found the time, never made the time.

Just look at them? I said. Just the changes?

Please try not to make any more lengthy additions at this point, Ada had asked, knowing my habit of sending through reams of last-minute requests, and although I had done my best to satisfy her on this front I was nervous about the chapters that I had added to. But still the days passed, and Patrick didn't get to these. I gave up asking; there wasn't enough time left. The final manuscript was due in on the same day that I was booked to fly to Paris to do an author talk. I didn't want to go. Although it was summer, I was exhausted from rushing towards the deadline and felt completely drained. My mind was elsewhere. It was impossible to focus on other things, to make small talk with a group of strangers. I always said yes to the wine at these events because it eased my nerves, but then it muddled my brain and I couldn't think clearly to answer anyone's questions and ended up with a terrible headache.

Besides, I said to Patrick, I can't decide what to wear.

Wear what you normally wear. You always look great.

What do I normally wear?

I don't know, you've got so many beautiful clothes.

I wanted to wear the silk shirt but it has a stain on it.

Then wash it.

I don't have time; I have to fly out tomorrow morning, I made an appointment at the hairdresser's and I've got to get the manuscript in before I leave.

I don't know what you should wear, then. It doesn't really matter. Just wear something that you're comfortable in.

But that's the point, I can't be comfortable in anything at these things.

I had thought of cancelling but people had bought tickets, everything was organised. I complained about this to Patrick.

But isn't this what you wanted? he said. Other people would kill for this.

I thought he might have been joking, he knew how much these events exhausted me. How I dreaded them for weeks beforehand. How I dreamt of them afterwards, castigating myself for saying such stupid things. How I increasingly disliked the feeling of even being in crowded places, of being glanced at, seen, of being visible. How I felt tired by the effort of making myself ready to be seen; even the expectation of being seen felt wearying.

This intolerance had spread beyond my professional engagements; in recent months I had started to find any busy public place especially exhausting. Busy rooms, busy trains, busy shopping centres. Once, the pleasure of stepping out, all dressed and ready, had been a source of energy. Patrick used to cheer me on, praise me. I was and always would be young in relation to him, if one were measuring just the years. But what I had been wooed by, what had given him that initial charm, what had swept me up, was his overwhelming and forceful belief in the bewitching potential of my future – all that I might become, but wasn't yet. In the intervening years this gap had closed and I suddenly found it inexplicably tiring to perform my appearance, even to myself, to have to fake this belief.

Really? No. You can't be, he had once said, showing his surprise at my youth. He seemed amazed by it. As if youth were magical, accidental, a lucky strike, as if it only happened to the chosen few. Back then I didn't understand that youth was not a virtue in itself, because he treated it like it was, as if I were virtuous because I was young – as though I had some inherent magic in me by way of this, and I made the mistake of taking pride in this notion, of giving myself credit for a biological phase that was in reality not mine, and did not mark me out but was entirely democratic in its manifestation within all of us, and equally fleeting. At the time he was far enough past his own youth for my very being to seem miraculous.

Eventually, however, that future caught up with us, with me. I felt his wonderment dampen. My youth was relative, defined in contrast to his experience. As my experience started to match his, and as my successes – by some measures – even exceeded his, the idea of my youth dissolved. The appeal of it. The young writers he sometimes worked with, however, were still the age I was many years ago, the kind of women who laughed at his jokes about certain books being structured like a male orgasm, women who were young enough to want to hear him talk about this, who believed him. Rising, rising, rising, he'd explain, and then *bang*. Everything said and done. Resolution was a version of him falling asleep on top of you. This was foolish literature, in my view, naïve, overly simplistic. He himself made light of this structure, and once added to a special guest lecture a plot diagram which, he said, echoed the female climax: more complex, nuanced, multiple. He was talking about a short story, I don't know which one. I only heard about it afterwards. Everyone heard about it afterwards. Apparently the women giggled while the men blushed. Young men they were, scarcely more than boys. They probably didn't even know what this was, what a female orgasm could look like. It would have been their innocence that was embarrassing, not the explicit content. Of course, such exuberances only made the women in that audience fall for my husband a little more, as I once had. Such exuberances only made them dwell on his knowledge, fantasise about it, imagine the theory in practice: his knowledge of the body, or of their bodies in particular.

And so that day, as I prepared to go to Paris, he didn't say to me, Oh wear those blue trousers, I love seeing you in those. Once, he would have said to me, Why don't you walk ahead of me, so I can see your arse move, misquoting a line from that favourite film of ours, *Day for Night*. The film we quoted to each other all the time. Alphonse says this to his fiancé as she walks down the hall. We loved that film. The way it gave you the feeling of being an insider, and you would only intermittently remember that the film about the making of a film was itself being filmed. *That man will use anything!* Later, on the cruise ship, Patrick would take my hands as Ferrand did Pamela's, and rearrange them on the ship railing, just as Pamela's hands are rearranged on the railing of the balcony. Ferrand held her hands so gently, he paid her such intimate attention, receptive to the mood of every gesture.

Instead Patrick said to me, as if to a general assembly and without looking at me, Yeah, anything will be fine. You'll look fine. They'll love you in anything. In fact, they probably won't even care what you wear and it will all be over soon anyhow. I mean, doesn't the whole thing only last an hour?

Look, he said, if it would make things easier I could drop the manuscript off for you. Save you the time.

Really?

Sure, he said, picking up a green apple from the fruit bowl and biting into it.

I remember, after the event, making the quick decision to alter my schedule and catch a late flight straight back. I felt uneasy for some reason and couldn't imagine sleeping in a hotel bed. I didn't yet know about the prize. At that time, when I flew home from Paris, it must have been around the second week in July. I hadn't given a thought to our anniversary. I'd been so preoccupied with trying to finish the manuscript that I was oblivious to anything else going on and was still mulling over some proposed changes as I hopped in a taxi at Gatwick. When I got home Patrick wasn't there. I showered and made myself some toast. Then I heard him fumbling at the front door: a man too drunk to fit his key into the lock. I opened it for him and he stumbled inside. He was surprised to see me, You? he said. He tried to stand up a little straighter. I thought you were, you know, I mean flying home in the morning? he slurred. He slipped his bag off his shoulder and let it fall to the floor.

I could see the manuscript was still in there. I was sure he'd been to the publishing house because he'd sent me a message to say he was dropping the package off on his way home.

You mean you went there, I said, and didn't take it out of your bag?

You know I thought I did. I swear it. I remember holding it out to her.

And then what?

I don't know, he said, I must have put it down, or gone to put it down, or maybe— we just got chatting, and she seemed really interested.

Really interested?

Yeah. Interested. I mean, she knew your books, and was telling me how much she loved them and wanted to, what's the word, if I was planning on you know adapting this one. I don't know. I must have held it out and somehow forgotten to put it down or put it down and picked it up. Or maybe put it back. Your publisher wasn't there. Ada I mean. I was later than, I thought maybe I needed to— I mean Annie said—

You mean Anna-Maria, Ada's assistant?

I think so.

You think so, but you know her well enough to call her Annie?

It all made sudden sense to me then. All the things I hadn't understood before but which had troubled me. His distractedness, his unusual fatigue, his reluctance to read my work – his strange and sudden desire to move elsewhere.

Why don't we move to LA? Patrick had said, three months earlier. Just think of the weather. The space. It would be the real deal, he said. Or something like that. A whole new start. He proposed this long before we stepped on to that cruise ship, and although it was spring when he came up with this idea, the weather still felt like winter.

Huh? I said. What for? It was late and I was busy, fixing up a scene in the novel. He was pacing the kitchen, looking out at the rain. I chewed on the end of a pencil while I scanned the page. The pencil was coated in shiny lacquered stripes, black and red, which I dented between my teeth. The taste of wood, lead.

You know I hate the heat, I replied, taking the pencil out of my mouth for a moment, my glasses slipping down the bridge of my nose.

But you'd be so great there, he said. Imagine.

Hang on, I told him. Listen. And I ran the pencil down the page against the section I was revising. What about this, and I read aloud the paragraph I had just rewritten. Yeah yeah, he said, waving his arm, that sounds great. Whatever you do with it will be great. I glanced up at him. He was standing by the window, his hand pressed to the glass, as if through this he might touch the rain.

Are you hungry? he asked then, not looking at me. His face was in profile. And I noticed, perhaps for the first time, how fame had aged him. Within the space of three years his hair had turned almost entirely grey. During that period, he had been flying somewhere almost every week and sleeping only in snatches. I had stepped in to help with work when and as he needed me, which was less and less, it seemed. In the daytime we carried on with our separate tasks – I kept on with my book, he zipped about, directing those stellar screenplays that I had helped him pull together, adding dialogue and new characters as required.

Not much, I said. He didn't ask why not, or if I was feeling OK or whether I'd like to go out to eat instead. He said nothing about his day. He used to tell me everything. He used to tell me that that was why he loved me, or one of the reasons – because he could tell me anything. But over the last few years things had started to change. And so while I watched him carefully stir the pasta so that it didn't stick to the bottom of the pan – not a task that required substantial concentration or silence – I said, Are you tired?

He turned to me, an absent look on his face, and replied, Yes, yes I suppose I am a little. And I suddenly realised that I could no longer read him. That whatever he had, up to that point, given freely had been swiftly withdrawn. I couldn't figure out if he had nothing to tell me or whether there were things he didn't want to tell me or whether, if he was tired, he just couldn't bring himself to speak, to muster the energy, or if my question in fact

provided him with an alibi, an excuse, and he decided just
to take this, seeing as I was offering it, just as I had offered
so many other things.

I had known for some time that our successes were out
of step. His work overshadowed mine for years, and so
when my own triumphs finally arrived I let myself look
away. I couldn't cater to his needs as I once had. By the
time we sat together in the kitchen that night, swirling the
pasta around our forks while the rain hammered against
the windows, the scripts he wanted me to check had piled
up on my desk. There were changes he wanted me to
approve, redundancies he wanted me to look at and edit
out. There were bills to pay and too many emails to respond to. I hadn't been able to accompany him to various
screenings because I had my own events to attend. And
although I was accustomed to him sharing everything
with me, I hadn't thought anything of his increasing
bouts of silence, his unusual fatigue, his periodic absences.
I hadn't had the time to dwell on this. I just thought he
had less to say, less to tell me, more commitments, or that
he knew I had a lot going on too and could see that I was
preoccupied. It never occurred to me to question him, to
suspect him of anything other than an excess of deep and
private thought, which I trusted he would share with me
in his own good time, because who else could he speak to
in the way that he spoke to me?

But perhaps this was my one mistake. My miscalcula-
tion. My hubris. He was one of the great directors of his
generation, but he was a terrible actor – a man whose attempt at a poker face always looked incontrovertibly false.
He poured more wine. What had changed in him? What

were those thoughts I could see him trying to keep from me? I didn't know. I couldn't tell. But I knew then that I had missed something and that he had made sure of this. We had been together for so long that by that point it was almost constitutionally impossible to properly surprise one another. We could give delight, we could thrill, we could share bursts of something one might call joy. I loved him. Deeply. But surprise – up until that moment when I could see him keeping something from me, surprise had long been lost to us. I didn't recognise the feeling at first: a sudden plummeting in my gut, my heart flipping in my chest. That feeling of being a child again, of something jumping out at you. From behind a curtain, from behind a chair. And you're meant to laugh at this, accommodate it, and instead you burst into tears.

22

We didn't talk that night, after I got back from Paris and he came home drunk, and I didn't ask any more questions. In the morning he went to a shoot and I worked until the afternoon, then took a taxi back to the publishing house and handed over the manuscript. Ada ushered me into the break room, locked the door behind us and hugged me while I cried.

His betrayal ought not to have shocked me in the way that it did. After all, I had once been that other woman in Patrick's life. He contested this – he told me he'd left his wife, that there was no one else: I was it. Forever and always. But I don't think Trudi ever saw it that way. She didn't know he would never come back to her. He used this line to convince me, to persuade me to do as he wished. But if this was the case, if I was the only woman, if he loved me as he said he did, then why did he need to hide me all those years before? That day, for instance, when I stayed over and he told me not to leave the flat. I obeyed him without ever asking why. I wanted to keep pleasing him as a way of retaining my own relative power, or what I mistook as power – how weak he seemed in moments of intense attraction, how yielding. How wrong I was.

That old apartment of his had been so neat and clean. I had plenty of time that day to inspect it. Even the papers on his desk were neatly arranged. There were no dishes on the drying rack waiting to be put away. No pile of clothes on the chair in the bedroom. Of course I didn't know him then as well as I would come to. But even from my limited knowledge at that time, his preference for order was evident – at least in his domestic life. This was a surprise, given the state of his office at the university where the books sat in haphazard stacks on the floor, the papers on his desk spread about or shoved into unstable piles.

What I recognised then as his need for domestic order continued down the years, extending even to the layout of our home. He liked a house where the kitchen was separate from the dining room, the toilet distinct from the bathroom, a study but never a desk in the bedroom. Everything needed its place, and these places should never overlap. Open-plan living would have been anathema to him: all the blurring, the potential for noise and confusion. In his professional life he was just the opposite, and maybe his line of work required this. It demanded a certain fluidity: the ability to dissolve boundaries or think across them, to infiltrate, overlay, borrow, steal and adapt. The order in one sphere allowed for the requisite transgressions in the other. It was all a question of contrast: unpredictability, shock, disarmament, the disruption of sudden change – it's all calibrated and relative. Life and art are never as different as we think.

I understood too well then, but perhaps too late, what I had been for him, and maybe what I was still – a younger, surrogate artist who had no right to supremacy. The vessel for his drives and desires, his right-hand woman, his editor even. I, in turn, had once seen him as my enabler, the man who would chaperone me towards the greatness that I wanted for myself. And now you whine about it, he had said, when I was getting ready to go to Paris and couldn't decide what to wear. I mean people would kill, *absolutely kill* for this.

And so what? I replied. What does that mean, how does that help? He was burnt out and I had made it. I had made it, as we say, not because but perhaps in spite of him – that long shadow of the sugar daddy. In truth I had always been more invested in his success than he was in mine. That day in the break room Ada passed me a box of tissues. I mopped at my face, blew my nose. My phone buzzed in my pocket. It was Joshua. I had forgotten he was coming for the weekend. He'd lost his key and was stuck outside the house in the rain.

I've been here for ages. Dad's not answering, he said.

OK, I told him. I'll be there soon. Next to me on the bench was a half-bottle of wine left over from a book club event. Here, Ada said, have some of this, and she poured me a generous glass. Cheers to the book! she said, and I started to cry once again.

Back at home I cooked dinner. At some point Patrick returned from wherever he'd been and the three of us ate in silence. Patrick drank. Afterwards, he stacked the dishwasher. Joshua came in looking for ice cream and Patrick turned to him smiling, as if nothing was wrong, as if the bad atmosphere was just something in our heads. For some months Joshua had been visiting every weekend because he was arguing with his mother and Patrick was eager to make him feel at ease, to make it clear, even that night, that his presence was no burden.

Do you want to play a game? he said. It was a diversionary tactic; any sign of irritation on Patrick's part had the tendency to set off Joshua's temper. It was also a way of shutting down the conversation that he knew we had to have.

Sure, Joshua replied. What about *Twilight Struggle*? Lucie, will you play? he asked me.

Lucie doesn't play games, Patrick replied.

What do you mean, doesn't? Sometimes I do, it depends what game.

But you never actually play.

I played that game at the pub the other weekend.

That was a game for under-fives. It was a guessing game.

I played it and it was fun.

You know what I mean.

Then why don't you ask me if I want to play so that at least I can refuse for myself?

He closed the dishwasher and pressed the start button. It's just too complicated, he said.

What, asking me?

No, the game. The game we want to play. There are too many rules for you.

I'm sure I could learn them.

I really don't think you'd like it, you don't like rules. You hate them. You'd only start playing and then get cross and stop playing and we'd then have to start the game all over again with two players rather than three and all the while we'd be aware of you sulking upstairs as if we'd done you some harm when it's just that you're being petulant and impatient, so that the fun game I had in mind would be ruined by your tantrum, which is not an exaggeration, because it always happens. It's true, he said. It does. Anyway, he continued, squeezing the dishcloth out over the sink. Hey Josh, he said, why don't you go into the living room and get the game set up.

I leant against the opposite bench, staring at Patrick's back as he wiped down the counter. You know it only happens when no one explains the rules properly, I replied.

They're not complicated.

They seem that way to you because you already know them.

The game is designed for *children*.

You could have just asked me. You could have just asked me if I wanted to play. I can speak for myself. Instead you made a claim on my behalf, belittling me, as if I weren't a person in the room at all. I said to him then exactly what I wanted to say, and all the things I'd never let myself say before. And you know what I hate about playing games with you? What I hate is how you go about policing me. It's like an excuse for you to police me. The breaking of rules is something you reserve for yourself, right? That's your prerogative. Everyone knows that, it's what you're *actually* famous for. To me, the thing you've done last night with that woman and however long before that, that's a game, that's you playing a fucking game. Maybe we should talk about the rules of that one? It would be good to have a better understanding of your affairs, as I have always called your business – I would love you to explain how it works now, the game of us. Because I don't think I know the rules any more, or maybe they have changed, or maybe we need to—

Oh don't be so facile, he said. And keep your voice down. He turned away from me and back to the sink, rinsing the chopping board. I could see his reflection in the kitchen window. I knew that Joshua was listening from the living room. Patrick glanced up, and in the mirror of the dark glass met my gaze. His face appeared drawn, his eyes seemed wary. Maybe this was his look of guilt.

You know, you've changed, he said very quietly. I just can't understand who you've become.

I held his stare. You've made me become this person, I replied. Whatever I am, I am because of you.

I haven't made you *become* anything, he whispered. He took in a sharp breath, like he was building up to something. Then he let this out very slowly, through tight lips, making a sound close to a hiss.

I glanced through the kitchen door towards the living room where Joshua sat rigid, staring at his lap. His face was flushed. I worried that our argument might set him off, start one of those strange tantrums he'd been having of late. On the coffee table in front of him two piles of cards had been dealt.

It was true, what Patrick said. I didn't play games well. It was also true that I didn't like rules, or rather, I didn't like the kind of rules that Patrick liked: logical rules that built on one another in increasingly complex ways until a whole universe of ordered systems had been established. He liked serious games which required strict obedience, I liked fast-moving games that I could play when a little drunk and that made me laugh. *Twister*, 'Who Am I', snap. Even outside games were preferable; stuck in the mud, tip, hide-and-seek. This had become, for him, a character flaw in me, as he saw it. Yet because of the peculiarities of his accent all I heard was flood. It was flood. I was flood. We were caught up in something that was flood, or flooded or was flooding, something that was so embarrassingly unsophisticated that he had to explain my flooded ways to his son.

In the distance I could hear the local church bells; I heard the wind first – heavy, gusting – then behind this the bells. Dusk was settling. I had had enough. I forgot something from the shop, I said, lying. I didn't need to lie – the impetus was not to deceive, but rather to reinforce my own privacy. I didn't want to have the conversation that went: Fine, I'm going out. I need some air. And he would then say, pretending obliviousness: Why?

And I would say, Because I need some space.

And he would say, From what?

Do I have to say?

I asked, he'd reply.

I just need a minute to myself.

What for? Can't you have that here, upstairs?

Will you stop?

Stop what?

And so on and so on.

OK, sure, he said. He wasn't wearing shoes. The best he could manage were wide-fit sneakers. Even these squeezed his feet too tight and made his back hurt, he said. And because his back hurt, it took him a long time to get his shoes on, so I knew he wouldn't follow me. He wouldn't chase after me. He wouldn't pursue me, as he once might have.

He sat down and reshuffled the cards. I took my coat from the hook by the front door and tugged my arms into it as I stepped out into the evening. The air was fresh and cool, blustery and damp. Leaves drifted down from the trees and clung to me as I walked. The road ahead of me dark and shiny in the rain.

Earlier that summer we had visited a gallery together. It was to see an exhibition of new sculptures made by an artist of considerable fame. The tickets were expensive and came with timed entry, so we had planned our day around this, taking the train and then having lunch, and afterwards seeing the show. We climbed the stairs and handed over our tickets to be stamped, then entered the vast atrium that was full of light. We paused for a moment, taking in the space. For some reason, and this has always been the way, when we enter a gallery together my tendency is to turn right and move anticlockwise around the room, while his tendency is to turn left and move clockwise. If one of us follows the other's path it feels wrong; the person taking the unfamiliar route feels disorientated, out of step. They have abandoned their own instinct – the wayward trajectory of their own curiosity – in favour of some kind of collective response, possibly just because they like the idea of this companionable looking, this shared attention, but also out of a continuation of duty: the train journey undertaken sitting side by side, the lunch shared together, the tickets purchased under the same name with the same credit card. It never results in an increase of satisfaction. We had learnt this. Besides, I was still blankly refusing to discuss the idea of LA, which he'd raised a month or so beforehand, and his irritation over this festered. So when we entered the gallery space, he split off to the left and I to the right.

It was a strange and impressive exhibition that lulled me into something resembling a dream state. I moved around anticlockwise, clinging close to the wall, and then, once this circuit had been completed, moved out into the centre of the room, weaving my way between the sculptures that were positioned here and there under bright lights. One might compare it to walking through a forest, circling ancient trees of a wide and spiralling girth, peering into the burnt-out hollows of their trunks. At a certain point I came to a standstill. There was a small print on the wall that looked to me like a preparatory work for one of the larger and most celebrated sculptures. I found myself transfixed by this black and white plan, more moved by this than by the great resulting mass of industrial steel that now hung in the corner. I don't know for how long I stood there, but at a certain point I became aware of Patrick beside me.

I was standing very close to the image, as close as I was permitted, and because of this my peripheral vision was reduced. I felt Patrick's presence as a sense of weight and shadow in my vicinity, just to my right, slightly behind me – but could not say that I saw him. He certainly did not reach out to touch me, and I thought this was possibly because he was as moved as I was by the image before us.

While keeping my eyes on the drawing I started to say something to him, something about the mass of dark lines and their energy. Only he didn't reply.

Don't you think? I said, pressing him, but still without shifting my gaze from the drawing. When he didn't say anything I at last turned to face him, only to find that what I had taken as the living form of my husband was in fact the sculpture of a man, cast in metal and life-size, six foot, maybe six foot two, I reasoned – almost exactly Patrick's height. A sign on the floor read Do Not Touch. A shiver ran through me, which was partly embarrassment that someone might have heard or seen me talking to what was, in the end, only myself, but the shiver was also one of mild horror, or forced recognition: I could no longer tell the difference between the listening, living body of the man to whom I was married, who sometimes stood just behind me in this way while he dried the wine glasses as I washed, and the dull force of an inanimate object – an iron man, or a tin man, or even a clay man, say. Or maybe he had become just a straw man, a logical fallacy without substance.

I returned from my walk to find them still at the kitchen table, playing the game. I continued up to my study without talking to either of them and took out my notebook. I wrote fast, putting down the whole argument almost verbatim. At a certain point I had to stop and rub the muscle at the base of my right thumb because it was cramping from gripping the pen so hard. I included everything he said, the comments about my inability to play games, a slight revision of his act of deceit, going over it to change key details for dramatic purposes and adding other things besides, as well as some of the stuff about the blue trousers – that outfit I wore to the event in Paris. Then I typed up the best bits and broke this into several sections and numbered these before identifying, for the senior editor, the paragraph breaks in the manuscript where each new section needed to be inserted: on page seventy-three, after paragraph two, insert new section number one; on page 120, after paragraph one, insert new section number two, and so on.

Then I printed this out and turned off the computer. I would give the corrections to Ada first thing the next morning, there would be just enough time. I heard Patrick coming up the stairs then and pushed the pages into the desk drawer only moments before he stepped quietly into the room. I sensed him behind me. He placed his hand on my shoulder – a warm, thick, meaty pressure. My stomach turned.

23

After the investigator hung up that night, I too eventually replaced the receiver on its cradle. I turned off the lamp and went back to my room and closed the door. I lay down in my bed and listened to the thwunk-thwunk of Lexi's sandshoes circling in the clothes dryer. Adam must have put them in there sometime earlier. I shook a sleeping pill from its white plastic canister and swished this down with the glass of stale water left on the bedside table. I plumped the pillow, turned off the light. Then I lay back and waited for that old loosening of muscles, first the neck and shoulders, then the back of the legs, the feet, the weight of the skull, the jaw unhinging, the eyes pooling heavy into their sockets, waiting for that whole long warm blanket of gravity to cast itself over me and let me be gone. The last I remember is the rain starting up outside; the wind tossing it against the glass like a handful of small pebbles.

When I eventually woke the next day, the bedroom was filled with bright sunlight. The nausea was there again – a deep, unsettling tide of queasiness. Certain movements seemed to make it worse. I rolled over and took a sip of water, then suddenly dry-retched into the wastepaper basket. I waited until I heard Adam leave for work. Then I got up and went downstairs. The house was quiet, the windows open, letting in the humid air. The thick scent of wisteria, mock orange, pittosporum. I stepped outside on to the balcony. The breeze stirred the trees. Like the kind one feels at the beginning of a journey as the train pulls out, picking up speed.

I never meant to go back, to come back, to return. Nothing should have happened as it did.

In the kitchen, May was making coffee while wearing sunglasses. Are you all right? I asked. Bad headache, she replied as she popped a couple of ibuprofen from their foil pack. She was hunched over a little, in an attitude of self-protection. Black coffee? she asked. I nodded in thanks and took the cup she offered me. This too was all I could manage for breakfast. The air in the house felt brittle after last night's argument about the scene at McDonald's. Tell Lexi and Jess that there's money for lunch in my purse? Then, nursing her coffee in both hands, she returned to her bedroom.

In those last days at May's house things started to rot. The muggy heat caused plant matter to decay; in the garden, leaves turned white with mildew. The pumpkin vine was spattered with blooms of fungus. Other plants decayed further down, where the stem entered sodden black earth. Yellow ladybirds gathered to eat what mould they could. From where I stood at the kitchen window I could see banks of dark storm clouds in the distance. The garden filled with an eerie yellow glow as the last of the sun broke through the weather; the light viscous and lurid before the wind and rain lashed the trees, bringing down the bounty of green plums. Around me the air felt thick and damp, hard to breathe. The smell of jasmine and wild ginger crushed under heavy rain. Later, after I had gone, the unripe plums would rot where they lay, pecked at by birds, swarming with black specks of fruit fly. But that was still weeks away yet.

For three days May stayed in her bedroom, coming out only occasionally for water or caffeine, her sunglasses still in place while her headache throbbed. Outside, the summer rains continued. The air remained humid. Low, dark clouds filled the sky. I took May her coffee in the mornings and opened her curtains so that she could marvel at the sight of the jungle garden through her dark lenses, at the pink hibiscus and acid-yellow dahlias, at the mottled pumpkin vine crawling wild over the lawn. And morning after morning I woke to a fug of nausea. A strange, intense nausea that increased if I moved too fast, if I turned my head in a certain way, if I brushed my teeth too hard. At the same time my sense of smell intensified, doubled, tripled: I could smell car fumes in my bedroom from the very distant highway, the smell of onions or fish cooking was unbearable. And each night I waited anxiously, hoping the phone did not ring, that no one would ask for me.

Meanwhile, Christmas was only days away and there were preparations to be made. I thought of Joshua and the Christmas that Patrick had promised him. It had been little more than three weeks since Patrick died, but it felt now like months had passed, years; the night of the accident seemed like it had occurred in an alternate life, a

near-fiction. An impossibility still. And yet the days continued. Adam's family would be arriving soon, just before
Christmas Eve. It was more than clear that May was not
up to this and that she couldn't manage it on her own. At
the same time, I knew I had to leave. That I needed to get
away. That it was time to go back, or even somewhere else
entirely. Another call would come, eventually. A constant
queasiness stirred in my gut. During the day I felt vague,
a little light-headed, disoriented.

On the third night of May's quarantine Adam ordered a
takeaway, the fridge empty but for a tub of Greek yogurt,
a wilted bunch of chard with its white stems still held
together by a rubber band, and half a litre of milk. What
do you want Jess, Lex?! he shouted from the computer.
And they both called something back, simultaneously.
He shouted again, I can't hear you! Come and look at
the menu! But Lexi wouldn't, or only too late, after he'd
already put the order in, and then she complained about
his selection, so that when the pizza arrived she moped
over it, picking off all the toppings and putting them on
Jess's plate, who then fed them to the dog, who sat with
his muzzle on her lap, waiting for gourmet titbits: olives,
marinated eggplant, capers and feta.

Where's Mum? they both asked, and I saw him shrug,
as if he didn't know or, perhaps, as if he didn't care, before
replying that she was in her room.

Still, he said. All conversation, all niceties that passed
between the four of us took on, during those few days,
a hollow ring. I could smell the cardboard of the pizza
boxes. The slightly burnt edges of the pizza base. Nausea
rose up again. All I could manage was a piece of cold, dry

toast. And, like someone readying a room and setting it in order before departure, I offered my help.

May! I called, later that evening when she had still not come out. I'd put the pizza boxes in the recycling and loaded the dishwasher. The kitchen smelt of bacon and grilled cheese. I took her a glass of water with ice in it and she held the cold glass against her closed eyes, listing off in a rushed blur all the things she still had to do, or organise, or had to remember to do, all the things she needed to see to for the girls, to make things up to them, to be ready for Christmas. The presents she hadn't picked up, the food she had to buy. The extra ribbon, the aluminum foil, the Christmas crackers. My eyes feel bruised, she said, rolling the glass back and forth and back and forth over her closed lids, These unbearable headaches. May, I said. Let me help. Let me go do the Christmas shopping. At least that. You're going to run out of time otherwise, and then everyone will be turning up on your doorstep. And besides, I said, there's something I need to get.

24

I always had the greatest respect for Patrick's medium. The pure visuals of cinema that create, unconditionally, an entirely separate reality – the framing that makes us attend to things that are right in front of us but which we would otherwise overlook. In particular, I admire cinema for the way in which its women do not need to explain themselves as the women of fiction are required to do. Why did Chantal Akerman have the film character of Jeanne Dielman murder the man she had just slept with? We all have our theories, but Jeanne is under no obligation to voice her thoughts. After the murder she sits very quietly. We watch her watching her thoughts, watch her having them, sitting so still at the glass-topped dining table. But we don't know what these are. She doesn't have to give this away. Maybe she herself doesn't quite know. When I am writing, when I am in the middle of a book, there is always something I am waiting to find out. Something that exists for me to discover. A thing I cannot put my finger on, a lost cause in the chain of causes, something I don't yet understand or have full knowledge of. I try to find that lost cause so as to make use of it and fill the gap.

But for a long time everything is murky. I am vaguely nervous, irritated. As if someone is keeping a secret from me, the universe conspiring in this game. Clues present themselves. I dream of a dark-brown cat and the next day see one in a nearby garden. I often dream of things, animals especially, and then encounter them in the days following. Like Jeanne, their thoughts are also not made known to me. This dreaming followed by a sudden, almost mystical appearance of the thing dreamt has also happened with inanimate objects: tarnished ivory-handled cutlery, a baby's bottle, a pair of white sneakers. Some call these omens: the trail of signs that lead you to the discovery. The secret the work is hiding from you. The thing that you have hidden so well from yourself.

I did as I promised: I took the shopping list, and the car, and made my way to the supermarket. The rain was so heavy that the windscreen wipers were almost entirely ineffective against the summer downpour; everything outside was a blur of fuzzy grey. Headlights. Slow-moving vehicles. Small, dark umbrellas bobbing on the sidewalk. At the entrance to the car park two girls in school uniform sprinted for cover, their tanned legs slick and shiny in the wet, their long, drenched hair making ropes down their backs. That morning, Ada emailed: she hoped I was resting well. I just wanted to say that I'm so sorry, she wrote, we should never have let you go ahead with all those events. Please don't rush back, she continued. Just take your time, wait until you're feeling yourself again. And don't write! she said. Seriously, you work too hard and deserve a break. Everything's fine here. Valerie sends her love.

I had to delete the message. Pretend it wasn't there. She'd never said anything like this before. There was always the question of what I was working on next, and when it might be ready, or else she would send me favourable reviews, or reports in which I was mentioned. I never liked to read them, but Patrick kept tabs. And now what? I felt disposable. As if I were suddenly irrelevant, or a liability. A woman from which one might keep a safe distance. I could just drive, I thought. I could reverse and hit the main road and just keep going. Somewhere, wherever, anywhere.

But now there was a line of cars behind me, nowhere to turn.

I pressed the button for the parking ticket, took the piece of paper from the slot and the yellow barricade lifted up to make way for me, letting me into the dark, dry underground of the building, the air heavy with the smell of exhaust.

May had pre-ordered the turkey and the ham. I bought goose fat and custard and cream and brandy. It was a relief of sorts to be burdened by someone else's domestic duties – in this way I could imagine myself into a life of rhythm and plenty. I pulled a trolley from the bay and pushed it towards the cold goods, the wonky left wheel making me lean on the handlebar to keep it heading in a straight line. The wheel ticked and ticked as I moved along until I reached the supermarket freezer, where I paused, looking down into its depths. I slid open the glass door and smelt that freezer smell: something clammy and stale and a little sour, dehydrated potato or breadcrumbs or fish. She didn't say which kind of peas we needed: baby or regular, minted or plain, 250 or 500 grams, or more than that even. How many people were coming? Adam's brother and wife and parents, she hadn't mentioned the number of children. And maybe an uncle and aunt. May had tried to get out of it, citing her health and fatigue, and possibly even my visit, my presence, not as a source of conflict but as a figure she wanted to indulge – a person she wanted to spend time with – and yet found herself being convinced by the expectation of hospitality, and by the promise of her own strength, or the potential of strength, the strength that only needed to be called upon, as any hero's strength is tested and questioned before it shows itself in its full power. Of course she wanted to be that. And this was what Adam had said to her, apparently, that she'd be fine, that she was always fine in the end, she knew she was, and besides, you're an amazing cook, he said, and really, you're getting better and stronger every day. The headaches or whatever, they always pass, he told me, and by Christmas, he said, she'd be back to her old self. She liked cooking anyway. And she'd enjoy it. You always say this, he told her. That's not true, she said.

But *afterwards*, he said. *Afterwards* you're always glad you did it. The whole Christmas thing. And everybody loved her food, and she *would* enjoy it in the end, he told her, You know you will, the company and the wine.

How is it that we find ourselves so easily persuaded by this idea of our own greatness, the vision of our invincibility, when really what we know we need is an acknowledgment of our real, if only passing feeling of weakness and incapacity? Simple humanness. I watched him flatter her into an idea of strength that she in no way possessed, not then, at that time anyway. But she wanted to be this greater thing without realising that her effort to become it only allowed him to evade the task himself. She did not ask him for the same display of greatness, of strength, no one did, it was not necessary, it did not need to be proven because it was assumed, there was no imperative to demonstrate the overcoming of frailty, weakness, fatigue. And so she exhausted herself doubly by trying to live up to this thing that she never really wanted for herself, but was convinced that she should want for herself, because someone else wanted it for her, even if they wanted this for their own unspoken advantage, and so she was persuaded, somehow, that this hidden and un-expressed power was part of her character, latent, waiting to be brought out by the challenge of Christmas dinner.

I reached into the freezer and took a jumbo pack of regular peas. I moved on from this to the fruit and vege-tables, where I found the Brussels sprouts contained in small netted bags made of yellow plastic mesh. Red cab-bage. Waxy potatoes. The mint was to be bought per sprig in a tiny sealed bag. The cranberry sauce was somewhere near the Vegemite, May had told me. Then I lined up at the cash register and placed one item after another on the conveyor belt. I put the bags of shopping in the trolley and pushed this towards the pharmacy that stood just next to the supermarket, under the cover of the mall. I left the trolley outside.

I scanned the shelves, trying not to look like I was searching for something in particular. An assistant asked if she could help me and I mumbled that, no thanks, I was fine. I found the pregnancy tests high up on the far aisle, among baby wipes and sanitary pads. On the way towards the checkout I picked up some toothpaste, a packet of tissues and some hair elastics, to hide the real purchase, to downplay it with the paraphernalia of everyday life. So that when I placed these items on the ledge near the register it would all just be a jumble of pink and white boxes. Still, the cashier beamed at me as she scanned the box. She was young, maybe just out of high school, and had plastered her eyelashes in thick, dark mascara, her skin smothered in beige powder. Good luck! she said, joyfully, as she placed the test into a plastic bag along with the other items. I must have looked surprised, because she immediately apologised.

Sorry! she said. I just mean, I mean, it would be so exciting, such a cool Christmas present. I didn't mean to, I mean I just meant – I think it would be, like, really nice to have a baby? She beamed at me again. Her teeth were very white, and when she smiled I could see the paleness of her gums. Thank you, I said, rifling through my wallet for the cash. Then I waved away the receipt and hurried out of the store.

Back at the house May was sleeping. I put away most of the cold food and boiled the kettle for tea. Then I opened the packet and read the instructions. I didn't need to take the test. I could already feel, inside me, the new state of things. Right at that moment my body gave little away. It wouldn't stay like this, though. My jeans were slightly too tight at the waist. The nausea was intense. All I wanted to eat were bagels with cream cheese or plain toast. I locked myself in the bathroom, peed on to the strip of plastic, then waited with my eyes closed. The line came up pink, the double line or the line with the cross, whatever kind of line that meant the test was positive after all. In your condition, she'd said – the woman at the police station in Japan. The one who brought me the persimmon and the buttered rice. I slumped to the floor and cried.

Often, when I am sitting in the cinema and the film ends, I feel myself adrift, lost, almost homesick, disoriented even. For a brief moment I am unable to remember quite where I am, and what I had been doing before we sat down, and what I have to go and do next, once it's all over. I dread this moment, the moment of the film ending, because I always want to stay inside the film. I want to carry on as an observer of those lives forever, to see what happens next, to be relieved of this responsibility for myself, in my own life, to not have to think about my life, not have to plan, or make decisions, or ruminate on the best or worst course of action, or regret actions taken so far, dread whatever has to be done later that day, or the one after, or the one after that.

When the film ends this reprieve is also over, and with the appearance of the blank screen just before the credits start to roll I always feel a jolt – so strong as to be almost physical. I believe in the film too readily, too entirely, and the ejection from the world of the film always surprises and troubles me. I dislike this transition so much that sometimes, when Patrick asked if I wanted to go and see a film, I would refuse just so as to avoid this sensation at the end. It wasn't so bad if the credits ran across the final scene, so that the rolling list of titles and names was superimposed over the characters and the landscape, giving me time to adjust, to reconcile the fictional and the real, to recognise the artifice and break free of it, pull back. But it was unbearable if the screen just went dark and then the white text appeared, cruising over this blackness. In that moment I had to work back to remember where I was, or else sometimes the sudden realisation of real life going on outside, the life I was supposed to go back to, would fill me with unjustified foreboding. The ordinariness of it all, the low levels of feeling, the lack of a soundtrack. The longer I sat through the credits the worse the feeling grew, and I preferred to cut this short by leaving the cinema quickly, before the credits were finished. I liked to stand up as soon as they started to roll, before the lights came on, and make my way along the aisle, stepping over people's handbags, then turning towards the exit and the tunnel of light which I could see now that the usher had propped open the door. I could be at the toilets first this way and avoid the long line at the tiny art-house cinema we liked, the one that only had two stalls for the women. I could have a moment alone in the bright lights of the bathroom and shock myself back to daily life. Patrick, though, he liked to sit through the credits to the very end. He watched right up until after the logos appeared at the very bottom of the credits and the screen went blank. He liked to sit through all this, he said, so as to feel the after-life of the movie in the last songs. The transition between the experience and its ending never bothered him. The shift between representation and real life never tripped him up. He knew it was a film. He knew that outside the cinema there was our ordinary existence. He didn't mind this, the gap. In fact he liked the long segue between these states that the credits allowed. And so I would leave him sitting there, all alone in the dark, while I rushed out to stand under the bright lights of the bathroom and check my appearance in the mirror. Reaffirm it. I would splash cold water on my face, reapply my lipstick, touch up my hair. You see women doing this all the time in public restrooms. But you never notice any significant difference between the version they first present with and the touched-up one with which they depart. They appear a little jauntier, maybe, the head held a little higher. But nothing much changes, nothing essential. They have simply taken a moment in between one phase and the next – before moving to a different room, or on to a new task, towards a different city – just to check that they are still there, that the feeling they carry inside them, of evaporation or dilution or erasure, is false. That their outline holds. They pause at the doorway, then step forwards and look for the real person who promised to wait for them. I'll stand here, he always said, under the clock.

I wrapped the test up in the plastic bag that the cashier had placed it in and dropped this in the bin. I washed my face and gulped cold water from the tap. In the kitchen I could hear Lexi and Jess arguing. There was still the rest of the food to unpack. I couldn't think clearly. I felt sick. I tried to count back, by weeks. Then forwards, by months. The question of when, and then how. It must have happened during that last month or so, in the final lead-up to the cruise, when it felt like we had at last reached some common ground, when we had tried so hard to find our way back to each other. We loved each other well then, or so I thought. What we had between us, Patrick told me, meant everything to him, he never meant to sabotage it. I

forgot then all about the changes I had made to the manuscript, and the note I had sent through with the proofs.
I thought everything would be OK. Now I just wanted
May to get up and take charge. To be strong and unailing,
as she was when we were girls. Instead I returned to the
kitchen and put away the pantry items, then removed all
the tupperware containers with half-eaten or rotting food
so that I could fit the rest of the shopping into the fridge:
cured meat and cheeses and fruit. The smell of the ripe
mangoes made bile rise in my throat.

Some hours later, May emerged from her room and
took up a place on the couch, an old blanket pulled to
her chest despite the summer weather. Adam said he'd
barbecue the turkey but May said she didn't trust him. He
shrugged and took a beer from the fridge, not so keen on
the task that it was worth an argument; he'd happily settle
for the assumption of his own ineptitude, even if this was
a quality that he refused his wife.

I can cook it, I said to May. Not because I wanted to,
or because I even knew how, but because it was better to
be busy, because I couldn't think of what else I was to do,
because I was waiting, just waiting now, and because all
the family was arriving the next day and it was too late
to tell them not to come. Too late for me to leave at short
notice.

25

On Christmas Eve I stayed in the kitchen as cars pulled up on to the kerb and loud greetings were made at the front door. The air conditioner swivelled an icy draught into the dining room, blowing napkins and Christmas crackers to the ground. Carols played on the stereo, the kitchen extractor fan roared at maximum setting, pointlessly sucking up smoky air as yet more and more heat was created. I basted the turkey, but in the rush of attending to the vegetables and the steamed pudding I forgot to cover it. When the timer went off hours later it came out looking as though it had been put through a dehydrator. The legs, over which there had been much bartering, were a dark, unhealthy shade of brown, tending towards black, so that the skin appeared like a cling film pulled tight over sinewy flesh. When I poked what should have been the fattest part of the leg, the skewer went straight through the skin, as if popping it, and into air – the meat having dried up and shrunk against the bone. The rest of the bird fared little better: there were some softer, slightly juicier parts at the breast, but otherwise it was, as some little-known relative at the table said, like chewing on genuine boot leather. He laughed, I swallowed my wine. I thought then of the frost on the heath. Of the crisp morning walk Patrick and I might have been taking now. Of the milky-blue winter sky. The icy grass crunching underfoot. He would have kept his arm round me for warmth. It could have been a completely different Christmas, like the kind we used to have – intimate and loving. And now there I was sweating in my sister's house, exhausted from making a festive dinner for a family that was not my own. The sprouts were too soggy, the potatoes not crisp enough. To help soften the blow of this, I filled people's glasses liberally. One after another and another, and still more. At least, May said, there is dessert. Our father had given May the thruppenny bits for the pudding, the same ones we had spat out as children year after year and tried not to swallow. At the end this was brought to the table, set alight, its brandy-blue flame flickering. Hardly anyone actually ate it – it was too rich and heavy for the middle of summer, too strong for the children. But the actual eating of it, the finishing of it, May said, didn't really count. Everybody liked the first mouthful, she said, and maybe that was enough: the performance of it. People ate the custard. They spat out the coins. I looked at the shiny metal globs, still coated in masticated dried fruit, and thought, I will be the one left to wash those. Lexi snuck into the kitchen and drank the remaining custard straight from the carton – taking it from the fridge, folding back the cardboard spout and pouring the cold yellow goo directly into her mouth, wiping her lips as she sat back at the table. By then everyone was drunk enough to be interested in the jokes that came with the crackers. They read them aloud. Wait, I've got one, Adam called. I had started to gather up the plates to take to the kitchen and in the clatter of cutlery and china I missed the punchline, a good one clearly as everyone laughed hard, and as I carried the plates from the table I heard Lexi call out, Stop! Stop! I think I'm going to wet myself!

Just then the phone rang, and because my hands were full, someone else answered it. It was for me. I put the plates down, wiped my hands on the damp tea towel and picked up the receiver. I can't remember whom I spoke to now, or exactly what they said. I remember thinking that no one was meant to phone on Christmas Day, but maybe it was Boxing Day, maybe it was Christmas Eve – to be honest I can't say for certain when May and her family chose to have their festive meal, at some point it was meant to be on Christmas Eve. Which means, given the time difference, it might have been an ordinary day in England, not a holiday or a festive day, or maybe the man calling had forgotten about such festivities, or wished to avoid them; perhaps he was drowning in paperwork and just wanted to get through it no matter what. Maybe this was the only spare moment he had, when no one else was around, or he could have simply been working late, too late, keen to escape the ordeal of Christmas, whatever that was for him, in his home with his family.

His voice was slightly phlegmy. Not the same man as before. As soon as he started speaking I felt the most extraordinary fatigue, the kind that made me feel I might collapse, faint, wither where I stood. Don't they normally surprise you? On the television news and in the movies such a man turns up at your door. On the footage your face is blurred, pixelated, made unrecognisable. A series of tiny moving squares. It is more than one man, normally. You see one man on either side of the faceless woman. You are given no warning, no explanation. I can't remember his name now, or what he said exactly, but I've said that before, many times in fact, this part is on record – what I remember is not being able to remember clearly, not being able to make sense of things, and so everything afterwards remains a jumble. Shock, my lawyer said. Delayed shock. Something different from unreliability. The man on the phone had a slight accent but I couldn't place it. He made it clear that he knew things about me without telling me how he knew, and used this information as a way of bargaining, trying to gain my trust, I suppose, wanting me to believe what he told me and do as he instructed. This isn't a choice, he said. It's a warning, a fact. Listen to me when I say I'm doing you a favour here. You can make things easier. It would be wise to prepare yourself. These, at least as far as I recall, were some of his phrases. Otherwise someone will be there soon, he told me. By tomorrow afternoon I expect. It would be good to keep this hushed up a bit, he continued, nobody wants a scene. Just do this quietly. What I tell you to do.

New footage had turned up. A fellow passenger who'd been out filming the storm and later posted the clip to YouTube. He gave it a soundtrack and red captions. He didn't see the two dark figures in the background. On the deck. That night, almost four weeks ago, or so the man on the phone told me.

This is complicated, he said, by anomalies in the autopsy reports. There were some concerns. Some disparities.

One report said heart attack, which would have caused the fall. Another said drowning. The first said heart attack as a result of the temperature – the shock to the system – which can't therefore rule out the possible involvement of another person. And then the body, some signs of struggle which were agreed upon in both reports. The torn muscle of the right arm, indicating he had tried to hold on, to not fall, or to pull back. The scratches indicating conflict and maybe self-defence. I put one hand to my belly, thinking of the possibility, of the child. It's likely that charges will be laid, the man said.

I hung up just as May came into the kitchen carrying another load of plates. She scraped the leftovers into the bin, which was already close to overflowing.

I'll take that out, I said. She stepped back and piled the dishes by the sink and I leant over the bin and unfastened the bag liner. I took the corners and tied them into a knot. The plastic was thin and white and sagging under the weight of its contents – too much liquid, with a small dark dribble escaping from the bottom corner. I carried it quickly through the back door. Outside it was raining. The summer dusk was setting in. We had eaten early, on account of the smaller children, cousins of one order or another, and the day had been something of a disappointment to them due to the weather. No one had been able to use their new pool toys after all – a large inflatable alligator and a giant purple unicorn, along with a polo set – and as a result they had spent the afternoon tearing round the house, high on sugar and cross with this unexpected confinement. The rain was not cold though; I could feel it on my face: fat, warm drops as I took the path down the side of the house to where the bins stood between the fence and the garage. They could have swum after all, and treated it for what it was, a day of monsoonal showers. But in truth, no adult wanted to spend their afternoon in a state of near-hyperventilation, blowing up those pool toys in between drinks. I saw then that the wind had thrown open the lids from the bins, and two fat crows perched on the contents, stabbing and dragging at the refuse. The ground was littered with debris: the plastic wrapping from the bacon, the oily foil packaging of the butter, the old chicken carcass from some days ago that I had tied up in another bag before depositing it outdoors, but which had now been found – the smaller bag torn open by the birds, the bones scattered over the concrete. One crow stood keeping watch while the other pulled at some dark, wet piece of trash. I tried to shoo them away, waving my arm and calling, but they just looked at me with their beady and unblinking eyes. Shoo! Shoo! I cried, kicking the bin, and slowly, lazily, they hopped down and flew a few metres off, where they stood, waiting for me to be done with my business so that they might return to theirs. I tossed the plastic bag into the garbage and replaced the lid. I knew then that there would be no second chance, no starting over. Events that I couldn't control were now under way. From here on there would be only repetition, revision, the qualification of facts, alibis, the question of motive or its absence. Even if it came to nothing, even if the thing that the man on the phone threatened, or that he predicted, rather – even if this never eventuated, the possibility of it had been brought into existence by his suggestion. I could not stay at May's any longer. I could not, as I had once thought or imagined, just begin again as if the accident and Patrick's death had never occurred. I could not, in reality, take to the road or the mountains. If you do as I suggest, the man had said, everything will be easier. Say nothing, or make some excuse. Don't bring anyone else into this. You don't need any more attention than you're going to get. Trust me. Let's just try to keep this quiet for the time being, he said.

I went inside and dropped a handful of ice cubes into a Scotch glass, then I turned on the kitchen tap and filled the glass with water. May was making tea and coffee. The dishwasher was already on, but the pots and pans were waiting in the sink. I told her I was happy to do them later, but that I was feeling really tired now, that the day had finally caught up with me and that I just needed a minute to lie down.

Back in my room, I waited for the ice to melt a little then pressed the cold glass against my forehead, the ice softly popping and cracking in the water. For a moment my body registered this sound as its own; as if the bones in my skull were hinging open a little, coming adrift by small increments. This error brought its own relief – a momentary conviction that the dark matter of my brain was giving up its tension, that the bones of my skull were widening a fraction so as to give my thoughts more room. I packed my suitcase. Then I went to the bathroom and collected all my toiletries: creams and deodorant and make-up. I used a tissue to wipe off the excess gunk of toothpaste from around the edge of the nozzle and closed the cap. I washed out the plastic canister which held my bar of soap and packed another smaller toiletry bag for my hand luggage – a jar of face cream, lip balm, saline spray.

At last I lay down and turned off the lamp. In the hall-way I could hear people saying their goodbyes. The light on the porch was shining into my bedroom. They would wonder where I was, and very soon they would forget I had not been there to see them off. Car doors opened and closed. Headlights moved across my bedroom wall. Pat-rick had often waxed lyrical about the force of the tragic in everyday life – the pulse of its aliveness. Its power to move. The problem of complicity. He liked to marvel at it from the sideline, without necessarily feeling the force of it in his daily life. He liked to stand up and applaud at the end of the show. He was a spectator, not an agent; an observer of the greater ambitions of art, its loyal witness. All the rest, I see now, he left to me. I did not know what I would say to May, how I would tell her, what I would offer in my own defence.

It's easy now to see the events of that night from a distance. To recognise a trajectory of inevitability that was closed to me at the time. Late at night, when everyone here is sleeping, I let my mind stretch out into the darkness and it feels almost simple to unpick the details that once seemed unapproachable, unthinkable. All around me the building is quiet except for the soft scurrying of mice in the wall cavities of my room. They scratch about, hidden from sight, making strange rasping noises that give me the shivers. Each summer they call in the pest man to lay poison. But everything is so old here, and there are so many small crevices for the creatures to come through that the problem is never solved. I need to pee. In the toilet I switch on the light and hear the mice scurrying before I catch sight of them; there is a gap between the awning and the door jamb and they rush for this. A slip of a tail. A pointed snout; the things I see in the sudden brightness. Then they are gone, back into the shadowy cracks of the building.

He read it on the cruise, my book. Or at least he read those last-minute changes that I had made in the heat of the moment and then forgotten about. It was the day before the storm; the weather was muggy, and we were lying out on the deck. I thought at the time that the cruise was working. That being stuck together in a small cabin in the middle of the ocean had given us back what we had lost: that intimacy, that total knowledge. While we lay next to each other he reached out and held my hand, his touch so very gentle. I felt the relief of this in my whole body; a new lightness. Even Patrick seemed to have relaxed. He didn't set out that day to read the book from the beginning, but took the copy I had in my bag and flicked through it, as one does, holding the spine in the fingers of his right hand while fanning through the pages with the thumb of the left. It was meant as a gesture of admiration: Look what you have done. He stopped here and there, on one page or another, and scanned the words. This was how he found the additions, some of them, but not all. Of course he was furious.

26

The floating world. In Japan, I had heard people use this phrase as a way of referring to life on earth. A brief passage. The cherry blossoms, they said, lasted only three days. Like human life, the petals are fleeting. After snow, there are more flowers; an eternal cycle of blossoming and decay. Of force manifest and then dissolving.

When I booked the cruise, I chose Japan as our destination because I thought it was something that Patrick would like. While he'd once been a voracious reader of thick novels, for some time he'd been finding it hard to concentrate and had turned instead to poetry, and haiku in particular. It brought him back, he said, to his cinematic roots: the collision of objective images that could, when placed next to each other, disintegrate the totality of an event. Sometimes he would read these to me at night while I drifted off to sleep. Silent autumn air . . . here and there among the hills rising thin blue smoke – Gyodai. Or, better yet: By abandoned roads this lonely poet marches into autumn dusk – Basho. And then my favourite, which now seems too prescient, as if we secretly knew what we were moving towards, and the contact with the poem, as with any art, was a way of readying us for what lay ahead without our realising it: On the last long road when I fall and fail to rise . . . I'll bed with the flowers – Sora.

The night before I left May's house to return to London, I dreamt of a long walk through unfamiliar countryside. It was springtime, the air mixed with warm and cool currents, the sky pale blue. It was the afternoon, and I remember the watery sunlight, the bright green of the hillside and the light through the foliage. I had set out on my own to look for a prized landmark. Although I walked for hours I found nothing, so returned to Patrick and told him of my failure. We then set out again, together. Dusk was settling in by that time, the landmark was not supposed to be far away and I couldn't understand how I had missed it when, after all, we had travelled so far to see it – this was the whole point of our journey. Look, he said, there– there it is. But there was nothing to see, just a white fence delineating a lump of ground. We stared for a while at the pile of turf then turned back. I was starving but had brought nothing to eat and fretted about this as we walked on and on, somehow missing the turning to the house where we were staying. The path was muddy and overgrown. I felt weak with hunger. Patrick walked ahead. Suddenly I stopped, for there was something in my way: Look, I called, there's a loaf of bread! I picked it up; it was soft and fresh and smelt of sour rye, the top dusted with white flour. I was about to eat it, so happy that I had found food in this way, perfect, recently baked food, bread that had perhaps accidently fallen from someone's shopping bag, or else been left just for me on the path.

Stop! Patrick said as I lifted it to my mouth. You can't eat that.

Why not? I asked, entirely bewildered.

Because, he said, you don't know who has pissed on it.

On that last day, the day of the accident, I had been reading a book by the pool in the midday sun. The light shone directly on to its pages. You should put a hat on, he said, coming up behind me. Or sunglasses. He ran his finger along my collarbone. It's not good to read with that bright light on the paper. It burns your eyes. The rays or whatever. Hm, I said, ignoring him because I was absorbed in the story. Or I didn't care. But he kept on. I can go get them for you. You really shouldn't read like that. You'll go blind. Why don't you come inside? Maybe it was his way of trying to be conciliatory, given the argument we'd had the day before about my book and what I'd written.

I looked up, squinting. Relative to him I had young eyes and he had once wanted to protect these, wanted me to be able to keep seeing him and to see everything, to go on seeing everything about him right up to the very end. Come inside with me, he said again. You know it's cool down there, in the cabin. We always did have extraordinary make-up sex, mind-blowing even. I'm fine, I replied, as I lay back, soaking up all that dangerous light. Why don't you go get yourself a drink? Later of course, I followed him.

★

In the morning I made an excuse to May. I said a problem had come up with a contract, just book stuff, and that some clause had to be renegotiated. It was too difficult to work it out by phone. My rationale was sudden and not wholly convincing. Are you sure? she said. Are you sure that's all? Did something upset you? Was it something last night? I'm sorry I've landed you with so much this last week, I didn't mean to, I'm so sorry, and you've been amazing taking it all on – I've hardly been hospitable. No wonder you want to make a run for it. I mean, she said, I'm sorry, I don't mean it like that. I just don't know what I would have done otherwise. I probably shouldn't have asked it of you, unless it's something else? Did Adam say something? He can be completely tactless, especially after a drink or two. Awful sometimes, actually. Please, tell me if there's something I can do to make things better. But seriously, what will you do? I mean afterwards, once the contract is sorted out?

I had already called a taxi that would take me to the airport. I'm sorry, I said, pushing my sunglasses down over my eyes, my throat tightening. I'm so sorry for the suddenness. It's just this thing, I said, rifling through my purse to check I had my credit card. I mean, it's complicated. More than I thought.

May was crying. I'll tell you everything later, I said, I will. I'll call you, I promise. As soon as I land.

I'll never forget the light that morning as the taxi pulled away. After the rains the world seemed washed clean. The light clear and luminous. It cut brightly through the trees, glittered over the surface of the pool. As the taxi reversed then turned out on to the road, I glanced back to the house and saw the darker hillside reflected in the wide glass doors, the image slipping and tilting. A giant wave skimming the edge of my vision before disappearing from view.

27

I had to ask him to repeat it. That last night on the ship.
What? I yelled through the storm. What did you say? He
said it again and still it made no sense to me. The rain was
torrential. The ocean and the thunder so loud.

She's pregnant! he called out. I said she's— He was
soaking from the overflow of the waves. The ship leant
violently. I'm sorry, he shouted through the storm. I
didn't mean for— I held on fast to the railings, slipping
a little. I'm the— he said, but the wind carried his voice
away. We had just spent the afternoon below deck. We
had been happy, even deliriously so. Now the lies massed
in my brain, a swarm of errors: the before and after, the
moments in between. He must be wrong. Or else she was
lying. Of course she was. But when did he know? Unless
it was, unless he meant for it to happen this way, if he had
planned it or if— He couldn't be saying this, couldn't be
serious, not after everything. If you hadn't, he started to
say. If you'd only— as a giant waved slammed against the
railings. I thought of what we'd just experienced together,
the reunion I thought we'd shared.

Another part of me took over then, the shaking body,

electric with rage, my pulse thumping in my neck. The facts unwinding then coming back together again. You can't be— I started to yell, as water rushed up over the railings.

In that moment I wanted just to be free. To be free of him, and our marriage and all the ways in which we had come to burden one another. How much I resented then everything I had done for him. He had encouraged my own greatness, promised it even, all that time ago in the taxi. Did he even remember? Just imagine, he once said, what you could become, what we could be together. But that ambition – I understood that it had come at a cost; to think of all the things I had sacrificed because for years I had been so devoted to him, to us, to the idea of our art. To think he could have even asked me to move to LA when he would never return with me to my own country. I realised then, perhaps for the first time, exactly how much I had given up: my father, my sister and her children, the possibility of my own family, a quiet and wholesome existence of the kind that so many other women aspire to. I had believed him. All that ambition, which he encouraged, fuelled an ascetic tendency that now sharpened my life to a point. I had turned forty earlier that year. Patrick had bought me pearl earrings that didn't suit me but which he liked to see me wear. That night, on the ship, I was almost the same age Patrick was when we first met, give or take a little. I realised then how much adult life he must have had before me, how I was only one small part of this, a blip. And yet he had been the whole of mine.

The storm was worsening. Patrick! I yelled. What are you doing? We've got to get inside. I reached out to him, but he pushed my hand away. I felt the totality of his rejection burn through me and in response I made some hollow threat. He lifted his face towards me then and said something he perhaps would not have said were he not so out of it. Something he must have been storing up. Something he must have been trying not to say. Something he must have thought of frequently, but at intervals.

You know if it wasn't for me, he said, you'd have come to nothing.

You don't mean that, I told him. You're really drunk. But then he yelled it again. It's true, he said, and you know it. We'd have been better off with a child.

I stepped back a little, scared and disbelieving.

I had to get away from him. We need to get out of the storm, I yelled as I stumbled towards the door. He moved fast then and grabbed my wrist, his grip hard. Don't, I said. Don't do that. I pulled myself free and he lunged at me again, a tiger lashing out its paw.

You know this is all because you wouldn't, he said. It was the one thing I asked of you, and you wouldn't!

The boat tilted and Patrick vomited again then wiped his mouth with the sleeve of his bathrobe. Somehow, at some stage, I had made the error of thinking that to become a great artist one had to learn to renounce; to forsake carnal distractions in the name of some more abstract principle and to practise this in so many different ways until the work called on you for real. To forsake sleep or money, or meat or wine in order to become, at last, a pure channel, an empty vessel, a force of nature. To forsake children. He loved me more as an artist, I always reasoned, than he ever could love me as a mother to his child. And there I was, thinking the cruise had returned us to each other; that we might again be what we once were. The one thing? I screamed into the storm. The one thing? I said, shoving at his chest. You think you've only ever asked me for one thing?

Hey, he said, raising his arms. Let's just treat this as our last hurrah. His words were slurred. He was more drunk than I at first thought. Maybe out of his mind. I said this, Are you out of your fucking mind? What the fuck? I screamed as I shoved him harder, and harder still, his hands coming down as he tried to ward me off. You think you've only ever asked me for one thing? What the—

My father always said that I didn't know my own strength. Although I was older than May, I was always smaller – slight and lean, with a wiry energy. Sometimes when we fought I would shove her or hit her. She would cry every time, fake tears, I always complained, that nevertheless drew our father's attention and he would scold me: You might not have intended to hurt her, he'd say, but you don't know your own strength. It was a kind of compliment masked as criticism: he wanted me to be strong, but not show it like this, not display it. I was to keep my strength a secret and learn to rein in this dangerous thing, even if I myself did not feel that strength and had no physical awareness of it. I knew my own hot temper, but not what it could do. Or so my father claimed; I ought to check myself for this power that I didn't know I had.

Maybe May's tears were real. Maybe she didn't make herself fall, those many times. Maybe I pushed her harder than I meant to. After all, a girl and later a woman is taught not to become too familiar with her own strength, not to invest in it, not to identify herself by way of it. Of course I didn't know what I could do.

28

Because of the suddenness of my departure, I had to take whatever flight was left. It was a crazy long-haul zigzag that went via the US and then Frankfurt before arriving at Heathrow. When we at last landed and I stood up to make my way down the aisle, I realised I could hardly move my legs. The best I could do was collect my bags from the carousel and check into the airport hotel, too wasted to even consider navigating traffic and the rush-hour commute on the Tube. I took, once again, a white plastic room card. I scanned it and the tiny light above the door handle flashed green. I pushed the door open and stepped inside. The room stank of cat piss. In the foyer the hotel was advertised as being pet-friendly, although I hadn't seen any animals when I checked in. Now, though, their presence was obvious. It was a high smell, a tomcat in a nervous state marking his territory while his owner took in the view: the neon-red sign of a neighbouring hotel, the dusk sky. And once I could smell cat, I found myself looking for other signs of animal life – the scratches on the wallpaper near the window, the darker brown marks on the tan carpet. I boiled water in the coffee machine because there was no kettle. I mixed powdered creamer into my tea. White flecks floated on the surface. I drank anyway, scalding my tongue, then I undressed and stepped into the shower.

In the mid-point of life, one becomes universal. I mean this in the sense that at a certain stage your decisions no longer seem original, your sufferings no longer new or unusual. If anything, it feels that these sufferings and decisions are not yours, and do not belong to you, and have not been made by you, but are the remnants left over by the family that came before you, the unlived matter that you have somehow gathered, accumulated, inherited, imbibed, and now must live out one way or another in order to close some troubled circle, and at these junctures the only conversations worth having seem to be the impossible ones with the dead and with the missing.

Back in the days when I sometimes used to teach, I would give my students Henry James's famous adage as a point of instruction: 'Be someone on whom nothing is lost.' I would tell them this as a command, an imperative, a challenge. A lesson for the artistic life. In class, this conversation would sometimes segue towards a different philosophical challenge, which was to work out what to do with the world one observes, with those details one has saved and retained: how then to live? On a few occasions I found myself rounding off this discussion with the equally famous words of Rilke: 'You must change your life!' My students loved this one the most, even if they, like me, knew little of how to achieve such a thing. What might it really mean, what would this really look like? What would the risk be?

★

Two days later I was charged and brought to the mag-
istrates' court where I pleaded not guilty. Due to good
character and the fact of my pregnancy I was released on
bail and the case was transferred to the Crown Court for
criminal trial. In those first newspaper articles that came
out after the charges were laid, Patrick's life was well covered, scrutinised, and he himself was fawned over even in
death, while I was identified not by my own work, the
work I had done under my own name, but as the wife of
Patrick and as the daughter of the late scholar Dr H.K.
Blackwood. It was as if by being charged I had forfeited
the power to exist in my own right. In widowhood I had
at first been granted some privileges, but now everything
had to be reconsidered, including my own story, and the
appetite among the press was insatiable. The shift in narrative made for a media frenzy: journalists felt they'd been
made fools of, after having described me so generously as a
tragically bereaved woman. The public were angry – who
was I to take such action against a handsome and loving
husband who had granted me my every wish? This was
what the press wanted the people to believe, what they
wanted Patrick to look like: the rich and famous man, the
gallant knight, the great storyteller who had given us all
so much through his films. It was a version of those fairy
tales we all know so well, in which I was then cast as the
ungrateful child, the selfish daughter, the vain wife.

The media coverage continued around the clock. It's a
fucking circus out there, Valerie said, on the morning that

the Crown proceedings were to begin. She had picked me up from that airport hotel and after I was granted bail she stayed with me the whole time. Ada would have been there, only she'd had to go abroad at short notice to see to her father who'd been taken ill, and so had organised for Valerie to look after me. It's fine, I'd said. There was no need to apologise, in fact I was glad it was Valerie who kept me company then. She was quiet and soft, while Ada tended to swoop in – brisk and organised and always ready to take charge. Valerie was what I needed then. Now she was peering through a gap in the curtains, the press already waiting for me outside the house. Some witnesses, passengers on the ship, had been ruled out from testifying because they'd sold their story to the tabloids. Other new witnesses came forward with whatever they could proffer. May had wanted to come and support me, but I couldn't have her see me like this. Besides, I said, your girls need you more.

You should eat something, Valerie told me, coming away from the window. But I was too nervous and already dressed. My hands were shaking, and I worried that if I ate anything I'd only make a mess of myself. I wanted it over with. I said this, that I couldn't stand waiting any more. The traffic might be bad, and I didn't want to risk running late.

OK, Valerie said at last, pulling on her scarf and checking her watch. Ready when you are. Then I did what you see women doing as they hurry towards the getaway car, holding up a handbag or a magazine to shield their face from the cameras. I had the magazine, Valerie covered me further with her open coat. She drove. Before we stepped up into the building and through the metal detectors she straightened the collar of my shirt and smoothed back my hair where the wind had blown it out of place.

It's true, no one took my blood alcohol reading that night. It is also true that there are things I do not remember. Human failure is hard to tolerate, not least in oneself. But I didn't mean for it to happen this way. The mess of the whole thing. I really didn't. Maybe, I said to the court at one point – not that day, but later, when it was at last my turn to testify – maybe if I'd gone with him, when he first went up on deck. If I hadn't stayed in the cabin. He wouldn't have drunk so much then. Or if I'd insisted that he take the anti-nausea pills when I did. If I'd led him to the bathroom instead of letting him go outside. Maybe if I'd not followed him. If I'd not gone when he called but left him to his own devices, adhered to the warnings, stayed inside. If I'd not insisted, on the holiday, on doing something special for our anniversary, on taking the cruise that was also an urgent attempt to save the very marriage we were meant to be celebrating. If I'd stayed home and just let him carry on with his work and with his other commitments – I suppose I could call them that. If I'd not asked him to drop off the manuscript. And then all the little things beforehand, the things I might not have said, not have done, not have written. But by then it was a kind of foolishness, such thinking.

Afterwards, I said, I got stuck inside. After the, I mean— when the door slammed shut. It was so heavy. But finally I managed to open it and went out again, to see if— It had been so hot that day, the day he died.

357

29

Here, he had said, the morning before the storm, we should toast this. It was very bright that day, and I remember feeling a little giddy: so much heat, so much sun, too many martinis. He held the book in his right hand and flicked through the pages with his left. I know I've said this before – it is an image that stays with me. A gesture meant to flatter: Look what you have done. There was the initial scanning of random sections. Then the second faster, more attentive flicking through. Then he turned to the end pages, where I had included an Author's Note, just before the acknowledgements. Although I knew many of his films contained autobiographical elements, he was famously guarded about his personal life. He had always assumed that I too would toe the same line, keeping his confidence. When he realised I had disregarded this he was livid.

As a novelist, there are few formal avenues through which I can control how my work is positioned. Unlike his earlier critical writing, my books don't come with introductions or abstracts that set out the terms of debate and frame the reception. The best I get is a blurb, which, in the desire to establish intrigue, often turns out to be grammatically incorrect. I don't write them. I have sometimes suggested we remove the number of adjectives. Lessen the tone of female melodrama. So I decided to put this note at the end, by way of explanation. It was only brief, hardly offensive. Just direct and to the point. Which is unusual, I suppose. It was here that I discussed the structures of power which a woman's art must wrestle with before it is permitted to flourish, which was a way of explaining why this particular book had taken me so very long to write. The gap between books, like the gap between babies, is assumed to signal some biological problem, a weakness of sex, of function, a lack of commitment to the cause; she is guilty of weakness before proving herself otherwise. It is something that draws attention, a talking point, the starting place for questions: what happened to you? I wanted to pre-empt this. In truth, even though I did so less than I had at the start of our relationship, I still helped Patrick a great deal with his work. I wanted to take charge by stating this fact and considering its implications.

It wasn't like I didn't think about the consequences of publishing this. I must've written and scratched out those paragraphs more times than I can remember. The first versions are in a notebook somewhere. What ended up going to press was a shadow of those earlier rants. But that did little to console Patrick, who felt deceived. He had never meant to keep me from my own work, he said, and yet I made it sound deliberate – a plot on his part. He resented too the way in which I took credit here for his achievements, making it known just how much of a contribution I had made over the years. It was only fair, though, that I got some recognition for his ascent. In doing so, however, I reversed an idea he was very attached to – the idea that he had made me who I was – by instead suggesting I was the one who made him.

It wasn't like that, I explained. It's not like that. But he wouldn't listen.

Or is this one of the things you added afterwards? he yelled. To get back at me? To try to make me look bad? To make room for all the others to come out of the wood-work and accuse me of whatever thing I stopped them from doing too?

Sometimes, in my line of work, I've found the need to consult the archives of writers who have come before me. I have gone to their work in search of answers to problems I have created for myself and pored over their manuscripts, my hands in those white gloves, careful to leave no trace. What I find there has often surprised me. On the published page their work appears faultless, which is why I chose to pursue it in the archives. And yet what I have often discovered is a mess as good as any I could create – sentences scratched through and rewritten, whole sections deleted. Pages illegible with crossings out. After this I could never again see their books in the same way – or else I preferred the doubleness of the archives, alternate words penned in the margins or above and below the words on the line, so that when I returned to the published version it seemed thinner somehow, less resonant. Too straightforward. In our books we are expected to hide our labours, to eradicate lesser and alternate versions. I could footnote such a thought, perhaps, and suggest that we are expected to conceal these efforts so as to have something more to talk about, another story to circulate at festivals and whatnot, satisfying the public's endless appetite for the story of the story. The infinite hunger. It is how we sing for our supper. Although this theory, in itself, risks oversimplifying. Any craving can easily be abused. But whatever the reason for the eradication, once you know these alternate versions exist, once you have seen the labour and the crossing out and the rewriting, once you know they are there – the years upon years of drafting and revising – these details ghost the page irremediably.

Our marriage, on the ship, felt a little like that. A story I desperately wanted to perfect, only I knew too well how much I had reorganised the narrative and how much I had compressed, which is not quite the same as omission, but nor does it equal the dynamic of repression with which each of us is in some way familiar. At the time, these two versions – the perfect and the damned – were at war in me, one rising up while the other rested, only for the rested one to then wake, revived and bitter, ready to take out its twin. It was hard to tolerate the way in which Patrick had shifted the direction of our story without asking. He had turned it into a narrative I didn't like and couldn't abide and from which I could only be ejected – a bit player, as his life carried on replete with the progeny I refused because I wanted to avoid the disruptive presence of a child, only for that to be one of the things that ruined us in the end. There was nothing to equal the rage I felt when I realised he had taken our own story away from me.

Ultimately, in our marriage there could be no real winning, no resolution, no synthesis of component parts.

And I cannot now edit and revise my life as I would like, as so many of us wish to do once it is too late. Of course, Patrick must also have struggled to override what had gone on between us; he must have tried hard, that last day, to forget what I had written, just as I had tried, for months, to overlook what he had done. Maybe this was why he seemed suddenly irritable after the sex – that incredible sex, that make-up sex, the kind of sex in which you take everything out on each other – on that final day as we sailed unknowingly towards the storm. What he felt as a betrayal couldn't be easily or quickly quelled. The knowledge must have surged up in him again. Maybe that was why he went above deck without me and drank. Unless it was something else, something in that moment, after the sex, when he rolled away from me to check his phone.

We had an agreement, Patrick and I, that we were free to use each other's lives in our work but that our identities in those instances had to be disguised. We knew we couldn't very well censor our own creative impulses – one had to write about the things one had to write about. For each other, our work was all the richer due to those inside jokes, all the borrowings and exaggerations of character. But we had another deal on top of this: that whatever we took from each other and incorporated into our art had to be done honestly. We couldn't display our feelings in our art and then refuse to talk about them, refuse to acknowledge them as real and not fictional. But what if the fictional was the trigger of all that then became real? The Author's Note subverted our pact; I said things there that I'd never said to Patrick's face – truths my characters imagined long before I had the power to state these for what they were.

But it's fair to say here that while we had clear rules about what we could and could not do in our art, we never marked out any comparable rules for life. Patrick would have none of that. How could he make films, how could he have any vision if he was always thinking about how he was and was not allowed to live?

I know the Author's Note was more personal than Patrick would have liked. It wasn't just that he disagreed with the point I made; he resented the details I used to bolster this claim, begrudged the autobiographical emphasis. But it was always hard to tell where our marriage ended and my work began. I often dream now that I am drifting in a dark sea, the water around me lukewarm, like blood.

30

Inside, the courtroom smelt of leather and furniture polish. There was the bustle of paper, and people murmuring. I could feel my face heating up, everyone staring at me. All rise.

After the initial formalities I sat down beside my defence barrister, a young, fierce woman, thin and gristly, who gave nothing away. I entered my plea, and the jury was sworn in. It's not for us to win, the barrister had reminded me, but rather for the prosecution to lose. Then the prosecuting barrister stood and, pacing back and forth in front of me, outlined the case. He opened his hands to the court, palms showing, his voice deep. Your Honour, members of the jury—

There was a dry lump in my throat and I swallowed down hard. As if from some distance, I listened to the prosecutor tell a version of my own life. Beside me the barrister made notes, every now and then giving a small grunt of disapproval. I thought of Valerie, behind me somewhere in the public gallery. The prosecutor spared nothing, neither in his description of me nor in his reminding the jury of Patrick's renown: a man of esteem, widely celebrated, whose films were loved – a man who gave back to us the stories of our own lives. A good man, he told the court. A man who went out of his way to support the interests of his young wife. Who was known to dote on her, and who was instrumental in her own success – her first benefactor, one might say. This was a man who showered his wife with gifts: jewellery, clothes, even a cruise to celebrate their anniversary, little knowing that this particular gift would lead to his own death.

The cruise wasn't Patrick's idea, I knew that. But what proof was there now? He didn't even want to go. I made him. I begged him even. Still the prosecutor continued, pitting Patrick against me – emphasising his fame and the contribution he had made, the high regard in which he was held. By contrast I was turned into a shrew: a resentful and vindictive writer who sought to deliberately misrepresent her husband, even going so far as to publicly mock him – quoting as evidence a passage from my Author's Note.

He went on and on. I felt myself slumping. I put down here the worst of what I remember, but no doubt there was more. The transcript is there, should these recollections ever be queried or corrected. But God forbid I should ever have to return to this, to go back over all those details. Make no mistake, the prosecutor said, or something to this effect – the woman before you now made her fortune from fabricating and blatantly using her husband's life as fodder for her own work. A woman who has traded, quite literally, in the currency of falsehoods.

Then he launched into the backstory. My life. The instability of my childhood. His rhetoric was artful: Let

us pause here, he said. Let us open up the scene. He stilled
the moving image. In my own head I could see it unfold
and expand. Look at what happened to the child. To
me. Or maybe not. Maybe one doesn't want to know.
Maybe I don't. Maybe everything in my body has closed
down around that knowledge. Locked it in, compressed
the musculature, squeezed the ribcage tight around the
heart. Until life repeats and repeats and repeats the sequence. Until someone says, until you can't remember
what someone said when they asked you, when they asked
about what you remember. Until the pictures in my head
slip neatly over the top of one another, merging, sliding,
morphing. One disappearance after another, in life as in
fiction. The prosecutor pushed on. But I knew as well as
he that the linear story is always an illusion, a selective
retelling. Filmy. As Fellini said, I'm a liar but an honest
one. There are always so many ways of ending things,
and the end is never without means, although the means
can be without end. The ending of a poem, say, so often
seeks to propel one outwards, ever onwards. The hum of
it living on in the bloodstream. But in other areas of life
we have a preference for order and resolution, for all the
threads to be tied up and tucked in, no signs of thwarted
labours or good intent that has lost its way.

The prosecutor described Patrick as my rescuer. He
drew attention to what could be interpreted as my subsequent ingratitude, my lack of moral fibre, an inability
to recognise boundaries that other healthy people would
honour: psychological boundaries, emotional ones. How
I was prone to overstep, which is a common symptom
of—

The defending prosecutor stood up. If I may, Your Honour, this is argumentative.

Upheld.

The prosecutor paused only momentarily, then started again. The evidence will show that Ms Blackwood—

My heart was beating too fast. I tried to sit very still with my gaze lowered. The room was stuffy and overheated, the air heavy and thick in my lungs. I felt like I was about to faint. I bit down on my tongue to sharpen my attention, tried to slow my breathing. The prosecutor's voice carried on, but I couldn't seem to focus on what he was saying. I remembered that moment when I was being questioned in Japan. I remember watching the investigator's face while I talked: how he appeared very animated as I spoke, how he lifted his eyebrows, then squinted in concentration and pressed his lips together. I was hardly aware of what I was saying. I had been telling him about the sex. I remembered this now. I had forgotten. To think that all that was on record, the detail, that the prosecutor must have read this, or heard me on tape. I had gone on to explain that afterwards Patrick had seemed suddenly angry. His mood changed very quickly. I know that on record I said he'd seemed irritable, but it was more than that. Suddenly he didn't want to touch me at all. Like there was something wrong with me. He turned away from me and checked his phone. I started to cry. He showered. Then he took a bathrobe and said he was going up on deck for a swim and a drink. I was too ashamed to tell them this, to have this part written down or recorded. The feeling that in that moment – rolling off me, rolling away – I had become somehow abhorrent to him.

I looked up at last and the prosecutor met my gaze. In Patrick's films he liked to use close-ups of the actor's eyes. At crucial moments the camera would zoom in and show a single, troubled eye in great detail, blinking, watering. It was meant to suggest that we could now see into the mind of the character, that we were as close to their thoughts as the camera could get without the camera actually becoming the eye, which was the direction my own work tended to take. We often debated these tactics, but it almost tricked me every time, that close-up – the voyeur, the man with the camera, leaning in towards your face, pretending he knew what was going on inside of you. The prosecutor turned away and spoke to the jury. He wanted me to appear in a certain way, and took pains to represent me as a particular kind of woman: as a woman who expressed no outward sign of grief. Instead, he said, I went to parties, I went shopping, I went swimming. He portrayed me as a woman who lacked all sentimentality – so cold as to appear ruthless, even dissociated, in the pursuit of my own ambitions. Accusing me as a woman of all that which, as a writer, I had been denied – if my writing had often been deemed too feminine, I myself was now not feminine enough. At my core, I was always guilty of one failing or another.

Without missing a beat he then called to the stand the first witness. Of all people, it was our neighbour. I was taken aback. That miserly old woman who'd lived in the adjoining terrace for fifty years, long before the area was gentrified. A gossip and a scrooge. She hated the renovations we'd done, she disliked the manicured garden, she couldn't stand all the dogs that everyone had these days and was disgusted by the cool influx of money that had made her feel out of place in her own street. More than anything she hated me. I was never much good at staying up late, always preferring to get an early night and then set to work at dawn. Our house and hers had an adjoining laneway down which we would drag the bins every Wednesday, for the Thursday morning collection. The laneway was next to my and Patrick's bedroom and each week, for years on end, she would roll her bin slowly down this path at one or two in the morning, waking me and setting the dogs barking, ruining my morning's work because I couldn't ever get back to sleep. Patrick never noticed this because he slept so deeply. And then the following day, rather than return the bin in the morning, she'd drag it along the path hours after I had gone to bed, waking me again.

I lost track of how many times I spoke to her about this, until eventually I took to moving her bin myself, only for her to retaliate by dumping her bag of Wednesday night garbage in our backyard because the bin had already been taken, by me, to the kerb. When I asked her about this she acted as though she couldn't hear me, or couldn't understand what I was saying – was she deaf or senile? I wasn't sure, but I said this to her once. Clearly, though, she understood everything the whole time, because that day in court she was a wellspring of rumour and hearsay.

Of course, Patrick had always charmed her, carrying her shopping up the steps and bringing the paper in from the rain – it was me whom she despised. The press gave a full report on the statement she made from the witness stand: how she'd heard us arguing, how the arguments had escalated of late, how it was my voice that was most often raised. The sound of this frightened her – I could be very domineering, she said. In recent months, she told the court, there was often the sound of things smashing: furniture being pushed around or kicked over. Once, she'd been so worried that she came to our door on the pretence of needing help unscrewing a jar, and Patrick opened the door just as I threw something at him – which I had done once or twice, hurling a mug or a book, some harmless object that always missed its mark. But she didn't report it as such. She said that whatever I threw was heavy and metal, because it thumped hard on to the floor behind where Patrick stood, hunched over the ancient jar, trying to open it. There were scratches on his face, she said, and on his chest, just above the neckline of his T-shirt. It looked, she said, like they went down all the way to his chest.

The prosecutor paced, his robes sweeping out behind him as he summarised and reinterpreted this statement and others for the court, drawing attention to gaps in the story, to signs of rage. I was, he said, a violent woman that you trust at your peril. Did her husband call her out to the deck in the storm? Or did she in fact pursue him, even try to grab him? She says he was wearing slippers. The autopsy shows a glass cut on the sole of his left foot. And eczema on his chest? The defendant's DNA is in those scratches. Scratched raw. But not only that. As you will now see, this is a woman who allowed the public and all those around her to be deliberately misled, not for hours or days but weeks. Right up to this point, to this very moment, the defendant has continued not only to lie but to deliberately deceive, constructing – in keeping with her profession – a fictional version of her husband's death that she insists on passing off as the truth.

Just when I thought he was nearing the end of his summary, he called Trudi to the witness box. My breathing became fast and shallow. My body felt rigid, my pulse thumped in my neck. Trudi took her oath and squared her shoulders, but I have blanked out almost everything she said.

31

When I at last took the stand the next day I was exhausted and weak. I hadn't wanted to testify; I knew everything was against me. But the defence barrister insisted – the trial, she said, had sought to dehumanise me, and wrongly so. I needed to somehow re-establish my character. The one thing the jury had not yet heard was my own story in my own voice; my testimony needed to be both a disavowal of the charges and a plea for mercy. Disclose yourself, my barrister told me, as best you can. In my own head I ran those last days on the ship backwards and forwards, checking, memorising, smoothing out.

But the prosecutor anticipated this. Each time he asked me for the story, he asked it from a new angle, for a different reason, and very soon my own versions, no matter how good or true, failed to match up. I got confused as he started to dig into what I had thought was ancient history. I didn't mean that, I said. It was complicated, I explained. The marriage. Of course we fought. Yes, that's correct. For that, no. We always planned to collaborate. I didn't know that about his ex-wife. His son never really warmed to me, not really, I don't think. The pregnancy wasn't planned. No, he didn't. Neither of us did. Not by then.

I'm sorry, I will try to speak up.

Yes I would have told him. That's right, I don't know.

The child is due in June. All healthy I am told, thank you.

And can you please recount for me, the prosecutor asked, the last things said between you and your husband on the ship? The last conversation.

I nodded, then reached for the glass of water that had been placed next to me. It was empty. I asked for more. The usher stepped forwards.

I well knew that these were different things: saying words and conversing. Is a conversation the same as what we writers tend to call dialogue, or is dialogue closer to the things people say? The distinction between the two is subtle and one that Patrick liked to interrogate, just for the chance to refer to Hitchcock and that line he adored: *Wives don't nag, they discuss.* He liked to quip this at me now and then. Words rather than phrases.

There is a difference, I wanted to explain. The characters in those great Victorian novels have what we might call conversations – long, rambling exchanges in which suspicions are unpacked, positions detailed, histories developed. They last for pages, carrying on across rooms and through buildings. Or else these conversations are undertaken on long walks through grimy cities, wealthy estates, public gardens.

Whereas dialogue, on the other hand, or what you might call speech, never sustains itself in this way, never floats and drifts. If conversation might be a means without ends, dialogue is functional. Characters pass the salt. They make reference to the weather. They debate who has the gun or the drugs. Dialogue serves to break up the lengthy sections of prose. Only in art-house films do characters have exchanges without an end in mind. Those movies can go on for so long, and the steady shots of trees in the distance, or of branches blowing in the wind, or a damp field in the morning, are always so beautiful. We would watch these movies, Patrick and I, in rapt silence, and afterwards the effect was so powerful we had nothing to say. Only days later, once the experience had settled in us, would we talk about what we had seen and heard. And even then, we would tend to talk in fragments, expressing just joy or bafflement. We would do this while holding hands, walking by the river, and the knowledge of the experience, the thing we shared, seemed to just pass through the contact of skin. We never really said anything.

To be honest, I told the prosecutor, it is very hard to recall our last conversation in full, or the last exchange of words that might be called a conversation. We had argued, if that's what you want to know. In the lead-up to the cruise we had argued often. It was true, although I spared the court the petty details. We had been at each other since spring, since he'd started ranting about LA, long before his unfaithfulness had been made apparent. Once I had even thrown my wedding ring at him in the street. I threw it at him to make a point, although the argument was in no way over. The ring hit him on the chest then bounced off and rolled across the footpath into the crowd. I marched ahead of him and he ran after me.

Look, he had said, I really want to finish this argument, but I need to go look for your ring. And he went back. He returned to the spot where I threw the ring, and where he thought he saw it hit the ground, then he got down on all fours and crawled along the footpath, searching for the glint of gold. People parted for him. People stared. Eventually he found it wedged against the side of a donut stand. He stood up, put the ring in his pocket, smacked his hands together as if to clean them, and brushed off the dirt from the knees of his trousers. Right, he said. Where were we?

I didn't go into any of these particulars that day in court. Nor did I bother to explain to the prosecutor the timings, that this argument happened on the way home from that gallery visit in the summer, the one where we saw the sculptures, and almost two months before Ada would phone to tell me about the prize. We were walking to the Tube – it was drizzling and generally unpleasant weather. We both felt the disappointment of this after looking forward to the summer for so long. At that time, in June, I was still making changes to the manuscript and feeling the pressure of this. I only had four weeks before I needed to hand the whole thing in and was tired and irritable. Patrick still wouldn't let up about LA despite my refusal to even consider it. He went on and on. The awful weather didn't help. But his relentlessness on this front drove me crazy. I didn't yet understand his motive. Maybe I still don't, whether he wanted to escape temptation or drive me away.

But to answer your question more directly, I replied. By that point on the ship, I'm not sure that you could say we were having conversations. By that point perhaps all that passed between us was, in fact, dialogue. Then there was the seasickness and the alcohol and the sex. Although not in that order, mind you. At a certain point in a marriage one ceases to expect or to rely on conversations, and this is not always a bad or disappointing thing. Sometimes two people simply become telepathic. Still conscious of the fact of love and everything else. Hardly needing to talk about it. Sometimes not wanting to.

If I remember correctly, our last 'conversation' was about the cherry blossoms. Their fragrance reminded him of the sugared almonds, covered in marzipan I think, that his mother would give him at Easter time when he was a child. The eggs were different colours: pastel-blue, pale pink, sherbet-yellow. The same kind that people sometimes throw over newly-weds, like confetti, to remind them of the bittersweetness of love. They came in a little wicker basket, the Easter almonds, with cotton wool padding the nest. He hated the taste of them, but loved the colours and the smell, and remembered rubbing the sugared almonds one at a time against his nose, the marzipan shell very smooth and delicate.

This private memory didn't match Patrick's appearance; it didn't fit the mould of the radical intellectual and rogue. Every generation has an image for this type of person, this character. Or at least, and let us be clear – every generation has an image for this type of *man*. But underneath he was someone else. And I alone was the woman who knew this other version of him, who was the sole audience for this different person. A quiet, loving man full of deep reservations. A man who liked to swim for miles out into the ocean through warm, choppy waters. A man who liked to listen to Handel's arias in the bath. A man who liked his feet rubbed and other parts of himself licked as though I were a cat at a saucer of cream, a man who read the great poets to me aloud at night. A man who proposed to me on the Pont Neuf in Paris, down on his knee. Tourists stopped to take photographs. He could never admit to this romanticism, not in public, where his very identity was built around a hunger for critique and experiment. But I knew that this had become mere posturing, and he knew that I knew. I was his relief, his true north as we sometimes say. This was the secret we shared. The private life. Which is, whatever anyone might tell you, the only real life that any of us ever have.

I felt myself stalling and leant forwards a little, rubbing my forehead, trying to clear my thoughts. Sometimes I find that I replace a memory with a scene from a movie or television series, or even an ad. The screen image slides over the real memory and erases it, removing it so effectively that I can never find it again. Sometimes, if the erasure is interrupted, I am left in limbo so that the memory and the image blur at the seam and create a confused recollection. I tried to continue, there was more to say in my own defence, but I felt my voice failing me, dropping to a hoarse whisper. The prosecutor took advantage of my apparent weakness and launched in with his questions.

But didn't you just tell us? he began. And wasn't it the case that—? Only a moment ago you told the court that you agreed to—

He paused, paced and turned to face the jury. I think, he said, that something is missing. Can I remind you, Ms Blackwood, that you are under oath.

I felt heat rising up my neck, colouring my cheeks. I knew there were things I hadn't said, things I couldn't put down on paper or admit even to myself. I knew I wasn't thinking straight when I was first questioned. The chain of events didn't make sense. And now? At one point in the court proceedings a witness had said that when they saw me struggling with the door I was soaked and shivering, and I suppose I must have been, but in my own recollections I'm bone-dry. There is always a lag between an event and my understanding of it. Sometimes that lag can last a decade, if not more – culminating in my decision to sit down and write about it, and only through this do I understand what came to pass. All truth cannot be captured in fiction, but I know I am more honest with myself when I am being fictional, rather than pretending to be real. Which is, I suppose, how most of us try to be most of the time, an attitude that only leads us to lie, or is a lie to begin with – the pretence of the real – and we just live on, digging ourselves deeper. But it takes time, to do this, to get to that place where I can at last arrange the events in order and see them for what I think they were. The distance lets me recognise the points that mattered, the things that had the power to remain alive inside of me, and then I can let go of all the rest.

I felt a headache coming on. I was tired. So incredibly tired. There was the taste of bile at the back of my throat. Can I ask you, the prosecutor said, to once more walk us through the period leading up to the cruise?

I took a deep breath and, in an effort to show my willingness to give the whole story, went back further than I perhaps needed to. There had been a terrible row, I explained, between Patrick and Joshua – in which Patrick hit Joshua with a rolled-up magazine. Not long after this Joshua went back to his mother's house. Neither Patrick nor I had made a serious attempt at keeping anything from him. He knew about the affair. It was possible that he knew about it long before I did, and that this was one of the sources of his rage – the recognition of my own betrayal, just as his mother had been betrayed before. He felt, I told the court, like his father had failed him. Joshua was still young and idealistic enough to believe that adults ought to be upstanding, and that Patrick should be the most virtuous of all. He was furious at him. And there Patrick was, preferring to pretend that this was a normal adolescent response to the world. I knew Joshua must've heard us arguing that night, while he was waiting for Patrick to come and play the board game. He must've gone home and told Trudi everything, because she was the one who recounted all this in court when she took the stand: the details of the affair, and the fight between Joshua and Patrick. She even recalled the fact that I was locked out of the house at the time, and that when I was finally let inside, Joshua accused Patrick of hitting him, after which that terrible argument erupted between Patrick and me and the neighbour knocked on the door. We were alone in the house then, once Joshua had gone. It's probably fair to say that at that point all bets were off.

But after a marriage as long as ours, the greatest of moods – the most savage accusations, the worst insults, even real hatred – can be given room and accommodated, rationalised, tolerated and perhaps forgiven, in a way. The simple feelings die off and are replaced. Surprisingly perhaps, and it is surprising when it happens, one can start to feel affection and even something like loyalty for this more nuanced state and the history it reminds you of that cannot be acquired elsewhere, or ever replaced. The meat so densely marbled with fat that it can't be cut off or extricated in any way.

It was not long after this particular fight that I booked the cruise, I explained. I booked it in a strange lull of exhaustion. In the aftermath of that argument we were kind to each other – partly, I think, because we felt eviscerated: we had fought so much we had nothing left. I have to get away from all this, I told him. Can you do this for my sake, for us? He rubbed at the skin just above the bridge of his nose. Yes, he said.

I booked that anniversary cruise just to go somewhere else, just to be alone with him again. If we couldn't have a fresh start, we might still begin a new chapter, and Patrick was by then full of remorse, even loving. In the weeks following, he convinced me that he wanted to make amends. That it was nothing in comparison. That he needed me, which I knew he did. That was a fact, a statement of knowledge and truth on his part. It wasn't a line meant to persuade me. Every woman wants to know that she's needed, or more than that: to feel that the one she loves wants her so much he mistakes it for need, and can only feel himself complete when in proximity to her – thereby making her irreplaceable.

He said there was nothing going on any more – that he'd ended it, and that the night he went to drop off the manuscript was just a mistake, a slip-up. He used lines from the movies when he explained it to me, and I, the heroine, swallowed them whole. He was docile and complicit and unusually eager to please. So much so that he seemed to be behaving almost out of character, or too much like the younger version of himself that I had fallen in love with all those years before. He went to new lengths to help and appease – offering to take the author photo for the book, for instance, which was something he didn't have to do. I was grateful, but I felt on my guard. Anyone can see this from the picture on the book jacket. That tight smile, a little hardness to the eyes. Four weeks passed between Patrick taking that photo and the day we boarded the cruise. They were quiet weeks, each of us busy trying to finish things off before we left. I think I was hoping that everything would just go away, that if we didn't talk about it it would no longer exist and we would return to what we once were.

I fell silent then. The prosecutor paced back and forth, pausing before addressing the jury. I watched his feet. Six strides in one direction, pivot and turn. Six strides in the next. His shoes were polished to a high shine, a military shine. I imagined him taking a seat in the Burlington Arcade, hitching up his trousers a little as he made himself comfortable, the shoe shiner kneeling down before him and taking his foot in hand. I've often seen men spending their lunch break this way, and although I myself have occasionally wished to stop and rest and put my feet up and have my shoes made to look brand-new again, I've always felt shy, out of place. I never have seen a woman sitting on that throne, with a man kneeling before her. A woman paying a man to kneel down before her. A man who was paid not to flatter her, or to talk about himself, or ask her personal questions but to defer and acquiesce. I found myself thinking that if I were to be released from here, if I were let out of this place as a free woman, I would go and sit on that throne and have my shoes shined. I wouldn't worry about drawing attention to myself, or that people might wonder what I was doing – thinking about this in a way they never think about a man who stopped to get his shoes shined, because he was quite naturally entitled to it and was in the habit of enjoying this entitlement: the rest and the padded-leather seat on which he regularly spent part of his lunch break watching other people walk by. Tap, tap, tap, went the prosecutor's shoes. Tap, tap. Someone behind me coughed. In front of the judge's bench the stenographer typed away at a rapid pace, not once showing any expression. Reporters sat on the press bench, scribbling.

And then? he said. How did that lull, as you describe it, change?

After that, well, I said. We enjoyed the cruise. Until, I said, my voice cracking. Until, I tried again, on the day before—

I beg your pardon, Ms Blackwood. I wonder if you could repeat that?

Sorry?

Louder if you will.

Until, I said, on the day before the accident, we argued about something that I had written in my book. There was no way of resolving this, I couldn't retract it. And Patrick's anger was significant. To be honest I was wary of him when he was like this and on the day of the storm I spent much of my time by the pool, reading. That afternoon he wanted me to come down to the cabin with him, but I refused. Later, as you know, I said, we made love.

I remembered the investigator in Japan pressing me on this. After this episode was over, he had said, what happened? I had forgotten what I told him, forgotten the details. Not wanted to recollect them. Now it came back to me in a great rush, the realisation of scenes misplaced.

Patrick had an extraordinary singing voice, I told the prosecutor. A deep baritone. Not many people knew this. He used to sing to me sometimes when we were first together. And he was especially prone to singing in the shower. It was a sign of his happiness. Of the greatest kind. But I hadn't heard him sing for years. Until that afternoon, in the cabin. I wasn't sure what it was at first, and then when I realised I was overcome by the most terrible feeling. I didn't know the passcode to his phone, I couldn't read the message he had received – assuming it was a message he rolled over to check. I had a strong feeling of things being suddenly very wrong.

Do you remember what song he was singing? the prosecutor asked.

No, I replied. I can't see how that's relevant.

Maybe, he said, turning to me then, this might jog your memory. He pressed the button on a tape recorder and from this came the sound of my own voice, small and echoey, cracking a little with tears as I sang, for that investigator in Japan, the tune I heard coming from the shower the day Patrick died. I remembered the wind outside. The snow that the train later travelled through. It proved nothing to play this, to show yet another minor fault in my memory. But it stilled the courtroom like nothing else. As if the sound of me singing Patrick's song had brought his ghost into the room. Our song, I should have explained. It used to be our song. He used to sing it for me.

32

The prosecutor stopped the recording. And then, he said, Patrick went up to the bar and drank while you slept, am I right?

Yes.

And when you woke, the storm was about to hit, and you went in search of him.

Yes.

And you followed him to the deck, where you argued?

Yes.

What was it you were fighting about?

In my hands I nervously twisted a piece of scrap stitched cloth, similar in size to a woman's handkerchief when folded in half and then in half again. I wrung and scrunched it, the cloth absorbing the sweat from my palms. When we were children, and Joan cared for us, she was eager to never let us think that she wanted to take the place of our mother. It was not that she could not love us so well or as deeply as a mother might, but that she did not want us to think we ever had to renounce the memory or the idea of our mother simply because another woman was offering us maternal affection. My mother didn't take much with her when she left, and after a time my father had thrown away almost everything that remained.

But two dresses were left in the back of the wardrobe, behind his shirts and the winter coats. When my father was not at home Joan would sometimes let us play with them, dress up in them, and after we had grown too old for such games she unstitched their hems, cut off one long, deep strip from each and made May and me both a small purse, of the kind a child might use to keep milk teeth in, placing this under their pillow for the tooth fairy. Mine was made of a heavy yellow silk, shot through with red thread that looked as though it might have formed the pattern of leaves or birds on a larger piece of fabric. Because it was made from the fold of the hem, the fabric was marked and divided by a horizontal line that never left it, one half marking the outside of the dress that had been worn often and faded by the sun, and the other half much darker where the fabric had been kept hidden by the fold, brushing only against my mother's leg. It had long since lost the smell of her, the scent of her perfume, but still I liked to hold it, even now as an adult. While I endured the prosecutor's narrative I pushed the cloth purse into my lap and lifted the glass of water to my mouth. I tried to sit very still and not wipe away the beads of perspiration that formed on my temples. I touched my belly only once. By then my condition, as the press liked to call it, was plain to see. I was uncomfortable; the baby had wedged itself in an awkward position, its elbow pressing into my bladder. The room was hot and stuffy, the air difficult to breathe.

In my recent book, I had in fact created a scene that was disturbingly close to my life as it now played out.

The prosecutor was alert to this and pulled up a quote about the disaster that derailed the sisters' adult lives, the scene of a certain accident. Was this a form of premeditation? None of it was deliberate or intentional. But his question cut to the heart of my own anxiety: does fiction bring forth reality? To me, fiction has always felt to be the closest match to the form of consciousness itself. Maybe this is why it has such force. Or perhaps I should reverse this: consciousness, to my mind, has always felt fictional and therein lies its magic, its strangeness. Each is as potent and unreliable as the other. At the time of writing, this statement about the sisters was not real, as in it had not actually happened and I had only imagined it. I cannot help but give words to the things I see unfolding: in my own mind a daydream and a fiction appear proximate, the visual qualities indistinct. Perhaps my biggest fear is that in writing about a thing I make it happen, will it to life – that I have in me a power I do not wholly understand and yet am compelled by.

The prosecutor was a seasoned performer, but maybe not a literary man. Or perhaps he was such a literary man that he knew he could blur the line between my testimony and my work: he played to the jury as if they might be, as indeed some were, members of the reading public – another jury in its own right. It was true, what he went on to say: many of my books featured the same characters or extended the story of a fictional town or family that had appeared frequently in my work. Sometimes different characters – characters in different books – ended up with the same first name, not by design but just forgetfulness, although the prosecutor used this as a way of suggesting an accrual of intent. Either way, the voices were familiar and consistent – often circling around a mysterious incident such as a death or disappearance, say, or a secret, and mostly narrated in the first person, or by a series of first-person narrators.

With this the prosecutor provoked the jury and made out as if there could be no real distinction between my own first personhood and those characters that spoke in my books. As if one could not credit imagination as a true power, but only as a sham and outdated idea we writers use to cover our tracks, to voice our dreams and desires in disguise. A disguise that he would now tear away from me in order to show my true face.

I felt myself backed into a corner. Many of my peers were comfortable in discussing their work on these terms, they were prepared to be exposed or else they played to it, writing autobiographical books that worked hard to give a carefree and seemingly labourless account of their ordinary lives. I was troubled by this – troubled by the idea that, in order to gain literary status, confession or some semblance of it was once more expected, and of women in particular, only for our words to be used against us when the time came. Alternatively, should we shy away from such admissions and move in the other direction, too much artfulness could make it look like we were hiding something, and risk the accusation of inauthenticity. It was a high-wire act. As a woman writer I could be neither true nor false. However I said what I did, I risked being rendered illegitimate, seen to mislead on one count or the other – weakened by a poorly curated confession that was excessive or inconsistent, or else flawed by pretence.

The prosecutor knew this. It was his job to make it clear to the court that he understood the workings of my mind and that on the basis of this knowledge he could convince the jury of my guilt. If I can turn again to the evidence, he said, there's a final section I would like to quote, from a public statement you made. I started to feel queasy. The baby kicked hard. Its foot was digging at a rib, but I couldn't stand up and stretch so as to encourage it to move. The prosecutor continued. Ladies and gentlemen of the jury, he said, let me remind you that this is a woman who, in her acceptance of one of the most significant literary honours, spoke of her determination to finish what she started, a woman who in fact thanked her late husband for his encouragement, for helping her to see things through to their end. Let me read you this section of her speech in full.

As he spoke, I leant forwards to try to draw more air into my lungs. More air and a little deeper. It was so hot in there. The prosecutor's voice carried on in the background, the heels of his shoes tapping as he paced. I could smell his aftershave – strong mint and something like cloves. I thought I might vomit. The baby kicked again, harder this time. Deeper air now, gulping it further down into my body, as far as it would go, which wasn't nearly far enough, not even close, I could feel that, my body starting to gasp and suck until I heard someone call out, Stop, wait, help.

33

When I came to, my vision was blurry. I wasn't sure where I was. Faces were leaning over me. But they were indistinct, wobbling. There was the ceiling behind them, bright lights. Ms Blackwood. Ms Blackwood? Stay with us now. I knew that was my own name. I didn't know who was calling it. I felt a cool hand on my neck checking for my pulse. I closed my eyes for a moment. In the background was the sound of voices rising. The wooden hammer ordering silence, the court adjourned. A woman was beside me, clearing others away. A man in a medical uniform rolled up my sleeve. You're OK, darling, she said. Or maybe the man said that. I think it was the man. I could smell his cologne. You're going to be just fine, he said as he carefully rolled me on to my side. Who were these people? I heard them speaking together. The ground felt to be falling away from under me. Six months, the woman said, nearly seven. Then the man asked her something else. I couldn't make it out. Yes I can, she replied. We need to move her, he said. Get her comfortable and resting. I heard a swing door opening and closing, the suck and hush of its hinges. The room fell quiet. I can look after her, she said to the man. A familiar voice then, swimming through the air. If you can maybe just help me get her to the car.

Skip. Skip. Blank. Skip, blank. Blank. Skip, blank. There is somewhere a box of slides from our early childhood. The box is rectangular, so that two neat stacks of slides can fit beside one another. The lid is yellow, the rest white. For a long time I kept this box in the bottom drawer of my desk, taking the slides out every now and then to look at the grey images. The slides have a cardboard edging, almost a frame, in the middle of which is the semi-transparent image. Dark, almost black if you look at it straight on with a solid object behind it. But if you lift and tilt each slide individually, with the light shining through the plastic film, the picture appears – miniature and with its colours muted. Each image a little larger than a thumbnail and prone to disappearing back into its dark state. The image appears almost as a smudging-away of the shadows, a picture guessed at and interpreted via the patches of brightness: a baby's face, a mother's shoulder, a coastline with a stretch of pale sand, two tiny figures sitting on their beach towels. Slipped into the slide projector, the images ballooned. Sometimes my father projected them on to a white sheet, at some other point I remember a portable screen that made an odd wobbling sound like a sail in the wind if we bumped it, or if he had to reposition it relative to the projector so that the machine and the image were aligned, allowing the image to appear in the middle of the white screen, and not half on this and half on the wall – scenes of our babyhood, sisterhood, our original family life shimmering over the sideboard and the table, over the vases and picture frames, loose like water. Skip and click, skip and click. Sometimes he would let me drop the slides into their assigned slot in the carousel of the projector. I had to be very careful to hold them only by the glossy white cardboard edge, and not touch the grey square in which the image was held. No fingerprints. The grooves of the carousel were dark and narrow. I would peel a slide away from its stack in the box and gently slip it sideways into one of the slots. Then my father would press something and the carousel would whir and click, jerking the image into the light.

I thought for a moment that I must be delirious. I had this as a conscious thought. Dim sense of maybe hallucinating. The nausea. Heat in my face. I don't remember the car journey, nor the arrival. I don't remember where we parked, if we had to walk to the house. Blank, blank, skip. Skip. Blank. Let's just get you comfortable, she said. A memory of someone kneeling beside me, pulling my shoes off, then lifting my legs on to the sofa. I must have slept, and when I woke I realised that I was at Valerie's house.

There you are, she said, as I heaved myself to sitting. How are you feeling? she asked, stroking my hair back from my face. You certainly gave everyone a fright there.

I nodded, and said I thought I was OK now. I felt a little weak, dazed. The courtroom had been so hot and stuffy. I should have eaten something, like she said. She brought me tea, carrying it on a tray and placing it down on a side table.

The doctor said you need to rest, she told me. Dumb

advice really, all considered. But I'm being the messenger.

Outside it was getting dark, and the room was dim. Valerie stirred extra sugar into my cup and sat down beside me. For a while we were quiet together. But I could sense something bothering her, how she fiddled with the charm on her necklace, tugging it one way and then the other. Maybe it was what she'd heard, back in the courtroom. Things I'd said that she didn't know. That I should have told her. I felt both disoriented and dejected — filled with a sense of hopelessness. It was hard to imagine how any of it could have gone worse. How I could be made to seem any more monstrous. How could I turn up the next day? It would make no difference — my life was over, I said to Valerie. Or as good as. What's the point?

Don't. Valerie said, Don't speak like that. She got up to let the dog out, a small white thing that she doted on, then went to the kitchen to refill the kettle.

But really, I said, I owe you an apology. I should have — but Valerie held up her hand to silence me. Please, she said. You don't need to. She turned on the lamps, frowning a little, then sat back down and sighed. You know, she said, whatever happens next, however you feel now, you need to hold on to the idea of the future. To your own future, not forget that whatever the verdict, you will have a life afterwards. You will.

From where I sat on the sofa I could see through the kitchen and the large glass doors that looked out on to the narrow back garden. There were no curtains there, and in the distance, at the edge of a neighbouring property, stood a large oak tree. Its branches were empty and they swayed in unison in the evening breeze.

For weeks my life had felt unreal: as though I was seeing everything through some kind of veneer, as if everything were a hallucination. Too thin and sharp. It was as though I could sense the truth on the other side, tangible and waiting, but for whatever reason I was unable to break through. Now the room seemed to tilt a little, as if I were badly jet-lagged. I felt strange, tidal, like my own life was sweeping right through me and moving out to sea. As if everything I had thought, everything I had imagined, was possibly a mistake. All the decisions I had made.

A timer went off in the kitchen and Valerie got up to see to it. There was the sound of plates, cutlery. Then her footsteps on the floorboards. I blinked back my tears and tried to steady my breathing. Here, she said, passing me a bowl of soup, a spoon and napkin. Beside me she placed a glass of water with an ice cube floating in it. Try not to think about tomorrow, Valerie said, right now you should eat. Eat and rest.

34

The following morning the prosecutor gave his closing address. I wanted Valerie to take my hand, to be near me, but she was in the public gallery and out of sight. Joshua wasn't there – he was right to want nothing to do with me, and it's possible I'll never see him again. My back ached, my feet were swollen in my shoes. I didn't want to hear whatever came next. I wanted just to sleep. To drop from consciousness until it was all over. Everything, even the whole of life. That was how I felt then. The same sketch appeared with all the newspaper articles. A rough charcoal drawing done in profile, emphasising my hair pulled back in a ponytail, the arc of my belly, my spine slumping a little, the downturned mouth – a picture of discontent, or discomfort. I had tied my hair in such a way so as not to fiddle with it and show my nervousness. But in the drawing the ponytail only made me look childish. The newspapers commented on this: my fall from grace, my dishevelment, so far from the glamorous author I was seen as before.

My own barrister soon rose and spoke in my favour, but even I could tell that her words lacked the prosecutor's clout. She asked for understanding, for compassion, for attention to be given to the broader circumstances, reminding the court of Patrick's volatility and the ferocity of the storm, framing his death as a tragedy due to a freak event. But it was hardly satisfying, to blame it on the weather and the rain.

The jury retired to make its decision, and that afternoon returned with a verdict.

The pause between the announcement of this (Has the jury reached . . . Yes, Your Honour) and the revelation of the decision opened up a dark gulf into which I dropped. And yet my body did not fail me. I did not pass out, or vomit, or even wail as Valerie did. My barrister made a plea in mitigation, reducing the charge to manslaughter. Meaning that circumstances had reduced my culpability. Did I have a guilty mind? *Mens rea*, Latin: the intention or knowledge of wrongdoing. Cocktails. Happy hour, seasickness, sunstroke. Manslaughter by a dangerous act. Not wholly. This being the deciding difference between the charge of murder and what I was now deemed guilty of. *Found*. Found guilty. As if this were accidental, or happenstance. The found object. From the Latin *fundus*: bottom or foundation. To be made this way, at the bottom, to be made from this base. The experience itself being that – base, debased, the foundation of my— Or, in variation – as the French would have it, to smelt, melt, mix, to cast metal, from the Old French *fonder*. Although fond itself, as a feeling of tenderness comes from Middle English *fone*, (*fonne*, *fonned*), to be foolish or simple. Sentimental. Here stands the bronze cast of the foolish woman at whom you throw stones. Or, as if I myself might, by way of this declaration having been found, be now melted down, reduced to a base substance. And then there is the more recent interpretation of found which is *to discover*. From the expression to *find one's self*, variant of to *provide one's self*. As if, in the act of providing for one's self, there is the assumption of self-discovery. Fourteenth century that one, later adopted as an Americanism: the self-reliance of the convicted, who are discovered to have provided for their own ruin, reduction and smelting for the purposes of extraction. What is left. What is drawn out. What rises from that debasement. Certain leniencies were granted, on account of my condition. This is not to overlook the seriousness of the charge, the judge reminded me. Something was read out from a sheet of paper. And then I was taken away. Later, I signed a form giving Ada guardianship rights over the child.

I held her only for a moment, my daughter, after she was pulled from my body. I was too exhausted to gather her up to my breast. Someone placed her on my stomach and I rested a hand on her back, warm and slippery with blood and vernix. I saw her deep-grey eyes search for me, wandering loose into the space above, where I was waiting. Then, as the placenta came out, I started to bleed and was rushed away, my daughter removed from my arms. Transfusions and surgery followed. I couldn't look after her. They wouldn't let me. I was in no state. One or all of the above. I felt my daughter's mouth at my breast just one time before they took her away.

During the trial, and for some time before this, I had wanted no longer to see myself in the dingy mirrors of public bathrooms, or in the polished windows of shopping malls, or in the panelled mirrors of fitting rooms, or in the bathroom of an ordinary morning, or across the black surface of the television after I had switched it off. I found myself imagining a world before all this, before mirrors and glass, before screens, a world in which you would see yourself only in the gaze of others, in which you would learn of your worth only via the expressions on their face. You would not need to add to this or undermine it with your own scrutiny and doubt, your own sabotage by which you attend and give preference to the angles and details which you most dislike: the nose or chin or freckled mark. For that fortunate child, the one born into the mirrorless, glassless world, the steady marker of their own worth and beauty would be the mother's face as she gazes down with love at the babe in her arms. It is an archetypal image, that maternal gaze, one repeated and rehearsed; a memory perhaps held more by the mother than by the child, because it is an image that the mother believes in so strongly, even lives by, an image she holds so dear that she wishes it upon herself as well, even though this is never something that any of us can properly recall – not the exact moment of its happening, not the image itself. We hope that this maternal gaze fell on us, that it happened to us. I have to believe that this is a gaze that also fell on me. And how badly now I want my daughter to know that I myself looked on her in this way, that somewhere in her consciousness there must be the memory of this love. That moment when they gave her to me to hold and she nursed, just briefly, then turned to stare at me.

Now, years later, she has her father's beautiful eyes,

the sly and happy gleam of them. Each time Ada brings her to visit, my daughter seems more and more like him. This frightens me and at the same time gives me pleasure. Through her I can feel close to him, and at the same time distanced from myself. This is a good thing, for that glimpse of our own likeness, when I have felt it, has come more as a disturbance than a pleasure. Am I really that way? Is that likeness what I am? In such moments I feel concern above everything else, a fear of replication and repetition, the knowledge of the weaknesses, the faults of character. It is much easier, as a mother, as the mother that I am, to think of my daughter as sharing a likeness with her father and not me. I think of her, I want her to know that I think of her all the time. Even when I'm thinking about other things, even then. She is a constant flickering in the back of my thoughts, like the beam from a projector creating dappled patterns on the screen of my mind.

35

On account of my pregnancy, and then the child, and then my ongoing dull obedience during those first years of my sentence, I was assigned a place here in the open prison. Re categorised, as they call it. There are not so many of us here, a hundred at most. We are kept busy, assigned jobs that will prepare us for our eventual return to normal life. For some years now I have worked in the garden. In spring and summer I help care for the roses and the vegetable beds, and in the winter you find me in the greenhouse tending the seedlings. My father would be proud of me, I know how to sow a seed rather than bury it, how to blanch celery and force rhubarb. I have been taught all these things and proved myself to be one of the most eager students, the most dedicated workers. And for this I have been rewarded. At this time of year my room looks out on to greenness, and in the morning the sun streams through windows that are not barred. Tall miscanthus grass forms a high border between the garden and the building where I'm housed. There are guards there, on the edge of the lawn. In spring, when the grass has put out its plumes, the guards appear hidden, camouflaged. I am behind the grass, looking through it. There is something almost elemental in this, something primal, I know myself to be exactly what I am: an animal in hiding. Not the hunter, not any more, but the prey, seeking cover in dense prairie. The grasses lean together in the wind, then lean back again. It is impossible not to intuit their livingness, not to respond to this with feelings of love, as one might watch children running together in a park on a windy day. I imagine my daughter's hair flapping in the breeze. How I have seen her sometimes, pushing this back behind her ears when she visits. Long, silky hair. Quite dark. If you keep tucking it back that way, I once heard Ada say, it will make your ears stick out; Ada prefers her to have it pinned in place, and she has given her small clips with butterflies on them. She and Ada visit once a month and every week my daughter sends me a letter, or a painting that she's done at school.

It makes me happy, to think of her, and to think now of the life we might share. I can at last allow myself this, as my time here nears its end. It is a life I have envisaged in such detail, but which I have tried to keep at bay – a fictional design of sorts, passed off as a moral act. A kind of recompense.

Although part of me is afraid now that this might turn out to be nothing like what I have imagined. It's possible that too much time has passed – nearly the whole of my daughter's childhood. While my own years here seem to have warped and stretched. I try to run the figures differently: the time lived, the time paid off, the credit and the debt.

Like everyone in this place, my life has been reduced to

such tallies; one keeps track of progress by counting down the time – counting in years, then months, weeks, days. Now, at last, it has come down to the counting of hours. How slow this has been. Increment by small increment. Yet when I look back over this period it seems to have run at a different speed, faster somehow, even though nothing of any quickness has filled it. I wonder whether, after tomorrow, I will continue to count the weeks just out of habit. After tomorrow. Only what would I count down to? I don't know yet. It's hard to think of this. I might have to turn the counting the other way. Count upwards. The way some people hope to count their money, their good shoes, their accolades, their children.

I imagine what it will be like to be together at last, my daughter and I. Although I can't leave Ada out of this picture. I can't be anything but grateful for the love she has so freely given – the care, the cooking and feeding and nightly brushing of my daughter's tiny white teeth. The reading of bedtime stories, teaching her how to write her own name. And that is just the beginning. Ada had long been an excellent midwife for my books, and for years now has extended this same careful attention to my child. I know that because of this I can't ever wholly be my own daughter's mother. Not completely. Eight years is a long time. In a few years my daughter will move on to a new phase, and in another eight years she will be a young woman in her own right, trying to make decisions that are different from those I made, trying to be as unlike her own mother as possible. That is the way of things. Maybe it's even a form of love, of recognition. The knowledge of difference. She at last sees you in your own light, as a singular person. Although who knows what she will think of me by then. Still, there is a window coming up when I might yet get to love her as I have always wanted to, as I should or would have done from the start. I have come to understand, too late perhaps, that my life has been defined by the very relationship I'd sought to escape. In turning my back on motherhood, it nevertheless found me. Maybe none of us can help but become the things we are most determined to avoid, so fixated on what we don't want that we will this, indirectly. In the end I have lived out my own counterfactuals, or become them, in opposition to my conscious and professed desires – complicit in my own downfall, if I can think of it like that.

Today, on my last day, some of my final tasks are in the rose garden. I am retraining the roses so that they grow more evenly over the pergola, a job best done with two people, one to hold the rose cane while the other secures it with a garden tie. My companion is a sassy woman who goes by the name of Dolora. She has beautiful cheekbones, and skin that has been roughened by sun and alcohol. She too was a martini woman, in a past life. A deft hand at the lemon twist, or so she tells me, repeating the proportions required for the mix: two of this, one of that, two of this. Something for me to remember her by, she says. She is out in three months. All she talks of now is how her sweetheart will come collect her and take her to eat oysters. She can't remember the last time she ate oysters. We are nowhere near the ocean, but this seems an insignificant detail – her man will find oysters for her, just wait and see. The motorway is not far off from here, a few miles east, and at night, when the wind blows in a certain direction, I hear the traffic quite clearly as it moves down that road which I, and then Dolora, will also drive along soon. When I am very tired, or just emerging from a dream, I can forget it is the sound of vehicles and think I am again by the sea.

Dolora sings while she works and mutters to the roses when they do not bend in the way she wants them to, when they spring back and refuse to stay close to the poles of the pergola despite the garden ties. Yield! she says to them. Yield, you suckers! I pull harder, tie a triple knot. I am using old beige pantyhose that has been cut into strips, the laddered underwear that one warden or another had discarded. The strips stretch well and hold fast. What are you going to do, she asks, when you get out?

I can't tell her the truth because it feels too complicated, and because I will cry, and because she has always struck me as a good-time kind of girl, but not a woman to whom I'd make any genuine confession, not a woman to confide in. And so I tell her something that is not really a lie, that is close enough to the truth. I don't know, I say. I haven't let myself think about it up until now. I mean I've tried not to. Every woman here has some resolution, for how things will be after this. A secret resolution, for the untold part of the story, for the days that will not be on record, for their time not lived as debt. A period of great and greater happiness up ahead.

After we have finished our work in the garden I rest on the bench. In this brief reprieve, last night's dream comes back so vividly that it could almost be a real scene, misplaced and now reclaimed: Patrick and I discovering empty flower beds in the garden of the house where we used to live – beds that we never knew were there – and it was only as we were about to leave the house forever that we realised we had not planted flowers where we should; in fact we had not planted flowers at all. Zinnias, foxgloves, delphiniums, hollyhocks. How did we forget? Many of my dreams are like this: intense conversations with Patrick about things we forgot to do or shouldn't have said. Despite everything, he remains my interlocutor – the figure with whom I continue to debate. Very often, we seem to have these conversations near water – he on one side, me on the other. A swimming pool, a rushing river. Once, a large puddle after heavy rain.

I talk to Patrick now like I talk to other characters in my head. I have internalised him as my protagonist, the figure that I vouch for and interrogate, and will him, despite everything, to live on. When a book ends, I always want to feel that the character's life continues; the story may be over, but I like to think that their life carries forwards only privately, without an interloper. As if we, the readers, have simply lost track of them but can still sense their presence, imagine them out in the world.

I always did over-identify with my characters. Or even more than that: I gave myself to them, often in quite literal ways – I let them have my memories, my affections. My desires became theirs. We lived in and through one another. Perhaps now, in a similar fashion, Patrick and I have again become one – a single consciousness. Art always had this power for me – the power to make the disparate and the irreconcilable seem, if not whole, then at least continuous; experiences in motion, the sense of quickening. Because what else is the feeling of life and aliveness? I only ever wanted to be as near to this as I could; once, that was what Patrick gave me. Maybe it is still.

Around me now the air is cool. Dolora has returned to the dormitory. I shift position, my back hurts a little from squatting down by the plants. But there is still the laundry to do. On Tuesdays it's my shift. The machines are in the basement. I like the smell of the washing: the detergent and then the clothes drying, and sometimes the iron when it is set to steam. I open the door that leads to the stairs and flick the light switch. Neon tubes jitter to life. The stairwell is painted a greenish blue. It is a cold and sour colour. Here and there the paint has been chipped to show a cream undercoat and brickwork. There are black marks on the wall of the stairwell where furniture and machinery must have scraped against the paintwork in the process of manoeuvring such things down the narrow passage. I carry a large grey sack full of towels. This will be the first load. There are seven washing machines, five dryers – there's another laundry in the west basement. As I descend the stairs, the smell of mould intensifies. The air is chilly, but viscous almost – heavy with damp.

I empty the first lot of towels into the nearest machine, pour in the blue liquid and turn on the machine. I do this seven times. When the machines are all running the dank smell of the air is disguised by the perfume of the detergent. It is peaceful down here. They are industrial-power top-loaders, the machines. The towels wallop the inner metal edges, thumping round and round, and still the machines stay put; they do not beep or become unbalanced or skitter sideways due to the force. Ada used to tell me that my own child, as a baby, could be calmed by being sat near the front-loader. Ada would put my daughter in her rocker and let her watch the clothes and the bubbles go round and round, especially hypnotised, Ada said, by the spin cycle as the clothes moved from the sloppy middle of the glass circle to the edges and the bubbles became less as the sound of the engine grew higher and thinner.

Once the wash cycle is done, I load everything into the dryers and wait some more. Along with my skills in the garden, I have become known for my thoroughness in the area of stain removal and pressing. This achievement has brought me considerable peace; I am free to come here alone and sit quietly on the fold-up camp chair. On occasions I bring a pen and paper and write to May.

Later, when I've finished the laundry, I walk back the long way, through the woodland by the eastern boundary. The path here is muddy and there are cloven hoof prints of animals I cannot decipher: too small for a horse, or a pig. I squint a little to see them better, but even on a bright day the woodland can be dark, as if the trees held the shadows for themselves. The air around me is damp, a soft haze of rain forms itself out of the dusk; a drift of tiny wet droplets, cool pinheads, a haze. Trees creak and rub their trunks together. I listen for the rustling of small animals – birds, mice. Even the thud of a pine cone falling on to the ground echoes in the silence of the place.

I know I have changed here, and that this change began after my daughter was born. By that point I had lost everything. I couldn't even bring myself to write, and then, when there was nothing left at all, I found myself alone in that hospital bed with my child. Maybe I needed to be bereft and stripped of all I had known in order to make room for this new love. One I never thought, up until then, that I wanted. And yet it turned out to be true, what Valerie had said: the promise that there would be life afterwards. It is a different kind of life to anything I have known before. To anything I had imagined. Perhaps it's just that there was no longer, at that time, anything I had to exscind or police – not Patrick, not the experiences I once sought to wrestle into my fiction. A new space opened up in me, and because of this I suddenly found myself pointed in the direction of life and living. My desire was suddenly to be in the midst of this. The balance had tipped. It has stayed that way ever since, so much so that sometimes, when I have been walking back this way, I have been sure that I heard the cry of a small child. I stop and look about, listening closely – the sound gone. But then I walk on and the sound starts up again, the cry coming from deep within the forest, over behind the fence line, past the dark pond and the bulrushes and the swamp grass. I do not know whether or not this sound is real. I don't know of any children who live nearby – this is an isolated place, in a distant stretch of country. I know all women listen out for their children at all times, well beyond the point where they might feasibly hear them. Years afterwards, decades. For those women, for me, with the cry of a child all time collapses. The edge of the body stays attuned, alert, forever an animal in the woods. At other times I have felt my breasts swell and harden as if they were readying to let down milk, even though I know this to be impossible, miraculous. Or I am adamant that I smell the sweet newborn scent of my child – I think

I smell it on my fingers or on my face, as though I have been nuzzling her neck and cheeks after a feed. When she was a baby. The few times I was permitted to do this. When I could. Before the mastitis set in and the milk dried up, because I couldn't hold her often enough, hardly at all. Although I know that at this stage of her life such a smell is years gone. Washed away by the diligence of Ada's hands. I feel my eyes sting and walk a little faster, trying to think only of the good things that are now to come. Soon, so soon now.

Her face, in my mind. The lanky eight-year-old child. So much about the feeling of being alive depends on the experience of anticipation, whether we are permitted this or not, whether we can find it in ourselves. At the beginning I tried to squash this instinct, to just live out my time without measuring it, without stretching it forwards. This is easy to do when one feels oneself to be in some state of grace; time stops then. It expands in order to accommodate the magnitude of love. I felt this so much in the first years of our marriage. Against all expectations, I felt it beyond anything I had imagined possible when I held my daughter for the first time, her huge grey eyes searching out my voice. Since then I have done nothing, in any real sense, as I wait and wait and wait.

And now, as if all of a sudden, time hurries forth again. In so many days, I have said to myself, over and over, in so many hours and then I will see her again, properly, for real, forever, as we say. I rehearse my excitement. For years I refused to let myself do this and now it's all that fills my mind as I imagine and reimagine the scene. Because it is tomorrow. It will really be tomorrow. And in only so many hours that will become today. They will arrive together, Ada and my child. My husband's child too, Patrick's. They will wait for me outside. They will stand on the damp grass, squinting to catch sight of me. Ready. I play over the feeling of happiness, the one I think I will find there, testing it, feeling pleasure in my anticipation. Sometimes I romanticise the scene, as if it were a film: the sun is out, we run into each other's arms. I know it won't be like this, that it will be slow, and mostly happen inside, the administration of this, that there will be forms to sign and possibly delays. It may or may not feel anything like the thing I expect. So I rehearse it as if to try out the variations and prepare myself, inoculate myself even, against what the experience will really be like. Because I don't know. Because it is so soon now and I'm nervous. Tomorrow, after breakfast. I have rehearsed this so many times in my head that, as the actual moment nears, I find it hard to believe. My hands shake. It will happen, and then it will be done, and afterwards I suppose I will rehearse some other thing. As you do, before you go to sleep. Something simple, banal, of no significance. I look forward to this. Going to the shops, buying milk, bread, boiled sweets. She likes these, Ada says. One lives ahead of oneself by days, weeks, months, sometimes years. One can mark one's spot on these incessant waves of experience; now I am waiting for the next one, now I am coming down, now rising, now speeding forth, now looking back over my shoulder. My daughter will be waiting for me. Ada will be holding her hand. Or this is what I see, what I imagine. I might be wrong. I'm afraid of the lived moment differing from the imagined one. I'm afraid of it being the same. I want her to run to me, like you see in the movies. I will bend down and pick her up, her warm body, the heavy body thrumming with life. The smell of butter on her cheeks from the sandwich she has bitten into, a deep bite, with the whole sandwich held close to her face, held with both hands, the bread touching her face so that the open edges of the sandwich leave traces of jam on her skin, and as her hair brushes against me I will catch the sweet smell of this. This is what I imagine. The feeling I anticipate. The reunion. One day she will tell me what she thinks of me, of this, of this time in our life.

No regrets, Ada said to me in an effort to give comfort, and it is far easier to think now of these small things than to face the greater error that is too large to scale, to touch, to consider from any which way, to know how to talk about, what I will one day say. Whether I will expunge or remember Patrick in my work, whether I will give us the privileged status of a fiction, and in so doing set something free. Because desire passes down through the generations and evolves. Desire which can be pain or love alike: unrequited or fulfilled, as it came, as it happened. We try to live it out, which is a form of expulsion, almost a test, a challenge of sorts to see whether the living person can surpass the expiry of the inherited thing hovering, foreign inside them.

On the floor beside my bed my bags sit packed. When I leave there will be no fanfare. Because we don't do that here, and because I've asked for there to be none. I will just vanish. Walk out. No soft fade, no repetitions of stock phrases, no backward glance. Just a good clean cut. Severance. Neat ends. This is what I think, watching the scene over and over again, as I step outside and crouch down, arms open, and she runs towards me. It's her face I see. Her hair in the breeze. The grass around us, clear sky overhead. Just one image, then the next.

Acknowledgements

This novel came into existence with the help of many. Greatest thanks to my agent, Emma Paterson, who encouraged this book from the start, and who seemed to know what kind of book it was long before I did. Thank you so much for spurring it on and helping it find its shape. My great thanks to Monica MacSwan for your generous reading of those early drafts and invaluable feedback. Enormous thanks to everyone at W&N, with very special thanks to Lettice Franklin for your extraordinary enthusiasm, encouragement and sharp eye . . . and for reading more drafts of this book than any human should. Thank you to everyone at Hachette Australia and greatest thanks to Vanessa Radnidge for your gusto, friendship and support over many years. Thank you to Elisabeth Schmitz for your brilliant interventions, and to all the team at Grove Atlantic. Thanks also to Linden Lawson for such careful editing and Lucinda McNeile for managing the final stages. Working on this book with you all has been a complete pleasure and honour.

This novel was written with the vital and generous support of the Australia Council for the Arts, Yaddo, the Whiting Foundation, Asialink, the University of Melbourne and Tenjinyama Arts Studio in Japan. This support was essential to my being able to both start and finish the book. Thank you to the Oxford Centre for Life Writing at Wolfson College where many of the early ideas for this work were developed.

Thank you to T.G., G.S., Alice, Molly and John. Thank you especially to my children, Dashiell and Milla, for your enthusiasm and for suggesting essential plot developments – I owe you. Thank you, above all, to Boyd, this book is for you.